The Blood of Alexandria

RICHARD BLAKE

The Blood
of Alexandria

HODDER &
STOUGHTON

5157392 ,

First published in Great Britain in 2010 by Hodder & Stoughton
An Hachette UK company

1

A CIP catalogue record for this title is available from the British Library

Hardback ISBN 978 0 340 95116 3
Trade Paperback ISBN 978 0 340 95120 0

Typeset in Plantin Light by Hewer Text UK Ltd, Edinburgh
Printed and bound by Clays Ltd, St Ives plc

Hodder & Stoughton policy is to use papers that are natural, renewable
and recyclable products and made from wood grown in sustainable forests.
The logging and manufacturing processes are expected to conform
to the environmental regulations of the country of origin.

Hodder & Stoughton Ltd
338 Euston Road
London NW1 3BH

www.hodder.co.uk

I dedicate this novel to my dear wife Andrea, without whose support I could never have begun it, and to my little daughter Philippa, despite whose best efforts I was able to finish it.

ACKNOWLEDGEMENTS

The reference to Homer in Chapter 2 is actually from John Milton, *Paradise Lost*, Book I.

The verses in Chapter 7 are by the author.

The verses in Chapter 9 are from *The Seafarer*, an anonymous English poem of the 7th or 8th centuries. They translate as

> Let us consider where our true home is,
> And then how we may come there again.

The words ascribed to Euripides in Chapter 19 are an anonymous commonplace.

The words ascribed to Epicurus in Chapter 20 are from John Locke, *Second Treatise of Civil Government*, 1690.

The verses ascribed to Sophocles in Chapter 22 are by the author.

The verses in Chapter 50 are from *Antigone* by Sophocles, translated by Francis Storr (1839–1919).

The verses ascribed to Claudian in Chapter 63 are actually from John Milton, *Paradise Lost*, Book I.

PROLOGUE

Jarrow, Tuesday, 21 August 686

'You know, Brother Aelric,' Benedict told me this morning, 'you may be up for canonisation.'

I grunted and carried on looking at the draft manifesto one of King Aldfrith's clerks had given me to correct. It was dire stuff. Latin has no aorist, and you can't use participles to supply the lack. And that was probably the most literate error.

I think the Abbot mistook my silence. He brightened his voice, adding, 'Of course, I would never dream of wishing you called out of this life. For all your great age, the work you do for us here makes you irreplaceable' – he repeated the word 'irreplaceable', and emphasised it – 'but the common people are already calling you a saint.'

I'm now alone in my little cell, and free to think again. Benedict is a good man. I'm grateful for the refuge he gave me in his monastery, no questions asked. I'm particularly grateful at the moment for the stove he's had brought in to keep the afternoon chill away. If you think I was upset by his reference to the inevitable, you're as mistaken as he was. At ninety–six, that is something you've had plenty of time to consider. And *Saint Aelric*! It may not make death any less of the darkness it probably is. But it does have a nice sound.

The truth is, I was cutting off any renewal of the questioning. What *did* happen yesterday afternoon? Everyone is itching to know. Benedict first asked just after I'd been carried back here, and I lay dripping on to the polished floor of his refectory. All he got for his trouble was a blank stare. The boy who dared ask this morning got a box on the ears. But questioning by others is easily

I

handled. The problem is that I don't myself know what happened. Oh, the generality is easy: lack of air can do funny things to the mind. The question remains, though, of the attendant circumstances. How to explain those?

Well, as Epicurus said, facts must be described before they can be explained. Before I go any further, let me here – in the double privacy of this journal and of the Greek in which I keep it – set out the facts as best I have them. Since what I must explain happened yesterday afternoon, I suppose it is with the facts of yesterday afternoon that I must begin.

Generally, the Northumbrian summer is shite. So it was last year, and the year before that, and the year before that. I can't speak for the year before that, as I still had my summer palace in Nicea, and rain was the least of my worries. Yesterday, though, it was almost warm. And that's what had me out for a sightseeing tour on the banks of the Tyne.

Nothing there to see ordinarily, I'll admit. Even when not hidden in mist, the whole prospect is one dreariness of green with a great expanse of water running through to the sea. But let the sun be out, and it's here that the boys come to bathe and play. So, fighting off the stupor of beer at lunch, I stepped out of the monastery garden, and in my slow, rickety gait made my way down to the river and settled myself on a convenient stone.

The stone was too convenient. I was no sooner arranged than the beer won its battle and I nodded off in the sun. I can't say how long I slept. I don't know if I dreamed. But I woke to a sound reminding me in a smaller way of the great, collective wail that went up in Ctesiphon when we smashed through the southern gate. I propped myself up on an elbow and looked blearily at one of the boys standing nearby. Water ran off him as he hopped terrified from one foot to the other.

'What's going on?' I croaked. I was stiff all over. I could feel that my face and hands had caught the sun. Behind, I was cold and itchy from having rolled on to the damp grass. I think I'd pissed myself a little. Certainly, I could feel a sicky burp coming on.

The boy looked through me and turned away to look into the water.

'Well, come on, lad,' I said, louder now. I struggled to my knees, and, pushing my walking staff into the soft turf, heaved myself unsteadily up. Yes, I had pissed myself, and it was still dribbling down my legs. 'What's all this racket?'

All the boys, I could now see, were standing still and silent, and looking into the water. I squinted against the glare from the water and waited for my eyes to focus. It wasn't hard to see what had happened. Being so close to a strong tidal sea, the bed of the Tyne here is rippled with sandbanks. Stay on one of these, and you can walk far out at low tide, paddling in just a few inches of water. A foot or so either side, the water may be bottomless. One of the boys had walked out a few hundred feet. Then the tide had swept back in. The water had suddenly risen from his knees to his chest, and was still rising.

No problem there, I thought. If he couldn't see the sandbank now, all he had to do was step off and splash however feebly while the tide washed him back in. If he couldn't swim, however ... I turned back to the boys.

'Well, don't just stand there, you stupid buggers,' I said in Northumbrian dialect as I hobbled down to the water line. 'Get back in there and bring him out.'

I might have shouted in Persian or in one of the Slavonic dialects for all the effect my words had. They just stood there, surly looks on their faces. Some had turned now to face inland.

It was fear, I could see, of the Old Gods. It's only been a generation or so since the missionaries turned up in this part of England. Before then, the locals had drowned the occasional human offering in the Tyne – something to do with the fishing, or perhaps the harvests. If the boys rattle off their prayers well enough in class, they've picked up an older nonsense at home. They were terrified of going back into the water now that one of them was being taken.

I sighed. It struck me once again how ugly most of the boys are in Northumbria. The line put out from Canterbury is that we're all one people in England. My own experience is that the better

3

sort of barbarians who came here settled the south, the very best, I'm in no doubt, settling my own Kent. The further north you go, I find, the more runtish the people become. Why I'd bothered staggering down to look at those white, knock-kneed bodies I couldn't now imagine.

Meanwhile, the tide was still coming in. As if he wanted to keep as much of his body from the chill waters, the boy held his arms over his head. I might have heard sobbing from far out. Even by local standards, he was a pathetic specimen. I thought of quoting Lucretius on the evils of religion, and settling back to reflect on how rotten life can be. Then, as I strained to see more clearly, my stomach turned upside down.

It was Bede out there. What the sodding hell had he been doing in the river? With his asthma, it was a miracle he'd even walked out that far. I poked my staff sharply into the stomach of the boy most conveniently in reach. It was an unexpected blow, and it doubled him up.

'Get in there, you little shitbag bastard,' I snarled, 'or I'll see you won't sit down for a week. Get in there and pull him out.'

He simply ran up the bank out of further reach. The others huddled together. One of the older boys who'd sprouted a few muscles over his ribs began to puff and look ferocious. I suddenly recalled this was near enough how Brother Paul had got his head bashed in last summer. I looked desperately around. There were no adults in sight. I was in no condition to run off for help. The little churls and semi-churls around me couldn't be trusted to get any sort of message back to the monastery. It was a matter of standing impotently on the river bank watching as my best student drowned in some stupid accident.

When that toad Croesus grassed me up in Constantinople, it was annoying but manageable. The confiscation of goods, the loss of status, the midnight escape down the Straits, Catania, Rome and all the continued shuffling along the roads good or bad, never more than one step ahead of the Imperial agents – all that and more I'd borne with surprising equanimity. I'd even put up with Jarrow. But the loss of Bede, I knew, would be the end.

Take from me that scrawny little creature who'd been soaking up these past few years all the learning I could give, as a sponge does water, and that would be the end. It would be simply a question of how to bring on the darkness without embarrassment for Benedict.

I looked round again as if there might be any alternative. There was none. I kicked off my sandals. I gritted my teeth and stepped into the river. The water came up to my ankles. It was fucking cold, I can tell you! With so little flesh on my bones, the chill went straight through me. I thought at first I'd faint from the shock. No one could have blamed me if I'd stepped out again. For anyone but Bede, I'd not even have got my ankles wet – not at my age, nor at twenty years younger. I once watched a man put himself into a barrel and float over a waterfall. It did him no good, and isn't something any reasonable person would have advised. But there are times when you have no choice but to act in ways the whole world would call foolish. So here I was. I took a deep breath and fixed my attention on that terrified boy, then I stepped further into the liquid ice of the Tyne. The only noise I could hear as I waded further and further out was my own gasping breath. My robe was floating up and clinging to me. I pulled it over my head and wound it round my left arm. I'll swear I could feel the uncomprehending stares of those silent boys from behind me.

The water was now up to Bede's neck. I'd managed to stay on one of the sandbanks. Though it shelved about an inch every few paces, the sand underfoot was firm enough. The water spread around me in uncountable acres of cold silver. But it came hardly up to my chest even as I got within a dozen feet of the boy. I could see into his terrified eyes. I wanted to call something reassuring. But I had no breath to spare. I smiled and waved my staff. For all the response, I might as well not have been there.

Another few feet to go, and the sandbank seemed to give out on me. I prodded around with the end of my staff. He was standing on something. So was I. Between us, though, was some watery chasm. I pushed the staff at him.

'Take hold of this,' I gasped through chattering teeth.

He looked straight through me, as still and unresponsive as one of the carved figures in the monastery chapel. I pulled the staff back and turned it round. The other end had a kink at the top. If I got that into his clothing, I could pull him towards me.

Splash!

I'd leaned forward at just the wrong moment. A stray current had got me from behind and I'd overbalanced. One moment, I was standing a fifth out of the water. The next, I was several feet under. I opened my eyes, and looked up to see the sun-dappled surface of the Tyne rising higher and higher out of reach. From habit, I'd taken a lungful of air before my face hit the water, and I still had the skills of a swimmer. But the Tyne is not the heated swimming pool I used to keep up in my main palace. And age is age, there's no denying. I couldn't find the power in my arms to keep from sinking further into those frigid, black depths. Was now the right time for a prayer? I remember thinking as my chest began to hurt.

But the time came and the time passed. I found myself back on one of the sandbanks, pulling a now unconscious Bede by his hair.

There were a couple of the bigger monks waiting for me. Flashing scared looks at something behind me, they waded in to their knees and helped us out. I needed that. Without the water to support me, I'd have fallen straight down. They tried to pick me up and take me back to the monastery. But I had come this far. I wasn't leaving until I was finished.

Bede was lying still on the river bank beside me. His eyes were closed, his face wizened and a touch blue.

'The Gods' – the monk corrected himself and switched to Latin – 'The Devil has taken him, O Master. The Angel was too late.' He made the sign of the Cross. 'Come back to the monastery. Your body is all blue from the cold.'

'Not taken anywhere yet, I think,' I snapped back at him in a surprisingly clear voice. 'Get the boy laid out on his front.' I knelt over Bede, all sense of how cold and stiff I was banished from my primary attention. I reached out to the fleshless, white skin of his upper body and pressed with both hands. I pressed hard, and

6

hard again, as if I were a servant making bread. Again and again I pressed, until I thought my thudding heart would just stop.

I suppose that was another opportunity for prayer. Again, I passed it up. Then Bede was coughing and spluttering and vomiting water on to the grass. I rolled him over again and looked on my handiwork. The young are marvellous creatures. The colour was already coming back to his body.

I wanted to promise him a sound whipping for what he'd done. But I now really was at the end of my strength, and I flopped helplessly on to the grass. Those monks had me wrapped in warm clothing and back to the monastery before I had time to think what was happening. Then straight to a bed made up beside the bakery oven and Abbot Benedict to watch over me until I was wakeful enough to bear the full weight of his anger.

Bede's family came by in the evening with a sheep and a whole barrel of salt fish. I heard the little speech Benedict gave on my behalf. He excused my accepting in person on the grounds that I was confined to bed in my cell.

I woke this morning feeling decidedly perky. I don't think I've been so with it in the morning since last Christmas in Canterbury, when old Theodore of Tarsus made sure to keep me off the beer. I glared at the novice monk who fussed around me, arranging food and asking endless questions.

Did I walk on water? Did I restore life by the laying on of hands? Did I expel the old demonic Gods from their last refuge in Northumbria? Did the Angel of the Lord say anything while I was all that time under the water that I might wish to share?

No and four times no! I wanted to shout at him, my good mood clouding over. But I didn't. So I'm now a candidate saint. There will be a sermon about me next Sunday. Aldfrith will come over in royal state and look pious. His clerk won't bluster when I point out his illiteracy. When I'm dead, I don't doubt they'll have my body on show till it crumbles to dust.

Basic Greek restored my spirits. I was on excellent form. Wrapped in a double cloak under the thatch roof, my students all sitting obediently before me on the floor of beaten earth, I chalked up one of the more nonsensical passages from Revelation, and demanded an exact Latin translation. That was my excuse to set about flogging the arse off every boy I'd seen by the Tyne. When I ran out of energy, I wheezed and gloated while one of the novices drew blood for me.

Dear me – I said I'd describe the facts before I explained them. But I haven't even described them properly. What *did* happen out there in the water? How was it I didn't drown? How was it that Bede still had his head above the water when I went under, and had managed to drown by the time I got him by the hair? What really happened between the moment I fell off that sandbank and when I found myself on another, pulling Bede behind me, back towards a shore thick with boys and monks, all bouncing up and down in some kind of frenzy?

Good questions. Only, the more I think about the answer, the more I realise that yesterday afternoon is not the right place to begin. If I'm to make any sense at all – to me as well as to you – I'll need to begin much, much further back.

I

The story opens on the day when we began to lose Egypt. It was Thursday, 10 August 612, and I'd been just over four months in Alexandria. And at twenty-two, the infirmities of age were things at worst to be read about or imagined.

Martin gave one of his dry coughs as, otherwise noiselessly, he came into the room.

'They're gathered and waiting for you,' he said.

'Come over and look at this,' I said, not bothering to turn. I waited a moment for him to cross the floor and join me by the window. 'Down there,' I said, pointing over to the left.

We were in one of the inspection rooms high above the Royal Palace. Its glass windows faced out over the city. The Sea Harbour and the Lighthouse were out of sight behind us. You had to be in the other inspection room to see those. This was, though, by far the best place for viewing the city called into being by the Great Alexander nearly a thousand years before – the city that, in age after age, had been the one place where Egypt and the West and the most gorgeous East came together for trade and for mutual enrichment.

Before us, the neat central grid of the city laid out as on some mosaic floor. Along the wider avenues stood the public buildings, their roofs glittering in the early light. In narrower streets leading off, you saw the houses and palaces of the higher classes. Where the main streets intersected were the public squares, some paved, others laid out as little parks with trees and fountains to give relief from the baking heat of the summer. Though, like all other places in my world, somewhat past its best, Alexandria remained a city of three hundred thousand people. If not all were now occupied or working, it still rejoiced in its four thousand palaces and its four thousand baths. Now Rome was a shattered dump, only Constantinople itself was bigger.

Over on the right, clouds of steam were standing up from the vast slums of the Egyptian quarter.

But I was pointing to the left. Yesterday, it had been almost dry. Now, snaking from far beyond and then round the Jewish quarter, the canal shone silver as it brought the flood waters from the westernmost branch of the Nile to flush out and refill the underground cisterns.

'It's later than we were told,' I said. 'But the Nile has risen. It's now only a question of how high, and waiting for the harvest estimates to come in.'

'I saw it twice when I was – er – when I was in Antinoopolis,' Martin said, turning the sentence to avoid recalling his time there as a slave. 'Herodotus said it's all to do with the shifting winds to the south.'

'I don't believe that,' I said, turning to face him. He'd cut himself shaving. I suppressed the urge to frown at him. 'According to Colotes,' I went on instead, 'it's the rains that fall every summer on the mountains where the Nile starts – the Mountains of the Moon. These swell the river and carry down the silt that refreshes the land. You'll surely agree, this is a more credible explanation.'

Martin smiled faintly at the appeal to the scientific followers of Epicurus. He might have asked who had ever seen these Mountains of the Moon. But we'd been arguing about the Epicureans for so long now, he'd not be rising to this challenge. The sun now full in my eyes, I squinted to see how far into the distance the canal might be visible.

'They are now gathered, Aelric,' Martin reminded me, a polite urgency in his voice. He would have said more, but he'd seen the burned-out lamp poking from my bag of notes. If this was a place from which the whole city could be seen, it was also a place that could be seen by those able to understand the signs.

'He got in again, past the guards?' Martin asked, his voice now sharper.

I nodded. 'You know these people make an art of going everywhere without ever being noticed,' I said. I poked the lamp deeper
into the bag and pushed the leather flaps together. I turned back
to the window, wondering how long it might be before my instructions had their effect.

Now obviously impatient, Martin coughed again.

'They've been gathered since the spring,' I replied, switching
from Latin into the privacy of Martin's native Celtic. 'If things
had gone as planned, it would have been a matter of reading out
the law and then taking questions about implementation. Thanks
to the sodding Viceroy . . .'

I trailed off bitterly, thinking about those endless delays, delays,
delays. Waiting for the Nile to rise was nothing like waiting for
a decision from Nicetas; indeed, there was less doubt the Nile
would eventually rise.

'You've seen the newsletters drifting in from Constantinople,'
I went on, 'and I don't think we've intercepted half of them.
Everyone's had time to know what's in the law, and to spend every
evening arguing and plotting against it.

'If I go in there now or after lunch, it's pretty much the same.
I'll be facing down an assembly of factions, most of them immov-
ably hostile.'

Martin looked quietly down. I turned back again to the window.
Above Lake Mareotis, a flock of birds was wheeling and darting. I counted twelve of them. If I'd believed in the Old Faith,
I might have called this a good omen. But I didn't believe. If
Martin had brought in the orthodox and the heretical patriarchs
of Alexandria, together with His Holiness himself from Rome, it
would have done nothing more to lift my spirits. There was no
recapturing my earlier peace of mind.

'Oh, what's the point in keeping them still further?' I sighed.
'Do go ahead, Martin. Prepare the way as best you can. I'll be
down in a moment.'

The Great Hall of Audience was an obvious addition to the
Palace. It had its own gated entrance from the square outside,

and a fortified entrance into the Palace itself. I think it had been put up by Cleopatra when the Romans were making life hard for her and she found it necessary to suck up to the natives. Whatever the case, it had been extensively remodelled by the first Imperial governors so it would project the New Order of Things. This remodelling had included a thirty-foot-high frieze running all round the place. It showed Augustus making his deal with the Senate that had finished off the Republic except in form.

Done in the Greek style of their best age, the frieze showed him as first among equals among the senators. There was no hint of the universal barbarian custom of making the ruler look bigger than his subjects. Submission here was conveyed by facial expression and downcast eyes. Augustus wasn't even in the absolute centre. That was given over to the various nonentities he hadn't thought it worth murdering before he'd got himself declared Father of the People. Only on the outer fringes, far down the Hall, could you see his family. They jostled at the back of the admiring crowd, most of them not even in full view. You did manage to see the whole of his ghastly wife. She stood in the gallery of the Senate House, looking almost maternal as she leaned over the children Cleopatra had borne to Antony. The deposed couple, you could be sure, were nowhere in evidence. Nor was the child she'd borne to Caesar. Like his mother, he'd not lived to see the New Order of Things.

Yes, the New Order of Things. It was now six and a half centuries old. And still it continued, in an unbroken and apparently unbreakable sequence of governors and prefects and dukes, and, more recently, of viceroys. And here I was from Constantinople to bring the glad tidings of its renewal.

The chair that had collected me on the roof, then carried me down the paved ramps that connected the floors of the Palace, paused as the double doors into the Hall were silently opened. As they closed behind us, one of the eunuchs who'd tagged along gave a gentle cough. Ten feet above, on the platform that blocked my view of the Hall, we were at last in business.

'All rise for His Magnificence Alaric, Senator, Count of the Most Sacred University, Legate Extraordinary from His Imperial Majesty to His Imperial Highness the Viceroy.'

Even before the echo faded of Martin's voice, there was a scraping and shuffling as a hundred and seventy well-fed bodies heaved themselves up and then pitched forward for the required prostration. As the echo did fade, Macarius preceded me to the top of the stairs leading up to the platform. I followed, still carried in my chair. Following me were a couple of black slaves to fan me with ostrich feathers.

As the prostration ended, the hundred and seventy called into my presence looked up to see me already sitting on a high chair of ebony and ivory. I sat in the beam of sunlight ever directed on this point from the mirrors set in the domed roof high above. The frieze of Augustus and friends was behind me. Against the wall to my left stood a colossal statue of Augustus. Over on my right stood one of the Great Alexander. Of exactly equal height, each looked across the Hall at the other, ambiguously soft approval on their faces. On a golden easel just behind me on the platform, an icon of the Emperor kept watch on the proceedings. Before me, presiding over my silver inkstand of office, Martin sat on a low stool, his eyes cast reverently down to a heap of papyrus rolls.

In that vast floor space, and with a hundred and fifty feet of ceiling height above us, it hardly mattered with what magnificence we'd arrayed ourselves. For that reason, I'd decided against the gold leaf and cosmetics. I'd chosen instead to rely on the natural gold of my hair and from the smooth regularity of my still clean-shaven face. As for the robe, it was mostly white, though with a good third dyed purple. Normally, the heavy Corinthian silk would have shouted wealth and taste and, above all, power beyond anything the grandest man in my audience could ever hope to match. Not here. The statued past and the architectural ever-present alike dwarfed us all.

As the slaves, now standing on each side of me, set up an almost imperceptible breeze, Martin rose and stretched a hand out to the audience. With a chorus of relieved grunts, the hundred and seventy sat back into their own chairs.

I sipped at the cooled, well-watered wine before handing back the goblet to Macarius. It did nothing to settle my nerves. I looked at the sweating, slimy faces of the Egyptian landed interest. In silence, they looked back at me. I looked briefly up to my left at the curtained-off gallery: was that a gentle tug on the painted silk? Or was it a stray morning draught? I took a deep breath; and thus, as Homer says, the great consult began.

2

'Gentlemen, friends, lords of the Egyptian soil,' I said in a voice that carried to every corner of the Hall, 'I am come before you to speak the will of Caesar. I speak with the permission and full knowledge of the Viceroy Nicetas, his cousin. Though it is not required by protocol, I am instructed to take reasonable questions at the end of what I have to say.'

And there'd be plenty of those, I could see. I cursed Nicetas again. Given half a say in the matter, I'd have had him shipped in chains to Constantinople, there to answer for a stupidity and cowardice indistinguishable in their effects from outright treason. But I continued.

'It is a fact well-known to Caesar that the Egyptian land taxes have been short since the time of His Imperial Majesty Maurice of sad memory. We are aware of the representations made by your agents in Constantinople, that the late tyrant Phocas was kept deliberately short of revenue. We are also aware of the material help you provided during the late revolution. You, however, will be aware that your taxes were due not to the tyrant *but to the Empire itself.*

'You cannot also deny that, during the two years since the revolution, the shortfall has grown still worse. In more settled times, Egypt contributes around a third to the Imperial revenues. At the moment, even though other provinces have been wasted by the barbarians or occupied by the Persians, Egypt contributes barely one-fourth.

'This is surely insupportable. Heraclius is acknowledged, by Church and by Army and by Senate, as legitimate Emperor. The taxes he is owed – for his own reign and for those of Maurice and of the tyrant – are his by law, and, I will say, by nature.'

For all the law was known in outline, there was a ripple of nervous shuffling throughout the Hall. Perhaps I'd come on a little strong with that nonsense about a government's natural right to taxes. I smiled and managed a perfect fall from the hieratic tone in which I'd begun.

'But gentlemen,' I said, 'I come before you not as the representative of a tyrant, eager to plunder you of your goods. I represent Heraclius, the Lord's Anointed, the Thirteenth Apostle, whose reign is and ever shall be known as the restored Golden Age of Love and Justice.

'Know, therefore, the will of Caesar.'

Deep under the folds of my robe, I moved my leg to give Martin an imperceptible kick. He opened the first and biggest papyrus roll to the marked place and read in his loudest, flattest voice.

Back in Constantinople, I'd counselled against the switch of official language from Latin to Greek. Bearing in mind the weight each had for many years had in the Empire, it made sense to have all communications from the government in the language best known to the educated classes. What had concerned me, though, was the greater chance of ambiguity and therefore of chicanery provided by the very riches of Greek.

Listening again to the marvellous clarity of the new land law, it was obvious I'd been wrong. Sadly, though, I don't think my assembly of landowners cared one way or the other about the style. What they hated was the content. Martin was barely halfway through the reading before the murmurs broke out. As I said, they'd had time to know exactly what was coming. But there were certain motions that had to be gone through. When Martin came to the rights and obligations of the enfranchisees, the shouting got really under way.

'Are you telling us,' one of the fattest in the assembly bawled, all thought of my position absent from his outraged mind, 'that, in return for letting us off a few taxes, we're to give our best land to the wogs? And do I hear right that you're even planning to arm them?'

As the horrified babble rose higher, I leaned slightly forward.

'Get that man's name,' I said to Martin, trying not to move my lips. He'd been one of the latecomers. I'd not had time to try sucking up to him; and he seemed genuinely not to have known the details of the law. 'Put him on the red list for the apportionment of lands.'

Martin nodded.

I wanted to single out another of the dissenters, but Apion was now trying to make himself heard.

'There is no alternative,' he was saying. 'The scheme has already been tried in the Asiatic provinces. Already, it has increased the revenues and ended brigandage.'

My biggest ally was Apion. If Nicetas had been wasting my time, I hadn't. I'd been hard at work on lobbying of my own. Apion had the biggest estates in Egypt. A few assurances about his own interests, plus the promise of a governorship for the nephew he'd sent off to study in Constantinople, and he'd come neatly on side. Now, he was doing his best to rally support beyond the richer landowners who, comparatively speaking, had less to lose from the reforms.

'You mark my words,' the fatty broke into the emollient flow, 'you give land to the wogs, and they'll let it go to waste. They'll be putting up heretical churches while they've money to spend. When that's run out, they'll turn up here in Alexandria. Give them arms – why, they'll cut the throat of every honest Greek in Egypt.'

The man had the nerve to put his hat on in my presence. He sat back in his chair and glared openly at me. All round him, the roar of approval grew in volume. Apion looked nervously at me for support.

If I hadn't been long in Alexandria, I'd managed to learn one important truth. This was that the less Greek someone looked, the louder he damned the natives. This creature's ancestors might well have bought a pedigree showing descent from the Macedonian settlers called in by the first Ptolemy. His dark eyes and swarthy face told a different story. Indeed, when not twisted in almost apoplectic rage, his lips had a slight touch of the Ethiopian about them.

But so it was with most of them. Their Greek was barely less harsh than that of the natives who spoke it as a foreign language. In private, their customs differed hardly at all. Even so, they had their Greek names and Greek robes, and they clung – at least in public – to the Orthodox Faith laid down at Chalcedon. They called themselves a Greek ruling caste in the country. And they didn't care to learn they might have to behave otherwise.

I held up my arms for silence. No one paid attention. I nodded to one of the guards at the back of the Hall. He drew his sword and beat hard against his shield.

That brought them all to order. There was a flicker from over-head as the sun moved round to be caught by another of the mirrors.

'Gentlemen,' I said, 'I must remind you that I am not here to negotiate with you, but to inform you of the settled will of Caesar himself. My Lord Apion has already told you that this is the law not merely for Egypt, but for the Empire as a whole. I will, however, do you the honour of explaining the purpose of the law.

'For the past three hundred years, the Imperial government has generally had one response to each successive crisis of the state. This has been to ensure continued production by tying the culti-vators of the soil ever more firmly to the soil, and putting them under the dominion of the great landowners.

'This may, in each case, have given a temporary respite. In the long term, it has reduced the bulk of the population from free citizens to something approaching slaves. It has also reduced the numbers of the population.

'I understand that this process was completed somewhat earlier in Egypt than elsewhere in the Empire. Indeed, it predates the entry of Egypt into the Imperial system.'

Well, that was certain truth. If you've ever seen those repul-sive wall carvings put up by the kings here before any foreign conquest, you'll know just how exalted every ruling class has made itself since time immemorial.

But, again, I continued: 'Whatever the case, the effect has been the same in all places. The Empire is fighting desperately for life on every frontier. You all know of our losses to the Persians. You may not be aware that, in the past year alone, we have lost our last part of Spain to the Visigoths; and our losses in Italy to the Lombards have put Rome itself under almost continual siege. But for the efforts of His Holiness the Universal Bishop, Rome would long since have fallen.

'We need soldiers to defend the Empire, and we need taxes to pay them. That means we must give the cultivators of the soil ownership of the soil they cultivate. Only then will they produce. Only then will they pay taxes. Only then will they lift a finger in defence of the Empire.

'As My Lord Apion has also said, there is no alternative. If the landed interest in every part of the Empire will not give up part of what it has, all of it will finally be taken away under the rule of barbarian and Persian invaders who care nothing for established orders.

'We have heard it said that native landowners will squander what they are given and settle in Alexandria. This has not been our experience elsewhere. The land grants and duties of military service will be inalienable. I do assure you, the natives will be tied more firmly to the land by interest than they ever have been by law.

'If this Empire is to survive, it must become, more than it has in recent centuries been, one of farmers and soldiers. Only those cities shall survive that have trade or manufactures to support them – and only so far as trade or manufactures can support them.'

I sat down to a deathly silence. Perhaps I'd been carried away when I dropped that little hint about ending the bread dole. I don't suppose anyone there gave a damn for the poor of Alexandria who lived or died by the free bread we handed out. But it was unexpected news that they'd have to feed their domestics out of their own pockets.

And no – it still wasn't finished. Leontius had now broken cover. He was, I knew, the real leader of the resistance. He'd arrived in town almost before the wax had set on the writs of summons I'd squeezed out of Nicetas. For months now, he'd been slipping from dinner to dinner, getting up a regular party of opposition. I was surprised he hadn't spoken already. Perhaps he was waiting to see what, if any, concessions I'd been authorised to make by Heraclius. He'd only speak after I'd done half the work for him.

'Your Magnificence, My Lord *Al-ar-ic*,' he began, dripping contempt for a name that, Latin or barbarian, was still from the West. A good thing I'd long since given up, except with Martin, on my English name: he'd have had fun with that opening diphthong.

'My most Magnificent Lord,' he went on, the flab around his neck wobbling as he shifted about for the right oratorical pose, 'the will of Caesar is, of course, our command. If it is his will that we resign the lands from which we have always fed the great city of Constantinople, and before then Rome, what is there for us to do other than bow and go quietly into the dark? If we are told that the natives to whom our dominion must be transferred will thereby be raised from their so far eternal vice and degradation to become like the great men of Rome who, in olden times, fought and tilled until they had conquered the whole world, who are we to disagree?

'But' – he'd evidently practised this oration, and thought its sarcasm ever so witty – 'we are unjustly put upon when accused of not paying our taxes. Whenever bread and gold have been required for the Sacred Armies of Our Most Noble Augustus, when have we ever stayed the hand of generosity? When have we ever withheld the six million bushels of corn that we send every year to Constantinople?

'Nay, when this year we were called on to supply not six but ten million bushels, did we stay the hand? We did not. Now is the time of year when, by ancient custom, the people of Egypt rejoice in the plenty afforded them by the Nile and by their labour. It is now that the Alexandrians rejoice in low prices of bread. If they now grow thin – if they worry that the supplies left among us will give out before the next harvest – is that the fault of us who own the land? Nor have we made these truths known to the people. If we are in any sense at fault, it is surely in our blind devotion to the

20

will of the Caesar who has sent his young and beautiful Legate to accuse us of disloyalty.'

There was another murmur about the Hall. And he was right. We had stripped the country bare. We'd had our reasons in Constantinople. But it remained that the Egyptians – or some of them – were buggered. It was a good question, indeed, how many Alexandrians would make it through to the next harvest. Still, though, Leontius wasn't done.

'If we have refused to fill the Treasury in Alexandria,' he cried, suddenly passionate, 'it is only from regard for the True Faith of Our Lord Jesus Christ.'

He looked dramatically round the Hall. If he was up to something, he'd kept it to himself. Every face was as mystified as I was. Again, I noticed that no one was standing close beside him. He might be leader of the opposition. That didn't make him liked.

'I am not referring,' he went on, 'to those separated brethren who accept the heresy of a single Human and Divine Nature for Christ. While they have strayed from the true orthodoxy, they at least accept that no salvation lies but through Jesus Christ.

'No, I refer to the Old Faith of this land. Our Lord Viceroy Nicetas is second to none in his observance. Who does not know of his conversations with His Holiness the Patriarch – His Holiness who is like unto his own brother?

'But what would Our Lord Viceroy say if I were to tell him that, even to this day, the government that he directs is pouring out oceans of our gold and silver for the support of a temple raised up in ancient times at Philae far in the south to the demon Isis?

'What if I were to tell him that our taxes, even today, are feeding an army of shaven-headed priests? And that the sound of their blasphemous chanting extends far through Upper Egypt, to the scandal of orthodox and heretical alike?

'Your Magnificence may seek to punish us with confiscation of our land for refusing to give more than we have for the worship of demons. But I say to you – as the Holy Martyrs of the Church said in the days of persecution – "What crime be there for them that have Christ?"'

There was a moment of silence after he stopped. This last point he had indeed been keeping to himself. The mystery had been total. No response had been planned. But the silence was only for a moment. If at first hesitant, the Hall soon filled with howls of almost convincingly outraged piety. Some ran about wailing and waving their arms. A few ripped their clothing. Others, with more conviction, swore they'd never again pay taxes. One even did a passable job of throwing up behind one of the chairs.

Apion and the party I'd bribed and cajoled into existence sat eyeing each other in shifty silence. The chaos about them was resolving itself into a ragged chant of 'No crime for them that have Christ'. I'd come here to scold a pack of tax evaders. Now, I was facing a mob of candidate saints.

Leontius ignored the shouting and looked up to the gallery. He held out what I took to be documentary proof of his claims. I wasn't the only one to have noticed Nicetas up there following this whole shambles of a reading. I was fighting the urge to send the guards in with the flats of their swords when the curtains billowed outwards and then fell still again. I ground my teeth in fury. I looked that piece of offal Leontius carefully in the face. One way or the other, I'd have him before I left this city. This morning, though, he'd beaten me. Even with Nicetas gone back into the Palace, there was no point continuing.

'Gentlemen,' I said bleakly, the louder troublemakers now running out of puff, 'this meeting is adjourned until further notice. You will, in the meantime, do me the goodness of not going far from Alexandria.'

3

'It's a fucking disaster,' I snapped for the third time at Martin. 'And if you can't see what Nicetas has done to us, I can only assume this climate has turned your brains to shit as well.' My robe dumped on the office floor, I sat naked at my desk. The blacks were fanning me like mad. Every so often, one of them would reach forward to sponge on more scented oil.

'Well, whatever Leontius was trying,' Martin said with another stab at the optimistic, 'the law is now in effect. The enactment clause says it's to come into effect by reading, and it was read.'

'This isn't Bithynia,' I said, now wearily. I took up the cup of unwatered wine. I noticed I was starting on my fourth cup. I put it down and stared again at my commission. Written on to the parchment in words of gold and purple, it looked as grand a thing now as when Heraclius had presented it in full meeting of the Imperial Council. Back then, of course, I hadn't seen the flaws in its wording. Now, if I scraped off the seal and washed off the ink with a sponge dipped in vinegar, I might at least have a useful sheet of parchment.

'This isn't Bithynia,' I said again. 'Nicetas isn't some pen-pushing governor who has to bow to me in public. He's the sodding Viceroy. At least an exarch is one down from the Emperor. Within Egypt and Alexandria, Nicetas *is* the Emperor. If the law comes into effect when read, it can only be implemented when Nicetas seals the warrants.

'And since we're alone, Martin, do consider taking at least something off. Even sit much longer in that robe, and I'm sure you'll have a stroke.' Never mind his shaving cut, which had started bleeding again – his whole face was taking on a purple tinge.

I got up and walked across the room. The slaves hurried behind me with their ostrich feathers. But the movement of air around me was a greater relief. I stopped by the window and lifted a corner of the blind. Even this high up there wasn't a breath of wind. I sat down on a little sofa and stretched my legs.

'Of course,' I said, 'Nicetas could argue that sealing any warrants would be unwise. Outside Alexandria, the entire government is run by these landed turds. With all this banditry and the troubles arising from the supplemental grain requisition, we can't afford to alienate the landed interest. You may have noticed that Leontius as good as threatened to raise the mob against us over the grain matter.

'If only, though, Nicetas hadn't delayed and delayed and delayed, we could have got the law through before the newsletters caught up with us. If only he hadn't insisted on formal consultation. If only he hadn't virtually specified the content of my speech . . .'

After a very brief knock, Macarius came into the office.

'His Imperial Highness regrets that he must decline the pleasure of your company,' he said, looking discreetly away from me, 'but he has urgent business with His Holiness the Patriarch.'

Martin scowled at Macarius and looked sharply at me. I ignored him. Yes, everything was awful. I had Nicetas to deal with. My own people couldn't get on. Then there was this ghastly climate – hot all day, hot with bloodsucking flies all night. I'd been here at least a month longer than I'd expected. Unless recalled in something approaching disgrace, I might well be here till Christmas. But the wine was doing its job, and I could easily see Nicetas, at last understanding something of the balls-up he'd arranged, running off to take sanctuary from me with Patriarch John. Laughter was out of the question. But there was an absurd side to it all. I turned to the slaves.

'Leave us,' I said in Greek, dropping the Latin I'd been using with Martin.

They bowed low and packed up their stuff.

'Do lock the door, Macarius,' I said when we were alone. I leaned back in my chair and looked at the ceiling. It was a good twenty feet above me. But still the air didn't circulate.

I turned to Martin, who was now fussing through a satchel of notes. It hid the sulky look he couldn't keep off his face. I took up a handy sheet of parchment and fanned myself.

'So, what's all this about payments to pagan temples?' I asked.

'It's news to me,' said Martin, still looking away. He shrugged. 'We've been investigating the trends and ratios of spending, never the budgetary details. Even so, I'd have noticed that sort of item.'

'If Leontius is telling the truth, the payment is buried under some innocuous heading.'

'If I might intervene, My Lord,' Macarius said, speaking smoothly, 'there *was* a Temple of Isis at Philae. This town was always on the fringe of Imperial control in the south. For some years now, it has been somewhat beyond.

'The temple was exempted from the law that suppressed the Old Faith. It was an important cult centre for the kings of Ethiopia, who would come every year down the Nile to worship there; and diplomatic considerations prevailed. My understanding, however, is that the exemption was ended seventy years ago, when the Ethiopians were brought over to the True Faith of Jesus Christ.'

'Thank you, Macarius,' I said.

He allowed his hairless, desiccated features the ghost of a smile. Was there any end to the man's usefulness? He'd come to me on my second day in Alexandria. From running the household, he'd progressed into a general adviser on all matters Egyptian. He and Martin stood looking at me in respectful but also anticipatory silence. I was their leader, and they were waiting to be led. I swallowed another mouthful of wine and thought quickly.

'I want full details of the subsidy,' I said to Martin. 'You will be aware of my dealings with Jacob, who is Undersecretary in the Disbursements Office. I quashed the investigation into his return to Judaism. That is a favour he will now be able to return.

'Go to Jacob. Tell him to do or promise whatever it takes to get the information. Make it clear we aren't interested in punishing whatever fraud or corruption attended the subsidy. I want my involvement kept secret, but I want the information fast. I want it preferably before dinner tonight – certainly by this time tomorrow.

'And the moment you've got it, I want a proclamation drawn up, cancelling the subsidy. Fill it with the usual attacks on the Old Faith and threats against recusants. Make a big point about how Leontius brought it to our attention. Call him "Our right trusty and beloved friend" and so forth.

'I also want an order unblocking his appointment to the Commission of the Nile. It's plain Nicetas messed up there, with his talk of "graduated pressure". The man's turned out brighter than expected. Threatening us with the mob wasn't the limit of his abilities. Making non-payment of taxes into a religious duty was almost admirable. We've lost our present campaign against him. We might as well give way in style.

'I want this done by you alone and in your best impersonation of the local chancery style. Again, secrecy and speed are of the essence. Ideally, I'd like both documents ready before dinner. I'll force Nicetas to seal them. We can get them into the Friday *Gazette*.

'As for you, Macarius,' I went on, 'I think it's time to forget all that bleating from Nicetas about "clean hands". I want you to investigate Leontius yourself. Reasonable caution, of course – plausible deniability wherever possible. But there's dirt on *everyone*. It's just a matter of finding it. He's the biggest man in Letopolis. He must be up to something dodgy.

'I want sworn statements, conversation transcripts, original documents. When I invite that man here again for a private dinner, I'll serve him a meal he won't forget.'

I put my cup down and smiled. I looked about me. Martin wasn't looking too happy. Then again, he never did. Macarius, though, was looking as pleased as his impassive face would reveal. Whatever the case, I'd spoken. They'd wanted leadership. Now, they'd been given it.

'Be aware,' I took up again, 'that Leontius has limited active support against the law. His threat of the mob was intended to scare us. At the same time, it will have terrified many others in that meeting. But the subsidy matter is important. We can't risk getting the priests involved in matters of taxation. You never know with Heraclius. They might just win.

'We cannot afford further delay. The whole thing must be knocked on the head before Sunday service. That being done, we go back to the main issue – preferably without Leontius against us. This morning, things went badly for us. That doesn't mean we've lost.' I had another thought.

'I feel one of my "anonymous" pamphlets coming on,' I said to Martin. 'I may have said this morning that Heraclius is not Phocas. They didn't seem that convinced. We can work on this. It may be useful to remind them how, when Caracalla turned up here, he organised a massacre in pretty short order. Diocletian was hardly the Lamb of God.

'There's something about Alexandria that brings out the worst in an emperor. This being so, dealing with me might be better than having to face Heraclius in person.

'Leontius must be made to understand that, if he draws it, his sword will have two edges.'

I stood up. I really had finished now. Macarius hurried forward with a towel. I let him wind it round my waist.

'Do arrange a cold bath for me,' I said, 'and something light and simple to put on. I'll be in the Library, if anyone needs me.'

It was early afternoon, and the streets of Alexandria were baking in the sun. Elsewhere, the heat would have driven people indoors for a rest. The hours of business in Alexandria, though, were always when there was business to be done. If I'd taken my official chair, or put on finer clothes, I could have relied on a clear path through the crowds. As it was, I was jostled continually to the street edges. Even in the fifty-yard width of Main Street, I had to push back at people to avoid being pitched into shops I had no intention of visiting.

The street demagogues didn't help. In this heat, of course, even they couldn't be really active. But enough of them had taken up their usual positions – and they'd attracted enough of the usual scum – to add to the general unpleasantness. As I tried to pass by one of them, I had no choice but to stop and listen. He was ranting on about the floods. Apparently – and he assured us all he was the greatest expert on the matter – the Nile had risen too late, and was now rising too fast.

'You mark my words,' he bawled above the chatter of the passing crowds, 'it will be evil as well as mud washed down from the south this year. These will be floods never to be forgotten.'

'What I want to know,' a strongly Syrian voice struck up beside me, 'is where the police have all gone. In Antioch, this liberty of speech among the lower sorts would never be permitted.'

The answer I could have given was that the police had no manpower for pushing the demagogues off the main streets. Most of them were manning the Wall that kept our own central district sealed off from the Egyptian quarter. The rest were down in the Harbour, keeping the Greek trash from rioting as the supplemental grain requisition was loaded. But I was in no mood today for putting a finger on the pulse of street opinion. I tilted the brim of my hat to cover more of my face and prepared to move off.

'Is it true the government is planning to require different grades of bread to be sold each side of the Wall?' the Syrian asked again.

I stopped and looked hard at the man. Where had he picked this up? It had been raised in the Viceroy's Council just a few days back. It had been a vague option, and the Patriarch and I had got it dismissed out of hand. But this was the sort of rumour that, Wall or no Wall, could set off intercommunal war.

I would have asked a few questions. At this moment, though, there was one of those tidal movements in the crowd that pulled me away from the Syrian and brought me to rest just a yard or so from a column of monks, dressed all in black, who were pushing their way towards some mischief.

'Blessed are the peacemakers: for they shall be called the children of God,' one of them cried, waving his club for emphasis. 'Blessed are they which are persecuted for righteousness' sake: for theirs is the kingdom of heaven,' another bellowed. I squeezed myself far back out of their path. Wherever they were going, they really were about no good. Besides, they were almost dripping vermin. Just looking at them made me want to scratch.

'Spare some change for the hungry!' came the practised whine.

I'd now got through the stationary crowd and was the other side of the statue put up to celebrate the Great Constantine as the Thirteenth Apostle. I'd been looking up at the colossal meekness of the thing, and hadn't considered where I might be treading.

'Piss off!' I snarled. I stepped smartly back before the beggar could lay scabby hands on me. I could have given him a lecture on the virtues of working for a living. But I'd had enough that day of explaining myself.

He shuffled back to his patch of shade and sat down again with as hard a bump as a starved body could manage.

His begging cry was soon lost in the noise around me. But soon it wouldn't just be the beggars who were hungry. There's a limit even in Egypt on how much grain you can take out before people begin to starve. For the moment, so long as I could keep Nicetas from signing his price control order, there was still bread to be had in the market. But it was hard to say how much longer the poor could afford to buy anything at all.

4

I looked again at the tattered sheet.

'I can't say I've heard of a Lake Smegma,' I said. I looked closer still at the sheet. Why was it, I asked myself, that papyrus always crumbled under the most important words in a document?

'I think you will find this helpful, My Lord,' Hermogenes quavered. He pointed to another of the sheets stretched out before us on the table. I shifted position, to see if the faded writing might look any better from another angle. How at his age he could read a word of this was beyond me. Then again, as Head Librarian, his job was to read far worse.

'Ah,' I said at last, 'a transliteration of an Egyptian name.' I'd raised my voice only slightly. But it echoed in the cavernous main collection room of the Library. Perhaps thirty yards away, some bearded scholar looked up and scowled at me. 'It gets us a little closer to what we want,' I continued. 'At least we can be sure it did exist. But we still don't know what it contained – or, indeed, exactly where it is.'

'That may be so, My Lord—' Hermogenes broke off as one of the lead weights shifted, and the map rolled shut. As he reached with palsied hand to keep it from moving any futher, he knocked it and a whole stack of rolls on to the floor. They fell with a crash that echoed through the room.

'No, My Lord,' Hermogenes gasped as he went down on all fours. 'Please allow me.' The rolls scraped harshly on the pavement as he tried with all the feeble uselessness of age to gather them all together again.

'I must inform you,' the far away scholar hissed with pompous self-importance, 'that I am here on work of the highest importance to Holy Mother Church. I do not expect endless disturbance from the prattle of some barbarian child. Show some respect as you breathe in the sacred dust of these four hundred thousand volumes.'

Hermogenes tried to get up and splutter a protest. But I kicked him gently in the side, and he went back to trying to re-sort his documents. 'Work of the highest importance' to the Church, he'd said? Well, he must have been pretty far down the scale of human importance not to have recognised me now I was wearing no hat. And if he had recognised me, a bishop himself would sooner have kissed the dust beneath my boots than call me a barbarian. I could have called for security and had him arrested. A good racking and the loss of his eyes wouldn't have been thought unreasonable to anyone told the facts of his treason. But I'd grown used to living in a world where my looks made me an object either of lust or of contempt. I turned my back on him and stared again at the racks that housed just part of the biggest collection of books in the known world.

Oh, how excited I'd been on my first visit here back in April. Here, at last before me, was the greatest research library in the world: the treasure house, begun by the first King Ptolemy, of all the arts and sciences. It was here that the standard text of Homer had been settled, here that the world had been measured, here that the secrets of the human body had first been laid out and classified.

It hadn't taken long however, to discover just how 'sacred' the dust was of all those books. The shelving racks might still have their ancient labels. Their contents had long since been replaced with the accumulated mass of the Arian and Monophysite controversies. Riots and civil war, religious fanaticism, fires and the general accidents of time – all had combined to diminish the ancient Library to a ghost of what it had been. As to the replacement volumes, few who mattered had thought them other than an improvement.

That should, officially, have been my position. Back in Constantinople, Sergius and I had decided to settle the

Monophysite heresy. It had long seemed impossible to bring the heretics to accept that Christ was both Human *and* Divine. Every means of persuasion, from discussion to massacre, had been tried – all to no effect. The belief that Christ had only One Nature – or that, if there was any tinge of the Human, it had been subsumed within the Divine as a drop of honey is dissolved in the sea – was ineradicable. Off and on, the dispute had been running for centuries, to the distraction of both state and Church in all the Eastern provinces. It had also periodically made for difficulties with Rome. It was a dispute that, in itself, should have moved a schoolboy to laughter. But it had worked itself into arguments over Greek cultural and political domination that were endangering the Empire. Now, Sergius was Patriarch of Constantinople. I had a certain influence in Rome. Both of us had the full ear of Heraclius. If Sergius had the advantage of actually believing in God, we had an equal facility for discovering new meanings in words that everyone else had thought settled. We knew the orthodox would accept a Single Will for Christ if the heretics would accept a watered down meaning of His Double Nature. I was here to impose a new land settlement on Egypt. But I was also quietly sounding out the clerics of every party.

And that was another reason for not having that beastly old scholar up for treason against the Emperor via rudeness to me. By local standards, he might count as a moderate, and my turning the other cheek might be in every legitimate interest.

But Hermogenes had all his stuff back in place on our table, and it was time to return to the matter in hand. I was there to discuss the old reserve stock. Its whereabouts had been lost in the fire and massacre that had followed the siege by Diocletian. It might have contained a hundred thousand volumes. If so, these might well have survived the shipwreck of the main Library.

Hermogenes unrolled the map again. He put a finger on Alexandria and traced a shaky path across Lake Mareotis. Then, from Apis, he moved more firmly about fifty miles south-east across the desert. He stopped just beyond the maximum flood mark of the Nile.

'It would have most likely been south enough to benefit from the dry Egyptian climate, but not too far outside the black land,' he said.

'That would put it in or around,' I said, looking at the tiny writing on the parchment map, 'Soteropolis. I don't recall that name from the tax records.'

'It was a place of ill fortune,' came the reply. Hermogenes closed his eyes and dug visibly into his memory. 'It was home to a recurrent pestilence not shared in the rest of Egypt. After an outbreak around the time of Diocletian, the citizens were resettled in the neighbouring municipality.

'It was the subject of a celebrated law case in my youth.' He screwed his eyes harder in an effort to recall. 'It was all to do, I think, with maintenance obligations for a road. No decision could be reached, as both road and town had been claimed by the desert sands, and no one could be sure how either had been connected.

'From the tone of these invoices, the reserve stock would not have been in the town. It would have been perhaps a few hundred yards outside the walls, in a compound of its own. Bearing in mind the pestilential air within the town, an outside location would make sense.'

I looked up. Between the topmost of the book racks and the high circle of windows that let in the continuous and warm glow of light, ran the inscription: *Of All Its Ills the Soul Shall Here be Cured*. Carved in letters a foot high, this had been put up on orders of the first Ptolemy. It was centred on a niche containing statues of the King together with the Great Alexander, one of whose leading generals he had been and whose successor, by speed and cunning, he'd made himself in Egypt. He stood, just half a head shorter, his eyes turned in adoration to the Great Conqueror.

'I could arrange five hundred labourers,' I said, looking back to Hermogenes. 'The Viceroy has decided to employ people during the flood season in digging out the old canal between the Red Sea and the Mediterranean. I could easily borrow a contingent of these for a month.

'But we still need to assure ourselves that Soteropolis is the right place. And we still need to know at least roughly where outside the town the reserve might have been. There is also the matter of content.'

'You reassure me, My Lord,' Hermogenes interrupted, 'that all the literary and philosophical works listed in the catalogue are still extant in Constantinople?'

I nodded. In Rome, I'd been shocked by the perhaps irreparable losses a century of chaos had made in the Latin classics. But the much larger Greek *corpus* had survived intact in the great City on the waters between Asia and Europe.

'If the reserve stock is just from those works,' I said, 'it's a waste of time to go looking for it. What interests me is whether it contains any of the scientific and technical works. From the accounts I've read of the University here, certain advances were made that may be of use to the Empire. There are, for example, reports of a powder that, when ignited—'

With a sudden whoosh of air and then crash of timber on stone, the door flew open. Puffing mightily from a brisk two-mile walk along those streets, Martin leaned unsteadily against one of the book racks. His face had turned a still deeper shade of purple. I poured him a cup of water and hurried over to him.

'Aelric,' he gasped after a long pause. He looked at the old Librarian and pulled himself together. 'My Lord Alaric, you are needed urgently. The Caesar Priscus has arrived without warning. He says he needs to see you.'

5

As I'd expected, I caught up with Priscus in the nursery attached to my own quarters. I walked in on the beginnings of chaos. The moment he saw me, Maximin broke loose from where Priscus had cornered him, and, wailing with fear, ran towards me. Over against the far wall, the nursery maids huddled quietly in each other's arms.

'My dear Alaric,' said Priscus, with a flash of his riddled teeth, 'how delightful to see you again.' He dropped the puppy – so far as I could tell, unharmed – on to the floor. It scuttled straight under a low table and stayed there.

I took Maximin into my arms and held him tight. I controlled my voice.

'Priscus,' I said, speaking slowly and deliberately in Latin, 'if you ever come near this child again, I'll kill you.'

'And what will Our Lord Augustus say when he has to find another Commander of the East?' he replied very smoothly, still in Greek.

'If he replaced you with a committee of his softer palace eunuchs,' I said, 'I doubt things could go worse than they have under you. I seem to remember you promised a shattering victory over the Persians in Cappadocia. The latest newsletters report a loss of the whole province.' I glanced at the low table. I could just hear the whimpering. 'But I see you can be brave enough when it comes to small animals.'

Priscus scowled, but put his knife away. 'My son is a Roman,' he said. 'He must learn to be strong.'

With an extreme effort, I remained calm, though I continued now in Greek; the nursery maids could hear what they heard and make of it what they would.

'Priscus,' I said, 'you stopped being this child's father when you had him dumped as a newborn outside that church. By law and by the teachings of every faith, *I am now his father.* If I see you so much as near him again, I swear I'll kill you, and I'll take my chances with Heraclius.'

I handed Maximin, his arms no longer locked about my neck, to one of the nursery maids. 'Put him to bed,' I told her. 'Try to get the dog to lie with him.'

In silence, I led Priscus along the endless and stuffy plush corridors of the Palace. Finding my bearings in the seven floors of the place, each one covering about an acre, had taken me days. Why the Ptolemies had built and put up with this gigantic oven was obvious: they were the richest men in the world, and they had to show this off to their fellow Greeks and to the Egyptians they and their Fellow Greeks lorded it over. The Imperial governors had no such need. They could easily have built something more convenient to the climate and to the needs of administration. For much of the time, there'd been no shortage of money. But it was too late now.

Martin was dictating some letters as we walked in to the outer office. He jumped up at the sight of Priscus and made a polite bow. The secretaries fawned low on the floor.

'Ah – Martin!' Priscus opened with smooth courtesy. 'How delightful to see another friend so far from home. You will surely let me compliment you on how well you are looking on all that Alexandrian food. But for the red hair, I'd barely have recognised you. Such a glorious thing, I've always thought, to have red hair. A shame it goes so quickly – don't you think?'

Martin's face reddened, and I noticed the little movement as he stopped his hand from its instinctive move upward. I glared at Priscus. He stepped forward and took Martin's hand.

'But we have no need to stand on outmoded ceremony, have we, Martin? In our new Empire of Love and Justice, we are all equal servants of the common good and of the Great Augustus!'

Martin swallowed and managed the appropriate form of words. But Priscus was moving again.

He crossed the floor and pulled open the door to my own office. Martin had ordered the blinds to be sprayed with rose water. This, plus the very light breeze coming off the sea, made my office almost endurable. I looked at Priscus as I sipped at my date wine and he fussed, as ever, with his pouch of drugs. I'd last seen him at Christmas in Constantinople. Then he'd been pressing every ounce of glory from his successes against the Persians, and predicting final victory once he'd finished tying them up in Cappadocia.

Just eight months later, and he was looking a decade older. The bounce had gone out of him. Oh, there was the same slimy gloss on his manners. Everything about him still screamed Powerful and Nasty Piece of Work. The cosmetics kept his face unlined and the same colour it had always been of fresh papyrus. But, while I hadn't bothered once to look back as I led him from the nursery, I'd almost felt the shuffling gait of an old man as he hurried to keep up with me.

I waited for the seizure from whatever he'd shoved up his nose to clear. One day, I'd often hoped, he'd find some mood-altering substance that would kill him instead of just slowly rotting his mind. As his shoulders sagged from the release of tension, and he reached for his own cup, I stared back into the tiny dots of his eyes, and passed from outraged father to senior official of the Empire.

'So, My Lord Priscus,' I said, 'what brings you to Alexandria, and with so little notice?'

He reached into his bag – had the man no slaves with him? – and pulled out a letter. He passed it across the little table that separated our chairs.

'I need you to provide me urgently with these,' he said.

I unrolled the document and scanned it. I rolled it up again and replaced the leather band before pushing it back across the table.

'You'll need to speak to Nicetas about this,' I said. 'He's the man with authority over Egypt.'

Priscus smiled weakly. He left the roll beside the wine jug. 'My information was that you were the effective power in Egypt,' he said.

'Your informants are misinformed,' I said curtly. 'However, if I did have any authority here, I'd have you put on the road straight back to Pelusium, and then pushed across the border into Syria, which I think is within your area of command.

'We haven't money at the moment to pay our own frontier guards. As for the corn, we already have riots brewing over a shortage here. If you can force an interview with His Imperial Highness the Viceroy, good luck. But you'll only get a longer and more formal version of the answer I've just given.'

Priscus looked awhile into his cup. For a moment, I even thought he'd cry. But the moment passed, and he was looking at me again.

'How much do you know about Cappadocia?' he asked.

'Only what you said during that supper with Heraclius,' I said, 'and the reports that have drifted here on the posts. You said you'd have the entire Persian Army holed up in Caesarea, where you'd starve them into surrender. Instead, I understand the Persians broke out and annihilated half the Army of the East while you lay in your tent, knocked out on those shitty drugs.

'I'm told it's now only a matter of time before siege armies turn up outside Damascus and even Antioch.'

'It wasn't like that,' said Priscus in quiet despair. 'You still won't or can't understand the scale of what I achieved last summer and autumn. With armies a third of their official strength, I harried the Persians. I pushed their smaller forces back across the Euphrates. The main forces I drew further and further from their supply routes. I bribed. I spread dissension. I fed false reports via double agents.

'I don't think any other general – not even Belisarius himself – could have done more with less. I had effectively the whole Persian invasion force and their Commander-in-Chief squeezed into the last place military logic suggested they should be. It should have been a question of waiting for the invasion to collapse, and then ending the war on favourable terms.'

'So what went wrong?' I jeered. All other involvements with the man aside, I had grown thoroughly sick of his strategic playacting at Christmas.

'Fucking Heraclius went wrong!' he cried with an involuntary look at the door. It was faced with padded leather. 'He turned up in person to take the credit for the surrender of eight Persian generals. I told him to wait. But the fool wanted a battle. He insisted it was "unseemly" to gain such a victory without a blow.

'And so challenge was laid and accepted, and the Persians marched out to discover that what they thought was an army of forty thousand men was instead a half-starved rabble of five thousand.

'Even then, I might have managed a draw. But our New Alexander confined me to quarters while he strutted round in a golden breastplate that must have weighed ninety pounds.

'We were lucky the Persians showed more interest in breaking free than staying to enjoy the fruits of victory. We'd all by now be on display to the rabble in Ctesiphon – we or our heads.

'And you are right about Damascus. I haven't a single fighting unit anywhere in Syria. With Constantinople itself in danger, all forces have been drawn to the north.'

There was no need for cross-examining about any of this. I knew Priscus was telling the truth. I could almost hear that voice – half sulky, half dreamy – as the Emperor laid down his childish notions of war craft. Sergius and I had managed to get a free hand in religious controversy by showing that letter I'd squeezed out of the Pope. Keeping him from military affairs would have defeated anyone, let alone Priscus.

Oh, if only Emperor Phocas hadn't been a complete duffer, he'd still be boiling his victims alive in the Circus, and I'd be back in Rome, playing the markets and sending books to Canterbury. As it was, we had Heraclius; and if his personal body count was much lower, he was proving still less effective at holding the Empire together.

I unrolled the letter again. We both served Heraclius. That brought certain duties – even to Priscus.

'I'll put in a word to Nicetas about the money,' I said. 'Gold can always be found if the need is pressing. I stand by what I said

39

about the corn, though. Until the next harvest comes in, there's a shortage we daren't risk adding to.'

'Thank you, Alaric,' he said. Unlikely words, these, from Priscus – and they even sounded genuine. He finished the cup and refilled it.

'There is one other thing not on my list,' he said, starting over with an echo of his old bounce. 'The Patriarch of Jerusalem turned nasty when I asked for a loan of the True Cross. You see, soldiers won't gather unless you pay or feed them or both. They won't fight – and certainly won't die – unless you give them something more. Have you heard about the first piss pot of Jesus Christ?' he asked.

'Er – no,' I said.

'Well' – Priscus smiled weakly and reached again for the jug – 'you know that when Herod had all those boys killed, the Holy Family came to Egypt and remained some years in safety?'

I nodded. I was already beginning to guess what would come next.

'The child Christ,' he went on, 'had a piss pot. After He returned to Palestine, this remained in Egypt. It is, I'm told, a relic of the highest power. You see, it received His excrements while His Human Nature was still undeveloped, but His Divine Nature was already perfect. The True Cross, by comparison, was in contact with a body that was fully half human.'

'My dear Priscus,' I said, trying hard not to burst out laughing, 'I don't think this heresy's been advanced even in Alexandria. What you are saying is that had Christ died as a baby, the Monophysites would be broadly correct. If, on the other hand, he'd made it to fifty, the true orthodoxy would be Nestorian. How lucky for the majority at the Council of Chalcedon that he died at thirty-three, when His Nature was a perfect balance of God and man conjoined in one substance!'

Priscus shrugged. 'How the priests sort these things out is their business,' he said. 'My business is to raise another army and lead it into battle with a relic beside me the men would run through fire not to lose.'

'I've not heard of this relic,' I said, 'and I've been here for months now, and spoken to hundreds of people. Where do you suppose it might be kept?'

'I believe it's secreted in the base of the Great Pyramid,' came the reply. 'I looked around for this as I entered the city. Perhaps it's smaller than I was told.'

I did laugh now. I really couldn't keep it back. I laughed until tears began to run down my cheeks. The thought of Priscus, wandering round Alexandria like a barbarian pilgrim in Rome, no guidebook in hand, looking for the Pyramids!

I got up and moved to the north window. I pulled back the blind and looked out past the Lighthouse to the calm, sparkling waters of the Mediterranean. I turned back to Priscus, whose face, I could see, had gone puce under the make-up.

'You must forgive me, Priscus,' I said, 'but the Pyramids are three days up river – five if the winds are against you. And you need to add a day for the sea voyage from here to Bolbitine, or half that if you're willing to take the Nile from Canopus. And though I haven't seen them, it's my understanding that the Great Pyramid was last opened three thousand years ago. No entrance has ever been found since then, assuming, that is, the thing isn't just solid stone. Christ lived here about six hundred years ago. You'd need a miracle to get the poor man's piss pot inside the Pyramid, another to let anyone know it was there, and another for no one in Alexandria to know what your doubtless very holy informant in – in Syria? – has told you.

'If you want relics, I'll get you an appointment with the local Patriarch. He might be more accommodating than His Holiness of Jerusalem. I believe Alexandria has the head of Saint Mark, both feet of John the Baptist, and three right hands of Saint John the Divine. But there's no holy piss pot that I know about – not of Jesus Christ, nor of anyone else likely to inspire your men.'

'My sources are confidential,' Priscus snapped, 'but I have it on good authority the relic is where I've said.'

I changed the subject. 'Have you any soldiers with you?' I asked. An interesting thought had come into my mind. I'd rather Priscus had been stuck in a tent somewhere close by Armenia. Since he wasn't, I might as well find some use in him.

But he shook his head. He'd come alone and in secrecy.

'Never mind,' I said. 'You are Commander of the East, and I doubt if any of the notables here have been introduced to a military dignitary close to your exalted status. You must allow yourself to be guest of honour at tonight's dinner. All the big men of Egypt will be there. And I think I can promise the Viceroy for you to sit beside.'

I took up the little bell from my desk and rang it.

'Ah, Martin,' I said as the door opened. 'The Lord Caesar Priscus will be in Alexandria for at least the next few days. Please ask Macarius to make all necessary preparations in the Palace.'

Martin bowed. He let his fingers rasp ever so lightly on the papyrus sheet he was carrying.

'A productive afternoon with our friend?' I asked.

Martin nodded.

I ignored Priscus and his unspoken query. 'That is excellent. My compliments to the pair of you.'

Again to Priscus: 'When my steward arrives, you will surely do me the honour of letting me accompany you to your suite. If I'm not mistaken, one of your rooms will be the office where Cleopatra killed herself.'

6

I was awake. At first, all was silent in the darkness around me. I was alone in bed. That much I knew even as my head cleared. With the Patriarch scowling away through dinner, there had been no dancing girls. And, out of respect, we'd used the older serving boys.

I'd come to bed alone. So why was I awake? Instinctively, I reached under the pillow. Then the tiny voice spoke out of the darkness: 'Daddy!'

I relaxed and focused on the dim shape. 'Maximin,' I said. I reached out and took his hand. As he clutched at me, I took him into my arms. There was no point in trying to get any sense out of him. I knew at once it had been another of his nightmares. With 'uncle' Priscus in town, it was hardly surprising. The man gave me bad dreams.

Now he was pushing two, the boy was finally growing bigger. Even so, he remained against my big barbarian chest and arms what that puppy was to him. Whispering comfort, I rocked him gently until he was asleep again. I thought to put him into bed with me and go back to sleep. But it would only have set the nursery maids into another panic when they finally woke. I waited until his breathing was completely regular, then slid out of bed and put on a gown.

The lamps burned low in the airless corridors. Night had brought no let-up in the baking heat, and the slightest movement had me dripping sweat. Maximin was normally light enough to carry, but holding him away from the furnace of my body was a strain that did nothing for my temper.

'I thought I'd made it clear to lock the nursery at night,' I hissed at the chief maid when I'd gently kicked some life into her. She opened her mouth to reply. I raised my hand for silence. 'We'll discuss this tomorrow,' I said.

I watched her tuck the child back into his bed and arrange the netting above him, and waited until it was clear he'd sleep without break until morning.

Was that a flash of light?

I went softly over by the window. But it looked into a courtyard. Far overhead, the stars burned steadily down. I stretched out for a better view. I could see the reflected glare of the half moon on an area of roof tiles. There was nothing otherwise to be seen from here. Leaving the shutters open, I gently pulled down the reed blinds.

Outside again in the corridor, I waited until I heard the faint click of the door lock. Going back towards my bedroom, I reached one of the corridor junctions. Turning left would take me straight back to bed. Right would lead me out of the wing of the Palace assigned to me and my household. I thought briefly. About a hundred yards to the right, I recalled there was a staircase going up.

The inspection rooms had the advantage of greater height. In this sweltering heat, though, I preferred the openness of the main roof. Its flat span interrupted by the various courtyards and by the big central garden, this covered most of the Palace area and was mostly paved. It was sometimes used for theatrical performances, though more often for transacting business where much light was needed. It might now catch the occasional breeze.

I leaned on the rail that separated paved from tiled areas. I was on the seaward side of the Palace, and stood looking roughly north over the Harbour. Over to my left, the Lighthouse shone brightly, its curved mirrors taking and concentrating light from the burning oil in ways that no one nowadays had been able to explain to me. Because of its much greater height, its beams would reach beyond any horizon visible from where I stood.

Or they normally would. Tonight, there was a storm far out to sea. Those repeated and intense if irregular flashes left no doubt what was happening. Far out, beyond my horizon, the sea and the wind would be running wild. No ship that had dared a night voyage would ever get out of that howling chaos. We'd skirted a few storms on our crossing here from Constantinople. If they'd been nothing like this must be, they had almost made me reconsider my prejudice against long journeys by road.

But if a great storm, it was far out. Here on land, there was scarcely a gust of wind. It was enough to scatter the reflection of a few stray lamps on the Harbour, but no more than that. Down in the parks that fringed the Harbour, the palm fronds hung still on the trees. Around me, the dust lay still on the moonlit pavements. Suffused with the aromatic scent of the shrubs dotted in bronze pots over that roof, the air lay about me with the hot stillness of a bathhouse.

What the bloody hell was I doing here? I asked myself. And I wasn't asking why I was out of bed. This whole way of life wasn't anything I'd once have chosen for myself.

Yes, I had power. Priscus hadn't been far off the mark when he said I ran Egypt. In the sense that I could squeeze any function of state into my commission, I was limited only by the time I could get with Nicetas to sign the required documents. But what is the use of power? If you stand outside government and look at all those levers and pulleys, you can imagine the good or evil that power enables. From the inside, all you really know is impotence. Either those ropes and pulleys are too immovable, or they pull easily enough, but aren't attached to anything that produces the desired effect.

Look at me with the new law. I had the Word of Caesar behind me. I could in theory have any one of those landowners taken up and flogged. In the event, I was reduced to negotiating with them from a position of structural weakness.

It was the same even at the top. Phocas had killed his way to the Purple, and had killed and killed and killed to stay there. In the end, he'd still been dragged out of that monastery to serve as first public victim of the new reign. And before that end, it was a quiet day when he wasn't signing begging letters to the Pope for money, or promising money he didn't have to barbarian raiders he hadn't the means to drive off by force.

I wasn't powerful enough as Imperial Legate to do what I needed to save the Empire. Even if he'd wanted and had known how to act, Heraclius was in no better position.

So here I was, wasting time that would never come again. I was giving up all but the most hasty pleasures of youth. I was giving up the more solid pleasures of learning in what had once – Athens always excepted – been the university town of mankind, and pre-eminently its museum and laboratory. If I'd read and was using those mathematical writings Hermogenes still had in his basement, how much more might they give up if I weren't spending so much of my waking time on that bastard commission of Heraclius?

I turned from looking over that boundless moonlit sea and walked back across the paved expanse. My sandals flopped loud on the marble. There might be a few guards on sentry duty far below at the gates who weren't dozing. Otherwise, I must be the only person awake in the Palace. How they could all be asleep on such a night escaped me.

But were they all asleep? I stopped and listened hard. Nothing. Night can deceive the senses, I told myself. I took another few steps, then stopped again. I wasn't alone up here. There *was* someone else on the roof.

I wouldn't call it chanting. I'd have heard that at once. It was more a sort of broken, rhythmical whispering. If I couldn't make out the words, I knew for sure it was in the native language of the Egyptians. Being in Alexandria, I hadn't bothered learning any of it. But the pattern of guttural, short sounds was unmistakable. It came from the far side of the roof. Because of a parapet wall that closed off one of the smaller courtyards, I couldn't see the far side from where I was standing. Moving softly now, I took myself over against the wall and moved round.

Long and thin, the moonlight gleaming on his scalp, someone leaned far over the rail, as if bowing through the gloom over Lake Mareotis at something in the vastness of the Egypt proper that lay beyond.

46

'Macarius?' I said hesitantly. There was little doubt who it could be. No one else I'd ever seen in the Palace matched that shape and size.

'So you can't sleep either?' I asked, trying to sound natural. He straightened and turned. The moon was behind him, so I couldn't see his face. But I could feel the close stare he gave me. He stood awhile in the confused silence of one surprised. I was preparing another comment to break the silence.

Then: 'The night, My Lord, is made more oppressive by the storm.' He pressed his shaking hands hard into the folds of his robe.

'Oppressive is just the word,' I said, stepping over beside him. 'I believe the nights grow more endurable from October.' My voice sounded loud. I dropped it to match the semi-whisper Macarius had used. 'This one is certainly bad.'

We stood looking over Lake Mareotis. The moon stood high above, and shone back at us from the perfectly smooth waters. Beyond was the dull gloom. Whatever Macarius might think he could see, I saw nothing.

'The storm will be with us by morning,' he said.

As if in response, there was another flash. It still came from beyond the horizon. We crossed the roof to the shore view from the Palace.

Was that a very faint rumbling I could hear? Hard to say. Macarius was speaking again.

'When these things blow up,' he continued, an abstracted, slightly annoyed tone to his voice, 'there can be an end for days to all contact with the world.'

I ignored his remark. If he thought at all as the other natives, he'd care nothing for the disrupted sea lanes. So long as the causeways into Egypt remained unsubmerged, Alexandria would not be entirely a place where Greeks looked outwards to the Mediterranean. I thanked him for his advice regarding that temple.

'I understand that My Lord's secretary was able to have the subsidy traced,' he said, now himself again. His face showed in the moonlight. It had its usual bland expression. Though fluent

47

enough, Macarius spoke the flattened Greek of the natives, and it could be hard to tell between a statement and a question.

I took this as a question and nodded. 'The subsidy was hidden away in the military pensions budget,' I explained. 'It seems to have been that way for three generations. But for Leontius, it might have continued another three.'

'And I understand the Viceroy sealed your proclamation,' Macarius said, 'and this will be published tomorrow.'

I nodded again. Dinner had been a ghastly affair. It had begun with a reading from Saint John Chrysostom on the horrors of gluttony, and then proceeded, to an accompaniment of loud, twanging music, through about fifty inedible courses. It had culminated with the mice in lead sauce that had been the last year's fashion in Constantinople. Missing out on the wine had been a bitch. But I'd sat beside the Patriarch, and had used the opportunity to match him in refusing all but bread and water.

To my annoyance, Priscus had struck up an immediate friendship with Leontius. They'd sat together deep in conversation as they drank their way through about a gallon each of wine. Afterwards, arm-in-arm, they'd staggered off together, doubtless to carry on till morning. So much for hoping the man might put the frighteners on Leontius!

Still, I'd got the proclamation out of Nicetas. Martin had brought it in, neatly written in perfect imitation of the local chancery style. Nicetas had sealed it without reading, then returned to pestering me and the Patriarch about the location of the soul between death and the Second Coming. It would be on the streets at dawn. Shortly after, it would be on a fast boat up river as close to Philae as could safely be reached.

If, shortly after, it might be floating back towards us, ripped and covered in shit, that was not a problem for me. All that mattered was the appearance of action here in Alexandria with the landed trash of Egypt. On the other hand, I'd seen to it that this Temple of Isis wouldn't get another clipped copper out of the taxpayers.

'Of course,' I went on, 'there'll be no investigation. But it would be interesting to know how the subsidy continued so long without comment. And it would be most useful to know how Leontius came to hear about it – and how no one else in that assembly appeared to have known about it.'

I looked at Macarius. I wondered again how old he might be. Fifty? Seventy? It was hard to tell from those shrivelled features. He'd probably looked much the same since he was my age.

'Did you not once tell me,' I asked, 'that you lived awhile in the south?'

'I did live there,' Macarius answered. I wanted to ask in what capacity. But he continued: 'In Alexandria and in all areas touched by Greek influence, the dispute is between orthodoxy and heresy. Go far enough up river, and the Old Faith makes up a third party in the dispute. I find it hard to believe that anything so important as the cult of Isis at Philae could be maintained as publicly as Leontius claims. But many of the old temples are quietly kept going.'

'So,' I asked, coming back to the main business in hand, 'how do you suppose the man got his information? Has he been sniffing round in the south?'

Macarius bowed slightly. 'I shall be better able to answer your questions the day after tomorrow,' he said. 'All I can report for the moment is that Leontius has recently been enlarging his manor house at Letopolis. Bearing in mind that his estate is known to be encumbered with various debts left by his uncle, it may be asked where he obtained the money.'

'Men can be very sensitive to news that their financial transactions are being watched,' I said. 'But I repeat, we are now willing to take a certain risk of discovery.'

'I can assure you that Leontius has been under close surveillance since our earlier meeting,' Macarius replied.

A sudden gust of wind brought a chill to my face. It stirred up the dust on the pavement. I looked out to sea. From behind me, the moon still shone bright. Now, for the first time it was reflected in a tessellated splash from the waters of the Harbour. Further out, the sky, empty of those bright, unwinking stars, was turning a brownish grey.

'The storm approaches,' said Macarius. 'It will be a great one. Even if not wet, I think I can promise a cooler morning than in many days.'

Stronger now, the breeze blew again. I shivered in the sudden chill. This had been an unplanned meeting, and it had run its course. Time to take my leave.

From the stairs just as I was stepping below the level of the roof, I looked briefly back at Macarius. He'd gone again to the southern edge of the roof. Once again, he was looking intently into nothingness.

7

Martin stared at me and pursed his lips again.

'Well, I don't like him,' he said. 'If you ask me, there's something dodgy about him.'

'Martin,' I sighed, 'please bear in mind that every local sneer you repeat about the natives is also made behind our backs about us. Are we also "wogs"?'

'What they choose to call us is their business,' said Martin with a sniff. 'Personally, I don't like the natives or the local Greeks. In my experience, there's nothing between them but the choice their ancestors made of which language to speak. But that isn't the point. What is the point is that you found the man wandering about the Palace roof at night in what sounds very like an act of sorcery.'

I gave up on the argument. Praying up a breath of air doesn't constitute sorcery – not even by the stupid laws Heraclius had just republished to great acclaim. And Macarius was, I'd tried repeating, highly useful.

It was mid-morning, and the storm had indeed cooled the air. The sun shone brightly as ever, but Alexandria was again a Mediterranean city. The sun was bearable, and slightly more than bearable. I was still wearing a hat, but had left my arms uncovered. We'd had business near the main gate that led to the Egyptian quarter. Now, we sat at one of the covered benches outside a wine shop. A hundred yards away, the police were checking the identity documents of the Egyptian workmen passing in and out of the centre. Some of the Greek trash had gathered, and were setting up a chant. It was one of those ritualised verse insults of the sort I'd heard many times pass between the Circus factions in Constantinople.

'If anyone's dodgy,' I said, looking back at Martin, 'it's that fucker Priscus. You know as well as I do how often the man's tried to have me done away with. He made three full attempts under Phocas. He'd no sooner come out for Heraclius when he tried again.

'Now he's here in Alexandria, and I smell trouble that makes yesterday's little reverse nothing by comparison. He—'

'From what you tell me,' Martin broke in, 'he's here with his tail between his legs. He's lost Cappadocia, and—'

'He's still head of the noble interest in Constantinople,' I went on. 'A few defeats don't change that. Heraclius may prefer to rule through outsiders like us. But he can't altogether snub the old families. Priscus is trouble on legs. And how did he get here? He turns up at the Palace with a change of clothes and has another ready for dinner, yet tells me he came alone. He says in particular he came without guards. Yet he must have come overland from Pelusium – and we know that road is notoriously infested with bandits. If I hadn't other matters to deal with, I'd have Macarius checking him out even now.'

I noticed that Martin wasn't paying attention. It couldn't be the trouble now blowing up over by the gate. He was mostly staring down with a worried look on his face.

'Are your guts giving trouble again?' I asked.

He nodded.

'I suppose it was the lead sauce,' I said. I'd called him back from his clerking the night before to finish dinner with us. He'd gorged himself proper on the mice.

'Do you think there might be a place of easement here?' he whispered with a downward glance.

'Oh, you don't want one of those horrid places,' I said airily. 'You'll have flies crawling all over you.' I stood up and looked round. As luck would have it, there was a potty man within hailing distance. Alexandria might be past its best in many respects, but it still had all the civilised amenities. I snapped my fingers very hard and gave the man a significant look.

'I can tell you, sir, you'll not find cleaner tools in all Alexandria,' he said, answering my question. 'Just take a look at this . . .' His slave assistant brandished the brass pot: it gleamed in the sunlight that was reflected up from the pavements. 'You could eat your dinner out of that.' The man stood before me, at once obsequious and calculating.

But he was right. For sure, I wasn't having Martin go and get his sandals all pissy in one of the public latrines. I fished into my purse. The bookseller had cleaned me out of gold. But I had a mass of goodish silver. I took out one of the smaller coins and put it on the table.

'Oh, sir,' he said, impressed though trying not to look too obviously at the coin, 'you can rest assured of a new sponge for your assistant.' He took one from his bag and waited as his assistant arranged the framework of curtained wood beside our table.

As he got reluctantly up, I gave Martin a shove towards it. The slave guided him in and fastened the thing shut around his neck. As Martin was forced by its weight into a squatting position, the cone made contact with the pavement. I raised my cup again and looked at his flushed, straining face. As we waited, a man at the next table looked up from his bread and olive paste. At last, with a long noise of farts and splashing, Martin emptied himself into the pot. And it was a long one. The whole framework about him trembled as, with purple face, he strained again and added to his deposit. I'd not have liked to be sitting downwind of that performance.

'Do you know what that chanting means?' I asked the potty man. I took another sip of wine and nodded at the growing crowd of Egyptians over by the gate. 'I think I can hear the word "Alexandria". Whatever it is, they seem to like the sound of it lately.'

'Don't know nothing of the wog language, sir,' he said proudly. 'Nor never been on their side of the Wall. But I'm told there's not a single bathhouse working on the other side – no, nor no potty men neither. If a wog gets taken short, why – rich or poor – he squats down and shits in the street. Pardon my expression,' he said hurriedly, 'but that's how it is.'

I glanced over at the Wall. In places twenty feet high, it bisected the whole city, and joined with the city walls. It had first gone up a hundred years before to keep the Greek and Egyptian trash from tearing at each other. Passport control at the gates and the cutting off of all public services had now made the Egyptian quarter into another world. We let some of the better workmen into the Greek side as often as they were needed, but always pushed them out again before dusk.

'But pardon me for saying it, sir,' the potty man went on. He'd now reached inside the framework with his sponge, and was rubbing vigorously. 'I don't think you's from round here.'

I made no reply. That much was obvious. My colouring screamed West. My accent should have said Constantinople. It wasn't surprising hardly anyone in the streets recognised me. In the capital, everyone below the Emperor was always going about in public. Here, just about everyone of real quality went about in a closed chair with an armed guard.

'Well,' he said, breaking the silence, 'I can tell you there is money on the other side of the Wall. The wogs ain't all low-grade scum. Some of them have big money. Can you believe it, though, sir? Some of them is rolling in gold, and nowadays they just won't turn Greek. I do some of them now and again when they come over on business. Not a word of Greek. They need interpreters even to get their bums wiped. Can you believe it, sir? They get money, but won't turn Greek. They don't believe nothing about the Conjoined Human Nature of Christ. Some of them even says – or so I've heard – that Our Lord and Saviour was just some ghost with God looking through the eyes. It ain't natural, I tell you, sir. It ain't like the old days.'

He was right there. The nice thing about orthodoxy is that, however nonsensical, it can be defined by an agreed set of words that have a reasonably agreed meaning. Monophysitism, though, wasn't a single heresy, but a heading under which any number of heresies took shelter. Some of these were so close to orthodoxy, they barely needed settling. Others were so radical and bizarre, they hardly counted as Christian.

It was here in Alexandria, while sifting through the rubbish that now clogged the shelving racks in the Library, that I'd fully appreciated the nature of heresy. Sergius and I had taken our sounding among the Syrians, and found that most of them weren't opposed in principle to a Single Directing Will for Christ. But this wasn't Syria. Here, we had against us all the ingenuity of Alexandria wedded to the fanaticism of Egypt. Getting these crazies even to discuss a settlement would be like herding cats.

'Oh, sir!' the potty man said to me, or perhaps to Martin.

I pulled myself out of a reverie that was branching into the decay of Greek as a common language, and looked back at him. He'd stopped his wiping. He rinsed his sponge again in vinegar and pushed it back inside the framework. Martin winced and groaned. The Potty Man took it back and held it up to me. It was covered in fresh blood.

'Cruel things is piles, sir,' he said to me. 'And these ones is hanging down like ripe figs. I'm surprised your man can sit down.'

'Martin,' I sighed in Latin, 'I have told you many times. Wiping isn't enough. You really do need to wash down there. A dirty arse, and in this climate – why, you're asking for trouble.' I would have said more. But it was now that the babble of Egyptian voices over by the gate took on an ugly sound. Perhaps the Greeks had given offence. I paid attention as they came to the end of their own chant:

> Let us ever recall for whom
> This city is the living room,
> And know ourselves the master race,
> And keep the natives in their place.

'Never a truer word,' the potty man said approvingly. 'Never a truer word.' He listened to more of the commotion, then recalled his business. 'I can recommend some truly good ointment for those piles.' He looked into his bag again and pulled out a small lead container.

I took it from his hand and sniffed the contents. So far as I could tell, it was opium in a kind of bird fat. It wouldn't do Martin any harm, and might lift his mood. I handed it back and nodded.

'Of course, there is some that disagree,' the potty man said as he set to work again.

I stared at him and frowned.

'Oh, I mean, sir, about the wogs. Why, it was just this morning that I applied this very cream to someone who told me the wogs too were God's Children, and we had more to bind than divide us. Right quality he was, I can tell you. He said that, with all the corn being shipped off to Constantinople, we'd soon all be starving together. So we might as well act together.'

For the first time, I pricked up my ears. Who was sowing concord between Greek and Egyptians? I tried not to sound too interested as I asked the question. I didn't succeed. But another coin got the man going again.

'A great fat man, it was,' he said, 'a fat man with a bald head and a red spot on his nose. Terrible piles, he had. He nearly screamed as I touched them. But he said the government was trying to fuck us all over – pardon the expression, but those were his very words. He promised me a reward if I'd spread the word of unity. "There's success in unity," he said, "success in unity."

'Me – I don't never mix with wogs. Nasty, dirty people, I say they are. Shit in the street: can you believe it? He was a generous tipper, though, sir. He even took a whole pot of my ointment. He said he was on his way to a journey along the Canopus Road. He thought it would help with the pain.'

I looked again over at the gate. About fifty of the Egyptians were getting up more of their chant about Alexandria. Even as they gathered, though, reinforcements were pouring out of the guard house, their swords already drawn.

8

'Of course it was Leontius,' I said. 'Who else is there to fit that description? Who else is likely to be going about preaching unity against us from both sides of the Wall?' I'd finished with my meeting in the Food Control Office, and we were now heading back to the Palace. I'd said I wanted the new land survey reports on my desk after lunch at the latest. It was now surely pushing towards the sixth hour of the day.

'But what can you do about him?' Martin asked. He tagged along beside me, sometimes cheerful, sometimes quiet, as the opium worked its magic on his fairly virgin body. I stopped. We were about to come from a side street we'd taken to avoid the public executions into the square containing the obelisk and the statues of all the Ptolemies. From here, it was a short walk along the Processional Way into the Palace square itself. I looked at a pair of yellow shoes in the glazed window of a shop. They were pretty enough, but I preferred something cut a little lower to show off my ankles.

'Among other matters Nicetas hasn't decided to share with me are security and public order,' I said. 'That means I can't just have the man taken up for suspected treason. But we had a threat of this yesterday – and Nicetas was watching. We now have some evidence that he's going through with the threat. Stirring up the mob, especially both sections of it, is something that even His Highness will accept requires action.

'I'll go and see him tomorrow. At the least, I can have Leontius kicked out of Alexandria. And unless we've pushed them over the edge of desperation, I don't think the dissident landowners will stand a moment by his side if they think he's actually planning to raise the mob against us.'

As we passed into the square, we bumped into the front of a long procession. There wasn't time to get past it. The best we could do was jump backwards out of its way. We stood in front of what had once been the Department of Medicine at the University, and was now a training college for missionaries, and watched it go by. It was soon obvious this would take some time. Led by three bishops I hadn't seen before, its centrepiece was a great wooden image of Saint Mark. It was smeared over in elaborate patterns of mud, its feet kept ever wet from pitchers of clear water. The patterns were repeated on the bodies of the humbler celebrants. Waving papyrus imitations of corn sheaves, they sang their thanks for plenty in the year to come.

If anyone there knew what I'd just learned about the black mould on the remaining stores of grain, he didn't seem inclined to spoil the party.

Still, there could be no doubt the Nile was rising nicely. The silver stream I'd seen the day before in the canal was become a dark flood. It gurgled loudly through the cisterns that ran under every street. Already, Lake Mareotis was seven inches up on the day.

Martin switched into Latin. 'What does this mean for your speculations?' he asked, a disapproving tone in his voice.

'Nothing at all,' I answered, following him into Latin, though the noise around us would have defeated the most intrepid spy. 'The contracts I made last month were for sale at the current, very high prices. The lower the forward price drops from now on, the higher the value of those contracts. As it happens, there's an excellent chance of a good harvest to come.'

Martin gave me one of his funny looks. So far as he understood financial matters, he took the view that I was profiting from misery, and probably increasing it. But this blessed change in the weather had cheered me no end, so I decided in turn to give him one of my little lectures on the science of enrichment.

'If you take the March price of corn in Alexandria during the past eight hundred years' I began '– yes, I've had those dozen clerks I commandeered extracting this for months now from the tax records – there is a fairly stable cycle. What makes it hard to spot is the quite independent cycle that correlates with the timing of the flood.

'But if you can separate these two cycles, and take account of plagues and other disturbances, you'll then be able to guess the future price. I'm not so fast as I'd wish at brute calculations, and I've applied the method to any past year chosen by lot. In eight-elevenths of cases, the answer has been sufficiently close to the actual price.'

Martin looked back at the image of Saint Mark. 'That sounds rather like divination,' he said still more disapprovingly, going now, for greater security, into Celtic.

'Not at all,' I said, warming to my theme. The flute and cymbal players were coming closer, so I raised my voice and went back into Greek, which is better for discussing these things. 'Divination and astrology and all those other frauds rest on the claim that one class of future events can be known from the study of present or past events of another class. Since there is no proven connection between any of these classes, the predictions made are all worthless.

'With the method I'm trying to develop, you can predict future events from the study of past events *of the same class*.

'Have you noticed how lucky I am at all games of chance? Well, if you throw a single die a very large number of times, the ox will come up one-sixth of the time, and every other side one-sixth. That's easy. But I've discovered that, if you throw two dice the same number of times, the chance of each combination will be—'

Martin broke in: 'The purpose of mathematics,' he said primly, 'is to supplement Revelation by letting us see – however darkly – the Mind of God. I don't think it was ever intended to assist commercial speculation. And didn't your Epicurus dismiss mathematics as useless?'

He turned his mouth down into a very sour look. I knew, though, his mood had been improving by leaps and bounds ever since the potty man had slapped on the ointment. We'd had this argument and others like it more times than I could remember. It was Martin's duty at this point to disapprove.

'Martin,' I said, trying to parry his attack on one of the few completely stupid things Epicurus had said, 'I do believe that, the usual miracles aside, everything that happens in the world can be understood by the use of reason. And I further believe that understanding allows prediction and even control . . .'

I trailed off. We were now on such familiar ground, words were hardly needed. Martin could have made his usual move: that Epicurus had been interested in rational understanding only as a way of diminishing fear of death, not at all of improving the comforts of life. But he wouldn't make the move. Even he must have seen how nice the afternoon would surely turn out.

We looked away from each other and crossed ourselves with varying piety as the image of some other saint was carried past. The procession would soon thin out, and we'd be able to continue back to the Palace. We could settle down after lunch to a long examination of how best to reapportion land in the Lower Thebaid region.

For the moment, it was enough to know I really had stumbled on a method that allowed vast personal enrichment without harming the poor wretches of Alexandria. They'd be able to fill their bellies in the season to come, and at low prices – if only, that is, they could get through this one.

'My sweet young Alaric, how delightful to bump into you!'

Oh shit! I ground my teeth. Priscus had worked his way through the dancing maniacs who made up the rearguard of the procession, and was now beside me. Flanked by a couple of slaves he could only just have bought, he was wearing something new of the best Alexandrian silk. One of the slaves carried a wicker cage containing perhaps the nastiest cat I'd seen in ages. It glared balefully at me through the strands. Holding the cage as far away as he could manage, the slave already had a deep scratch on his face.

'You seem to have found your way about town soon enough,' I said coldly. The cat reached out at me with an open claw. I stared back into the hate-filled eyes.

'Now, I thought you'd remark on that,' Priscus gushed. Except he had definitely lost weight since Christmas, he'd become quite his usual self again.

'Our mutual friend Leontius has proved most accommodating,' he said with a flash of his dark teeth. He put his face close to the cage and smiled broader still. The thing shrank back. 'Isn't she just a beauty? I had a most useful mid-morning snack with the dear man.

'He's a low sort, of course, even by provincial standards. I'd not think him at all fit to move in the exalted society that we inhabit back at home – but he's not without a rough charm. He gave me Margarita as a pledge of our new and happy friendship.' He poked a finger into the cage. The cat sniffed gingerly, before shrinking back again. Priscus laughed.

'You will not believe how greatly he esteems your efforts for our Sovereign Lord the Augustus,' he went on. 'I heard all about your performance yesterday. Everyone is discussing your divine eloquence for the scheme you and Sergius conceived of taking away their land.'

That wasn't at all funny. Perhaps I should have killed him in the nursery.

'I think I should ask you,' I said, 'roughly how long you plan to remain in Alexandria. I'm sure the Persian menace will not idly await your return to the theatre of war.'

'But how little you know of war, my young and golden darling,' came the reply. 'With pestilence in all their camps, and barely an ounce of food left for them in any likely direction of advance, their campaigning season is over. Unless they can attack from Egypt – and that's not very likely, is it? – Syria is perfectly safe. The Persians, I assure you, can't stir from their Cappadocian positions again until March. That gives me plenty of time to take in the sights here and conclude all the business we discussed yesterday.'

'Then I'll wish you joy of this place,' I said, trying to keep my voice as smooth as his. 'But Martin and I have an appointment I am not inclined to break.'

'We'll meet again at dusk,' he called after me.

'What?' I said, turning back.

'He being indisposed again, Nicetas says he must leave it in your hands to keep me entertained in a fit manner.'

'And Leontius?' I asked. 'Is he also indisposed?'

'It seems to be the case,' came the answer.

Was that a slight frown? I could hope.

'His travelling chair came for him just as we finished our shopping. He'll be on his way now on some business trip. That leaves no one but you to keep me company this evening.

'Now, my dearest love, I'm told the Egyptian quarter can be most charmingly exotic.'

9

So far as transacting the business in hand was concerned, the meeting went well enough. I'll not go into the details of what we did in my office. But there were seventeen ways of dividing up the taxable land of the Lower Thebaid, so that the tenants got viable plots and the current owners kept enough to maintain some position. I'd commissioned maps and reports showing each one of these. Every one had its merits. It was a question of whether, and if so how hard, we wanted to hit the dissenting landowners. Then, of course, there was the complicating factor of lands willed in perpetuity to the Church.

Back in Constantinople, with officials from half a dozen ministries sitting in and everything on the record, it would have taken days. Here, it was just the two of us at my desk with a couple of clerks, and we were able to get through the complexities with nothing carried over.

'Do come back a moment, if you please,' I said to Martin as he was about to follow the clerks from the room. I'd been considering this since bumping into Priscus. Now, there was something important I needed to ask him.

He looked significantly at the quilted leather on the door. He sat down again, just a foot or so from me.

'Aelric,' he said, speaking low in Celtic before I could make a start, 'I don't know exactly how to say this. But there are things that I believe you ought to know.

'I spent this last night going over those subsidy payments again. The Undersecretary in the Disbursements Office didn't want to tell me more than I asked. But he left me with enough documentation for me to work some things out for myself.'

'So, what was it?' I asked. 'Fraud or incompetence or superstition?' I resisted the urge to smile. Even straight up the arse, the amount of opium he'd taken was derisory. Now, he was gabbling away like a confirmed eater waking from his dream.

'All of them, and more,' he said. He pushed a sheet of his own jottings across the desk.

I glanced at it. I then read it properly. I looked up.

'Interesting,' I said. 'The subsidy has been located and cancelled five times in the past seventy years. Each time, it's been carried into another budget and continued unbroken. It seems we have a heathen conspiracy going on here in the Disbursements Office. It wouldn't be the first time, of course, this has come to light. Look at that stupid bugger of a Prefect – the one Heraclius burned to death last year for sacrificing to Apollo. If that still goes on in Constantinople, there's no saying what happens in the provinces.'

Martin leaned forward and dropped his voice still lower. I could smell the garlic sausage on his breath. A locked room, Celtic, whispering: these were natural precautions back in Constantinople; not here, though.

'Aelric, we're talking seventy-five pounds of gold here,' he said, 'seventy-five pounds of gold every year since the time of the Great Justinian. You don't need that to keep up a clandestine temple in the back of beyond. With one year of that, Priscus could have another army.

'And this subsidy isn't the end of it. Regular fractions of spending have been creamed off whole budget items. This isn't the usual petty corruption you expect to see anywhere. It's too consistent, over too long a time.'

I stopped him. 'This is all very interesting,' I said. 'But it's outside the terms of our commission. We were sent here to get the new land law into force, not reform the finances. We got the subsidy stopped because Leontius had set it in our path. Frauds in themselves on the Disbursements Office don't concern us.'

I looked again at the notes. There had been some very sticky fingers at work. I looked away and bit my lip. I looked for guidance at the silken hangings on the wall and the electrum water pitcher

I'd bought in the antiquities market. I looked back at Martin's heavy face.

'I suggest you drop the matter,' I said firmly. 'It isn't our problem.'

'Aelric,' Martin said, putting his face back into order, 'there's something I don't like about this. I can't give you evidence yet. But I know when things aren't right. We need to be careful.'

'Agreed,' I said smoothly. 'Egypt is a world in itself. Even Alexandria isn't completely part of the Empire. Augustus took the whole place over as a going concern, and no effort since then at incorporation has been a success. You only need look at the title and functions of the Viceroy to know this.

'Now, I do appreciate your concerns. But you've said yourself you have no evidence beyond this fraud. Your enquiries never took place, and will never be acted upon more than they have been already. After all, it isn't money that would otherwise find its way to Constantinople. If not for the Old Gods of Egypt, it would only be stolen for some other use.'

Martin stood by the door again. I got up and went over to him. I put my hands on his shoulders and looked into his face.

'Martin,' I said, 'I want you to forget all this. It doesn't concern us except so far as Leontius made it our concern. From tomorrow, he'll be closing up that shabby little place he lives in all alone while in Alexandria, and I doubt if our paths will cross again.'

Martin tried to protest, but I led him over to the window. On the fifth floor of the Palace, my office looked out over the Palace Square to the Church of Saint Mark. Down in the square, the Nile Festival was continuing with black belly dancers and a demonstration of fire eating. We stood awhile, listening to the rhythmical thud of the drummers. I waited for the continued breeze off the sea to bring him back to a semblance of rationality.

'I've a favour to ask of you and Sveta,' I said with an abrupt change of subject that brought the conversation back to where I'd wanted to start it. 'Maximin has been wandering again at night. Those useless bitches in the nursery won't do the job I've set them, and I don't see any value in having them whipped a second time. Can I ask the pair of you to take him into your own quarters while Priscus is about?'

All of a sudden, the cloud lifted from Martin's face. He'd be delighted, he told me. The boy always got on so well with their daughter, and, this time, she could surely be trusted not to pull his hair or stick pins in him.

I thanked him. I'd now have to put up with Sveta twice a day; correction, we'd have to put up with each other. Though the heat and flies remained a sore trial, she still found energy for evil looks and God alone knew what private slanders to Martin. The immense and continuing favours I'd done him didn't seem to register with her.

'So you go directly off to Sveta,' I said, taking him back to the door, 'and get things arranged. See that Maximin is settled in with you. I want you to spend the rest of the afternoon and all evening not thinking about survey reports or Leontius or anything else connected with them.

'I want you nice and fresh for tomorrow. The engineers will be coming round to discuss the reconnection of the Red Sea and the Mediterranean. Apparently, there is a difference of height between the two oceans, and we shall need to discover how the ancients managed the flow of waters.

'Now, do pass on my regards to Sveta. I will try to visit your quarters before whatever Priscus has arranged for the evening entertainments.'

Down in the Eastern Harbour, the supplemental grain ships were still loading up under armed guard. They would be ready, the senior captain told me, to leave within the next five days. Assuming normal winds, all would be in Constantinople in time for Heraclius to pacify the Circus mob with double rations, and to shell out as bribes to get the Avars to leave Thrace alone.

The Harbour area itself was walled and gated. The streets by which it was approached, though, were dotted with small crowds. So far, protest was muted. So far, it seemed to involve men from the almost respectable classes. The supplemental requisition was

66

little in itself. But it could easily be made an example of how the Empire was bleeding Egypt white. We needed to get those ships under way as soon as possible. Even before then, we had to get Leontius out of Alexandria and keep those landowners on side.

Now I was clear of all the dockyards, I looked over at the Lighthouse. If you walked westerly along the Embankment Road lining the shore, you'd pass some of the oldest and grandest buildings in the city, including the back of the Library. There was the old University Building. There were the old temples, all now converted into churches. There was the Spice Exchange. Then you'd get to the punctuated causeway that led across to the Lighthouse Island. A clever structure, this. It allowed easy access to the island without closing off access for ships to the Western Harbour. When it came to engineers – and, for that matter, to everything else – the Ptolemies had demanded and got the best the ancients had to offer.

But I didn't fancy crowds got up in their afternoon finery and the babble among them of greetings and pleasantries in a Greek so exaggerated yet so corrupt that I still couldn't listen to it without wanting to laugh. And Hermogenes and his message about more documents could easily wait another day.

I turned east, going back towards the Palace. It loomed before me, about twice as big as the Great Church in Constantinople. The elaboration of columns and statues and marbles of different colours never once took away from the knowledge that this was a vast, impregnable fortress, complete with access to its own harbour. It was the largest building in the city. For much of its history, it had been the most hated. In every park and square, and in every street in the city not too narrow or too twisting to block the view, it was a looming presence.

The guards at the southern gate pulled themselves presentable and saluted as they saw me approaching. But I looked at it. I thought of those airless corridors and those rooms with their heavy silk hangings. If Priscus wasn't sleeping off some new exotic drug or teaching his cat to scratch out slave eyes, he might come looking for conversation. Or there was Martin, jumping at shadows while Sveta nagged him viciously about matters that probably involved me. Or there were those clerks, sweating away together over the latest set of price ratios I'd given them to calculate. If not that, there'd be . . .

I turned and went back to the Embankment Road. I turned east again. Walking briskly, I skirted the Jewish quarter, and made for the Gate of Pompey. Here, I was recognised a few times. My dealings with the Alexandrian Greeks had so far been limited. I wasn't sorry for that. Except for Hermogenes and a few other scholars, I had little reason to deal with any of them. With the Jews, it had been a little different. One of the clerks in my preferred banking house almost bumped into me as he hurried about some business. Blinking in the sunlight, he stared up at me. With a muttered and vestigial obeisance, he turned and continued on his way. I looked at the rather dumpy buildings that surrounded one of the larger synagogues. But I had no business here today, so kept to the common faith area of the main road to the gate.

Being on foot, I expected I'd be allowed through without formalities. Normally, it was a matter of turning up and showing my face. With an obsequious bow, I'd be escorted round the heavy bar that blocked the gate by day and waved into the lush countryside beyond to continue my walk. Today, however, the guards had been changed, and a couple of unsmiling creatures looked hard at my passport. They didn't so much as nod acknowledgement of the golden ink on the parchment.

If delayed a little, though, I was lucky. On both sides of the gate, wheeled traffic was stuck in queues a hundred yards long. This was one of the days in the month when the priests had all the death bins outside the city gates opened. They'd been here with the dawn – scented cloths tied to their faces while they turned over the bodies of the unconnected poor and choked out the required words. The priests had long since staggered off to get drunk. However, the public slaves were still fussing with their buckets of quicklime. In the now recovering heat of the mid-afternoon, the smell and the flies were unendurable. I'd try to find out from Nicetas at our next meeting what was the idea of all this delay – not that he'd make much sense even if he knew and even if he were inclined to share the knowledge with me. For the moment, it was enough that I was soon through the gate, and the high, grey walls of the city were fading out of mind behind me.

IO

It was here, outside the city, yet within reach of its protective walls, that the very rich had once built their country villas, and the district had been quite a garden suburb. With the decline of population, and of order beyond the city gates, the villas had long been abandoned, and were now mostly fallen down. Slaves still toiled in the occasional cultivated field, growing lettuces and other delicacies for the city markets. Slaves still trod the occasional wheel, raising water from the low canals to irrigate the land. Otherwise, the area was a near-solitude of rocky green bordering the blue solitude of the sea.

About a mile outside the walls, the solitude became complete. The birds twittered in the little trees. There was a continual rustling under the bushes of lizards and small furry creatures. Over to my left, the sun sparkled on the sea. I was on a fairly narrow spit of land that separated Lake Mareotis from the sea, and the road to Canopus ran through this. But I was on a side road that ultimately led nowhere. Here, there wasn't a human being in sight.

It was hard to say what had got me out this way. Partly, of course, it was the joys of solitude. You got none of that in the Palace, and still less in the streets of Alexandria. If Martin had been working hard, so had I.

Then, it was the news I'd had of Leontius. He'd told the potty man he was setting out along the Canopus Road. Priscus had told me he'd not have set out till after lunch. Taken together, these might be significant facts. You see, no one ever set out by chair on the road to Canopus in the afternoon – not even with two relays of carriers to go at a steady trot. The Police Chief there had started locking the gates well before sunset, and was famous

70

for not opening them for anyone till the sun was well up again. By day, the road could be as delightful over its whole stretch as the countryside around me. By night, it was a haunt of bandits and God knows what other mischief. No one ever started a journey that would have meant being stuck on that road after dark. Nobody local was stupid enough to do that, even with an armed guard.

But if the potty man had been accurately reporting what he'd been told, Leontius was on a journey along the Canopus Road. Now, the settlements that had once lain between the two cities had been abandoned a good century before. If it wasn't Canopus, then he might well be up to something decidedly fishy.

I had thought at first to leave all this to Macarius. If Leontius was under continual surveillance, whatever he was up to would surely be known without my intervention. But little as I had any faith in his judgement, Martin's endless mutterings about Macarius were getting to me. Perhaps I could take some hand in digging up the dirt on Leontius.

I turned up a slight incline. It was about the only high ground on the entire spit of land that stretched east of Alexandria. From the top, you could see down on the other side over a longish part of the Canopus Road. I stood and looked up and down the road. It was as empty as the road I'd just left. No one, of course, would be going down from Alexandria. Neither, though, was anyone coming up.

Leontius would have been long since out of sight. That is, if he'd done other with Priscus than make a polite excuse from his company – hardly a surprising act.

I swore at myself and turned back to look over the sea. But no one can be really out of sorts when looking over that wonderful ocean that washes every civilised shore. It sparkled so prettily in the sun. About a mile out, a few coastal ships were hurrying into port from Canopus or perhaps further out. If I strained, I could just hear the regular beating of time for the oarsmen chained to their benches.

Uton we hycgan hwær we ham agen,
ond þonne geþencan hu we þider cumen

I sang in English. Other than for secret notes to myself, I hadn't used my own language in years. I no longer thought in it, though I believe I did sometimes dream in it. Now, its harsh sounds grated in my throat, nearly as unfamiliar and as menacing as Egyptian. I'd spent so long away from the language that any other Englishman who might overhear me would surely have thought I was a foreigner.

I fell silent. Once again, I asked what I was doing here. Again, the question had nothing to do with immediate circumstances. What was the point in this lunatic mission to stabilise the Empire by raising up the low? Hadn't that landowner been right? Perhaps there was a reason for the difference between high and low that went beyond human injustice. Give it as you will, would not the cultivators of the soil eventually lose the soil again?

What was I doing here? On the other hand, what else should I be doing? There was a question worth asking. If only I could think of the answer . . .

I turned from looking over the endlessly fascinating sea and walked over to the little ruin.

I'd come across the abandoned shrine on one of my earlier walks. I call it a shrine, but it might have been a tomb. After so many centuries of neglect, it was hard to tell what the thing once had been. Roughly the shape and size of a small house, it stood up here about fifty yards off the Canopus Road.

It had plainly been intended as a place of some importance. Now, its roof had long since fallen in. Its walls held, but were buried up to perhaps two feet above their original base. The inscriptions covering the inner and outer walls might have been younger than that inscription in the Library. But they'd been in the open, exposed to the sea air. Reading even a few words here and there had so far been as much as I could manage.

I sat down on a fallen column. With a wild olive tree for shade, I reached into my satchel and took out the bread and cheese I'd brought with me. As I chewed on the slightly stale crusts, I fixed my eyes on the least worn area of the outer wall and willed myself to make sense of what could still be read.

Was this a dedication *to* one of the Kings Ptolemy? Or did it record an erection *by* a commoner called Ptolemy? Who was Aristarchus? What significance had these repeated quantities of oil and grain?

Land redistribution, Martin, Priscus, even the spring prices – these were all forgotten. Perhaps, I thought, after an endless scanning and re-scanning of those broken words, the place had been neither a tomb nor a shrine. Perhaps it had been some kind of civic building. If so, however, why so far outside the city walls? I took a swig from my wine flask and got up to look again at the rear inside wall. There had been words carved here that I'd already tried to read. They might now make sense.

Behind me, over on the road, there was the crack of a whip and a shrill cry. I turned and looked through the boughs of the olive tree. It was a chair for longish distance travelling, and one of the slaves had put his corner down too roughly. I could hear angry scolding from behind the curtains, while some steward laid about the offending slave with one of those flexible leather rods you use when pain is intended rather than actual bodily harm. If there was still a queue back at the gate, it wouldn't be unreasonable for the owner of the chair to be thoroughly pissed off.

There was a sound of hooves further along the road. Still keeping behind the tree, I looked far to the left. Yes, it was a horseman. Dressed all in black, hood pulled over his head, he came on at a slow canter. So far as I could tell, he was alone. Or he might have been the first of several from round the far bend in the road. But unless those slaves were armed – and ready to fight – I doubted if their owner would be up to very much in the way of resistance, to one man or to many. I squinted into the now lower sun and looked at the monogram on the curtains.

Well, well, well, I told myself. Who was it but Leontius himself? He'd been telling the truth about his journey. And how late he'd set out! Well, if he were to get his throat cut, it would be no loss to me.

Even if it was a question of lifting his purse and personal jewellery, it would be a sight worth the journey to behold. I pulled myself back deeper behind the boughs of the olive tree and squeezed myself harder against its trunk. It would never do to be seen.

The horseman came level with Leontius. No sword showing, I noted with disappointment – only a salute. Another moment, and he'd swung off his beast and was standing on the smooth slabs of the road, stretching his arms and legs and brushing the dust from his cloak. Two of the slaves pulled the curtains aside and helped Leontius on to the road. He waddled forward as if to embrace the horseman. But the horseman stepped back. Going over to his horse, he dug into his saddlebag and pulled out a large package.

There was a conversation that I was too distant to hear. Then Leontius pointed straight up to where I was standing. I cursed and prepared to go down towards them. The thought of politeness to the man was enough to make the bread and cheese heavy in my guts. I'd not have put anything past Leontius, but I didn't expect I'd have any need of the sword I had at my belt. At worst, I'd have to cry off the dinner invite with the real excuse of Priscus. It was worth asking which of the two's company I least fancied for the evening.

But no – he wasn't pointing at me. He was pointing at the shrine. Leaving horse and chair and slaves behind, they were picking their way through the brush as they came up for some quiet conference. Given more time, I'd have backed round to the other side of the far wall. But there was no time. The best I could manage was to drop down on hands and knees and crawl as fast as I could over to the fallen column. If I squeezed underneath it from behind, it would need to be rotten luck if either of the approaching men were to push through those bushes and find me lurking there.

II

Leontius wasn't at all used to walking – especially uphill – and I heard his rough breathing from a good ten yards away.

'So, my friend, your journey was uneventful?' he gasped with an attempt at pleasantry. He evidently thought enough of his company to put on a comical drawl that wouldn't have impressed a barbarian slave in Constantinople.

'If you're asking if I was seen,' came the reply, 'the answer is no. I'm here for one piece of business. This being done, I've a passage booked on a ship calling at Canopus. You will understand my disinclination to savour the delights of Alexandria.' It was a deep, rather slow voice. The accent said educated Syrian. Something about it also hinted at time spent in Constantinople.

I felt a slight tremor above me as Leontius sat heavily on the column, and then another as, with a little yelp, he shifted position. He'd knocked loose a cloud of dust, and I had to suppress a sneezing attack. He sat where I had been, his back to where I now was.

'Well, my dear fellow, I think it's time we discussed terms for the no doubt excellent work you've done for me,' he said.

I thought from his tone he'd move to a boast about his estates and his position among the quality of Letopolis. Instead, he left his words dangling as he waited for a reply.

There was a silence. Then: 'Our terms were settled several months ago,' the horseman said, a hint of impatience in his voice. 'This meeting is to complete our business. As said, I have no wish to remain even outside Alexandria longer than I need. You have the gold with you?'

Leontius began one of his blustering speeches. He was allowed to run on a while.

Then the horseman broke in. 'You have the gold with you?' he asked again, not bothering now to smother his impatience. 'If you don't care to pay what was agreed, I can take myself and all I brought with me back to Canopus.' That shut up Leontius.

'You'll find it all in order,' he said, trying to sound cheerful. I heard the thump of at least one heavy purse. 'It was a large sum to gather in cash, and not all of it is the new-minted Imperial coin you specified. But weight and fineness are correct. Would you like me to help you count it?'

'I don't think that will be necessary,' the horseman said. 'With all my clients, I like to think I deal on trust. Let me give you what is now your property, to do with what you will.'

There was a rustling of smooth leather and then another silence. I was dying for a look at what they were trading. I almost had to hold myself from twisting my head up. Something was crawling on my neck. I hoped it wasn't one of those yellow bugs. They had a nasty sting.

'My, but aren't those big, heavy scrolls,' Leontius said uncertainly. 'What am I supposed to do with them?'

'When I am asked for information,' he was answered, 'my practice is to give it in full. If there is a lot here, it is because there was a lot to be gathered.'

'I will read all this,' said Leontius. He was still disconcerted. 'But could you oblige with a verbal summary?'

'Very well,' the horseman said. I could hear a little smile. 'Remember, though, that the written texts are the full report. Those are what you have bought. I hold out no warranties for any verbal summary.' As if getting back on his horse, he twisted himself astride the column and faced Leontius. His booted left foot swung maybe four inches from my face.

'Your target is not a natural-born citizen of the Empire,' he said. 'He comes from Britain, which I believe is an island to the west of Africa. Though this was in ancient times a province of the Empire, it is now given over, like much of the West, to barbarian occupiers.'

My heart skipped a beat. I'd normally have felt an overpowering urge to brush those bugs off me. There were two others now

– brown ones – crawling up one of my arms. But, frozen in my place, I hardly breathed.

'He is himself of barbarian stock,' the horseman continued. 'His claim to be descended from citizens of good quality is as false as the name he uses. His real name is also barbarian, but far less easily pronounced among the civilised. As for his claim to be thirty-five, that too is a lie. So far as I can gather, he is at least twelve and perhaps fifteen years younger.

'He arrived in Rome just over three years ago. He was secretary to a priest sent back to gather books for the new Church mission established in his country. The priest was murdered in circumstances that neither Church nor Imperial authorities will reveal to any enquirer. It is enough to say that Alaric emerged with credit, and was able to stay on in Rome as main collector of books to the Church mission in a place called Canterbury.

'He then moved about two years ago to Constantinople, again on Church business. He involved himself in the rather complex intrigues that ended in the replacement of Phocas with Heraclius. Since then, he has moved to a position of increasing importance in the Imperial Council. He is one of the projectors of the new land law. He has overseen its implementation in three provinces so far. And Heraclius is known to be impatient for his return to Constantinople, where he is needed to ensure good relations with the Roman Church.'

'So, he's the Emperor's bumboy?' Leontius cut in. He laughed unpleasantly. Sex was something anyone could understand. High politics, I'd known already, were beyond his provincial vision.

'According to how these things are measured,' the horseman said with quiet contempt, 'he is number four or five in the Imperial Council. You haven't bought my advice. But I will tell you free of charge to underestimate him at your peril. Despite his age, his reputation is for energy and efficiency.'

I nodded complacently at this. Those who spy never hear good of themselves, I'm told. That isn't always true. But the fucking cheek of it! Leontius had got someone down all the way from Constantinople to do for me what I was having done for him.

I was mortified. More than that, I was surprised. I'd never have thought him up to anything half so effective.

'I have little interest in his university reforms,' the horseman continued. 'But I am assured that he could, but for his turn to politics, have become the most brilliant scholar of this age.'

'I'm sure all you have to tell me is substantiated in your documentation,' said Leontius. 'However, I'm not sure if any of it is as useful as your associate promised it would be. My friends and I may choose to consider ourselves short-changed after so much promised.'

'You can all choose to consider what you please,' the horseman said drily. 'But what I've given you, properly used, can severely undermine the authority here of the Lord Alaric. Heraclius is far away and preoccupied with five concurrent wars. What confidence will remain in a representative who turns out to be an under-aged barbarian of dubious background?'

'Tell me about Priscus,' Leontius asked with a sudden change of tone. 'I mean the General Priscus.'

'A nobleman in his late fifties,' came the reply, 'Priscus rose to prominence as a soldier in the reign of Maurice. He switched immediately to Phocas and became his son-in-law and heir. When it still seemed a matter of choice, he then switched to Heraclius and was rewarded with control of the armed forces. Why do you ask?'

'Because he's here,' said Leontius. 'He's very interested in and sympathetic to my campaign against this barbarian child. I think he might be a useful ally to confirm all that you have finally brought me.' There was a long silence, broken only by the sound of the scraping of the horseman's boot against the other side of the column.

Then the horseman spoke again: 'You regard Priscus as your *ally*?' He laughed gently. 'I can only rejoice I came here in time to collect my fee. I will freely advise you, my dear if temporary client, to watch Priscus very closely indeed. I will confirm that he and Alaric are sworn enemies at every level. Indeed, it was Priscus who led opposition in the Imperial Council to the land law. But there must be whole cemeteries filled with those who thought Priscus might be useful to them.'

The horseman suddenly changed tone. 'You tell me you came here in secret?' he asked.

'Of course,' said Leontius.

'Can you tell me, then,' the horseman replied, 'what that half-eaten loaf is doing on the ground?'

I kicked myself. I should have noticed that. But Leontius was laughing.

'Some slave's lunch,' he said easily. 'You must recall that I am a man of considerable weight in this whole region. I have friends in every party. I have that even without developments that will soon force every party to seek my friendship. I don't think anyone would dare do anything so vulgar as spy on *my* movements.'

'A wealthy city indeed,' the horseman said with a sniff, 'where even slaves can eat bread of that quality, and have new linen for wrapping it.'

'Of course, I don't want the information you've brought me to discredit the little fucker,' Leontius said with a sudden shift to the defensive. 'Ultimately, the landowners and even Priscus don't matter a fig. It's the boy who is important to me. If I can only get him under my control, just a few days up river from here, Nicetas – even the Emperor himself – won't be able to lay a finger on me. Whatever I may have said to those who came up with the balance of your gold, I've commissioned all your dirt to turn the Great Lord Alaric into my own hunting dog. Do you suppose he will be open to such pressure?'

The horseman laughed. He swung his leg up and was sitting away from me again. Then there was the crunch of boots on the stony ground.

'But I think our business is done,' he said. 'Bearing in mind how the day advances, you will forgive my calling an end to this meeting.'

I waited until the sound of hard breathing and of that firm booted tread was gone. I waited until I could hear the shouted orders at slaves and the gentle clopping of the horse on the road.

As I stamped viciously on every one of those bugs I could catch, the words kept repeating in my mind: *Could have become the most brilliant scholar of this age.* Even at my age, those words stung worse than any bug. For the moment, they obliterated any curiosity I might have felt over the blackmail attempt Leontius had in mind.

Could have become the most brilliant scholar of this age. I almost had to fight back the tears.

12

'I beg you, My Lords, not to use Greek in public. If you must speak in front of others, Latin is safer. It may not be recognised. And please, at all times, stay close by me. Even those who live here can have trouble at night in these unlit streets. If you are separated from me, you will be lost in moments.'

We nodded at Macarius. Priscus had turned his nose straight up at the rather nice brothel I'd urged on him. It was the Egyptian quarter, he'd insisted, or nothing.

'There's a man who works out of a wine shop there,' he'd said firmly. 'He can see things, I've been told.'

So that was it. Priscus had suggested we invite Martin. Sure enough, he'd found 'an important domestic matter', that would keep him in the Palace. I couldn't blame him. Given half a chance, I'd have found one. Now, dressed in black, hoods pulled over, short swords hung out of sight, we waited for the police officer to unlock the side door by one of the gates into the Egyptian quarter.

'Standing orders is we don't go in there at night for nothing,' he said with a nervous look.

'I don't think we shall have need of assistance,' I said, trying to sound less edgy than I felt. We stepped through into the darkness. The smell was something everyone in the Greek centre of Alexandria experienced once or twice a month. It was a clinging miasma that drifted over us like smoke from a bonfire whenever the wind blew from the west. It was of uncleared and rotten waste of every sort, of unwashed humanity packed in too closely together, of poverty and hunger and despair, and sometimes too of pestilence. Then it was the time for incense and scented clothes and, for those who could afford it, of height.

But this was an experience always had from a distance. Nothing – not the poor districts of Constantinople, nor even most of Rome – had prepared me for the nearly solid horror of that smell at close quarters. I fought off an urge to gag as the door closed behind us. I pulled open my pot of scent and dabbed some on my sleeve.

'But this is glorious!' said Priscus in Latin. He breathed in deeply. 'How could you possibly have wanted to keep me away?'

I suppose it reminded him of that warren of torture chambers he'd presided over in the last days of Phocas. His voice almost dripped with anticipatory joy. He stepped towards Macarius. There was thin cloud in the sky now, and this shut off much of the moonlight. Even so, once my eyes had got used to the gloom, it was easy enough to see the main outlines of things.

'My Lord, are you quite sure of where you want to go?' Macarius asked, a dubious tone to his voice. 'Even in the Egyptian quarter, the man presides over an illegal gathering.'

'Don't be stupid,' Priscus snapped. 'We are the law – aren't we, Alaric?'

I made no reply. There was no reply to be made. I followed close as Macarius led us through those disgusting streets. He'd been right about their darkness and confusion. How it was he didn't get lost himself was a mystery. We weren't alone. All around us, dark shapes flitted. Sometimes, they passed quickly by. Sometimes, they'd stop for whispered conversations in an Egyptian so rasped and darting it almost chilled the blood.

We came once into a little opening in the streets that was lit with a central bonfire. Men sat around it, talking softly and drinking the local beer. They looked up and watched as we crossed the opening. I made sure not to look straight at them, but could see from the corners of my eyes how they looked at us. Small, wiry men of the sort you saw hanging round the palaces of the rich in wait for the food to be thrown out, they looked up to no good at all. They nudged each other and pointed at us. A couple of them got up noiselessly and seemed set to follow us back into the dark labyrinth of the streets.

But we were all three of us armed. Given the sort of weapons Macarius had insisted we put on, you don't worry about the attentions of slum trash like that. And there must have been something about our manner that said 'armed and dangerous: don't get involved'. The men sat down again and went back to whatever our appearance had disturbed.

'Isn't it just marvellous how our feet sink into this filth?' Priscus asked exultantly out of the darkness once we were alone again. 'Everything about this is just – just so very perfect, don't you think, Alaric dear?'

'Your tastes never fail to surprise me,' I snapped back at him. I was glad of my closed boots. They'd be a gift for the poor once I was back in the Palace. For the moment, I wished they stretched an inch higher up my legs. I went back to thinking about Leontius and his documents, and of what he had in mind for me. Getting me south for a few days under his control was what he'd said he wanted. He'd use me as a 'hunting dog,' he'd said. Beside this, the land law was nothing much. What was going on? I'd got back to the Palace too late to call for Macarius. Now, it was most provoking that he was a couple of feet in front of me, and I had no chance of speaking with him.

'This is the place, My Lords,' Macarius said.

We were outside a low building that seemed to go back a long way. Its windows were shuttered, its heavy door closed. For the first time since the door into this slum had been locked behind us, I felt a stab of optimism. Perhaps there was no one here, and we could go back for a change of clothing. If we hurried, we might still get to that brothel in time for the dancing cripples.

But Macarius was rapping some pattern of knocks on the door, and I could hear a shuffling and scraping on the other side. He pulled out a purse and turned back to us.

'Remember what I said about the use of Greek,' he urged. 'It is a hated tongue among the natives. If I believe it necessary, I will tell you in Latin that we must leave. If I do find it necessary, I beg you to do as I ask.'

The single lamp the doorman carried told me we were in a longish corridor. Though old and split in places, the doors leading off were surprisingly well made. The place must in the old days have been part of some fairly grand residence. Now, if possible, it stank still worse than the streets. It was all the usual smells, but concentrated and joined with something aromatic and still more foul. Again, Macarius spoke softly with the doorman. Another coin changed hands, and a door around a bend in the corridor was pulled open.

It was almost like stepping into one of those fogs Constantinople has in the autumn. I say 'almost', because it was worse. It was a cloud of steam made dark and oily from the many lamps in the room, and foul beyond any description I can attempt. A beggar's crotch at two inches would have been more salubrious. I rubbed my eyes and spluttered, and reached again for my pot of scent.

As my eyes adjusted, I could see we were in a large room. An oblong of about twenty by perhaps sixty feet, it had neither opening in its low ceiling nor any windows. It was hard to tell from the carpet of filth, but the floor seemed to be of crumbled brick.

The steam was coming from a low table to my right. Packed tight together, about a dozen men sat round it. Each with his neighbour shared a small bowl of liquid that was kept bubbling by the sort of charcoal burner used in better establishments for keeping depilatories soft. As one sat upright, the other would hunch over the pot and breathe in his share of the steam. The continual up and down motions, and the low chorus of pleasured moans, had a soporific quality even to watch.

I heard the door close behind me. I pulled my eyes away from the table and reached inside my cloak. Macarius gently touched my arm.

'That will not be needed, My Lord,' he whispered in Latin. 'I know the doorman's cousin. You are in no danger here.'

I relaxed. Once we'd turned left and were moving deeper into the room, I saw another of the druggies. He'd fallen away from his place at the table and sat on the floor, his back against one of the brick pillars that held up the ceiling. I looked at him. His clothing had gathered around his waist, showing the hard, throbbing erection. What was left of his lower face hung in folds, the saliva glistening on blackened teeth as he groaned from the long, continuous orgasm the drug had finally brought on.

'A mixture of Carthaginian berries and some of the metallic poisons,' Priscus said learnedly. 'Never tried it myself, though – all else aside, I'm told it can produce spontaneous castrations.'

A pity his father had never tried it, I thought. This was the last thing I'd imagined for the evening entertainment. I needed to get Macarius in private to discuss how to get hold of Leontius most effectively. Instead, I was stuck in some low drug den full of wogs and with Priscus for company.

To be fair, this wasn't just a place for getting doped. If it was hard to see anything approaching revelry, or even modest cheer, there were little groups of drinkers sitting on the floor or around other tables. Some of them even played, though at best with desultory interest, at throwing dice and moving stones about within the squared patterns chalked on the tables. Most of them sat silent, but for the rattle of dice. If any did speak, it was in the hushed tones you hear from a congregation in church.

Over in the furthest corner of the room, there was something approaching action. A small audience surrounding him, an old man sat beside a brazier. From the abstracted look on his face, and the uncertain motion of the food towards his face, it was obvious he was blind. A girl sat beside him, every so often arranging the food on his dish. The strong resemblance told me she was his daughter or granddaughter. Except she was dirty enough to have stuck to the wall, she wasn't that bad-looking.

'The man My Lord would question is here,' Macarius said to Priscus. He led us forward. We skirted the audience. No one looked up at us. Macarius took up two little chairs and arranged them, backs to the wall. Priscus and I sat down carefully. I sniffed at the cup that someone pressed into my hands.

'You may be assured,' said Macarius, 'it is just the free distribution wine.' Doubtless whoever had pissed this stuff out was drunk at the time. There the resemblance to wine ended, though. I put the cup down and looked at the act that was now making a start. The girl got up and scratched herself. As the old man finished coughing his lungs into the brazier, she struck up what sounded like a bored patter she'd had by heart since she was a child.

'She says,' Macarius explained, his face close to Priscus, 'that the Ancient One can see all with the eyes of his mind – all that is past or future or far away. He can also communicate with the dead, and even with the yet unborn. You have only to ask in order to learn the secrets of the world.'

'As if, with that sort of power,' I sniffed, 'I'd be showing off in this shithole.'

'Quiet, you fool!' Priscus hissed at me. 'You'll spoil everything.' He went back to looking intently at the Ancient One – who, bearing in mind how fast the lower classes grow old, might easily have been younger than he was. He swallowed another mouthful of the wine.

Someone who was sitting with his back to us had asked an involved question. In response, the Ancient One was muttering low towards the brazier while the girl relayed him in words that may have made a little more sense. Whatever the case, the questioner raised his arms in astonishment. He opened his purse and showed two silver coins. There was an appreciative hum from the rest of the audience. Someone else now asked a question. This time, money had to change hands before the stream of gibberish would start again.

Priscus touched Macarius on the shoulder.

'I want to know,' he said, speaking hoarsely, 'the whereabouts of a most holy relic. It is the first chamber pot of—'

'Oh, Priscus!' I called softly. 'My dear Priscus. I've thought you capable of most things, but never imagined you'd be taken in by this sort of shite.

'No, listen,' I went on, ignoring the outraged look he threw me. 'This is all just a fraud. The first question was a plant. It was there to set the tariff for whatever nonsense dribbles out of the old fool's mouth. Let's have a demonstration.'

I glanced round the smoky room. Priscus now had a sulky look on his face. Macarius looked worried. No one else, however, was paying any attention. The Ancient One was still babbling away into his brazier, while the girl babbled something different at her own speed.

'Macarius,' I said, 'tell them we want information about King Chosroes of Persia.'

As he put the question, several people now turned round to look at the seated strangers. I doubted if anyone here knew Latin or what it represented.

Still, I dropped my voice lower. 'Ask what Chosroes is doing at the moment.'

The answer came back that he was at dinner. An obvious answer – though surely a false one, bearing in mind Ctesiphon was far enough to the east for the evening to be much more advanced. But I overlooked this. I'd set up the line of questioning.

'Is the King a short man,' I asked, 'or a very tall man with a crippled foot?'

Came the answer: he was the latter. I smiled.

'Is he a man with white hair or with red hair?'

Came the answer: he was the former.

'Has he one eye or two?'

Came the answer: he had one.

'See, Priscus,' I said, trying hard to keep my voice low and suppress the note of triumph, 'see what garbage a few leading questions can produce. You've seen the pictures of Chosroes, just as I have. Shall we ask if Heraclius has three heads or five? Or how many teeth you have left?'

Priscus threw himself out of the chair and swore viciously. Macarius stepped back out of his path.

'I think we've seen enough here tonight,' I said, keeping my voice neutral. Seeing Priscus angry and baffled wasn't worth the unpleasantness of this evening. But it was some kind of offset. 'You must let me take you somewhere much more interesting for a late dinner.' I'd allow myself a good snigger once back in the darkness of the streets.

We got up to leave. If I'd got a few looks while having my questions put, we were now forgotten. No one looked at us. The girl was emphasising the Ancient One's latest answer by hopping up and down on one leg and flapping her arms like a bird. As we reached the door, I heard a rustling and a commotion behind me.

'Wait!' a voice called in Greek. 'Do not depart this place.' It was a loud, strangely impersonal voice – for all the world as if someone were speaking at a thin sheet of metal hung up before his face. It silenced the low buzz of conversation and clatter of dice. Even the druggies left off their bobbing and moaning.

13

'Wait if you would find the answer to your question,' the voice cried again, still in Greek. The flow of conversation started again, though for just a moment. It was now part angry and part scared. Then it died away. All was silent again.

'Time to get out of here,' I muttered to Priscus. I heard Macarius breathing hard behind me. But I turned back. I wanted to see who was speaking. Wouldn't you have done the same?

It was that girl. She'd left off her demonstration of whatever and had followed us halfway across the room. Now, she stood just before one of the gaming tables. A look of utter blankness on her face, it was as if the cunning imposter I'd seen by the brazier had suffered some kind of seizure while remaining on her feet. She was turned in my direction, though her eyes showed only the whites. She raised her arm in a stiff motion and pointed at me. I stepped over another of the fallen druggies to stand before her.

'If you would find your heart's desire,' she said, 'and all and more needed to save your world, seek it by the place on the map between the dead palms and the monument to human folly. Seek and you shall find.

'Beware, however, those who hate you, but trust in your friends and in those who cannot choose but to be your friends.'

She repeated the words '*but trust in your friends and in those who cannot choose but to be your friends*'. Her voice had reached every corner of that large room. She'd spoken a correct Greek – more correct than usually heard even from the Greeks of Alexandria. But it had been absolutely without emphasis. Imagine someone slowly and accurately reading out a text in a language he didn't understand, and you have some idea of the effect that girl had produced.

I looked at her. Everyone else in the room looked. All stood or sat or lay in frigid silence. Priscus shoved past me. He took hold of the girl and shook her.

'What the fuck is all this about?' he said softly yet intensely in Greek. 'What's this about maps and palm trees?'

Before I could get him from the room, someone darted behind me and pulled at my hood. As it came off and showed my golden hair, there was a shout of horror in the room. Someone else was yelling the Egyptian word for 'Greeks'. It seemed Macarius had been right about the effect Greek had on the natives.

Priscus was now shouting at the girl. But she'd passed out. She flopped loose in his arms. With a spluttered obscenity, he dropped her and wiped his hands in his cloak. The Ancient One had been up a while from his brazier and was shambling about. As he called something out, someone gave him a push from behind that got him sprawling over the girl. He ran shaking hands over her face and began to cry.

I thought Priscus would set about them both with a kicking. Instead, he twisted suddenly round to floor someone who'd dared lay hands on him. He threw his cloak back to get at his sword.

'My Lords, we must leave,' Macarius cried from the corridor. He looked ghastly in the dim light. I'd seen men look more composed at their own executions.

'I'll get Priscus,' I answered. I moved forward again. The room had dissolved into a chaos of shouting and movement. Everyone who could stand was on his feet, and holding a weapon or looking round for something to use as one.

A man swung at me with a broken chair leg. Straight away, I had my own sword out and gave him a shallow stab in the shoulder. He went down screaming.

'Keep beside me,' Priscus said in my ear. Now controlling himself, his voice was loud but calm. 'We back out of here together. Kill anyone who steps too close.'

Getting out of the building was easy. We were defending a narrow front in that corridor. No one could get behind us. The problem, I knew, would come once we were back in the streets. A shame we'd not been able to bar the door from outside the room. That would have contained the danger until we were well away. As it was, we were in trouble.

'You must run, My Lords,' Macarius shouted.

The cloud had passed by, and now the moon shone faintly on all about us. I looked at Macarius. That look of terror was now set on his face as if he'd put on a mask. I opened my mouth to speak.

He cut me off. 'Run for your lives,' he said. 'I'll try to hold them here.' He turned back to the doorway and shouted something in Egyptian. His sword glinted in the moonlight as he waved it at the men who were crowding the doorway. The doorman stood behind him, just into the street. He was calling out something that might have been a plea for calm or a prayer.

'Go, for God's sake!' Macarius shouted again, his eyes glittering blankly. 'There's nothing you can do here.'

I ran. Where to run was another matter. I heard a clatter of arms as I reached a street corner. Then there was a wild shouting and the padding of feet. I turned the corner and ran into the semi-darkness. It wasn't dark enough. They were after me. With every new twist in those streets, the mob grew larger. I'd left the building with perhaps half a dozen after me. Now, there were dozens. Roaring and howling, lit torches showing their way, they raced behind me through the labyrinth of the Egyptian quarter, not more than a dozen yards behind.

As I reached another corner, a few men jumped in front of me. I hit at one of them with the pommel of my drawn sword. He went down. I felt the other clutch at me, but I was too heavy and moving too fast for him to stop me. I ran blindly along those low, twisting streets, gauging my position less by what I thought was in front than by those terrifying sounds behind.

I took a corner. My foot landed on something unstable. I skidded. I grabbed out at nothing in particular as I tried to right myself. I fell on one side and rolled on to my back. I wasn't injured, and I was up at once. But those shouting voices were almost on me.

They must have been just a few feet round the corner. Which way to run? I cast desperately round, and started a dash forward.

'Not so fast, my pretty,' said Priscus out of the shadows on my left. He had my arm in that iron grip of his, and pulled me roughly against the wall. Another moment, and we were squeezed into a doorway, our faces pressed hard against the wood, in our black cloaks invisible to anyone from behind.

The mob went straight past us. I felt bodies brush against my back. But no one in that stampede could have stopped even had he thought there was reason. We waited until the shouting had lost its immediacy and until the slow and the lame had sloped past us in pursuit of the main action. Then we stepped back into the street.

The moon shone down thin but bright. I looked at Priscus. He'd shaken his hood off and was checking that he had his sword in the right way. His face shone with the sort of exaltation you normally saw in church – or in Priscus when he was especially pleased with himself.

'You saved me?' I said. There was no doubt he had. But for him, I didn't care to think what I'd now be having done to me.

'But of course I did, my darling Alaric,' he whispered close in my face. He stood back as if to savour the confusion the moon must have shown on my face. 'Oh, we may have our little differences from time to time,' he said with a careless wave upwards. 'But we are both members of the Imperial Council. We don't leave each other to be torn apart by the wogs.

'Now, talking of wogs, where is that man of yours? That was a most shoddy holding action back there. If he were one of my soldiers, I'd have him flayed alive on the field of battle.'

'I'm sure Macarius did his best,' I said, feeling guilty again I hadn't stayed to kill a few of the trash. 'But I'm not sure how we can get back without him.'

'Don't you worry your little head about that one, my darling,' said Priscus with a chuckle. 'We simply go back the way we came. Dear me, isn't it just plain you have no military experience? Lost, and in a shitty little dump like this? You should have been with me in the street battle I won in Amida. *That* was confusing!'

He paused and gestured at a shadowy dungheap we were walking towards. It looked like any other, and I had no recollection of having seen it on our way out. In any event, I'd seen very little, and couldn't imagine how Priscus had seen any more.

'The real question I'd like answered, though,' he went on, 'is where is the map that slut mentioned? What do you think of those dead palms and the monument? I'm not sure if the Oracle at Delphi used to give more crooked answers.'

'You'll surely remember,' I said, putting on a confidence I didn't yet feel, 'that she was speaking to me.'

'You were the nearest when she spoke,' Priscus said dismissively. 'I was the one there with a valid question. Your heart's content – assuming you have one – is not something it needs supernatural intervention to find.'

I didn't bother with a reply to that. I was beginning to wonder where the girl had learned her Greek, and why she'd brought on a riot. Had she been punishing us for making the Ancient One look stupid?

My thoughts broke off. As we rounded another corner – Priscus assured me this was the way – we came face to face with the mob. Perhaps someone had guessed which way we'd be going. We looked into a deep mass of menacing humanity, their torches still burning bright.

'Oh, shit!' I said. As I turned to run, Priscus had hold of me again. He already had his sword out.

'We stand together,' he said, still calm and now deadly. 'We go forward a step at a time, and we cut our way through.' He pulled a knife from his belt. I swallowed and drew my sword. I'd never yet come seriously to grief in street fighting. But I'd never been against these odds. There must have been dozens of these people. They didn't seem very well armed. But numbers like theirs must always count. Relying on Priscus was not something I'd ever expected. I found myself now hoping his own estimate of his military abilities was remotely close to the truth.

I remember the flash of steel in the moonlight as we stepped into the crowd. I remember the recoil in my sword arm and screams of the men we struck. I remember feeling the wave of panic that swept through the crowd as those at the front found themselves trapped against men who were still pressing forward. I remember the shrieks of fear and sudden pain. I felt the impact of something hard on my left shoulder. I had a moment of panic as I found it hard to move my sword properly in that packed mass.

But it was only a moment. We'd cut our way straight through. Priscus swung round and slashed at someone who hadn't pressed back as far as the others. With a crunch of sword on flesh and bone, the top of his head was cut as cleanly away as if it had been the shell of a soft-boiled egg. I lunged forward and stabbed at another. I think I got him in the side. He went down with a bubbling scream.

And that was the end of the attack. As quickly as it had formed, the mob now melted away. We were alone in the dim street. It was now just the two of us and perhaps half a dozen of the dead and dying. Priscus bent down to wipe his sword on the clothing of one of the bodies.

'Not a bad evening at all, my dearest Alaric,' he said lightly. He took my arm and led me along the street. 'After this, I'm sure you'll agree it's time to discuss how to end our rather sterile dispute and let young Maximin understand that he is blessed with two fathers. I suggest I should call again at the nursery—'

There was another pattering of feet ahead of us. I hadn't bothered sheathing my own sword. I held it up weakly, hoping Priscus wouldn't notice how it shook.

'Since the Legate of the Great Augustus is unharmed' – Priscus nodded again in my direction – 'I propose on this occasion to overlook your negligence in leaving us to shift for ourselves.'

His face impassive, Macarius bowed. The police officer drew his men into single file as they passed through the doorway back into the Greek centre of Alexandria. I looked at the bright streets and at the well-dressed men who moved easily around as they passed to or from pleasure or some late business, and breathed a quiet sigh of relief. Whatever else I had to do during the time I had left in Alexandria, it would not involve being again on the other side of the Wall.

'What is that chanting?' I asked in an effort to change the subject. My voice wasn't as steady as I'd hoped it would be.

The police officer looked back at the now closed and barred door. Beyond it, the mob had reassembled and was back at its favourite slogan.

'It's all about some wog prophecy, sir,' he answered. 'They've been told that Greek rule over the world will end when the mummy of the Great Alexander sheds tears.'

'The translation, My Lord,' Macarius whispered in my ear, 'is: "The tears of Alexander shall flow, giving bread and freedom." '

I nodded. So the word wasn't 'Alexandria', but 'Alexander'. I wished I'd taken the trouble on arriving to start lessons in Egyptian. But how could I have known I'd be stuck here so long? I thought to ask Macarius how he'd got himself away from the mob. But the police officer was speaking again.

'We would have come looking in more than one group,' he explained, filling up the silence that resulted. 'The problem is we're stretched rather thin tonight, what with the commotion outside the Great Synagogue – oh, and the murder.'

'Murder?' I asked. 'Why should that be taking up police resources?'

'But, of course, you won't have heard,' he answered. 'It was that big landowner – what's his name? Leontius, I think – horribly murdered, you know. Horribly murdered, and in his own bed.'

14

Priscus cocked his head to get a look at the corpse from a new angle.

'Nasty work,' he said appreciatively. 'By the look on his face, they must have kept him alive and awake till close to the end. I'd imagine he was being questioned as well as put out of the way.' He pointed at the screwed-up napkin. It stank of something that made my nose itch. 'Useful as far as it goes for keeping a victim conscious. Of course, I know better mixtures for that. I could manage better all round – but I'd need leisure and skilled assistants. Nasty work,' he said again.

'You say the guts are all arranged in those pots?' he asked the Chief of Police. He took up one of the lids and peered at the pale, slimy entrails. 'The brains as well?' he added, looking into another of the pots. He turned back for another inspection. 'How were those taken without spoiling the head?' he asked.

'I think it was Herodotus who said they are pulled down the nose with special hooks,' I volunteered. I gripped the back of a chair for support. I wondered again how much of the smell in the room was from a gutted Leontius and how much from what I'd managed to splash over myself in the Egyptian quarter.

'I defer to your greater learning,' Priscus said. 'But are you telling me poor Leontius was killed in some parody of wog mummification?'

'I'm saying no such thing,' I said carefully. 'In these cases, you make no inferences until all the facts available have been collected and weighed. As for your own inference, my understanding is that embalming went out of use after the Old Faith was abolished here. That doesn't mean all knowledge of the process has disappeared, or that such knowledge might not be taken as a guide for murder.

'Do have that crowd moved on,' I said, turning to the Chief of Police. His subdued yet anxious manner was getting on my nerves. 'I didn't like its look as I came in.' Indeed, I hadn't. That combination of silence and numbers might equal trouble. I thought of the mob in the Egyptian quarter and shuddered.

I heard a familiar voice in the hall outside. I called the Chief of Police back before he could open the door.

'And do get a blanket over that thing,' I said. 'There's no reason why everyone needs to look at it.'

'I was told you were here,' said Martin when the door was closed again. He looked at the large but now hidden mound of flesh. A dark stain was seeping through the blanket. He swallowed and looked away. He looked at me and also looked away.

I rubbed at the bruise on my left shoulder. I'd be stiff for days but, all told, had nothing to complain about. I looked at the Chief of Police.

'You'll need to leave a couple of men in the street,' I said. 'But I see no further reason for your involvement. This is a matter for the man's family in Letopolis.'

A look of relief on his face, he bowed his way out, muttering something about needing to make an entry for the next public order report.

'Well, my dearest,' said Priscus as he lifted a corner of the blanket for a final look at what had been Leontius, 'I think I'll take that as my own invitation to retire. It's been a glorious day, and I have so much to consider. Oh' – he paused by the door – 'did I overhear you back by the Egyptian quarter talking about Alexander's mummy? Do say that I did.'

'I believe it's been in the basement of the Library since the temples were closed,' I said. 'So far as nothing could be uglier, I suppose it must be an improvement on Leontius.'

'Decidedly!' he said with an appreciative smack of his lips. 'Well, I really must have a look at the great man. After all, we have so much in common, what with the Persian War and all.'

'Before you go, Priscus,' I said, 'I'll note that you may have been one of the last people to see Leontius alive. I hope you'll not mind if I call on you tomorrow for a brief discussion.'

Priscus stopped by the door and smiled. 'My dear boy,' he cried in mock alarm, 'you surely can't think I had a hand in this? I've told you I could have done it much better. Besides, aren't there the little matters of means, motive and opportunity? You did give me a most interesting lecture on these things. Don't think I ever forget a word of what you say to me.'

I grunted and rubbed my shoulder. I couldn't, I had to agree, think how or why Priscus might have murdered the man. But it was annoying – so much learned in one afternoon; so little hope now of following it up.

'Now that you're here,' I said to Martin once the door was closed again, 'I want you to help me go through the man's papers. In particular, we need to look out for a packet that may not yet have been opened and filed.

'Macarius,' I said, turning to the figure who'd been standing silent throughout, 'I want the entire household lined up in the big front hall. Sit them about a yard apart, and make sure they don't speak to anyone until I've had each one in for questioning.'

'The packet you seek, My Lord, will not be here,' he said.

I gave him a hard stare.

'I also observed the meeting between Leontius and his agent,' he explained. 'I was not so close as you were, and was not able to hear all that passed between them. However, I did follow Leontius back to this house. He was met at the city gate by another man on horseback who took delivery of the documents he had bought. I heard a reference to Letopolis, and assume from this that Leontius wanted everything taken off to his manor house in Egypt.

'Certainly, I had already discovered that he was planning a trip to his estates – this despite your instruction that no one should leave Alexandria.'

The things I wanted to ask of Macarius were beginning to accumulate like snow before an unused gate in winter. But they would need to remain unasked for the moment. He was continuing.

'I must, My Lord, inform you that all the circumstances of this murder indicate involvement by the Brotherhood.'

'What in God's name are you talking about?' I asked. Martin might have jumped as if he'd seen a ghost. I was wholly in the dark, and in no mood to be kept there.

'The Brotherhood,' Macarius answered, 'does not usually operate in Alexandria, and prefers in general to shun the Greek regions of Egypt. But it does maintain a strong presence in the south of the country, where, indeed, it is often the effective power.'

I took one of the entrail pots from the chair on which it had been placed and sat down. I rubbed again at my shoulder and looked round for something to drink. It was probably for the best that the only wine jug in the room was on the floor overturned.

'You'd better continue,' I sighed. 'Since I have no choice but to investigate the murder, I'll need to know exactly what this Brotherhood is.'

'It claims to be a very old organisation,' Macarius began. 'The story is that it was formed nearly twelve hundred years ago, when Cambyses of Persia invaded and extinguished the last native dynasty. For the next few centuries, it operated as a resistance movement, keeping hopes alive of a national recovery and largely confining the Persians to their garrison towns.

'When the Great Alexander invaded and expelled the Persians, he was at first welcomed by the Brotherhood and was offered much assistance. Greeks then were not hated by the natives, and their own victories over the Persians were taken as an example of what could be done, given the right spirit of unity. When, however, he died in Babylon and his general Ptolemy hurried here to make himself King, there was a reaction against the Greeks.

'The Ptolemies, however, turned out to be less hostile than expected to native customs, and the Brotherhood went into decline, reappearing only during the breakdown of order in the final reigns, when it operated as an order of brigands. It was suppressed by the Romans and, for centuries after Egypt's incorporation in the Empire, the Brotherhood was known only from old stories.

'It became prominent again after the closure of the temples, and has grown mighty since the decay of Imperial control over the south. It sometimes inclines to the Old Faith – and you know already that this continues in the south. More often, it is associated with the less compromising wings of the Monophysite heresy. Whether from Rome or Constantinople – whether by Latins or by Greeks – it remains pledged to end all foreign rule, and to restore Egypt to the sway of its own Pharaohs.'

'Very interesting,' I said drily. 'So we have a robber band that legitimises itself by attachment to something that may have existed in the past, but that probably existed only occasionally.'

'Not so, My Lord,' Macarius broke back in. 'The Brotherhood has rituals and an organisation that do point to long continuation. For example, every member must be tattooed on the small of his back with the name in the old Egyptian writing of the greatest native Pharaoh. More importantly, it is his duty to produce two sons. This done, he must pass the remainder of his life in strict continence. There are further rituals and customs of which the initiated never speak. But all the evidence is of long continuation.'

'For fuck's sake, Martin,' I snapped suddenly, 'do come away from those lamps. You'll have a fire going if you don't stop knocking them over.' It was no excuse that I'd fancied a look myself ever since ordering them in to illuminate the murder scene. Like everything else in the house, they were in the hideous style of the ancient Egyptians. Some of the stuff, mind you, was impressively solid. Forget the workmanship – one or two pieces, such as this array of lamps, must even have been valuable on account of their materials. If Leontius hadn't furnished the whole place from tomb excavations, I'd have been surprised. Quite fitting, I thought, Leontius had come to the end he had. No doubt the style of his murder had been prompted at least partly by the surroundings.

'Macarius is right,' he blurted out. 'This is all to do with the Brotherhood.' He stepped back from the array of lamps. 'These people were big in Antinoopolis. No one crossed them – no matter how big he was with the government in Alexandria.'

'So, what do you know about the Brotherhood?' I asked. It was nice that even he knew of some organisation I'd been here months without so much as hearing about.

Martin looked back, his face pale in the light of a dozen lamps. 'I've been looking again into those payments we were discussing,' he said. He stared at Macarius. After some internal struggle, he decided to go on properly with his explanation. 'That subsidy to the Temple of Isis – you know it's been cancelled five times. What I've now found is that every official who signed the cancellation order was murdered. Only one case was ever investigated, and the report is missing from the archives.'

I sat awhile in silence. Macarius was his usual impassive self. He'd not moved from the position he'd taken on first coming into the room with Priscus and me. Martin looked, as ever on these occasions, undecided between shitting himself and passing out. I stood and walked back over to the corpse. The fine blanket had settled over its contours, and it really might as well not have been covered at all. I lifted the blanket and looked under at the twisted, staring face. Priscus knew his business, and I had no doubt Leontius had been kept alive far into the murder. What I did wonder was how he'd been kept quiet.

Yes – there were questions to be asked of those scared, silent slaves I'd seen lurking in the hall.

'It seems to be the case,' I said, making sure to emphasise the mood of doubt or hypothesis, 'that we have one of those instances where two separate intrigues come accidentally together. Somehow, Leontius had got to know about the subsidy. How he got to know may be connected with his interest in Egyptian antiquities. With his known talent for understanding the wider implications of his acts, he used this to trip me up in yesterday's meeting. Those parts of this Brotherhood adhering to the Old Faith were consequently angered. He has now been punished for setting events in course that led to the sixth cancellation of the subsidy.'

I thought back to the conversation I'd overheard outside Alexandria. It would have closed matters if Leontius had been intending only to blackmail me into backing off from the land law. But he'd been planning to blackmail me into leading him to something that would make him powerful. That was one of those leftover details that tends to wreck neat explanations.

Something else worth asking was how extensive the Brotherhood's network was within the Viceroy's government. What Martin had turned up was certainly disturbing. But I checked the train of thought. I looked again at Martin.

'I told you earlier, Martin, to drop your investigation,' I said in my very firm voice. 'I trust you will now do so. Nicetas sealed the order. It looks drafted in the local style. Even so, our own involvement must be at least suspected.'

I paused, letting the implication of this sink into Martin's already scared mind. The door opened and a slave crept into the room, carrying a tray of refreshments. Macarius took them and pushed the slave back out. He sniffed at the jug and nodded. He poured wine into a large cup and handed it to me. I drank. An opium pill would have been nice to settle my thoughts and take away that dull pain from my shoulder. But the wine would have to do.

'Even so again,' I said, now in lighter mood, 'this Brotherhood seems to have struck, and in as public a manner as can be imagined. No doubt, the subsidy will once again be reinstated when the fuss has died down. If and when that happens, it will be none of our business. And, Martin – you will this time make it none of your business. For the rest, we have other work entirely. So far as its effect will be to raise the condition of those from whom the Brotherhood appears to draw support, I don't expect any untoward consequences for ourselves.

'Now, while I have no intention of bringing anyone to justice, there are certain things I must know about Leontius and his final movements. Martin, I want you to go and secure any papers you can find in the house. You will not object, I hope, if Macarius takes your place as secretary when I interview the household.'

As I got up to move to the door, I caught sight of my face in a little mirror fixed to the wall. No point moaning now at Macarius, but it would have been useful to be told about the smears of dried blood.

15

I glanced at myself again in the mirror. A little more sleep would have come in handy. But the masseurs had managed to press most of the youth back into my features. And if my bruised shoulder was hurting like buggery, it would have hurt still more without the opium. All told, I looked better than I felt, but didn't feel as bad as I might have.

'His Imperial Highness will be pleased to see Your Magnificence,' the eunuch trilled in an effort at the grand style of Constantinople.

I grunted and walked past him into the Viceroy's office.

'Greetings, my dear Alaric, many greetings,' Nicetas called in Latin from his chair. He waved me to the seat opposite and fell back exhausted. Like his Imperial cousin, he was from Carthage, and could be trusted to fall into his native language whenever Greek proved too much of a strain. This morning, his leg was giving trouble. The smell alone as I walked in had told me it had turned bad again. His shaven face was pale and haggard. That the remnants of his dirty blond hair had been carefully dressed to cover his scalp only added to the appearance of broken-down health. A monk was intoning prayers while slaves retied the bandage.

'Patriarch John has loaned me the little finger of Saint George to have bandaged next to the flesh,' he added, noticing my look at him. 'I'm sure it will have more effect than these worthless doctors.'

Saint George? I asked myself. Saint George? There were so many of them out here, it was hard to keep track. Wasn't he the sausage maker – or was it the arms dealer? – who'd been torn apart here by a mob back in the time of Julian? No point in asking.

Nicetas reached over to a low table and picked up a scrap of parchment.

'I've had a letter,' he said, 'from some trader among the Saracens. He lives in one of the inland towns.' He broke off and looked at the map of Egypt and surrounding territories that was a mosaic covering the entire wall on the far side of the room. I followed his glance. Someone had been at it recently with coloured chalks. All the Red Sea ports of Egypt had been circled and connected by lines to ports on the facing coast.

'Anyway,' Nicetas said, passing the letter over to me, 'the man tells me that God has been sending him messages these past two years via the Archangel Gabriel. Apparently, the pagan rulers of his home town don't like his efforts, and he invites our support.'

I skimmed the letter. It was rather a quaint production. Written in a debased Greek, with a few Latin characters thrown in, it went on and on about these alleged messages. The recipient plainly thought himself in good standing with the Almighty.

'I'm thinking to send the man a set of the Gospels on fine vellum,' Nicetas added.

'I'm sure their effect will be most edifying,' I said. 'However, your cousin the Emperor has interests in Arabia that suggest a more substantial gift. Saracen mercenaries are useful to the Persians as well as to ourselves. Promoting the True Faith among them will further our efforts to bring them into at least friendly neutrality.

'I would therefore recommend in addition a small sum of gold – oh, and perhaps some dancing girls. I'm sure they will go down very well if our man is having that bad a time.'

Except for the monk, who'd been mumbling away throughout, we fell silent. Nicetas had the best rooms in the Palace. Though the weather had turned hot again, with nearly fifty feet of ceiling height and those big northerly windows, the heat was less than intolerable.

'Heraclius mentions you again in a letter that arrived the other day,' he said, beginning again with a sudden jerk. 'As ever, he speaks very highly of you. He instructs me to continue giving all possible help with implementing the new land law.' He paused and looked over at the bigger of the three windows.

I glared at the monk. He gave me one of those 'fuck you' looks that favoured clerics always try on their betters. It didn't work with me. I glared steadily back. At last, he made the sign of the Cross over the bandaged leg and got himself out of the room. With low bows, the slaves followed.

'I understand it was at the urging of Priscus,' Nicetas continued once the doors were pulled shut. 'Even so, you have been here long enough to know the folly of going into the Egyptian quarter at night.' He tried to say more, but the effort was too much. He sank back again exhausted.

I refilled his wine cup and put it to his lips. He swallowed a few times and closed his eyes. I thought for a moment he'd nodded off on me. But the lids flickered and he was back again.

'The death of Leontius,' he said with a change of subject, 'is something I had been expecting since he worsted you in the Great Hall. Certainly, the document you had me seal the night before last might as well have been his death warrant. The Brotherhood seldom acts openly in Alexandria, but does not welcome any harming of its interests. Am I right that you propose to investigate his death?'

I shook my head. I'd slept on the matter, and was even surer that this was one of those things best left alone.

'I am glad,' said Nicetas. 'You may think that his death has been of some benefit to our project. The opposition is now without a leader. Indeed, I had a deputation earlier this morning of his followers among the landowning interest. They assured me of their loyalty and of their active desire to help maintain order both in Alexandria and in Egypt. This being said, there remain other considerations which I am too unwell at present to discuss with you. While my cousin urges the land law upon me, he must understand – as must you – that our primary concern is the maintenance of order and of stability in the wider sense. I am inclined, therefore, to proceed more cautiously.'

More cautiously indeed! At the speed he had managed so far to allow, more cautious would have meant going backwards.

'And I've spoken with Priscus,' he added. He looked away again. 'He believes there will be a Persian attack on Syria come the spring. The exports of grain are too important to risk at any time, so we cannot afford trouble in Egypt.'

'And what might Priscus have advised on this occasion?' I asked, keeping my voice very steady. 'Might it involve further delay?'

'He always has the best interests of the Empire at heart,' Nicetas said evasively. 'I know that you operate under the direct orders of the Augustus. Even so, you must see that the unsettled state of things here may require some special dispensation from the law.'

'Are you suggesting that Egypt should be exempted from the land redistribution?' I asked, a touch of nicely judged menace now in my voice.

'Not exempted,' came the stammered reply, 'just given more time for the implications of the law to be considered. Surely, bearing in mind Egypt's unique importance, we should see how the law works in the other provinces. I agree that it might bring substantial improvements in tax collection and military service and in general order. But surely we need to bear in mind local circumstances for the short term.

'Perhaps I should write again to Heraclius. He ignored my first letter. Perhaps this time . . .' He fell silent again.

'We cannot have any further delay,' I said, breaking the silence. 'The will of Caesar is that the law shall apply without exception throughout the Empire. If you are concerned about order in Alexandria, you might seal those orders for the dispatch of the grain fleet. It will be ready to go in the next few days. Already, it's causing trouble. You may care to remember how the granaries are running short, and how many months we have until the next harvest. If the grain fleet is delayed, it will hardly matter that Leontius is no longer here to stir up the mobs and the higher classes on both sides of the Wall.

'I might also mention once again your policy of sending forces out of Alexandria. I have no doubt the Red Sea ports are important. But I am not sure if we have enough men here now to suppress a rising of either of the mobs, let alone both.'

Nicetas shut me up by putting his hands over his ears and looking ready to cry. There was no point continuing. After four months of this, I knew his ways. I waited for the tantrum to pass. It did. He moved his leg a couple of inches. He winced from the sudden pain.

'You must understand,' he said, 'that I am responsible for Alexandria and the whole of Egypt. After two years in the post, I know far more than Heraclius about local conditions. I'm not sure how, in present circumstances, I can seal those warrants you keep setting before me. The murder – the death – of Leontius removes one difficulty, but raises others. The country is so unsettled, so horribly unsettled. There are so many things about Egypt I should have explained to you before all this happened. If only I had more time . . .'

He trailed off again. A distracted look coming over his face, he picked up that letter from the Saracen. His lips moved quietly as he read it over to himself.

16

'But, my darling, are such cruel words appropriate for the man who saved your life?' Priscus asked, sitting back in his chair. He raised his cup in a mock toast to the dust-covered boxes piled up against the wall.

'I do assure you, my dearest Alaric, that I made not one mention of your land law this morning. If Nicetas called me into his presence, it was on other matters entirely.'

I breathed deeply and took another swig from my own cup. There was no reason to suppose Priscus had made his way here specially to block in Alexandria what he'd so bitterly opposed in Constantinople. He'd just taken advantage of a situation that had presented itself. Perhaps he was even telling the truth. It wouldn't have surprised me at all if Nicetas had thought up the latest tactic for delay all by himself. Bloody Leontius! I thought again. Alive or dead, his talent for getting in the way was endless. I refilled my cup.

Just as I was opening my mouth for something really cutting, the door opened and Hermogenes came in. We dropped the matter and stood, composing our features back into the polite interest proper to this occasion. Behind Hermogenes, about half a dozen slaves were puffing and muttering as they carried in the heavy box. The lid was covered by a good quarter-inch of dust. But the sides were of polished ebony, and, if broken in places, the bronze handles were of elegant – and therefore very old – design.

'I do beseech you, My Lords,' the Head Librarian said anxiously, 'to be most careful in your inspection. Even the slightest handling can be ruinous for something so delicate.'

'Get it open,' Priscus said shortly. He was looking hard at the box. He might even have been trembling. 'You' – he pointed at one of the slaves – 'bring those lamps closer. I want to see properly.'

We looked in silence at what had, nearly a thousand years before, been the Great Alexander. He'd been brought in from still deeper into the Library basement than the room in which we'd been settled to wait.

'That is him, isn't it?' Priscus asked softly, not taking his eyes from the dark, shrivelled thing in that box. 'I expected it would be bandaged all over.'

'The embalming, My Lord,' Hermogenes explained, 'was carried out by his Greek physicians in Babylon. They steeped the whole body in aromatic honey, having first prepared it by some art of the ancients now lost to us. The method was less intrusive than that of the Egyptians. So long as the honey was kept replenished, I understand that the body retained its living freshness and even suppleness for many centuries.'

I pointed at some dark puckering on the right thigh. 'According to the biography written by King Ptolemy,' I said, 'he took an arrow here in one of his Indian battles.' I stretched my arms out. 'And, even if we assume a degree of shrinkage, this does confirm the general claims that he was below normal height.'

'He conquered and united all of Greece,' said Priscus, still speaking softly. 'He liberated the Greeks of Asia Minor. He conquered Syria and Egypt. He smashed the Persian Empire. He marched through regions lost before and since in the realms of fable. Had he lived and gone west, Rome itself would never have been known as other than the head town of some Italian league.' He looked up at me, awed at the mere summary of the man's achievement.

I ignored him and continued looking at the face of Alexander. There could be no doubt this was him. The documentation Hermogenes had brought in earlier was conclusive. The body had been ordered to be removed from display by Caracalla on his visit. It had been taken from its temple on the legal suppression of the Old Faith by Theodosius. There was an unsealed order for its burial in the necropolis – unsealed because of some dispute among the bishops about what to do with a body that had been so long worshipped as a god. Since then, it had been down here in the bowels of the Library.

It was the man. There could be no doubt of that. But I could look and look at the thin and brittle flesh that held to the skull, and at the lips shrunken back over the teeth into a perpetual snarl, and still see nothing to remind me of the statue by Lysippus set up outside the Imperial Palace in Constantinople. Stone is for ever, bronze for as long as a new shape isn't found for it. But – Greek method, Egyptian method – the embalmer's art gives somewhat less than immortality to the flesh.

Priscus was speaking again. 'I know a lot about Alexander,' he said. 'I am, after all, supposed to repeat him in smashing up the Persians.' He paused and glanced at me.

Still I said nothing.

He continued: 'When Augustus came here, he scattered flowers on the mummy. He was asked if he wanted to see the mummies of all the Kings Ptolemy. He said: "I came here to see a king, not a row of corpses." ' He took a gold ring from his finger and placed it carefully on the mummy's chest. It rolled slightly and settled into a depression between two of the ribs. It glinted up at us in the lamplight.

'Get this sealed up again,' he said, turning to Hermogenes. 'Keep it safe. I will be back when I have destroyed the Persians a second time.'

As the door closed, leaving us alone again, Priscus sat down. He reached for his drug pouch, and was soon lost in fussing over which blend of powders might most likely produce the mood he wanted. If going into the streets was out of the question, it was decidedly chilly down here. Alexander might be kept in a dry place, but with the waters rising just a few feet below in their brick vaults, this room was bordering on the dank.

I walked over to the far wall of the room and peered into one of the loosely stacked boxes. More old books, I noted. I took one out and read the tag attached to the papyrus roll. It was the volume in which Tacitus narrates the reign of Caligula. I hadn't known there was a Latin section here. It might be worth looking through what was left of it for rarities.

'So, my dear, what further thoughts have you had regarding last night?' Priscus suddenly asked behind me.

'I questioned the slaves,' I said, not bothering to turn. 'Apparently, Leontius came back unexpectedly from his Canopus trip, and sent all the slaves out to a religious ceremony. He was then alone in the house, except for an old crone in the kitchens, who is deaf.'

Priscus put his cup down heavily. In the silence that followed, I turned back to him.

'Don't trifle with me over this,' he snapped, for a moment losing control. 'I haven't come all this way to be fucked over – not by you!' He pulled himself together and laughed. I think it was intended to be light and mocking. The drugs, however, plus the unerased emotions of our viewing, left just enough of his real nature still showing.

'My dear young Alaric,' he said, trying hard for his usual slimy charm, 'if you suppose I give so much as a rotten fig for Leontius, you are sadly mistaken. His death hardly stopped the flowering of a beautiful friendship. I am referring to that slut and her message about the piss pot. You will surely agree that is a matter of greater importance.'

'Come now, Priscus,' I said, sitting opposite him. He pushed the jug forward. I filled his cup and then my own. There are times for jollying someone along, and times for trying to talk some sense into him. I'd never quite got the balance of this right with Martin. How to begin with Priscus? Having not the foggiest where his piss pot might be, or how to set about finding it, I decided to try for the second.

'What we saw in the Egyptian quarter was nothing more than a marketplace trick,' I said earnestly. 'Go back there tonight in a different suit of clothes, and you'll get more of the same. Don't ask how she knew Greek and put on that funny voice. But we've both seen marvels of conjuring at dinner with Heraclius. No one can explain how the tricks are done. No one assumes on that account that silk napkins really are burned to ashes and then produced without so much as a scorch mark.'

'And is it because they are such frauds,' Priscus said, now in his tone of menacing lightness, 'that someone fitting your man what's-his-name's description was seen handing them money this morning, since when they haven't been seen?'

'I'll question Macarius about that when I see him,' I said as smoothly as I could manage. Indeed, I would question him. Whatever could he have been up to?

'Now, what else did I hear when I was with Nicetas?' Priscus continued. 'Ah, yes – that you'd got him to seal an order to dig out some old canal, and then diverted five hundred of the workmen, complete with digging equipment, to your own ends. Would you mind sharing with me what those ends might be?'

'Priscus,' I said firmly, ignoring his nasty look, 'I'm having those men for something that is of no interest to you and that was planned long before you showed up here on your quest for that wretched piss pot.' Macarius and his doings were still uppermost in my thoughts. I was also beginning to wonder, though, if Nicetas was entirely as useless as he'd always seemed. I dismissed the possibility. As Viceroy of Egypt, he'd surely get the best intelligence reports to be had. As Nicetas, he'd still be an unintelligent slob.

'No,' I finished, cutting off the reply Priscus was forming, 'I promise that, if I ever stumble across the first chamber pot of our Lord and Saviour Jesus Christ, I will have it wrapped in purple silk and sent to you, together with your weight in whatever you've just shoved up your nose.' Not, of course, I wanted to add, that Alexander had needed any piss pot other than his own for conquering not just Persia but the whole East. But you don't really push your luck with someone like Priscus.

'After Nicetas, I went to the nursery in your quarters,' Priscus said, with a change of subject and of tone – he was now all aggrieved reasonableness. 'I was told Maximin was with Martin. I was stopped at the door of his quarters by that ghastly woman of his. I'll swear she's on her way to becoming as fat as he is.

'You know, Alaric' – he was becoming easier and more natural in his manner – 'when the Great Augustus does eventually get as sick of you as everyone else did two years ago, the worst you have to expect, in our wonderful new order of things, is being shut away in a monastery. This isn't a privilege, though, that stretches down far enough to touch your secretary and his family. Come the day, I'll see that bastard Celt and his bitch wife walled up in an oven with that child of theirs. I'll even provide the oven – the one I showed you back in Constantinople, with the inspection window I had fitted. Since Heraclius probably won't have you blinded, I'll allow you to watch.'

'Well, really, Priscus,' I answered, trying to match his mood, 'you overestimate the space you take up in my thoughts. I had Maximin moved for other reasons. I have no objection to a short visit every day after his afternoon nap. But it all depends on your further conversations with Nicetas.'

Priscus smiled.

There was no point trying to extract any promises from him. If he'd broken oaths made in church, why should I dream of trusting his word? But the implied threat might be enough.

'So, here at least, we do understand each other,' he said, getting up from his chair. 'Now, my golden young stunner, shall we walk out of here arm-in-arm – a most edifying spectacle of unity in the Imperial Council? And will you do me the kindness of showing me where you get your perfumes mixed?'

17

Even by his own high standards, Patriarch John had preached a fine sermon. It was all about the parable of the talents, and in the Greek of Constantinople. He'd turned it very cleverly to an injunction to give to his relief fund for the distressed churches of Cappadocia. Beyond making sure everyone saw what I dropped into the collecting box when it came past, I'd paid no attention to his use of the parable. I was instead reflecting on how much sense can be found in Scripture – if only you have the patience to look for it.

Martin was going over the fine points again to me and Sveta as we sat in their quarters for an early lunch. The two children played happily at our feet, Maximin looking up every so often to make sure I was still with him.

'I had that Chief of Police go through the Egyptian quarter last night, and again this morning,' I explained when Sveta and the children had finally left us alone. 'He seems to have vanished.'

'No great loss, if you ask me,' Martin sniffed. 'I told you he was dodgy. Didn't you say he knew the doorman in that place? Well, he was probably in it with the sorcerer and his girl.'

'That doesn't explain why Macarius should have chosen simply to disappear,' I said, ignoring the challenge. 'No body fitting his description has turned up in any of the usual places – not that I believe he's the sort of man who could easily be murdered. It's all most puzzling, and more than a little inconvenient.'

I looked again at the pile of document boxes on the table. Martin had done his usual efficient job in securing every scrap of written material from the house of Leontius. He'd also taken full notes during my second interrogation of the slaves.

'So what do you think all that stuff means?' Martin asked, waving at the largest box.

'We might be able to know if Macarius was at hand,' I said, lifting out a stack of papyrus. There was sheet after sheet, all covered very neatly in the pseudo-Greek alphabet used nowadays by the Egyptians for writing their own language. I sorted through it and pushed one of the sheets across the table to Martin. 'This one is in Greek,' I said, 'and it may be a translation of something else in the box.'

'Then shall the breath of Sekhmet roll over the red land and the black; and the men of neither land shall be smitten – yea, the very flesh shall be divided from their bones,' Martin read. I raised a hand to stop him. There was no point reading more. It was probably all in the same wild and rhapsodic style.

'Some poem, no doubt, from before the natives took up the Faith,' I said. 'If that's a fair sample of what they write, I'm rather glad not to have learned any Egyptian. You saw from all those ugly antiques in his house that Leontius had an interest in the ancient history of the country. It wouldn't surprise me if he knew the language.' I smiled. 'It wouldn't much surprise me if it turned out that was what he spoke in private.' I put the sheets back into their box and replaced the lid. I reached across the table and pulled open one of the boxes where everything was in Greek.

'Now, we have a problem,' I explained, returning to our hushed discussion of its contents as we'd wandered back from church. 'His accounts show that Leontius had liabilities about three times larger than his assets. And some of those liabilities were falling due in the next month or so.'

'I still don't follow how so much of what he owed was to you,' Martin said.

I sighed. I had tried to tell him about the forward contracts. Evidently, I'd failed once again to hack any path through the thicket of his financial ignorance.

'It seems that his rebuilding expenses in Letopolis were financed by loans from the wealthier landowners,' I said. 'Most of his creditors were willing to hold off foreclosing so long as he fronted resistance to the new law. Some of them, however, wanted at least part payment – and even part payment was more than he could manage.'

I took up a letter from a Saracen banking house on the other side of the Red Sea. I waited as Martin read it again, hoping he'd understand the promise of a big payment from some person or persons unknown – but only in October, and on condition he disclosed nothing of the payment in advance. What he was supposed to deliver in return was unstated, but it seemed to have been somewhat more than just keeping me at bay: it may have been goods as much as services. Indeed, there was a certain eagerness that came through the standardised commercial phrasing. I wondered if this might have been the matter that would have concerned me had the man lived.

'To tide him over,' I said, dropping the letter back on the table, 'he entered the financial markets; not a wise move for someone as thick as he appears to have been. My own positions were taken through those Jewish bankers. This should normally have kept me in the clear. You can always trust Jews to keep quiet about who their clients are. But the bankers used by Leontius told him who my people were. That, plus the contract I got Nicetas to award them to handle the customs arrears in Ptolemais, provides at least the ghost of a trail for anyone of intelligence to follow back to me. Leontius wasn't clever enough to follow the clues. His executors may not be so stupid.'

'I warned you not to get involved in speculations on the price of bread,' Martin said, finding something at last he could understand and condemn. 'When the people learn you've been behind the price rises, there will be endless trouble.'

And that – in spite of what I'd told Nicetas and everyone else – is what had me still investigating Leontius. Who had murdered him and why were matters of no importance. What he'd been up to that involved getting me out of Alexandria would normally have been of some importance. What really concerned me, however, was the avoidance of scandal.

'Martin,' I said very patiently, 'I have explained many times that my speculations have been on lower prices come the harvest. I've been selling corn in advance at lower prices than others expect, but at much higher prices than I know will be the case. Generally, speculating on future prices has the same effect on those prices as bets on a charioteer have on the speed of his horses. If not, the only effect such speculations can have on present prices is to lower them from what they would otherwise be. If prices are rising at the moment, it's because the corn is actually running short.'

'So, if you want the prices to be lower,' Martin asked, clutching at random words, 'why did you oppose the price controls?'

I sighed again, and put my thoughts into order. I needed to settle this with Martin. If I could persuade him, I might have an excuse ready for everyone else if the worst came to pass.

'Martin,' I said, 'there will be a good harvest. I've already explained how I know this. Therefore, speculating on the fact will tend eventually to release stocks of corn on to the market that would otherwise be stored longer than was needed. Fixing the price by law, on the other hand, will either encourage the people to be less thrifty than they should be, or give merchants reason to withhold stocks from the official market. It will turn shortage into famine.'

Oh dear, I'd lost Martin for sure. He wasn't stupid, and he always tried to think the best of me. If I couldn't make myself plain to him, what chance might I have against those landowners in persuading any of the Alexandrian mobs?

Martin opened another of the boxes and took out a document written on parchment. He looked at it and frowned.

'This is in Persian,' he said.

I looked. He was right. There was no mistaking those neat squiggles. It had been covered all over the other side in Egyptian writing that may have been a translation. A shame it hadn't been translated into Greek.

'I think you should hand all this over to the Intelligence Bureau,' he said.

I shook my head. Bearing in mind what we knew of these documents, I didn't fancy having so much as a sniff of their contents pushed under noses that answered to Nicetas.

18

'There's another one coming up on the right,' said Martin in his depressed tone.

I looked up from the shitty brown water and followed his pointed finger. At first, the reflected glare of the sun was too much for me. But I squinted and looked again. Sure enough, it was another body. Its belly was puffed up like an inflated bladder, and it bobbed about, face just visible beneath the water. I watched as the current from the south and the wind from the north drew us closer and closer together. It passed by about a dozen yards from the prow of our boat. I forced myself not to turn and continue looking at the bloated face and the white, bulging eyes. Not a pretty sight, I said to myself. Still, it affected Martin less than the occasional crocodile.

It was the second day of our journey up the Nile to Letopolis. After a little trouble with the winds of the sea crossing, and then a brief difficulty over further transport, it had been a smooth and uneventful voyage from Bolbitine. I'd somehow imagined the Nile as about the width of the Tiber, and passing between masses of lotus plants and various reeds on either side, with wide expanses of black land beyond. I hadn't fully appreciated the scale of the annual floods. They'd swollen the river as wide in places as Lake Mareotis, and had covered up the black land almost to where the desert started.

We were now coming out of the Delta – that immense fertile plain watered by the seven branches of the Nile. As its branches came closer together, the river itself was more embanked and no longer so impossibly wide. Even so, it remained wider than I'd expected, and I now understood that the undivided Nile above

Letopolis would continue wide. Moreover, since we were leaving the great flood plains behind, the narrower waters had wholly covered up the black land. On each side of us, the desert was increasingly evident – a line of red, its interior hidden by the heat haze.

If I hadn't conceived the details of their appearance accurately, I knew well enough that the waters would eventually recede, leaving behind them a thick layer of mud. This would be the virgin soil in which the harvest would be sown come October, and from which, come March, the fabulous wealth of Egypt would be reaped. If those who sowed and reaped it had never yet seen much of this wealth, that, I told myself, I was here to change.

Here and there, the tops of the taller palm trees poked above the waters. Every so often, we'd pass little clusters of dwellings crammed on to artificial mounds, looking for all the world like islands in the sea.

'Boats setting out from the left bank,' Captain Lucas called out in his flat Greek. I stopped myself before I could look to the left. We were passing up the Nile, I reminded myself. Left and right here were defined by the position of one looking downstream. Over on my right, a flotilla of tiny canoes had set out from one of those artificial mounds. Each one carrying a man and a few runtish children, they rowed close beside us. It didn't need any grasp of the language to know what was wanted. With piteous wails, the children stretched out their arms towards us, now and again pointing into their unfilled mouths.

Had I seen this a dozen times already? Two dozen? It was hard to tell. On that dreary, unnaturally silent expanse of water, all events of the same class blended eventually into one. I know that the first time we'd come across these desperate wretches, I'd told Lucas to throw our waste into the river. He'd shaken his head. Do that, he'd assured me, and they'd follow us up river until their strength failed. So now, as before and a forgotten number of times before that, I looked steadily down until the cries were out of hearing.

'I haven't known the waters to rise this high so quickly,' Martin said, giving me one more of the rare scraps of experience from his time in Antinoopolis. 'They might not have had time to gather in all their stocks of food – assuming, that is, the tax gatherers left them anything at all.'

'So, what happens then?' I asked. Even as I asked, I knew it was a redundant question. I wondered why the people couldn't get by on fish when corn was in short supply. The waters might be poisonous from all the stirred-up filth of those African mountains. But if that didn't kill the fish, why should the fish kill us? Come to think of it, what about all the ducks and other birds I'd seen in those wall paintings done by the natives in ancient times? I hadn't seen any so far on the journey. But they had to be somewhere. Or had they already all been eaten? I glanced over at the women, who were huddled together on the land. Unlike a few miles back, they hadn't been sent out in the canoes to offer themselves to us.

'I'm sure there were many more people when I was last here,' Martin said.

Imperfect as they were, I knew this already from the census returns. Taxable households were down from three million in the time of Justinian to just under half that now. There was little doubt the numbers would drop still further before the new harvest. It's one of the marvels of Egypt that you can sow and reap nearly the same amount of corn with whatever the number of hands. But I was beginning to realise what was behind the calls for delay from the dissident landowners. Almost certainly, they couldn't get the new law cancelled. But if they held out long enough, they'd lose far less in the reallocations of land.

'You should get out of the sun,' I said to Martin. 'Even with your hat, your face is looking red.'

'I was about to say the same to you,' he replied, gently stroking my neck. 'Skin like ours wasn't made for this climate. Alexandria's nothing by comparison. And it gets worse.'

We went back to the awning placed above the middle of the deck. Though only about ten feet wide, it was a longish boat. It would never have done for any work at sea, but was built for speed up and down river: sails and a dozen oarsmen in reserve for the journey up, a tiller for the journey back. The accommodation was hardly luxurious, but I'd been more interested in speed than in comfort when arranging the boat.

I sat down on one of the cane chairs and poured two cups of wine. It was the poor, local stuff. Too much, or drunk too fast, and it was sure to give a headache. But the water we'd brought with us didn't bear considering.

'We should be in Letopolis early tomorrow morning,' I said to Martin with a nod at Lucas. I tried to sound reassuring. I failed.

'I don't like him one little bit,' Martin whispered yet again in Celtic. 'You didn't see the really nasty look he gave you just now when your back was turned. It's not my place to say, I know, but I did think you'd book a military ship. If we need to be there just one day, does the journey have to be so fast?'

'Oh, Martin, Martin,' I said. I wiped the sweat from my face and poured more wine. 'You really are like that shepherd boy in the fable. You've taken against everyone who's come your way since we first docked in Alexandria. One of these days, you'll meet a right villain, and no one will listen.'

It would never have done for Martin's nerves if I'd admitted that the day might now have come. The requisition I'd ordered back in Alexandria had referred me to one Lucas, Captain in the Nile Postal Service. On the dockside in Bolbitine, I had met someone calling himself Captain Lucas. His documents had been in order. He'd scanned mine and saluted very correctly as he took me for an inspection of the *Southern Argos*. Like Martin, I'd expected something larger. But I'd also said I wanted speed. There was no doubt this looked a fast vessel.

Lucas had struck me at first as thoroughly professional in his management of the boat and its crew. It was only as we proceeded further up this desert of shining water that any doubts had emerged. The beating he'd given one of his men for pissing on the deck had seemed rather much for the offence. I'd told Martin to look the other way as the hooked strap rose and fell, and had done my best to blot out the screams and the smell of vomit. Afterwards, Lucas had stormed up and down the tiny deck, hissing and muttering away in an Egyptian that chilled the blood.

Even the trim beard that had looked so reassuringly Greek at first was managing somehow to appear in a different light.

I glanced over at the right bank of the river. It was slipping by about a half-mile away. And, if I'd laughed at Martin's fears, there were crocodiles in that filthy water. They broke the surface less often than the corpses. They were out there, even so, and they scared me.

I opened one of the wooden chests I'd brought along. Big, heavy things they were. Lucas had taken one look at them before telling me how the loading of his boat required them or our slaves to be left behind. That's why I was having to pour my own wine. I took out a sheaf of papyrus. I went through it and put it back, taking out another. From this, I took out three of the larger sheets. I passed them over to Martin.

'It's the Devil who puts thoughts in idle minds,' I said with a stab at piety. I cast around for a definite text from Scripture to reinforce the point, but could think of nothing appropriate. 'Now,' I continued, 'since there's nothing very scenic to look at in any direction, we might as well get on with some work. You may disagree, but I think we can reconcile these two sets of land measurements if you assume that one of them uses the units abolished by Diocletian. Why anyone should still have been using them two centuries after the event is a question not worth asking . . .'

And so we worked productively away for the rest of the afternoon. I was vaguely aware of the orders Lucas was shouting in his maniac voice and the rapid movements of the crew as they went about their pulling on ropes and shifting of sailcloth. I ignored the periodic cries from still more of those wretched flotillas. Every so often, Martin would set about himself with his flywhisk. Once or twice, he may have killed something.

At dusk, the flies came down in earnest. It was then that the fine mesh netting was let down around us and the smoky charcoal was set alight in the brazier next to us.

'It would be most pleasing if you could spare the time to join us,' I said to Lucas as he watched Martin dishing out our food.

'I'm not eating *anything* connected with the river,' Martin had insisted in Celtic while our stuff was being carried on board. 'If you don't want the runs all the way there and back, you'll take your own food along.' I'd given way to his urging. After all, he had lived in the country, and might for once be expected to know what he was talking about. And so, while everyone else ate food that, cooked down in the little galley kitchen, smelled divine, we were grimly munching our way through increasingly stale bread with olive paste and dates pickled in honey.

Lucas bowed and touched his forehead. He quickly rearranged the netting once he was under the awning and squatted on the deck in the Egyptian manner. It was one of those alien touches – nothing in itself, but cumulative – that had set Martin off, and was progressively undermining my own composure.

'With the river as it is,' he said, leaving the hard bread untasted, 'we can put straight in at the makeshift dock that Letopolis has outside its walls this time of year. I understand, however, that My Lord has business at the house of Leontius. This is a fortified compound a mile outside the walls. With your leave, I will arrange chairs to carry you there. To be sure, it is sad news you carry to the household.'

'I assume the news has not preceded us,' I said, looking steadily at Lucas.

He stared impassively back.

'It seems to have preceded us along the coast from Alexandria,' I added.

'He was a man of note in his own district,' came the reply. 'He was famed far beyond for the attention he paid to the boundaries of his estate, and to his collection of rents and customary dues. He was a man of considerable note in other ways – learned in the ways of Egypt, and assiduous in collecting objects from its days of glory. News of his death reached Bolbitine some while before My Lord's arrival.'

'But it will not, I think, have reached so far up river yet as Letopolis,' I prompted.

'It is sad news for the household that My Lord carries,' came the reply.

I darted a look at Martin's scared face. I took another sip of wine, and asked about general conditions in Letopolis.

'Though I have, in the absence of your slaves,' Lucas answered, 'undertaken to interpret for you, I can assure you that Greek remains well enough known in and around the city. I do not suppose that my services will be required for any confidential dealings.'

I nodded and chewed hard on my bread. To keep the conversation going, I asked if it was true that no one had Greek any more as a first language south of Oxyrhynchus.

'My Lord and his secretary speak the language to each other,' he answered, 'but neither of you, I think, is Greek?'

'A Greek,' I said firmly, 'is anyone who speaks the language and follows the ways of the Greeks.'

'Or whose ancestors began to do so long enough ago for the taint of wogitude to be forgotten,' Lucas added with a smile.

'There was a time,' he went on, 'when the Greeks came upon Egypt like the Nile flood. Then, they went where they pleased and were irresistible. But their flood has for many generations now been ebbing. And, again as with the Nile, the ebb exposes more and more of the hidden land of Egypt. It is, perhaps, a land enriched by the Grecian flood. The Greeks leave us the Christian Faith, and their alphabetic writing, and the concept they took, I think, from the Latins of a determinate and written law. But it will be Egyptian land.'

He put his hand up to refuse the wine I was offering. Most natives, I'd found, would drink anything offered them that wasn't actually poisonous. Many, though, were oddly abstemious. Lucas, I realised, was one of these. The evening before, I might have sent Martin to dig out some of my kava beans. I'd brought them along, though hadn't managed an infusion since leaving Alexandria. But it was the present evening, and I decided to leave them packed away.

'So, you think the Greeks will eventually lose Egypt?' I asked, drinking the wine myself.

'To every nation is appointed one day of glory,' Lucas said. 'The Jews and Latins each had theirs. Whoever and wherever they be, your people may, in some future age, have theirs. It is obvious that the day of the Greeks is now coming to its end.

'To every nation is appointed one day of glory. To some, God allows a second. Such is the case with the Persians. Who can tell if such is not also the case with Egypt?' He rose, saying there was much to be done if we were to sail through the night for a morning arrival.

Martin clutched at the little silver cross Heraclius had given him as a coronation present. I stirred honey into the wine and drank deep from the jug.

19

As I'd expected, they came for us around the midnight hour. There was no point resisting. I could have cut a few of them down. But the numbers were against us, and we were on their territory. Martin would never have dared follow me into the Nile – not that I thought those dark, infested waters were any safer than giving in quietly.

'I didn't notice any odd tattoos on your men,' I said, trying to keep some air of normality to the proceedings. 'But I might more usefully have examined your own body back in Bolbitine than your documentation.'

Lucas smiled grim in the moonlight. He gave another order to his men, who now began pulling in earnest on their ropes. I felt the boat slow and then turn towards the left bank.

'There are many things of which you know nothing,' he said.

'I think it reasonable to assume,' I said, holding up my bound wrists, 'that you were ordered simply to deliver us to your masters. You could have killed us at any time after yesterday afternoon. Instead, you've waited until we are almost at Letopolis. I take it you know who I am, and why I was sent to Alexandria?'

'We have, of course, been watching you since you arrived,' said Lucas. 'Perhaps you suppose your mission will have endeared you to the children of the soil. Do not suppose, however, it has endeared you to their legitimate representatives. Had he not over-reached himself by revealing what should not have been revealed, our favour would still have extended to Leontius, your leading opponent.'

'I see,' I said drily. 'Where you people are concerned, "worse is better and better worse".'

'Euripides was a fine poet,' came the acknowledgement of the quotation; we might, for that moment, have been back in Constantinople, playing at who was most learned. At least it wasn't some low cutpurse of a wog who'd taken me in. 'You will have noticed, though, that, like all other Greeks who are to be admired, he died a long time ago. But you are right,' he added. 'We are not interested in reforms that will only sweeten the gall of foreign domination.'

'So,' I asked with a look at the fast approaching left bank, 'is it worth asking what's to be done with us?' I didn't think it worth asking what he'd meant about Leontius. A few words had clarified all that hadn't made sense when I was sitting beside the body. The temple at Philae was funding the Brotherhood. Leontius knew this because he was with the Brotherhood. He was killed for revealing its secrets.

'Yes,' I repeated, 'what is to be done with us?'

'That is a question you should consider saving for later,' Lucas said. 'According to Leontius – and according to someone else of whom I will not speak for the moment – you possess information that is of the highest value to the cause of our independence. And you should also work to ensure that your answers will be in order.' He raised the lid of one of my boxes. One of the crew stood forward with a lamp so he could make out my scrawled note on one of the sheets.

'Is there anything confidential in here?' he asked. 'You will appreciate that lying would not be in your interests at this stage.'

I sniffed and looked up at the now almost full moon. I couldn't be bothered to explain it was all routine stuff. A shame, though, it would pass out of my hands. I'd put a great deal of effort into making sense of it.

We were now only a few dozen yards out. Over on the bank, the lights that had guided us in were still bobbing about. We were beginning to pass under the blanket of heat that covered the land. After so long on those foul waters, the land had a dry and bitter smell.

'Do exactly as they say,' I whispered to Martin in Celtic. 'At the same time, try to stay as close by me as you can.' I'd seen sheep

132

on their way to slaughter with less apathetic faces. In his position, I'd have thought very ill of the man who'd got him into this. Being Martin, he was probably recalculating his tariff of sins and wondering if they only merited Purgatory, and, if so, how long there.

The crew stayed behind with the boat. But they were obviously sailors and of no use on the land. Lucas came along with us, now with about a dozen big, rough-looking men. The moon shone on what showed of their faces above the beards. Dressed in dark clothing against the sun and the desert winds, they bowed low before him, and a rapid conversation started up. There were looks in our direction and more bowing. Then they set us – still bound – on camels. Since the Nile was on our right, we were heading back north along the military road that ran above the highest flood point.

I'd seen camels before. That was in Constantinople. There'd been a parade of them in the Circus when Priscus had his Triumph after the previous year's successes. The things are best described as resembling a misshapen horse. They're rather bigger, with a tall hump on the back. They terrify real horses and smell like death. Their big advantage is that they don't need the same watering as horses, and so are ideal for desert terrain.

They don't ride much like horses. Even without being tied at the wrists, it would have been hard enough to keep hold. As it was, we had to be tied to the harness to keep us from falling off. I could hear Martin behind me. When not gasping from the pain of bruised haemorrhoids, he was praying softly in Celtic. I'll not say I felt calm inside. There was no telling what this wog Brotherhood had in mind for me. But the mention of 'information', had made it hard to believe we'd be done over straight away like Leontius.

As the sun came up, I looked around. Not much chance of escape that I could see. The Nile rolled massively by a hundred yards to our right. There were a few boats out there, but nothing with the slightest military look about it. Immediately on the left, patches of low, broken rock stretched up a slight incline to the reds and yellows of the boundless desert. The men before and after us on the road might have been born on camel back. Even if they were the bound ones and we the free, they'd have been able in no time to outride us.

As it rose higher in the sky, the sun turned baking. Lucas rattled out some orders and we stopped for refreshments and what I took, by the spreading of rugs, to be a longish rest. The water looked clean enough – not that I was inclined by now to fuss over anything I was given to drink. More welcome were the hooded cloaks the men had tied over me and Martin. Back in Alexandria, I'd seen some nasty cases of sunburn on northern slaves. I'd made sure to limit my own exposure there. Now we were further south and in the desert. In places like Jarrow, the sun is a welcome friend. At all times in Egypt, it can be the most terrible enemy.

'So you really don't think we're to be killed?' Martin whispered back when I'd finally trailed off from my mixture of apologies and reassurance. 'You know I'm not brave like you. But I understand when the Will of God is made manifest. What must happen will happen. I was told many years ago that I'd be dead before my thirty-second birthday. That will be next month.' He groaned loudly and pushed his head between his legs. By the look of him, it didn't surprise me he was thinking of death.

But thirty-two? With his bald patch peeling under that hood, and his puffy face, I'd forgotten he wasn't somewhat older. But that was a secondary point. As with Priscus a few days before, I found myself wondering how to begin reasoning with a view of things so systematically perverse. This wasn't the time or place to talk about the mad old woman who'd told me outside Richborough I'd be dead within ten days. That was when I was twelve. But Martin hadn't finished yet.

'If God chooses in His Infinite Mercy to spare me,' he added, 'it will be because He truly has reserved you for some greater work, and that I am needed to assist. That must be our only hope.' I left him to his renewed praying and munched on the unleavened bread one of the men had tossed in my direction. Sad to say, it was the tastiest thing I'd eaten in days.

'I trust you are enjoying your view of the real Egypt,' Lucas said. He stood over me, not bothering to squint in the sun that shone straight on him. The rather fussy official I'd met in Bolbitine was a fading memory. He strutted before me now, almost blazing with hatred and triumph.

'My dear Lucas,' I said, smiling up at him, 'would it be worth – even at this late stage – offering you a bribe? I'm sure I could get you a promotion within the Imperial Postal Service. Captain Second Class might suit your abilities.'

'My true name, be aware, is not Lucas,' he said, the sarcasm lost on him. A shame this, as anger can unlock the most cautious tongues. And it was – you'll agree – a matter of some importance to get whatever information could be had. 'I am known among the discerning – and shall be acknowledged by all when the Greeks are driven out – as Meriamen Usermaatre Setepenre.'

'Well,' I said, still smiling into his lunatic eyes, 'that's a bit of a mouthful, isn't it? I'll bet your father called you something much closer to Lucas than to that. I hope you'll not mind if I go on call-ing you Lucas.'

'The name has been corrupted by the Greeks – as is their way with all names foreign to them – into Ozymandias,' he said with a scowl. 'Perhaps you have heard of him.'

Of course I'd heard of Ozymandias, the Egyptian King of Kings. 'Isn't he the one,' I asked with mock reverence, 'whose name is tattooed above every arsehole in the Brotherhood? You surely chose well!'

'You are not a Greek,' Lucas said, still refusing to be drawn, 'yet you side with them. Have they not also been a sore trial to your people?'

'And why do you side against them?' I asked, turning the ques-tion. 'Why all these woggy airs and graces when you can almost pass for a civilised man?'

I'd finally got to him. Just as he was about to let rip, though, there was another commotion behind him.

'Oh dear' – I nodded at the bearded figure coming towards us – 'it seems your followers are getting uppity again. Do you suppose another flogging might be needed to put them in order?'

With a scowl, he turned away. I was right. It was another argument. I had no idea what was going on. But the servile manner those men had shown Lucas at the landing had been turning sour. Now, with the Nile behind us, Lucas was having to insist on his authority at almost every step.

Yes, we were now headed away from the Nile. Once we'd slept through its worst heat, the sun was before us, though very slightly to our left. We were heading west. At some point, we turned southwest, and then south. All the time, we were pressing further and further into the outermost desert. As with the Nile, I hadn't done a very good job of imagining this. I'd thought of it as rather like the prettier beaches you get on the Mediterranean shore: all flat, white sand, but much more of it. My first impression was of a great and rather scary ugliness. We were on a sort of road that snaked off into the far distance. On either side of us, low hills of jagged rock rose and fell in undulations that stretched again as far as the eye could see. Here and there were patches of what might have been dead weed, or weed that had somehow managed to survive at a low level of growth.

As for the sand, I think it's best described as an accumulation of very fine dust. It fills up the spaces between the rocks, and is stirred into almost invisible but choking clouds at every breeze or other disturbance of the air. I got my first real lungful of the stuff some time in the latish afternoon. As we rounded a bend in the road, we came upon a group of the desert nomads you find all over those parts. We'd been hidden from each other by one of those low hills. Now, we came in full view. In white robes that covered their bodies, dark bands securing the scarves on their heads, they sat still as stone on their camels. They watched our approach. Then, as they came within hailing distance, they wheeled suddenly about and were off.

That was when I saw for the first time how fast camels could move. The ones I'd seen in Constantinople had shambled round the Circus with bundles of heavy swords heaped on their backs. Our own party had so far gone at a steady trot. These nomads, though, could get up the sort of speed you see in horses only at full pelt over level ground – and they were off the road and on stony ground. One moment, they were sitting watching us. The next, it seemed, they were a vanishing blur in the distance.

All that remained was the cloud of dust that drifted towards us, and that I breathed straight in. I nearly fell off the camel with my choking fit. I coughed. I sneezed. Tears ran down my face. I couldn't breathe. If I'd breathed in freshly ground pepper, it wouldn't have burned and paralysed so. And all around me, I heard the high-pitched giggling that passes, even with grown men, among the Eastern races for laughter.

'Drink this,' said Lucas, riding beside me. He raised his leather water sack and let a small trickle fall into my mouth. 'Rinse and spit,' he said curtly. The next trickle was a little more generous. It was becoming clear that water out here was not for quenching any but the most pressing thirst. I strained to remember the maps Hermogenes had shown me a few days before. Assume we were just north of Letopolis when Lucas had dropped his Imperial service act. Assume perhaps another twenty miles north, and now ten miles west. That would put us on the road to Siwa.

Most likely, we weren't going all the way to Siwa, but were headed into an area that I knew was thick with tombs and temples put up during the Old Faith. Here seemed as good a place as any for a Brotherhood encampment. It would have to be pretty far out into the desert, though, if water was being this strictly rationed. We might be another day on this road. At some point, I realised, we'd be passing Soteropolis. It wouldn't be quite the visit there I'd had in mind.

20

We stopped once more in the late afternoon. I thought at first we were to pack up for the night. Martin looked ready to die again, and I was now hurting all over. But I soon realised this was just another pause in what was turning into an endless journey into the desert. We'd come to a mostly fallen-down building of mud brick. While his men squatted, all looking remarkably glum, Lucas stood on a little mound of stones and packed sand. He took in a deep breath and called something out in a rhythmical and even a somewhat liturgical chant. He called out once without any response. As he was going through the whole chant again, an old man shambled into sight. I think he'd been sleeping in a hole in the ground. He'd been asleep, I could be sure. He was blinking about in the now moderate light as if it had still been the high noon of the desert.

'Some desert hermit,' I told myself. Perhaps it was time for a blessing of the Brotherhood's efforts in rounding me up for the completion of whatever it was Leontius had put in everyone's mind regarding me. But, no. I looked harder at the old man. He was bald enough and shrivelled enough for someone who'd left the baths and company of civilisation behind so he could seek the Love of Jesus Christ. But the pattern on his tattered robe, and the hooped cross in his hand, told me this was one of the priests of the Old Faith.

I couldn't follow the details of what passed next. But the outlines were clear. There was an offering from Lucas of flowers and dried fruit. In return, the old priest set up a long chant filled with references to Isis and Horus and Sekhmet and other divinities of the former national religion of Egypt – a religion now proscribed under penalties that made the wilder extremes of the Monophysite heresy by comparison a matter of petty theft.

Not surprisingly, since he'd called for the ceremony, Lucas took all the words and gestures in absolute earnest. He'd pulled some headgear from his saddlebag and put it on. It was too big for him, and the gilded snake that jutted out in front was continually over-balancing and pulling the whole thing down over his face. But, unaware of – or perhaps indifferent to – how ridiculous it all made him appear, he danced around and joined in the responses, a look on his face of demented exaltation.

His men took it very badly. They sat with their backs to him. One of them took out a rosary and counted its beads. Two of the others muttered to each other, every so often crossing themselves. The others sat in glum silence until the service was over. Without a word, they got us and themselves mounted again.

I managed to twist myself round once to look back. Though we'd covered about a mile, I could see the old priest, standing on the mound outside his temple. Still dancing in his arthritic way, he was now waving like a sailor sending messages to the shore.

'Is not the desert beautiful?' Lucas slimed at me as his men were packing up after another rest. It was now the very late afternoon, and he'd told me we were to travel through the night. I looked at the untidy bleakness that stretched all around.

'It takes all sorts,' I said morosely. 'Any chance of untying me?' I asked, holding up my bound wrists. 'I doubt I'd get very far in this waste, even if I could break away on that thing.' I nodded at the camel. 'Besides, I've no doubt your men have better things to do than wipe my arse.'

'But surely a man of My Lord's high station cannot find such hospitality unwelcome?' Lucas replied with another stab at sarcasm.

I grunted and went back to an inspection of the desert. Now the shadows were lengthening, its reds and browns had been joined by patches of black that gave the whole scene a thoroughly diseased look. No wonder all the monks who'd settled out here went barking mad in the end. Perhaps that was how the old priest had started, and ancestral recusancy was the form his own madness had taken.

'The desert is, of course, part of Egyptian life,' Lucas opened again. 'It is the red lands that mark the boundaries within which our life has always gone on. For ten thousand years, we worked the black lands watered by the Nile. Except when invaders swept out of the desert, we lived in brotherhood and freedom. Always, the invaders were cleared out again. Always, the clearing out was followed by an age of glory. Do not the Holy Scriptures themselves record how once we ruled Syria as far as Jerusalem itself?'

'Brotherhood and freedom?' I snorted. 'Nothing else in all the known world lends itself to tyranny and extortion so much as the Nile Valley. There's a natural demand for officials to keep records of the flood and for surveyors to measure out the land afterwards. And with nowhere to run if these turn oppressive, it's hardly surprising if the people become little more than two-legged farm animals.

'Now, I don't know any of your language,' I went on, warming to my theme. 'But there are histories of Egypt written in Greek. You can insist till you're black in the face that they are all lies made up to justify foreign rule. But I've seen any number of those temple carvings and statues. They perfectly corroborate what I've read. You're welcome to spout all you like about brotherhood and freedom. It only becomes true if you put meanings on words that would shock a theologian.' I reached both hands up together to brush away some large fly that was flapping ineffectually about my face. Lucas gave me a thin smile. If he'd been expecting meek assent to the sermon he was trying to preach, he'd have to address himself to someone else.

'You are mistaken,' he said, lunacy back in his eyes. He put his face close to mine. For the first time, I noticed the smell of decaying teeth. The teeth I could see, though, were white and sharp. Unless the back ones had gone, he might be rotting away within from some disgusting cancer. It would have been nice to speculate whether this had begun to hurt yet. But Lucas gave me no time.

'You are mistaken,' he repeated, now emphatic. 'The loyalty of the people to their Pharaoh was always freely given. How else could we have endured in peace and plenty for ten thousand years? How else could we have developed all science and all mathematics that the Greeks then stole from us?'

I laughed outright. Oh, he could have reached forward and struck me. But that would have broken the mood of triumphant dignity he was trying to impose. And if I was eventually to be done away with in some grotesque way, oiling him up wouldn't make that any better. But pissing him off might be both enjoyable and useful.

'Freely given?' I sneered. 'Ten thousand years? I'll tell you this, my lad: Phocas himself never put up images of himself standing three times the height of his nobles, nor the nobles three times the height of the poor bloody people who worked to make their lives easy. All government, in every time and place, rests on fraud and force – the force of soldiers and officials hired by the rulers, and the fraud of the priests who assure everyone that the force is just. You'll need to work much harder to convince me you didn't have ten thousand years of that, before you had a thousand of the same from the Greeks.

'As for what you dare call science and mathematics, you had nothing beyond the crude ingenuity to build those pyramids and all the other ugly things that haven't yet fallen down – and to build them with slave labour. Before the Greeks showed up, you were as ignorant as any other barbarian race of mathematics as an abstract science able to explain all of nature. Your cosmology involves a flat earth with some naked goddess stretching over it as the sky. Your history is of kings ten feet tall and reigning for a hundred years. The glory you speak of is just more of the usual plunder mixed with bloody murder.

'And, let's face it, my poor, dear Lucas, you can no more read the picture writing of this literature than I can. All you have to read in the alphabetic writing your people learned from the Greeks is a mass of third-rate polemic against the Acts of the Council of Chalcedon. What little they know about your brand of heresy makes you an embarrassment to the Monophysites of Syria. You've already acknowledged the debt you owe for alphabetic writing. Well, just accept that you owe the Greeks everything else in your culture that isn't actually a joke.' I paused to draw breath. I didn't bother swivelling my eyes: I could *feel* Martin's look of horrified despair. But I was enjoying myself, and I did have a more constructive purpose.

'It has never, I'm sure,' I went on, 'crossed your tiny minds that there is in human affairs, as in the world around us, a natural order in which your kings and their priests – of whatever faith – have no place.'

His mouth was working. But Lucas had no words to throw at me. So I let my own roll straight forward over him.

'Let us imagine a state of nature,' I said, 'that is, a world in which all are at "perfect freedom to order their actions, and dispose of their possessions and persons, as they think fit, within the bounds of the law of nature, without asking leave, or depending upon the will of any other man".' I was quoting here verbatim from Epicurus – his *Second Letter to Scatodotes of Cyrene.* 'This being given, let us suppose that everyone uses his freedom to supply himself with all his needs. Some he will abstract directly from the earth, which is common to all. Others he will acquire by free exchange with others. Therefore, some will raise crops. Others will take materials from the ground. Others will refine these things into other products. All property in this state of natural freedom will be based on the efforts of the possessor.

'Men may gather together to appoint judges for those disputes that cannot be resolved by good will or by individual force of arms. They may further appoint generals for the defence of the whole community. But they'll never voluntarily establish the system described in the Greek histories of your country or shown on your monuments.' Well, that wasn't direct quotation from the Great Man, though it was fair summary. I could have gone on to my own belief about the limitless improvement that might result from free exchange and the steady use of reason to understand the world about us. But it didn't serve my purpose, this being more attack than exposition.

'Don't waste more of your hot air on how all this is for the people of Egypt,' I said, my voice rising to a shrill scorn that could be noted if not followed by his men. 'If that poor bugger you tore apart on the boat is any guide, I know exactly what you think about the people. I've heard that your sort refer to Greek rule as a cup of abominations. That may be a fair description. Perhaps the Greeks haven't followed through in their actions the ideas they gave the world. But, let's be honest, you don't want to dash that cup to the ground. What you really want is to transfer it from Greek hands to your own with as little spillage along the way as can be managed.'

'You lie! You're worse than the Greeks you love. You lie! You lie!' Lucas was on his feet, shouting now like a maniac. Two of his men were openly laughing at him. They couldn't understand what we'd said – but they probably knew that the loser of an argument is the one who starts shouting first. Martin, I had no doubt, was praying the earth would cut out the middleman and swallow him up without pain. I smiled up happily, waiting for the spasm of rage to pass.

'You lie!' Lucas snarled as he brought his voice under control. 'When I – the second, and the greater Meriamen Usermaatre Setepenre – put on the double crown of Egypt and—'

'Oh, so that's your plan, is it, Lucas?' I cut in, still smiling happily. I'd got him at last. 'Cupbearer won't be good enough for you in this new order of things. You want the cup carried straight to your own lips. Well, I wonder if the Elders of your Brotherhood know about that?'

He was silent now, though breathing very heavily and fighting to keep control. I leaned over to one side and looked round him.

'If it pleases Your Majesty,' I said, with another look up at his sweating, hate-contorted face, 'two of your subjects are coming to blows over who gets first use of the shit shovel. Why don't you go and offer yourself as judge in their dispute. I can't pronounce the stupid wog name you've given yourself. But you come back other than covered in their shit, and I'll hail you as King Arsehole the First, the New and greater Solomon.

'And so my faith is that of *Jesus Christ*, our *Lord and Saviour*,' I said loudly as a couple of his men came closer to try to follow what we'd been arguing about. 'Mine is the faith that was born in *Bethlehem* and made glorious in *Jerusalem*.' I carried on, throwing in as many names and places as seemed relevant. 'And I utterly abjure the *Satanic* names of *Isis, Horus, Sekhmet* and all the other demons from Hell.'

Lucas stared at me as if I were the one who'd lost his wits. But his men looked on thoughtfully.

21

'Aelric, have you gone mad?' Martin wailed softly once we were alone. 'Are you trying to get us killed?'

'Shut up!' I hissed. 'And do try to keep a stiff upper lip in front of these wogs.' I ignored his jabbering reply and kicked him hard on the shin. 'Look, Martin, they've got us trussed up like slaves brought to market. Only one of them understands any language that we know, and he's mad. Meek obedience will get us nowhere. Pleading for mercy won't work either. We're already God knows where. Tomorrow, we'll be God knows where else and with more of these people, facing God knows what. It's obvious the people who are taking us there are under orders that involve keeping us in one piece. The people there may have other ideas. This being so, we have no option but to provoke a chance that doesn't seem likely to present itself.

'Lucas is plainly part of the Brotherhood that sticks to the Old Faith. His men are Christians. It may not get us anywhere. But working on that flaw within the Brotherhood structure is all we can do.'

I could see Martin was crying as we were tied back on our camels, and it wasn't his piles that had brought this on. And except he was now screaming at his men rather more than he had, Lucas was still taking no risk with us.

The wind came up as the very late afternoon shaded into evening. For some time, I'd been aware of the deepening haze that moderated the sun. It deepened progressively, until the sun became a patch of dim red just above the horizon, and the little hills about us a blur. The chain of mountains that had lowered all afternoon in the far distance were now gone from sight. All around us, as if the land itself were crying out, there was a low moan of wind brushing on rocks.

As the first gusts began to stir up the dust into swirling clouds, I heard Lucas giving orders, a note in his voice of anger, though also of concern. Someone grunted back at him. I heard the sound of spitting. Further back, two men were beginning an argument. Someone reached from behind me to wind a sheet of cloth over my lower face. Then he prodded more life into my camel, and I had to lean hurriedly forward to avoid falling off.

Except it was dry and there was no thunder and lightning, it was just like a storm at sea. The winds howled around us with a terrible noise. Great clouds of dust were now whipped up to blot out the late remainder of the sun. The camel continued stolidly forward, but its head was down and it made little of its earlier speed. Ahead of me, men were shouting. It was the angry shouting of an argument that neither side wanted to concede.

Another while of this, and then we stopped. I felt arms reach up to pull me from the camel. I hit the impacted surface of the road with a heavy bump. I opened my eyes just a little. They were stinging from dust that had mixed like some caustic cement with the tears.

'Get down there,' Lucas shouted above the howling. He motioned at the outline of some rocks that were the nearest approach we'd find to shelter. 'Put your cloak over you and keep your face down. Try anything funny, and I'll kill your secretary.'

I did as I was told. The storm was now at its height. Keeping that cloak even over my mouth was as much as I could do. It was as much as I needed to do. Over my legs and trunk, I could feel the cold softness of the dust – or, after all, I should perhaps call it sand. Dust isn't the right word for something that moves and settles like this stuff was doing. At first, it was a welcome softness. Then I began to worry about being buried alive. There was a whole army of Cambyses, I recalled, that had vanished in these deserts during a storm. After a thousand years, no one had come across the bones.

It was now every man for himself. We all cowered as best we could in the growing darkness. No one was paying attention to me. Time for what I guessed would be my only chance. I wriggled and stretched until my bound wrists were in my left armpit. It was there that I'd secreted the razor shortly after dinner on the boat. It had been the best I could do in the circumstances. While Martin was left to keep up his desperate pretence of normality, I'd slipped off to the stern, ostensibly for a shit. While alone, I'd stuck the razor there with a dressing from our medicine chest. Of course, my knife and sword had been taken as soon as the trap revealed itself. But I'd given such appearance of not noticing the preparations around me, that no one had thought to make a closer search. Now, it had been chafing and cutting me all day. Using it on the leather thongs wasn't easy. Once or twice, my heart beat fast at the thought that I'd severed a vein. But once I'd got the first effective slice at the leather, the rest was easier. Still lying in the shelter of those rocks, I rubbed at the sore flesh and clenched and unclenched my fists.

Looking for Martin, I had to cut one throat. It wasn't something I wanted to do. We'd been treated well enough so far, and I didn't want that to change if I found myself back in captivity. Luckily, Martin's was only the second mound of sand I'd disturbed. Now I had a knife, he was free in no time. It would barely have mattered in those winds had he shrieked like a eunuch singing in the theatre. As it was, he was remarkably calm.

'I've been waiting all day for this,' he whispered in my ear. 'I knew God would help you think of something.' He'd altered his tune! Such, though, was Martin. But what next? If the storm was losing its main strength, the sands were still blasting everything uncovered like a rain of quicklime. If we waited for them to fall still, we might as well tie ourselves back up and hope the dead man wouldn't be held against us.

'This way,' I shouted, pulling him towards where I'd seen the camels tethered. Could I get one of the things to move in this storm? How fast could it go with the two of us on its back? How much distance could we cover before we were missed? The storm over, we'd have the full moon directly overhead. We'd show up in that desert like lice on white skin.

All questions worth asking, but to be answered as and when.

'If the sun is up there,' I said, 'this must be the way back to the Nile.' I pointed uncertainly at the horizon. It looked like every other view from the top of the dune we'd managed to climb. We were in the middle of some vast, burning waste. Go where we pleased, its borders seemed to move with us, keeping us ever in its middle. If only that fucking camel hadn't taken off as soon as we'd got down to nurse our sore bottoms.

'Well, at least we had the water with us,' I said, trying to sound more positive than I felt. I shook the heavy skin. There was still about a half-gallon. I'd stopped sweating some while ago. But we'd agreed it might be for the best to be economical with its use.

'I did read somewhere,' Martin croaked, 'that the natives in the desert cover themselves in sand during the day and travel by night.'

I ignored him and squinted to see more of the horizon. We were now in desert roughly as I'd imagined it. There were still rocks to fall over if you didn't keep looking. But the rippling sands spread out around us now, almost as white in the sun as a snowfield. Mostly, they lay flat. Here and there, though, the wind had piled them up into dunes fifty or sixty or perhaps even a hundred feet high. There was no wind now. From a perfectly clear sky that seemed almost black by comparison, the small disc of the sun burned steadily down from directly overhead.

'Do you think we should even try pressing on in this heat?' Martin asked.

I nodded. We'd also tacitly agreed it would be for the best to keep going. Lucas and Company might be miles behind us. Or they might be over the next dune. Perhaps hiding for the day was the right thing to do. But I felt an overpowering impulse to keep going as long as we could.

'Aelric,' Martin said, now in Latin, 'I really do feel that God has reserved you for some higher purpose – and I suppose we have been in worse troubles – but I want to say now while I still can how grateful I am to God for having brought us together. If we are to die here, I want to say what an honour it has been to know you.'

Typical of Martin always to look on the gloomy side of things, I thought. But at least he'd stopped babbling about the supposedly miraculous wind sent to overcome the unrighteous. But the 'honour', of having known me! If he'd only kept himself from being sucked into that stupid plot with poor dead Lucius, he'd still be snug in the Papal Chancery back in Rome. He'd have known me a month, if that. Being a slave of the Church can't be fun. But there are few better masters.

'You'll not be dying out here, or any other place soon,' I snapped back at him. 'I promise you, we'll be back in Alexandria soon enough, drinking beer made in the German style. I've no doubt before then Sveta will have made you wish you *had* died. But you'll live to tell this escape to your grandchildren.

'Now, since we are still north of the equator, and the sun still rises in the east, I do say the Nile must be over there.'

'It was God, I tell you, Aelric,' Martin said as I shook my tunic again to get the sand out of it. I was having little success. Even without the sand that had settled on the great blood smear from that cut throat and that had now set like church brocade, the cloth was permeated with the stuff.

'God made them go right past without seeing us,' he added with a pious expression.

'Then let us give thanks in the appropriate place,' I said evenly. 'However, you will have seen that they didn't have that camel with them. This being so, they weren't looking for two men on foot.'

Burying ourselves in the sand had also helped. It was a stroke of luck we'd paused before reaching the peak of the dune we were climbing. We'd heard the recriminations in plenty of time as they rode slowly up the other side towards us. I'd allowed myself one look at them. Lucas was almost jumping up and down as he'd screamed at his men. Most of them had looked half-inclined to jump on him. One had even shouted back at him. We'd waited until the shouting died away before digging ourselves out. Now, relief was mingled with discomfort. I'll not mention the bastard flies that had been hopping all over me and biting.

'I grant it would have been best not to have seen them at all,' I continued, giving up on rubbing at myself. I was brushing as much sand on as off, and just a few moments in the sun were making my back feel tight. 'But it does show we're on the right course. It's plain they were trying to cut us off before we could get back to the water.'

Martin began one of his edifying lectures on the Grace of God. Since I didn't fancy skulking here until dark, I thought I'd put his claims to the test by carrying on through that burning waste – even if every step in it was beginning to feel an effort. Though I'd made sure we had good sandals on before we were taken, you need special boots for walking in the desert. Our lower legs had soon turned an alarming shade of red, and the soles of our feet were hurting as if we'd been dancing on crumbled pumice.

'What I want to know,' I said as we rested just below the peak of another dune, 'is how the Brotherhood knew we were going to Letopolis. I know it has its agents in the government. But the orders I issued gave less than a day's notice, and our voyage to Bolbitine was as fast as can be imagined. I can't see how notice could have outrun us – certainly not to produce the level of organisation we met there, nor so far up river.'

'Do you suppose those documents were left with Leontius in the knowledge that you'd feel drawn out of Alexandria?' Martin asked.

I took the tiniest sip of water and moved it about with my tongue. I had been wondering that myself for a day and more. But to get all this arranged, the Brotherhood must have worked faster than the wind. The natives had never struck me as good for anything beyond whining and a bit of casual violence. Macarius had always seemed more than a cut above the rest of them.

Yes – Macarius. What had become of him? If he hadn't chosen to vanish when he did, he'd have been there on the journey. With him in tow, we'd never have been suckered into that trap set by

Lucas. It wasn't worth setting Martin off again – not here, at least – about the worthiness of any native to receive my trust. Even so, I went grimly over the piece of my mind I'd make sure to give Macarius when he eventually did turn up again.

It beat reflecting on my own catastrophic want of common sense. If I'd been less eaten up with worry about those documents, we'd never have left Alexandria.

22

It was as we climbed over the third – or perhaps it was the fourth – dune after our shock about how much water we had left that we saw the monument. It was one of those granite things you see all over Egypt, of a man sitting stiffly in a chair, a false beard stuck to his chin, some elaborate crown making his head almost as long as the body. It was leaning over pronouncedly in the sands, and might have been there since the beginning of time.

Size and distance just aren't things you can gauge in the desert. With nothing comparable around them, things stand purely in their own terms. It seemed an age to get to the monument, and it was huge. It may have been half the height of the Royal Palace in Alexandria. There was no sign of any buildings around it. Perhaps they were buried in the shifting sands.

'Never mind the picture writing,' I said to Martin, fighting to keep the eagerness out of my voice. 'It's probably the same flatulence you see on the bilingual inscriptions in Alexandria. Look at this!' I pointed down near the base. It was carved so low that it was half buried in the sands. It was a patch about the size of a large paving stone, where those endlessly varied bugs and crudely depicted plants within their ovals had been smoothed out and overlaid with Greek.

I brushed some sand out of the letters and read the opening of the inscription, which was in hexameters:

> They died like rats confined, the men
>> Who crawled away from Assinaros,
> No roof they found to hold the autumn sun:
>> Nor straw to keep the winter frost

From off their shrivelled, naked bodies.
And the quarry choked with corpses,
     All among the stinking shit unburied.
And, brought to see what poets mean by Nemesis,
     Children came to see the living suffer,
          And, while its glowing embers long shall remain
To dazzle generations with their brightness,
     O proud City crowned with violets,
Your flame of glory died that day with those
Who crawled away from Assinaros.

'What the fuck is that supposed to mean?' I asked. I scrubbed more sand away from the bottom of the inscription. If I'd seen the Latin version of the Creed there, it wouldn't have surprised me more.

'It's a lament on the failure of the Sicilian Expedition during the Peloponnesian War,' Martin said. 'It's taken from the *Theseus* of Sophocles.'

'No, it isn't,' I said. 'I know that play very well. There's nothing there about the Sicilian Expedition.'

'You've read the standard edition,' Martin said with his first smile in months. 'This is in the version that he rewrote for a revival towards the end of his life. He was in pessimistic mood at the time, and thought the defeat in Sicily marked the beginning of the end for Greece as a whole.'

I deferred to Martin's greater learning. He'd read through some very obscure stuff when he was still helping his father run that school they'd had in Constantinople. I stood back from my scrubbing and read the attestation right at the bottom of the smoothed area.

'Well, whoever wrote it in the first place,' I said, 'it was put here by Hadrian.' I pointed at the attestation. Hadrian it had been. He'd passed by on one of his Imperial tours not far off five hundred years before. The blown sands had smoothed out nearly everything but the hexameters. But Martin stood beside me to see it as well as he could, and read what he could.

'. . .caused to be placed here among the lone and level sands . . .' was the last line of the attestation we could read. After this, the words came to an end.

'A pity it's the Greek that has worn away,' I said. 'All that horrid Egyptian stuff has survived well enough.'

'Your friend Lucas might wish to comment on that,' Martin quipped.

I looked at him and reached for the water sack. He was still smiling, and this was the first joke I'd heard him make since Christmas – and then he'd been drunk. Perhaps the sun was getting to him.

You might ask what on earth we thought we were about. We were still lost in the desert, still running out of water and, for all we knew, ready to dry up like slugs in the sun. We were still being hunted down by the agents of what we had no reason to deny was an implacable and highly effective conspiracy. And we were dancing before some wog monument that had taken an Emperor's fancy half a millennium before. I suppose it was because anything bearing a human mark was welcome after so much wandering in that sandy void. It also suggested the possibility that we weren't so far from the Nile. Or perhaps the stress of everything had got to both of us.

It was as we were arguing over reconstructions of the missing words – and, more importantly, over what could have led Hadrian to put up something so utterly incongruous – that I heard the jingling. It came from the other side of a dune that rose above the height of the monument. We fell silent and looked at each other.

'If we bury ourselves in the sand again,' Martin said with shaking voice – his piety wearing as thin for the moment as the inscription – 'they might not see us.'

'That's not the sound they were making on their camels,' I said hesitantly. We both listened hard. It was more a jingling of bells than of harness. It was the sort of thing you heard in the more sedate religious processions.

'Let me look over,' I said. 'My hair is almost the same colour as the sand. It saved us once.'

★   ★   ★

We pulled back below the peak of the dune and looked at each other.

'What the . . . ?' Martin asked in a whisper.

We looked over again. There are many things you expect to come across in a desert. There are bandits, of course, and soldiers. There are merchants, with their trains of camels or of slaves. There are the natives as they shuffle from one water hole to another. The last thing you expect is a carrying chair with white silken curtains. Carried by four strong blacks, it moved briskly along with two camels behind to carry some rather light baggage. Around the chair four maidservants walked, their bodies swathed in white robes. It was the sort of thing you didn't give a second look back in Alexandria. How else do fine ladies get to church? But out here, and in the middle of the desert?

'We can't be far at all from the Nile,' I said, with a doubtful look to the still unvaried horizon. 'I wonder where the other attendants could be? Come on,' I said, getting up. 'We might beg a bite to eat, along with a few directions.'

The bearers saw us waving as we hurried down the dune towards them. They looked briefly at us and then back down, not once breaking their pace. The four women responded with a shrill twittering in a language I hadn't before heard. They pointed to us and looked back at each other – again, though, not breaking pace. I couldn't see their faces. But their hands were as black as the bearers.

'Hello,' I cried in a voice that trailed off to a croak. I stepped clumsily and the sand gave way. I fell flat on my back, before rolling forward and then sideways. I came to a stop at the foot of the dune. Martin got there shortly after and helped me up.

'Hello,' I cried again, trying to ignore the loss of what little skin the camels had left on my bottom. 'Do any of you know Greek?'

About six yards from me, the front curtains of the chair fluttered. Holding a little gold stick, a white and decidedly female arm stretched out briefly to tap one of the bearers. The procession stopped. The bells that were dangling around the top frame of the chair suddenly stopped their jingling. There was another movement of the curtains.

'Greek is a language I have not heard in many years,' a voice said from within. 'I think, nevertheless, I may still be able to understand it.' It was a deep, though again a decidedly female voice. The Greek wasn't that of the natives, nor of the Alexandrians, nor of any other city dwellers I'd heard so far. It had a finely judged fluency, and was in the odd, lilting accent I'd once heard in Constantinople from an old man who'd studied in Athens before the universities there had been fully dispersed.

'Come closer, young man,' the voice said again from within the curtains. 'Say what you would ask of me.'

'I, er . . .' I'd not expected that question. I glanced at the tiny and almost festive party around the chair. 'Madam,' I said, trying to sound more composed than I felt, 'I must ask you to consider the danger of your situation. You are lost in a desert that is filled with bandits. If you would care to accept my protection—'

The curtains shook with the peal of laughter that came from behind them.

'Young man,' the voice said again, now mocking, 'I have travelled without want or molestation from beyond the limits of Abyssinia. I am now accosted by two beggars evidently lacking both arms and supplies, and warned to look for my safety. You might consider speaking again.'

Martin clutched suddenly at my arm. I turned and looked back up the dune. Silent, mounted on their camels, Lucas and his men looked steadily down.

'Oh, fuck!' I said. I reached to my belt for the knife I'd taken from the murdered man. It was hardly worth the effort of pulling it out. I looked at the four bearers. Their black muscles rippled hugely in the sun. But they were, so far as I could tell, unarmed. I looked uncertainly back at the curtains.

'Madam,' I said, 'these men surely mean you no harm. If you would only start again on your journey—'

Cutting off my words, the voice gave curt orders in that unknown language. Two of the attendants drew the curtains aside. Another produced a little sunshade and positioned herself.

Covered from head to toe in white silk, her face covered with a white veil, the owner of the chair stepped delicately on to the sand. I heard it crunch beneath the fine leather of her sandal. From habit, and exactly as if we were outside one of the Constantinopolitan churches, Martin and I bowed as she stepped past us. The robe of the maidservant who carried the sunshade brushed against my bowed head.

The owner of the chair stopped at the foot of the dune. From her general manner behind the curtains, I'd expected someone at least of middle years. Yet what I could see of her trim figure, and her firm tread on the sand, showed a woman barely older than me. She looked up, her veil fluttering in the gentle breeze that had come on suddenly. There was a long silence. Lucas stared back at her and then at me. There was an odd look on his face. Then one of the camels beside him made a spitting noise as its rider wheeled it round. From further along the line of silent riders, there was another movement. I heard the rustle of hastily disturbed sand on the other side. In an instant, Lucas alone was looking down at us.

The owner of the chair raised her arms towards him. It might have been in supplication or in mockery – when you can see neither face nor body, motions are hard things to gauge. Lucas stared back a moment longer. Then, with a snort of his own camel, he too had wheeled round and was gone.

The afternoon was pressing on. The sun was no longer so high above us. There was now a soft moan of the rising desert winds. In the midst of all this, we stood alone.

There were further orders to the maidservants, who now began fussing with one of the camels. The owner of the chair turned to me. I'll swear I felt the long look she gave me through her veil. I felt Martin's hand reaching nervously from beside me. I took it in my own. I suddenly noticed how cold my hand had become.

'It is, you will agree, a universal custom,' the owner of the chair said with slightly suppressed amusement, 'that those who rescue strays take on further duties for their welfare. You will not, there-fore, refuse my offer of dinner, nor of safe conduct tomorrow morning to the nearest town.' She pointed over to some dead trees in the middle distance. The water hole that had once sustained them was long since dried up. But the shelter would be useful.

'Your name, madam, would be most welcome,' I said, remembering my manners.

'My name is not important,' came the reply. 'Most who have reason to address me, though, call me the Mistress.' Without another word, she turned and began walking towards the two nearest of those dead palm trees.

23

I finished stirring at the cold ashes. A slave took the charred stick from me and wiped my hand with a piece of clean linen.

'It was still smouldering when I arrived,' Macarius said. 'The locals identified some of the household. The others were too badly burned even to show if they had also been tortured.'

All told, it hadn't been a very productive trip up river. The Brotherhood had been ahead of us at every step. I bent again and took up a scrap of charred papyrus. I thought at first it was in Greek. A closer look showed it was in Egyptian. I let it fall and stood back on to a less cluttered part of what had been the dining-room floor.

'Then I suppose we'd better start back for Alexandria,' I said bleakly. Whatever documents Leontius had kept here were now either one with the general wreckage of his house or irretrievably in the wrong hands.

'If the past few days are any guide to how fast the Brotherhood moves,' I said after a pause, 'I imagine word of our escape will be in Alexandria long before we arrive. Even so, I can order an investigation as to who grassed me to these people. We might at the least be able to save on a few salaries and pensions.'

A voice broke in.

'If you are using an official transport, I will accompany you. I have business of my own in Alexandria.'

I kept myself from frowning. It was the Mistress who'd spoken. Though I was curious to see more of what lay under those white robes, I was decreasingly pleased by her determined and thoroughly masculine way with those around her. Wherever she came from, it seemed that women there had little notion of how to conduct themselves in public.

I'm not saying I wasn't grateful. Somehow, she'd scared off Lucas and his friends. She'd then got us directly to Letopolis, where I'd discovered Macarius hard at work on making sense of the devastation of nearly all that Leontius had once owned and that the receivers of his bankruptcy would never now be able to touch.

The Mistress had joined in my enquiries, Macarius answering her pointed questions as if they were from me. Now, one of her maids holding up a sunshade, she stood on the cleanest part of the floor. Her right foot was slightly forward, and I could see the large emerald that adorned the ring on one of her toes. It was, bearing in mind what I'd read about the heat of Abyssinia – never mind what lay beyond – an astonishingly white foot. Again, I wondered how and why she could have made her home in so strange and distant a place.

'Our boat is, of course, at your disposal,' I said, trying to sound as if I were making the invitation. It was reasonable to suppose there weren't many shops as far south as she lived. I'd at least have the joy of silencing her with the range and quality of the frocks and cosmetics on sale in Alexandria.

'I hope My Lord will not be offended if I touch on the unwisdom of leaving Alexandria. I do hold myself responsible, however, in that I left without telling you my business.'

I grunted and made what I thought might pass for a non-committal wave. Macarius had finally managed to get hold of some opium in town, and this had almost restored my mood. And though I remained aware of the sunburn and the raw patches, the pain was largely bleached out.

We stood in one of the few streets in Letopolis that was now inhabited. Before us, the church rose from the ruins of an old temple. Behind us was the dilapidated block that served as the administrative building. I turned and looked at the place again. An old woman hurried past us, a bundle of mouldy reeds on her hunched back. She crossed herself and looked away as we drew level. Once she was a few yards behind me, I heard a clearing of aged throat and the spatter of flob on the crooked pavement.

'You will understand,' Macarius added, 'that I am breaking a confidence if I say that the Honourable Mayor's illness is entirely diplomatic. In part, he is embarrassed that his Greek is not sufficient for receiving an official of My Lord's station. While there is no one else qualified to replace him, he fears that a report of his inability to do more than write set sentences in the official language might count against him in Alexandria.

'In part, he fears the effect it might have on the Brotherhood if it were known he had rendered you active assistance.'

'So who is this Lucas?' I asked. I looked at the low mounds of what may once have been the bathhouse. Yes, it must have been that: you could see the remains of the water cistern that had supplied it.

'He goes under so many names,' the answer came, 'that you might as well call him Lucas. The real Lucas, I have no doubt, will by now have been found outside Bolbitine with his throat cut. News of your evident hurry must have been leaked from the government, and this would have been regarded as justifying the risk of discovery.

'But you ask about the man who called himself Lucas. His position in the Brotherhood is officially rather low. His energy and ambition, however, have made him its effective leader in much of Egypt. In this respect, if you will pardon the comparison, he is not unlike My Lord. He is even about the same age.'

'I did at first think,' I said, 'that his purpose was to trade me to Nicetas for some of the cash I inadvertently took from his people.' Macarius stood awhile in silence. That had made sense, I thought. Very little of the gold the Brotherhood had been leaching out of Alexandria could have been needed to keep a dozen scabby priests in whatever slops their faith allowed them to eat. But for raising and keeping in being the sort of conspiracy I'd brushed against, it wasn't gold that could easily be replaced by a tithe on the starving people of Egypt.

'However,' I said as we arrived at the top of the street where it simply ran into the desert, and turned back to the centre, 'he echoed Leontius in saying that my real value lay in my ability to lead whoever controlled me to something important.' I wondered if it might be worth sitting on one of the stone benches that had, back in the days when Letopolis was a populous commercial and administrative centre, been set before the church. But this was the only clean robe anyone had been able to set hands on that came near to fitting me.

'I am not entirely sure of his intentions in this respect,' Macarius said at last. 'A ransom might have come into it. But I have thought much since our last meeting beside the body of Leontius regarding the Brotherhood's interest in My Lord.' He paused again to collect his words.

I raised my eyebrows and tried to look quizzical. I was still slightly rattled by the stupidity I'd shown in putting myself into the hands of the Brotherhood. Now I was back in control of events around me, I was determined to avoid any show of an unseemly curiosity. I waited for Macarius to begin again.

'Even before the late disaster in Cappadocia,' he said, 'news had spread through all Egypt of the Persian military successes. This revived hopes that the empire established here by Alexander and renewed by Augustus might be coming to an end. It was believed within the Brotherhood that My Lord's arrival – on a mission from Caesar himself – had less to do with changes to the ownership of land than with the search for a very powerful object. This connects with a prophecy that the object will be uncovered by a man from the West fitting your appearance.'

'Now might that happen to be the first chamber pot of Jesus Christ?' I asked with an attempt at a grim smile. This couldn't have anything to do with Priscus. News of his own interest wouldn't yet have spread far within Alexandria, let alone through Upper Egypt. But he'd assumed my interest in diverting those five hundred workmen from digging out the old canal was to do with the piss pot. It was perhaps only natural the Brotherhood – and Leontius – had made the same mistake.

'It might, My Lord,' Macarius answered. 'The object is said to be of the highest potency. In Imperial hands, it could be used to turn the tide of war against the Persians. In Egyptian hands, it could be turned against the Empire and, at the least, drive the Greeks from Egypt.

'This may have prompted Lucas to his daring attempt on My Lord. Doubtless, however, there were other motives. You might have been held to ransom. Of course, the Brotherhood has every reason to fear the results of any redistribution of land; and the moral disgrace of your capture might have added to the already considerable difficulties of implementing the new law. Otherwise, the approaching end of Greek dominion might have been advertised by showing off its most eminent representative in a cage. It might also have been hoped that torture would prompt the appropriate words of support.

'But I also believe that the Brotherhood is under the impression that you know, or are on the verge of discovering, the whereabouts of this most powerful object. This, I am sure, is what weighed heaviest in the calculations that Lucas made. To have achieved any of the other purposes would have raised him higher within the Brotherhood. Taking possession of the object in question would have established his complete supremacy.'

'Is it because of this,' I asked, 'that you paid off the old fraud and his daughter back in Alexandria?'

'My Lord is well informed,' Macarius said with a respectful bow. 'I knew that His Lordship the General was making enquiries of his own. It struck me that it would complicate your own operations if the Lord Priscus were able to disturb the peace of the city with his continued enquiries.'

'I haven't seen any of the other landowners in this district,' I said, changing the subject. 'Not all of them can be in Alexandria.'

'Indeed not, My Lord,' he said. 'They keep to their own fortified manor houses. Though useful politically, Leontius was a man of evil reputation in these parts. His neighbours consider his death and the effacement of his estate as no loss to their order. Otherwise, they are guided by the same considerations of embarrassment and fear as the Honourable Mayor. They will not come out unless commanded.'

'You say there is a boat touching in here tomorrow morning?' I asked. I'd seen enough of Egypt for the moment. Since it meant skipping dinner with them, I'd ignore the insult from what passed for the local persons of quality.

'There will be a postal vessel on its way down to the coast,' Macarius said. 'It will be fully suitable to carry My Lord and his party.'

The door of the little church opened and Martin put his head out. He'd seen us, but his face carried the abstracted, holy look that I knew indicated a wish to be ignored. We carried on past him, to look over the lower and uninhabited part of town. Much of this was now under at least a few inches of the flood waters. Earlier floods had eaten away the mud bricks of the houses, and only the broken line of the city wall could now be made out.

'What can you tell me about this woman who calls herself the Mistress?' I asked, changing the subject again. The fact that she'd got so far without molestation – and had even scared off Lucas and Company – indicated she was of high status. I'd got bugger-all out of her, though, in the way of hard fact during the few days it had taken us to get here. How she'd acquired such excellent Greek – even better in some respects than my own – was one mystery. How she'd managed this with so hazy a knowledge of anything that had happened since the establishment of the Faith was another.

'The Mistress,' said Macarius, slowly choosing his words, 'travels from regions unknown even to the Egyptians of the south. Her purpose in travelling is not for me to say. I only know that she rendered valuable assistance to My Lord when it was needed, and that she will now continue, as an honoured guest, to Alexandria.'

Somewhere behind us, I could hear children at play. They sounded like children everywhere, and their shouted calls to each other were the jolliest thing I'd heard in days. No point in going back to look at them, though. One sight of me and, like everyone else, they'd be scuttling for cover.

I let the matter drop. Macarius had always struck me as a man of strong common sense. This being said, I preferred not to discuss the details of how and where I'd come across the Mistress in any conversation that referred back to what that girl had said in Alexandria. The faintest tinge of superstition was enough to connect the most disparate facts into a seamless narrative of the miraculous.

I looked silently over the waters. I didn't want to think of Lucas or cages or piss pots. All I wanted at this moment was the nearest approach to normality possible in this flyblown dump of a town. So I looked over the waters and forced my thoughts into the course I wanted. Varying between two and eight feet below these waters lay some of the richest land in the world. Some of this had been owned by Leontius. Over much else he'd had secondary and often still valuable rights. Not all had gone up by any means in the flames of his manor house.

'Macarius,' I said in my briskest and most irresistible tone, 'I want you to arrange a meeting with the local Mayor. Tell him I'm not interested in the possible deficiencies of his Greek. If it is as defective as you indicate, you will have to interpret.

'His main duty is to ascertain the land boundaries once the flood has receded. Since I control the central records in Alexandria, he might care to make one or two adjustments to the survey reports ...' Not being quite a creditor – and certainly not a preferred creditor – I might be about to take a hit on the contracts I'd made indirectly with Leontius. Now, Macarius listened intently as I outlined my scheme to offset what would otherwise be a considerable loss.

24

I was a child again in Richborough. I think I was about ten. I huddled on my bed of filthy straw in the corner of the building where King Ethelbert had dumped us all after killing my father. On my right, just out of reach, my two younger brothers lay sleeping in each other's arms. Over in the far corner, my little sister – my half-sister, that is, got by Ethelbert – lay sleeping with my mother. Through the unshuttered window and the unrepaired hole in the roof crept a dim light that heralded the coming of the dawn. With it came the sound of winds and the heavy crash of Channel waves on the nearby shingle.

I was cold. Even huddled as I was, I couldn't pull the thin blanket over my head without uncovering my legs. I was hungry, and my belly ached with the habitual pain of those who live on the edge of starvation.

I sat up and looked at the outline of things. There was the water jug with the broken handle. There was the pile of wooden slats on which I was being taught my letters by the renegade monk Auxilius. There was the workbox where my mother stored the things she used when mending clothes for the few people who lingered in what had, before the coming of our people, been the main gateway to the Province of Britain.

It was all as I remembered it. Or did I need to remember it? I was a child and I was there. Everything was as it ought to be. There were things at the fringes of consciousness that I knew I should call into full understanding. But, try as I might, they remained on the fringes – a blur that confused without abolishing my sense of being in a perfectly natural present.

I lay back in the straw and squeezed my eyes shut. I was hoping for sleep. But I was now too aware of the cold and hunger. I looked into the darkness of the roof timbers. Everything would brighten soon enough, and then we could all get up. The sun might shine this day. There might even be a scrape of fatty gruel for breakfast.

'Aelric. Aelric,' the voice called. I'd been aware of it for some time. But, as with the breaking of day, it was one of those things that is already known before it is noticed. I held my breath and strained to hear what was, as a cause of distress, overtaking that unease about who and where and when I was.

'Aelric. Aelric,' the voice called. I heard it clearly. It was a woman, her voice soft and long and hypnotic. She sounded my name twice each time, before pausing, and then – after just long enough to make you think it was all over – starting again. Her voice came from a distance, though it seemed also to come from nowhere in particular. And with each repetition of the call, I had a feeling that the distance was growing smaller.

'Aelric. Aelric,' it came again. It was louder. I looked over to the right. The younger of my brothers had his face towards me. Eyes shut, he was breathing gently through his mouth. If the call really was growing louder – or was even there – I alone could hear it.

I sat up again and pressed myself against the wall behind me. I pulled the blanket to my face. The faint smell of piss was oddly comforting. Without lifting my face, I looked up at the still and familiar things around me. They were exactly as they were. They always had been so. They always would be so.

But they weren't the same – not quite. There was a new shadow. Confused as I still was, I knew the pattern of light and shadow in that room at every time of the day or night. This was a new patch of darkness in the room. About eighteen inches from my sleeping mother, it had no obvious relationship with any other object. Still not lifting my face, I looked and looked. Like a spreading stain, the shadow grew. And insensibly, as it grew, it was changing shape, and acquiring substance as it changed. It seemed a puff of smoke. It seemed a ball of dark wool. It grew and changed and took on substance. And all the time, I sat on my bed of filthy straw, my lower face pressed into the blanket.

'Mother!' I wanted to call. But I had no voice. I could move my uplifted eyes from one place in the room to another. Otherwise, it was as if I'd been turned to stone. The mass of blackness was finishing its transformation, or perhaps its arrival. Without seeing eyes, I felt the close inspection. I felt the cold menace. In a weak, hesitant step towards me, it moved.

But it had moved too soon. It was like smoke again in its partial disintegration. It paused. Now, I could feel the impatience of something forced to wait for what had been thought so easy.

Still soft, the voice was urgent now. Its steady pulse of calling and then silence hadn't broken or altered in any way. Yet between two beats of this pulse that, if far apart, were not that far apart, the Dark Thing had managed its entire appearance out of nothing – and had done so in what seemed a very long time. It was as if I were within two distinct streams of time, each moving at its own speed.

The voice came now from behind me. Between each call, I could hear breathing. It was a long, soft rising and falling of breath. My back was pressed hard against the wall. It was a wall built in the old days by men of the race we'd driven out. Through those courses of stone and brick and stone again, you don't hear anything. Yet I could hear breathing from behind me. I wanted to jump up and run. I wanted to run to my mother. Or I just wanted to run. The Dark Thing was moving again. It was a shuffling but now confident motion as it closed the distance to where I sat. Still, though, I had no strength to uncurl my legs from under me.

There was a flash of light above and behind me. Suddenly, I could at least move my head. I looked up. Without any breach in those courses of brick and stone, a woman's arms – bare and white – had come straight through the wall. It might have been mist for all the resistance it gave. There was no head or body. It was just the arms, and they shone white as if bathed in the glare of the moon at its fullest. At first, they moved around over my head as if feeling for something. At last, they found me, and fingers that were ice-cold and unyielding fluttered over my face, and began closing themselves round my throat and pulling me back through the wall.

The Dark Thing was itself reaching out to me as I felt my head bump against the hardness of the wall. Then the hardness yielded, and, as if through honey, I was passing through the wall into – into—

I woke screaming. I screamed until my throat was raw and my voice cracked. As I fought to control the terror, some inner cordon snapped, and it came back into my understanding that I wasn't Aelric any more, dispossessed starveling in England, but Alaric, Legate Extraordinary of His Imperial Majesty. The familiar things of the dream had been dispersed four years ago following my mother's death. My brothers had been dead for years. My little half-sister – what had become of her was a question I couldn't begin to answer, never having seriously asked it. And it had all been a dream. I wasn't back in Richborough, some little child waiting to mature into the most literate bandit Kent had ever known. I was in Egypt, where my word was often close to law.

But I still wasn't in my own bed in the Letopolis administrative building, or in any other place where I was in control. I was in motion. Beneath the hard, wooden surface on which I lay, there was the rumble of wheels on a paved surface. Close by was a hubbub of voices, all speaking Egyptian. I flexed myself to sit up. My head banged hard on the wooden boards as I fell back. As on that journey into the desert, I was bound again at the wrists.

While I was trying to work out in my still fuddled mind what was going on, the canopy that had kept me in darkness was pulled away. My eyes adjusted slowly to the light of the Egyptian day that was all about me. It was some while before I could see for sure that it was Lucas grinning at me through the bars of the cage in which I was shut.

'Has My Lord slept well?' he asked as I rolled back into a seated position. 'Was he calling out perhaps for breakfast? Or for the ministrations of some native harlot?'

'What the fucking hell . . . ?' My throat was too raw for me to get out more than a few words. I pulled myself on to my knees and looked out through the bars. We weren't in any part of Letopolis that I knew. Except it was still Egypt, we weren't in any other place I'd visited. Pulled by two oxen, the wheeled cage in which I was the one exhibit rumbled down streets as crowded and as wide as those of Alexandria. On either side rose buildings of an opulence that had nothing in common with anything of the Greeks, old or modern. Lucas walked beside me. Children danced round and about, keeping roughly level with our slow procession, their elders looking on in angry excitement. In starched loincloths, their bare torsos burned a reddish brown by the sun, some of them called eagerly at Lucas. Others bowed low before him.

Lucas had turned from me and was shouting something in Egyptian that had more of those alien, jabbering faces looking in at me.

'Do you suppose you could escape the Brotherhood?' Lucas asked when he'd turned back to face me. 'Did you suppose you would be safe anywhere in Egypt, or in Alexandria itself? Your sorceress friend has powers that do not reach this place.'

'What are you going to do with me?' I gasped. There was much else I might have asked. But this was the first real question I could get out – and, I suppose, the most important.

'Drink before speaking,' said Lucas, pushing a cup of something liquid through the bars. 'You'll not be needing eyes to see the places where you'll be seen. But you will need a voice for proclaiming the end of Greek dominion and the restoration by me of the people's ancient and most perfect freedom.' He dropped his voice – as if it mattered what he said: we were as far beyond the hearing as the reach of any Greek.

'But let us continue our debate of the other day. You spoke about your own state of perfect freedom. You may wish to explain to me how, if there is no room here for kings or any government, you have allowed yourself to be sent among us as the representative of the most powerful king in the world. Is there some subtlety in your argument that my wog mind is not up to appreciating? Or is there just the smallest touch of hypocrisy in what you say?'

'Fuck off, shittybreath wog!' I snarled. 'Laying hands on me is high treason.'

'Not the answer, I confess,' said Lucas, speaking very even, 'I had expected from a subtle and learned student of the Greeks. But let it be as you declare. My real interest in speaking with you is to discuss your possible release, and even safe return to Alexandria.

'You have in your possession, I am reliably told, an object of considerable value. The moment I have this in my own hands, let me promise you—'

'Now, why should I trust your word in anything?' I asked, checking the obvious protest that I had no idea whether this bloody piss pot existed, let alone where it might be. 'I'll consider giving you what you want when I'm in a better position to rely on your side of the bargain.'

Lucas shrugged. He turned and shouted out a rapid stream of orders. With a frantic pulling of oxen, the wheeled cage came to a stop. The crowd about me thickened, and those dark faces pressed in closer and closer against the bars. I could see the blank ovals of their eyes, and smell the stale garlic on their breath. From every side, hands reached through the bars. Even cowering in the dead centre, I wasn't out of reach of those sweaty yet chill hands as they plucked at my clothing, uncovering and touching and squeezing every part of my body.

'Behold how the Day of Reckoning is at hand!' Lucas was shouting above the babble. For some reason, he shouted now in Greek. 'So the last shall be first, and the first last. Indeed, O ye children of soil, the last shall be first and the first last.'

I could already smell the charcoal when I saw the man with the blinding instruments – who had appeared as if from nowhere – standing beside Lucas. They conferred in hushed tones, with significant looks at me as I lay bound in the cage, trying desperately hard to blot out the horror of those cold sweaty hands still at work on exploring every part of my now naked body.

This time, I really was awake. I lay in my bed, safe on the top floor of the Letopolis administrative building. The netting hung white above me in the moonlight that streamed through both windows. There was a regular chirruping of insects from outside. The air about me was sultry in ways that no Alexandrian could have imagined. But I lay there freezing and unfreezing with terror. With every beat of my rapid pulse, there were bright flashes of pain in my head.

I couldn't really have been crying out. That would at once have brought people into my room. Instead, I lay alone in the moon-lit silence. But my throat was parched as if I'd been shouting all night. I scrambled out of the netting. The flies it was there to repel had long since gone off to sleep. I lifted the cover from the wine jug and drank deeply. I forced myself to ignore the sour taste of the local vintage and drank again. Feeling better, I got up and went over to the window through which the moonlight shone most directly.

I looked over the low huddle that remained of Letopolis, all colours bleached out in the whiteness. There was the street where I'd been speaking with Macarius. The church lay at the far end, where the street forked before leading down to the Nile. The moon looked pretty on the water, for all I could smell the mud.

Was that a shadow that had moved? It had been on the edge of my field of vision. My heart began its hammering again, and I clutched at the stone sill of the window. I looked straight ahead and ignored what might have been two glowing green eyes. If I'd never gloried in danger, and if I'd usually had to deal with an attack of nerves after what I thought an unreasonable danger, I'd always so far managed the combination of resolution and trusting to luck that passes for courage. Now, for the first time, I realised what it was to be a coward. I was jumping at shadows. I knew there was no one and nothing out there that intended me the slightest harm. And I was shitting myself with fear at the sight of Letopolis in the moonlight.

I took another drink and breathed deeply. I really was awake, I told myself. I'll grant there are dreams that seem real enough – I'd just had two of them. But they can always be known after-wards as dreams. What distinguishes them from reality is a lack of full self-awareness, or some observed deviation from the laws of nature, or, failing that, a set of events that cannot be related in space or time to the rest of my experiences. But here I now was – in a place where I expected to be, at a time that followed on from that dinner with the Mayor. Whatever I thought I could see outside could be dismissed as tricks of the moonlight on a heated mind. I was awake, and I was safe.

But I was still cold, and still dripping with sweat. And I could feel another fit of the shakes coming on. There was a faint doubt in my mind.

'How much of that filth have you been taking?' Martin asked sharply. He sat up and stared into my eyes. I wasn't sure what he could see in the dim light, but he already knew what he was looking for.

'It was dried resin,' I muttered. 'You can't always judge the dose when it's not an apothecary's pills.'

'You're as bad as Priscus in your own way,' he said flatly. He poured me a cup of sour fruit squash and watched as I drank it. He was still angry at the shock of being woken. But he was growing calmer, and I could hear a slight satisfaction in his voice as he went on.

'You first told me when we were living in Rome about the Richborough dream,' he said. 'You've been having it since you were still a boy in Richborough. I think you had it most recently in Alexandria, just before the floods began. Did the monster take hold of you this time? Or did you sit in that bright room, talking with the woman?'

I shook my head. You can dream about having had dreams, and you can dream about having had dreams about having had dreams. I needed Martin's assurance that I wasn't suffering some disorder of the mind. It was just the opium working with the after-effects of a difficult few days. I remained sitting on the bed. I was feeling better with every breath. I was even beginning to see the absurdity of running to Martin – of all people – with an attack of the vapours. But I didn't feel inclined to go back to my own room.

Martin sighed. He got back into bed and held the curtains open for me. I got in beside him. I could smell the stale sweat of his body. It was oddly reassuring. Suddenly very tired, I cuddled up close beside him.

'You saw me coming out of church this afternoon,' he said. 'God spoke to me again. He explained how He acts in the world partly through direct miracles, and partly through what you call secondary causes. I know perfectly well that you don't believe in these either, and that you only mention them to avoid upsetting me with your belief in a world governed by purely natural causes. But there are secondary causes. There are times when God works through events and even persons for His Will to prevail without the intercession of the obviously miraculous.'

Martin was still softly lecturing me on the Workings of Providence as I drifted off into a now dreamless sleep.

25

'Perhaps your husband grows concerned at your long absence?'
I said. I sat behind the desk in the front cabin of the – now genuine – Postal Service boat. The stack of papyrus on which I'd been
writing letters all morning had a most satisfying look.

'My poor young Alaric,' came the laughed reply, 'I trust your
official enquiries are less transparent than this.' The Mistress
kicked off her sandals and stretched back on the couch.

I tried not to move my eyes as I looked to see if her feet were
showing. I took in a mouthful of rich Syrian wine and struggled to
take my thoughts off the taut yet voluptuous shape that, however
faintly, was outlined by the thin silk of her robe.

'I wasn't aware,' I said, with a sudden shift of my attack, 'that
there was ever a Greek colony so far in the south.'

'Nor I,' said the Mistress. She popped a date into her mouth.
Her veil moved slightly as she chewed. I stared at the jewelled and
impossibly elegant fingers.

'Then it would much interest me,' I said, now feebly, 'to know
where you managed to learn such good Greek. The schools of
Alexandria, and of the cities of Egypt, do not, I believe, take
women as students.'

'Was it ever thus?' she asked. She reached out towards the dish
of sliced melon. 'Must the ladies of Alexandria remain unlearned
and even unlettered?'

'A long time ago,' I said, 'about two hundred years back, there
was a woman professor of mathematics there. She wrote interest-
ingly about the relative weight and density of liquids. But she was
murdered in a riot. Women since then have been barred from all
places of learning in Alexandria.'

'How perfectly barbarous!' said the Mistress, managing to sound almost scandalised. 'It was the view of Epicurus that both sexes could benefit equally from instruction. Do you not think our modern world so very corrupt?'

I'd almost jumped at the mention of Epicurus, and wanted to ask how she could even know the name. But there was a knock at the door. Martin came in, carrying a big papyrus roll. He bowed low before the Mistress and looked at her for further instructions.

'Do continue about your business, Martin,' she said. 'I was only just thinking how fortunate you must feel to have Alaric as an employer. His resourcefulness, yet gentility of manner, are surely the talk of your – what is the place called? – your Constantinople.'

Martin blushed. I looked down and scowled at my letters. I'd expected him at least to keep a little distance. He'd snivelled very promisingly halfway to Letopolis about sorcery. Then he'd decided she too was an agent of the Divine Providence. Now he'd doubtless have painted her toenails if asked.

'I think we'll soon be approaching Canopus,' I said with an attempt at blandness. 'If I'm not mistaken, the waters will now be high enough for us to take the canal into Alexandria.'

I leaned on the rail and looked morosely over the vast, shining expanse that the Delta had become. I hadn't been mistaken about the waters. They might not have risen that much more since the journey up river. But they had undeniably widened. Except for the endless series of those mounds, where the wretched natives huddled, we really might have been at sea. If I looked ahead hard enough, there was a blur on the horizon that I knew was the spit of land separating Nile from sea. Canopus was built where the two merged. We'd be there before the afternoon. From there, it would be the dozen or so miles to Alexandria.

There had been another storm out in the desert. So far down river, it had shown in little more than a brisker wind from the north and a haze high overhead that had dulled the glare of the sun. It was now clearing, and the sky was taking on the happy blue that it always had in the realms washed by the Mediterranean. I asked again what could have persuaded my own people to invade the chilly dump we'd made into England, rather than follow the Vandals and the Goths into that warm light.

I gripped hard on the rail as there was another great shudder. The boat stuck again. I'd gone up river from Bolbitine because its branch of the Nile was wider and better for speed. The Canopus branch we were taking back down would have been slower at the best of times. But with the river banks now under water, it was hard to keep in channel. Men ran to the left-hand side of the boat and pushed out with long poles to get us off the mud.

'No, My Lord, we're headed for Canopus,' the Captain had said, replying to my suggestion that the Bolbitine branch would be faster. 'The posts always go to Canopus. They have always gone to Canopus. Not the Viceroy himself can change the order of the posts.'

I'd been in no position to pull rank. Having no documents with me, the Captain had at first refused to take us on board at Letopolis. It was only when the Mistress intervened that he'd caved in. Now, she was queening it in the best cabin, with the whole crew to do her bidding. She'd even had the boat stop to take in more fruit and fresh bread for her. Doubtless, she could have had us diverted down the Bolbitine branch. But that would have meant putting myself still more in her debt.

Did the extra day matter? Probably not. Even going at full tilt down to Bolbitine, I had little enough chance of outrunning the news. I'd now be well behind it. I was sick of the Nile, and my heart rose at every thought of seeing the Mediterranean again. At the same time, I dreaded the return to Alexandria. As in everything else, Greek is a language rich in scornful epithets. *Dickhead, Fuckwit, Shit-for-Brains, Wanker* . . . You could fill half a papyrus roll with writing them all out. And I could imagine every one of them whispered about me behind my back.

From the moment Lucas had let his captain act start wearing thin, I'd been kicking myself. But I'd always had other matters to claim my active attention. There was trying to get away from Lucas and the Brotherhood. There was our shamble through the desert. There was sucking up to the Mistress all the way to Letopolis, where I then had the business I've described. Now, on the journey back, there'd been little else to do but dwell on how the ludicrous disaster – which needed no exaggeration – would appear in Alexandria. The public baths weren't a place men of my station frequented. But I'd heard enough on the streets of the ruthless mockery that began there and was sharpened there.

I'd gone out from Alexandria to deal with two highly contingent threats to my reputation. I was going back with my reputation in shreds. If the full story of my dealings had been put in the *Gazette* – if this had been followed by the whole packet of dirt on me Leontius had commissioned – the effect couldn't be worse than a plain telling of what I'd let happen to me during the past twelve days.

'I've just realised, looking at the date of your letters, why you're so eager to get back.'

I gave Martin a blank look. I'd supposed he was somewhere below, juicing dates for the Mistress or whatever.

He put his bag down and joined me in looking over the Nile. 'Tomorrow is Saturday,' he prompted. 'Saturday, 26th August,' he added.

I pulled my thoughts off the approaching horrors of Alexandria and tried to think what on earth the man could be getting at.

'Maximin's second birthday?' he said at length, a shade of disappointment in his voice.

Of course it was! I relaxed my grip on the rail and thought of the boy. How could it be just two years since Martin had brought him back to the Legation? Taking in all that had happened since, it seemed more like ten or even twenty years. But count back just two years, and we were in Constantinople, on our 'mission', from the Roman Church to gather readings and arguments for a refutation of heresy. That was before I met Phocas and was taken up by him, and before I made the leap – last of all in the City, if most glorious – from him to Heraclius. Yes, forget the vast drama in which I was the one visible and completely unwitting player: just two years ago, and I was an obscure visitor from the West.

What could have prompted Martin to take the little thing up from outside the church he never had been able to discuss rationally. Then again, I'd been shocked by my own behaviour. I'd barely drawn breath to insist the child be taken back and dumped where found than I was announcing his adoption. He'd been so small and defenceless – and so very beautiful.

So I'd adopted the boy and named him after the poor, dear Maximin – correction: *Saint* Maximin – who'd saved my life in Kent. His first birthday had been a joyous and even triumphant occasion. The Emperor himself had attended the festivities and presented him with a golden box for his toys. Not even having to put up with Priscus skulking round my palace and muttering hints about being regarded as an 'uncle', had spoiled the occasion. There was no doubt he'd be pleased to see me again in Alexandria. He was one person who'd run to me squealing with pleasure. He was the one patch of brightness to lighten my return. And I'd clean forgotten about his birthday. It was fortunate I hadn't had time yet to drink very much. It wouldn't do to shed tears in front of Martin. I gripped the rail again and looked at a point far out over the swirling waters.

'The way this journey's going,' I said, 'we'll be stuck in mud until his third birthday.'

There was a shrill cry through the wall of the cabin behind us. I looked up. It came again – a long, bubbling cry, now followed by silence. It was quite loud, especially in the general silence of the river. Some birds who'd been bobbing around on the waters now took off with an answering splash and were climbing fast into the sky.

'What in God's name was that?' I asked. I turned and looked at the smooth planking of the cabin wall.

'The Mistress!' said Martin.

Certainly, it was her cabin. Women can make the most peculiar noises, I'll grant. Give one an ivory comb, and she'll probably give every impression of going into labour. But this sounded more than a little distressed. We hurried along the deck and turned left to get to the entrance. The door was guarded by one of her huge blacks. Unarmed and almost naked, he practically hid the closed door with his bulk.

'Your Mistress,' I said, 'I need to see if all is well with her.'

If the man knew any Greek, he did a good job of not letting me know. He put up an arm to hold me back and opened his mouth in a snarl that showed all his teeth – very white and filed to points, they were. He flexed his hips. It was then I noticed the erection bulging through the skimpy white of his loincloth. I tried not to look at the spreading dark stain. I've never been much into that sort of heavy muscle; and the teeth and that web of tattoos on his shaven scalp were hardly a come-on. Then again, those gold nipple rings were well over this side of the exciting. But I remembered myself.

'Stay here,' I said to Martin. 'See if the door opens.' I ran quietly back along the deck to the stairway that led to the small upper deck where the Captain did his notional directing of the boat. As I'd expected, he was nowhere to be seen up there: he was probably down in the hold, praying again before his icon of the Virgin for deeper waters. Again as expected, the little window that threw light into the Mistress's cabin was shuttered. But there was a little hole in the wood I'd noticed the day before, and I'd been idly wondering if there was any chance of an unobserved look through it. Now, the chance was come, and so was the need. I got down on my knees and put my right eye to the hole.

At first, I saw nothing. What I heard, though, was a soft piping, as of some exotic flute. It was too low to be heard through the plank walls of the boat. But it was a low, throbbing sound. There was nothing about it I could recognise as tuneful. But its complex moaning was joined by the soft tapping of a drum. I strained harder to see anything at all through that little hole.

When I'd adjusted to the gloom, I had to pull back and rub my eye to make sure I was seeing straight. It was the Mistress. There could be no doubt of that. Still veiled, and still in her full robe, she stood in the centre of the cabin. She stood with each foot on the back of one of her maidservants. Naked, they lay face down on the floor. All were on the floor but one. Also naked, she was hung by her bound wrists from one of the overhead beams. With a terrified whimper, she twitched her feet, and the motion caused her whole body to swing gently round.

Red on black doesn't show well at the best of times, and the light was very poor. But the dark stains splashed all over the Mistress told me the truth about the gleam on the maidservant's body. It was as she stepped forward on to the third naked back that I saw the Mistress had a knife in her hand. It glinted dull in the lamp-light, and more blood dripped from it on to the spoiled whiteness of her robe.

There was a shuffling on the cabin floor as one of the prone women shifted position and held something up. The Mistress bent and took the cup. As she did so, the fluting ceased, though the drum continued its gentle tapping. I pressed my face closer to the hole and looked round for the musicians. They must have been directly below me, as I couldn't see either of them. The drumming continued a while longer without accompaniment. Then it too fell silent.

As if for half an age, the Mistress stood absolutely still in the silent gloom of her cabin. I think I saw a regular fluttering of her veil, as if she were quietly praying. The black bodies trembled and twitched all round her on the floor. Then she stretched full upright and raised the cup in both hands. She set it under the veil to her lips and drank. She tipped her head back as she drank and then drank again. As she did so, the drum and then the flute began again. Now, it was something still more complex and utterly alien. It was a while before the beat was firmly established. There was the dull sound of metal on wood as the Mistress relaxed and tossed the cup away. Now, she turned and – standing ever on the backs of those maidservants – began a slow wheeling dance. The steps were elaborate and sedate. The wet robe clung to her legs. The chief movement was in her arms and upper body. At every variation in the fluting and her step, there was a renewed moaning from the women on the floor, and another whimper from the bound woman.

The Mistress was certainly talking now. She spoke low and not in Greek. It was some language I'd never heard before. It sounded neither Egyptian, nor like the language of her maidservants. The words might have been a poem, or they might have been some ritual chant. Not understanding what she said, I couldn't tell. But the chilling, sinister tone was enough. The elegant coquette who'd lain in my own cabin, talking up the virtues of a diet of bread and fresh fruit, was a world removed from this bizarre and horrifying creature. The whole thing reminded me of something I'd read in one of the sicker Alexandrian poets.

Because they'd been so still, I hadn't noticed the male slaves before. Except the one on duty outside the room, they stood, also naked, against the one wall that had no fixtures. Gold rings trembled on the tip of each gigantic and unattended erection.

Forget the old Alexandrians. Forget even the wilder stuff I'd seen or read about the Old Faith. This was out of all experience. And, since I'd now accounted for the mistress and all her attendants, who could the musicians be?

'What can you see?' Martin hissed close behind me.

I jerked suddenly up and struck my head on the top of the window frame.

'Nothing,' I croaked. I tried to ignore the white flashes at the back of my eyes. I got up and wiped shaking hands on the back of my robe. 'It's just – it's just their religious observances. I – I feel ashamed to have intruded on them. I'm sure you wouldn't wish to repeat the intrusion.'

I led him back to the stairway down to the main deck. The Mistress was a foreigner, I told myself – and I'd known any number of Greeks who had an odd way of keeping order among their slaves. But it was probably for the best if Martin was kept away from that shuttered window.

The whole boat shook slightly and then turned free in the water. Sailors ran about again, pulling on ropes to let down the sails for some reason. There was another bump and we were still again.

'Martin,' I said, 'there are some letters I need you to put into the correct official form. If you could have them ready by the time we get to Canopus, I'd be grateful. And I feel a headache coming on. I think I'll retire to my cabin for a little rest. Do tell anyone who asks that I'm not to be disturbed.'

26

There was a time when Canopus was the main pleasure resort for Alexandrians of quality. The breeze it took straight off the sea made it so pleasant a change in the summer months from Alexandria. Long before then, I believe – back in the time of the native kings – it was a main trading port. With the building of Alexandria, that source of importance had quickly disappeared. But it had more than compensated with its shops and brothels and temples. It also drew benefit as the nearest exchange point, by land or water, between Alexandria and the Nile. Before its branch began to silt up, it was both the nearest and by far the most convenient exchange point.

Then, the canal dug by the Ptolemies to join the two cities had been kept clear at all times, and poets had sung of the flotillas of gay barges that, throughout the day and night, would pass and re-pass the silver thread of water. Canopus was now in much reduced circumstances. It had lost position to the more distant but generally more convenient Bolbitine. Its people had withdrawn to a walled centre. Outside the walls, the old pleasure gardens were given over to fortified monasteries or overgrown wasteland. The place survived as a satellite port for Alexandria, and because no one had ever thought to reorder the posts along the Nile.

Except when the floods came and raised the water level the old canal was choked with reeds and rubbish and the usual connection was now by sea or by the road I've already mentioned. But the floods had now come, and the docks at the Alexandrian end retained some of their ancient elegance. It couldn't be described any more as the best way of entering the city after a journey down the Nile. But if now used as warehouses, or divided into single rooms to house the poor, the palaces once built to stand close by the docks still impressed on first inspection. And it had, for me, the one advantage of privacy. I wanted to be back in my office, putting some kind of gloss on my adventures, before anyone noticed I was back.

As our barge rounded the last bend before the docks came in sight, I realised I was in for another disappointment. Not only had the news of my adventures raced ahead of me, but so had news even of my return. During the last few hundred yards of our approach, the mass of bodies that clustered round the landing place resolved itself into something like all the official and well-connected of Alexandria. I almost thought of joining the Mistress in the one covered place on the barge, and ordering the crew to take us straight past the docks into the Eastern Harbour. But then the cheering started. It began as a concerted buzz from the front of the crowd, then rippled back through the less important dignitaries, until there was, billowing across the closing distance of the water, a continuous roar of greetings and adoration.

'Put that box down,' I said to Martin without moving my lips. 'Get up here and look happy.' I'd already set my face into a smile and was nodding complacently back at the shining faces now clearly in sight.

'My darling Alaric, how glad I am to see you looking so well!' Our lips brushed as we kissed, and Priscus kept my hand to his chest as he stepped back a few inches. He was at his most convincing. The bystanders must have thought us the very dearest friends. 'But you must tell me the whole story once we're alone. What little I've picked up is absolutely shocking. Such rough and even impious behaviour to a person of your quality – it chills the blood.

'Oh,' he went on, answering my unvoiced question about the healing but still red gash across his forehead, 'I can't claim anything so dramatic as your own capture and escape. But the security of the Egyptian roads makes some of the places I've campaigned almost tranquil by comparison.

'And, no,' he added, now dropping his voice and leaning into another embrace, 'I didn't find it. I did learn much of value. But if I'd found what I went for, you can bet your life I'd not have arranged this homecoming for our impetuous little barbarian.' Priscus followed my glance at the armed guard that surrounded the two chairs that had obviously come from the Palace. He smiled.

'You must understand,' he said, 'that your safety is no longer something to be taken for granted, even in Alexandria. I'm afraid there can be no more casual wandering about the town. Besides' – again, he stretched forward and dropped his voice – 'there have been troubles while we were both away. There was nearly a riot yesterday in the Eastern Harbour. It was as much as the police guards could do to keep the grain fleet safe.'

'Hasn't it gone yet?' I asked. 'It should have been ten days at sea.' I smiled graciously at one of my Jewish agents. I'd scare him and his friends shitless when we were alone. For the moment, I smiled again and gave him my hand to kiss. There were a couple of the greasier landowners behind him. They made nothing like so good an effort as my Jew or Priscus as they congratulated me on my survival and return.

A flash of steel drew my attention sharp left. All this milling about had left a momentary gap in the crowd of well-wishers. Looking through it, I could see the armed cordon, and, behind this, the much, much larger crowd of the poor. Held back in one of the wider avenues that led to the dock, all stood silent and grim. One thing I'd learned early in my stay was that you don't let a crowd that size assemble in Alexandria. If it does, you break it up. I looked back at Priscus.

'Main forces are in the Harbour,' he explained shortly. 'And no, the fleet hasn't gone out yet.' He came close again for another embrace. 'If you can talk any sense at all into the wanker,' Priscus whispered into my ear, 'you'll have the entire Council in your debt. Nicetas has kept the grain fleet in harbour pending his further instructions. The effect it's having on the mob doesn't appear to concern him.'

We were interrupted by Martin, who pressed a message into my hand. In a firm though somewhat odd script, the Mistress thanked me for the journey down the Nile, and said she'd send for me when she felt ready to receive guests.

I bit back the angry reply I was about to make. I could see Priscus was trying to get an upside-down view of the note. I stood on tiptoe and looked over the heads of everyone else in the crowd. That might have been her chair going off towards the centre. Or she might have disappeared already into one of the smaller streets. I had offered her rooms in the Palace. Since she hadn't said no, I'd assumed her acceptance. Now she was gone. I hadn't thought she knew Alexandria at all – let alone well enough to have got herself lodged already. And she hadn't collected the emergency passport I'd had Martin draw up for her. She'd not get far without that. All told, though, it might be for the best if she weren't to be in the Palace. The various households there were pretty broad-minded. But her notions of slave management would have raised eyebrows anywhere.

'It's nothing,' I said, turning back to Priscus and waving Martin away. 'I need a bath and a change of clothes. Then, I think, we might both profit from dinner without an audience.'

'We are quite at one, my blond pot of love,' he replied as we closed for another embrace. 'You'll see that everyone is keen to be away before dark. The mobs are gathering all over the place by night. So far, it's just speeches. But you haven't seen what's going on in the Egyptian quarter. I'm *so* glad,' he breathed softly, 'that we can work together at last. We'll both have what we want – and be out of here before the place bubbles completely over.'

Though half gone now, the moon was still bright enough to show all the streets below. I stood on the roof of the Palace, looking down. Priscus hadn't been wrong. The streets were almost alive with people. With torches to make up whatever light the moon didn't supply, the crowds swarmed around the main squares. I couldn't make out the words of the leaders as they stood on the fountains or clung to the legs of statues. But I could hear the angry buzz. In Constantinople, the custom was for trouble to start in the Circus and then spill on to the streets. Here, it began in the streets.

Because the days were so hot, it made sense for protests to take place in the evening.

'Without actual provocation,' Macarius had told me earlier, 'it will be just gatherings and speeches. There is hardly ever serious rioting except in the spring.' He was probably right, I thought, still looking down. On the other hand, I knew that food supplies had barely ever been so short except in the spring. Nothing would happen tonight. It was too late. Priscus had told me of his meeting with the Police Secretary. There weren't the forces to disperse the crowds. But so long as they could be kept apart, nothing at all might happen. But rioting was something no person of quality in Alexandria ever wanted to see. Even when the city was new and still mostly settled by Greeks who hadn't yet had time to go rotten, the mob had been a fact of life. The reason the Ptolemies had built the Palace so close to the harbour was so they could make a quick getaway to Cyprus or Cyrene if the mob got out of hand – which it had been doing periodically ever since.

'You'll have to make it clear to her,' I said, turning back to Martin, 'that, whatever she says in private, she just can't go about the whole Palace making threats against the Emperor's Legate.'

'I think I've talked some sense into her,' Martin said uncertainly. His black eye shone clearly in the moonlight. 'I can promise she'll not embarrass you again with Priscus.' He tried to say something more, but trailed off and turned back to an inspection of the streets. A column of armed police was pushing its way between a dangerously large crowd in the Square of the Ptolemies. Divided in two, it might soon disperse of its own accord.

'It really is because she was so worried for the pair of us. You see, I did tell her we'd be away just a few days. When we didn't come back in the time I said, she grew worried. Then Priscus came back early, and he kept turning up at the nursery. Then news of our difficulties began coming through in Alexandria. You can't imagine the things Priscus said to her when she locked all the doors and kept Maximin under her own bed.'

'Let's drop the matter,' I sighed. Imagining what Priscus had said was something easily within my capacities. Back in

Constantinople, I'd made an agreement with Sergius to get Martin and his family plus Maximin shipped straight out in the event of my fall. There was money pledged to get them all the way to Rome, and even, if need presented itself, on to Ireland where Martin might still have a few relatives who recognised him. Priscus was now in Alexandria, where I'd never thought it necessary to make any plans at all.

'I'm told Nicetas is under absolute orders now from Heraclius to get the grain fleet under sail,' I said with a nod at the far side of the roof. At least from the Harbour side of the Palace, the streets were dark. 'I'll speak to the Captain tomorrow about it sailing at night. I think we can still get it out safely if we start the Christmas distribution early and call it something else. But the longer it sits down there stuffed with grain people here think is better directed at their own bellies, the harder everything becomes.'

I looked round at the soft pad of feet on pavement. It was the nephew or son of one of my Jews. Demonstrations or none, my lamp in the inspection room had worked its usual magic. I'd known someone would come, but hadn't expected a reply till morning. I took his knife and opened the letter.

'I look forward to seeing Isaac at the time appointed,' I said at last. 'Will you be staying here till morning?' He wouldn't. He always looked more Greek than Jewish. Dressed as he was now, no one on the streets would have given him a second look. And that was a big knife. I was surprised he'd been let in with it. Still, Jews always find a way. I shrugged and wished him safe passage back to the Jewish quarter. Even if his kinsman didn't, he deserved some courtesy.

'Leontius wasn't made bankrupt after all,' I said to Martin. There was no point going beyond the basics. But he was looking interested, and it took our minds off Sveta and what she'd said to and about Priscus. 'That draft he was expecting from non-Imperial territory across the Red Sea came through early just after we'd left. Given that some of his larger creditors have refused payment, it's enough to settle all outstanding debts.'

Martin didn't ask about the oddity of refusing payment from a solvent debtor's estate – not that I could have answered him: it made damn-all sense to me. He did ask about the deal I'd made with the Mayor of Letopolis. But since there were two possible answers to that one, and he'd not have understood either, I looked back over Alexandria to Lake Mareotis and the dark but horrid mysteries of Egypt that lay beyond.

'I've decided,' I said, rolling the letter up and putting it under my arm, 'not to bother with an enquiry. The Brotherhood, we've every reason to suppose, has agents throughout the whole government. If I order an investigation into who leaked our travel plans, it will only rumble on for months. Some low clerk might be sacrificed for Nicetas to burn to death. But we'll never get to the bottom of things. This being so, we might as well not bother even going through the motions.'

Martin nodded.

I continued looking into the darkness of Egypt. I'd had a lucky escape – all told, a *very* lucky escape. Lucas and his friends, I had no doubt, would haunt my dreams for years to come. But they were somewhere far out in Egypt, and I was back in the safety of Alexandria. The less I brought myself to their attention, the better it would be for me and mine.

'One useful outcome of dinner with Priscus,' I continued – and this was agreed after the guards had removed Sveta – 'is that he'll do his best to help get Nicetas to seal those warrants. Now Leontius is out of the way, the landowners have no convenient single voice for their opposition. With the warrants sealed, we can set the surveyors and lawyers to work. All that in motion, we can start preparing a return to Constantinople. The various deals I've made are safe enough in the hands of my agents.'

'God be praised!' said Martin.

All through my own inspection of where Egypt began, I don't think he'd taken his own eyes off those swirling, moderately angry processions of torches down in the main streets. I leaned forward over the rail and looked hard right. I could see the southern fringes of the Egyptian quarter. There was some vague light coming off there. For the moment, however, the protests seemed to be a purely Greek matter.

Things might be better, I told myself. They might also easily be worse.

27

'After Rome, Constantinople and Jerusalem, we have the biggest collection of relics in the whole Empire. They took over a century to catalogue, and the supplements fill two shelves in my library. But if we have never heard of such an object, belief in it is surely proof of its existence.'

Spoken like a true Father of the Church! I thought as the Patriarch wittered on about the piss pot. Come tomorrow's Sunday service, I had no doubt there'd be a good half-dozen of the things on sale, each with its crowd of attested cures of the blind and the lame. Two of them, I was equally sure, would be snapped up by Nicetas. No – if he carried on crossing himself and exclaiming like this, he'd buy the lot, and believe all the miracles.

But I'd thought too soon. The Patriarch had now changed tone, and was sounding horribly like one of the senior clerics in Rome. With the provenance criteria he was setting out, you'd have had trouble authenticating the True Cross in Jerusalem. If only the Church had thought of these back in the early days of establishment, the Faith might not have become such a joke. Stated now, they were a wretched inconvenience. If I'd supposed I could pass off any old piss pot and get myself out of this mess, I'd have to suppose again.

The Viceroy's Council was reaching the end of its meeting. I'd just finished my report, thereby putting flesh on the skeleton of lies Priscus had called into being for me. Now, a word of advice, my Dear Reader – and I speak with greater authority today than I'd had back then in Alexandria – there is much occasionally to be said for the full truth; and you should, as often as possible, keep to it. When that is not possible, however, you should lie while keeping as close to the truth as you can. A lie appears always to best effect against a background of truth.

I confirmed that I'd travelled south, that I'd fallen into the hands of pirates in the services of a seditious conspiracy, that I'd been carried out into the desert, from where I'd escaped and made my way to Letopolis. All perfectly true, you'll agree. All that was missing was the connecting thread of a desire to get my hands on those various documents that Leontius had possessed at his death. Oh, and since she'd now vanished, the Mistress too was missing from the account, together with my less than glorious last meeting in the desert with the Brotherhood.

Added was some romance about my attempt – successful, by the way – to throw the Brotherhood off the trail of the first chamber pot of Our Lord and Saviour. The idea had come to me, I implied without actually stating, in a vision sent by Saint Mark himself. Anyone with an ounce of common sense would have rejected this new connecting thread out of hand. For minds nurtured, though, on the lives of the desert saints, it managed just the right note. Nicetas believed me. The Patriarch believed me. Whatever they might prefer to think, or might suspect, the landowners had joined in the chorus of holy praise. If anyone in the public baths dared say otherwise, he really could go fuck himself.

'Whatever the case, we must have it,' Priscus struck up. 'We can't have a relic of such holy importance in the hands of this wog conspiracy.' Someone nodded and stroked the heavy gold crucifix about his neck. Nicetas looked set to start babbling nonsense again. But Priscus wasn't paying attention.

'We must have it,' he repeated, now looking down. 'Isn't that so, my little Margarita?' He pulled the cat towards him and buried his face in the horrid thing's fur.

'No, my sweet pretty,' he went on, 'Daddy can't have it in wog hands, can he? It's too good for unholy trash like that. It's for him – all for him so he can fuck the Persians over.' I thought Priscus would drift off into a reverie of smiting in the Service of the Lord. Instead, he picked up the cat and held it out before him at arm's length. 'But what is Daddy doing?' he asked in a tone of shocked horror. 'Pussy's had no lunchy munchie yet. Oh, wicked, neglectful Daddy!'

Setting the cat down again, Priscus reached under the table and pulled up a small lead box. Opening it carefully, he took out a mouse. There was a gasp further down the Council table. The Patriarch, sitting beside Nicetas, stood suddenly up. Quite understandable, this – mice can be a great embarrassment if you never wash and insist on going round in this climate wrapped in about fifty yards of heavy cloth. But Priscus had the creature firm in his grasp. Holding it in his right hand by the tail, he pinched a back leg hard between his left forefinger and thumb. The mouse must have dragged itself barely nine inches over the table before the cat was upon it. There was the usual dabbing and biting while Priscus cooed on his encouragement. As if frozen, the rest of the Council looked on in silence.

'If it may please Your Imperial Highness,' I said, when the cat had finished walking up and down the table, a mouse tail hanging from its mouth, 'now that the main business of the meeting is over, there is the matter of the grain fleet that awaits your permission to leave for Constantinople. His Magnificence the Commander of the East and I have taken the liberty of discussing this at some length. We defer absolutely to your greater knowledge of circumstances in Alexandria. But it does seem to us that the continued presence, down in the Harbour, of the fleet is an excuse for disorder among the lower classes.'

'Indeed,' Priscus said, looking up from an embrace of his now purring cat. Except for the spot of blood on the whiteness of his painted face, he might once again have been gracing the Imperial Council back home. 'I must concur with His Magnificence the Imperial Legate. I too have little knowledge of the particular circumstances here. But I do have much experience of city disturbances. Given the evident paucity of forces in Alexandria—'

'But Priscus,' Nicetas broke in, as moved by this suave formality as by my own, 'you claim ill of yourself by speaking so low of your abilities. Though your right to sit in this Council is of some ambiguity, it would be a crime against the good of the Empire if we were to do other than take advantage of your wisdom and experience. Isn't that so?'

There was a buzz of agreement through the room as Nicetas threw the discussion open. As it faded away, the Trade Commissioner coughed and tapped significantly on the pile of documents he'd been fidgeting with all through our discussion of the piss pot and associated matters. The Master of the Works got as far as opening his mouth to speak. But this was it. Even before a couple of monks were shown in for Nicetas, one with a stack of icons, the other with a bandage, it was plain the meeting had broken down into a series of conversations.

Slumped at my desk, I stared blearily up at Martin and Macarius. The padded door of the office was shut, all the slaves on its other side. Macarius looked less than his usually composed self. Martin shuffled nervously. I took a sip of the second lot of wine I'd had sent in and grimaced. I put the cup straight down. Not a big one, I reflected, but another annoyance, this, to add to all the others. I screwed my eyes shut and opened them. I sat up and spread my hands on the cool wooden surface.

'Well, Martin,' I asked, 'any messages from God about this? The Patriarch knows nothing. How about you?'

'If I might be so bold,' Macarius answered for him, 'did the Lord Priscus receive *any* guidance from the Monks of Saint Antony? Their desert monastery is of the highest repute.'

'He did,' I snapped. 'He was granted forgiveness for all his sins – and a confession of those would explain why he was away almost as long as we were. Otherwise, he was told to follow "the Light from the West". Sadly, he took that as another invitation to get me on the job.'

I looked at the bronze bust of Alexander my Jewish agents had hurriedly sent over after I'd finished shouting at them about their negligent near breach of confidence. It was a pretty object, and there was every reason to believe the claims that it was made by Lysippus himself as the draft of one of his full statues. If it was genuine – and it probably was: a dealer had confirmed it from the casting method – it would be the most valuable single object I owned. If I'd been asked to give that up in exchange for the genuine piss pot of Christ, I'd have had to think hard. Anything else, though, I'd gladly have given up at that moment.

'We are required,' I said, pulling myself into a more positive mood, 'to find a relic that nobody appears to have known about before this year, and that therefore may not exist. If it does exist, nobody appears to have seen it or to know where it is. However, both Priscus and the Brotherhood believe that I am able to find it, and have been competing in their own ways to secure my assistance. Priscus has now won, and I am not able to doubt that giving him the first chamber pot of Jesus Christ would serve every interest with which we are connected.

'Consider' – getting into my stride, I held up one finger as I made each point – 'whatever good it may do Priscus against the Persians, the thing can do the Empire endless harm if the Brotherhood gets to it first. At the least, we'll never get the redistribution law implemented if the people can be brought over to back the landowners. If we get it first, on the other hand, the Brotherhood will have suffered a moral defeat, and our own credit will go through the roof. In return, I already have that promise of help from Priscus. He's even said he'll put up with having Sveta in the room when he visits Maximin.'

I might have added that I did owe Priscus something for having spread just the right mix of vague and solid untruth for me to complete. But I'd said enough. What I had now to do was find something that looked like a piss pot and that I could squeeze through those bastard provenance rules.

'Macarius,' I said, sniffing again at my cup, 'do make sure the next wine you have sent in here is imported. I'm not too drunk to notice the taste of river mud in this stuff.'

Macarius bowed stiffly and turned to leave the room. I raised my hand to keep him. I had work for him yet.

But first – 'Martin, as you often used to tell your students, when there's no short cut to be had, you start at the beginning. I want you to draw up and seal a request from me to the Patriarch, giving you unlimited access to every collection of relics in Alexandria. You may care to begin with looking through the catalogue. His Holiness may insist that our relic isn't mentioned there. I'll believe those words more when I've heard them from you. In any event, please arrange for a physical inspection of *everything*. A catalogue that size is unlikely to be wholly accurate. Alexandrian scholarship isn't what it was, and our relic may turn out to be hanging beside the altar of the Patriarch's own chapel.'

Martin nodded, an exalted look coming over his face. Able to pass days and days, going from one object of the utmost holiness to another – if this didn't lift the burden of his sins, I could see him thinking, nothing would. Good luck to him, I thought. For myself, I could find better uses for time than looking at several thousand pickled body parts and bloodstained implements of torture.

'Macarius,' I said, taking up a letter I'd written in my own hand early that morning, 'I want you to deliver this in person.'

He looked at the tag on the sealed boards enclosing the papyrus and raised his eyebrows.

'Deliver it in person,' I repeated, 'and wait for a reply.'

As I stood up, there was a knock on the door.

'The Lord Priscus begs a moment of your time,' the secretary called out, omitting his bow.

As he stood away from the door, Priscus walked in. He'd left his cat behind this time, and had put on a robe of shimmering orange silk. His eyes flickered briefly over Martin and Macarius. I nodded at them. As the door closed behind them, Priscus threw himself into the chair just in front of my desk and grabbed at the wine jug.

'You know, my dear boy,' he sighed, 'until I actually met Nicetas, I could never work out how Heraclius won the race from Carthage to Constantinople and became Emperor. Mind you, the quality of everyone else in the government here leaves much to be desired. I'm astonished the wogs didn't kick us out centuries ago.

'It may have been the Brotherhood,' he conceded, noticing the look I gave the gash on his forehead. Now he'd taken off the lead paint and replaced it with a green wash to set off the robe, the gash showed again. 'Bear in mind that I only heard of this movement when I got back to Alexandria. But I do think it was bandits. I kept one of them back for questioning. Despite my very best endeavours' – he smiled, giving his face a less lugubrious appearance – 'I was unable to persuade the piece of filth to say a word of Greek. If it was the Brotherhood that waylaid me, it might have been to hold me to ransom as well. But as we both know, only you can lead anyone to the piss pot.

'And this brings me to the main subject in hand. What progress can you report?' He sniffed at my explanation of what I'd set for Martin. 'The little slut in the Egyptian quarter referred to a place in Egypt,' he reminded me.

'Until we know which place,' I said emolliently, 'we search for leads in Alexandria. You know perfectly well now that Egypt is rather large. When you came in, I was about to begin my own search. Bearing in mind its nature, it isn't something I thought suitable for Martin or anyone else outside the governing class. Since you're here, though, it might be something for us to share.'

'I'd be delighted to assist,' he said. He sniffed at the wine. 'You know,' he added thoughtfully, 'this stuff smells and tastes just like a poison I've often used called Tittymilk of Hera. Shall I tell you what it does?' He sat watching my face change colour several times, then laughed.

'Oh, my dearest, darling Alaric,' he said, dabbing at his eyes, 'if it really were Tittymilk of Hera, we'd both be twitching on the floor. I just couldn't resist the look on your face. Welcome to the grown-up world where every cup and every corner is suspect, and where every bed is one in which you might never wake. Now, let's have another cup of this doubtful but probably not deadly vintage, and then proceed with the search you mentioned.'

28

With a very correct bow to me and to the seal, the Keeper of the Archive handed me back the original of my commission from Heraclius.

'My Lords will forgive the long wait,' he said apologetically, 'but this is our second most restricted file. Copies must be taken of all application documents.'

'It's beastly hot down here,' Priscus complained as the man went back into his office to fuss with a box of lead seals. He took up a sheet of papyrus and fanned himself. 'Do I guess right that the heating is on – at this time of year, and in Alexandria?'

'The archives don't just cover the ground floor of the Palace,' I answered. 'There's also a labyrinth of rooms in the basement underneath. I've never been down there, but I understand they reach under the whole of the central gardens. There's special heating all year to keep off any damp from the cisterns.'

Priscus grunted and pulled at the gold threads to loosen his collar. The green wash was beginning to migrate on to his chest. I explained again about the effect of damp on papyrus, and that it was through the records contained here that Egypt had, since the first Ptolemy, been governed often against the settled will of the natives, but always unshakeably – and always could be, despite the best efforts of fools like Nicetas.

'I must ask My Lord,' said the Keeper, coming back from his office, this time with the file, 'not to go to your usual seat in the colonnade. This file can only be taken into the glazed viewing room, and I regret to say that I must observe you at all times. I must also insist on your leaving all writing materials with me.'

'So how did you discover this?' asked Priscus as we took our seats in the glass box.

'I came across references to it while looking up something else,' I answered. 'As you know, they fled to Egypt after the birth. Like most Jewish immigrants, they ended up in Alexandria. They were then caught up in the arrests that followed the uncovering of yet another Jewish sedition.' I positioned the overhead mirror to shine more light on to the table. There was adequate lighting, but only from a row of lamps placed in holders on the outside walls of the box. Beyond these, the Keeper watched us very carefully. 'I had been intending to have a look at the arrest file. You can see, though, the trouble involved. And I didn't feel there'd be much here of interest for an idle viewing.

'The official report of the Trial and Crucifixion, of course, *would* be interesting. But Constantine was in Italy when he established the Faith, and he was able to lift these records from the Jewish War section of the archives in Rome. I'm told he then destroyed them.' I untied the boards of the file and spread the pages on to the table.

'But this is the original document?' Priscus asked with a catch of his breath.

'No,' I said. I pointed to the wording at the head of each page. 'Constantine got his hands on this one as well. But he wasn't personally in Alexandria, and the archivists were able to insist on the normal practice of taking a full copy. I suppose the compromise he had to make was restricted access for ever.' Hands shaking, Priscus lifted one of the pages close to his face and read. For the first time, I noticed that, like me, he read silently and without moving his lips. I followed his rapid scanning of this page, and then of another.

'Nothing here,' I said, 'to shock the most scrupulous orthodoxy. Nothing here, indeed, to shock anyone – except those inclined to doubt whether Christ existed. And there aren't many of those, now the schools in Athens have all been closed down. Still, I can see why the file is restricted. If the heretics can twist any meaning they like into the Plain Word of Scripture, there's no telling what they might do with a set of semi-literate police reports.'

Yes, I know, irony on these matters could be unwise, even with Priscus. But the irony was lost on him. In his position, I wouldn't just doubt if there was a God: I'd be desperately hoping there wasn't one. With what he'd been up to these past forty-odd years, there'd be a whole section of the Lake of Black Fire cordoned off and waiting. Yet here he was, desperate to lay hands on the smallest contact with the Prince of Peace.

'It's not an original,' he muttered, 'but I do know the rules. Anything that has touched anything holy becomes holy itself.'

It would have been easy to agree with him. With this in his hands, he might have been persuaded to forget the piss pot and bugger off to Syria. There, he could have tied the file to his lance and ridden straight – I could hope – to his death. But if not the Patriarch himself, there was any number of experts to put him right on this one.

'Afraid not quite, Priscus,' I said. 'If you can prove beyond reasonable doubt that Joseph touched the original statement when signing it, and that the original document was brought into contact with the copy by an authorised person, you'd have one of the most powerful relics there can be in your hand. But, you see, there's no evidence that Joseph knew any Greek or was able to sign his own name. He'd have made the statement in Aramaic, and then assented to it without touching the written translation. Beyond that, the clerks used for the copy back in the time of Constantine wouldn't have been Christians, let alone ordained; and the chancery practice, as I've seen it here, is for one clerk to read and another to copy. Beyond saying it's a first copy, this has no more potency as a relic than your own copy of the Scriptures.

'Oh' – I pointed at the purple seal at the foot of each page – 'I think this means that nothing can be taken away except by the Emperor in person, and then with the correct requisition order witnessed by a Patriarch. There's an autograph letter of Saint Paul,' I explained, 'in Constantinople with something very like that seal.'

I moved to a brief commentary on why the document authorising Joseph's release from custody might have been copied in two hands, each separated in style by about fifty years. When you've spent as much time as I already had in libraries and archives, these are points you pick up and use as clues to a fuller understanding. But Priscus wasn't listening.

'I can't find the Inventory of Goods,' he said. We rearranged all the pages on the table and turned them over one at a time, to see if what we wanted had been copied on the reverse. But Priscus was right – no inventory.

'Perhaps the Holy Family was too poor to make any inventory worth the effort,' I suggested. 'Joseph must have come here with his wife and the three children, and precious little else.'

'Doesn't matter,' Priscus insisted. 'When I ran the Treason Police under Phocas, we *always* took an inventory. If it's just their clothes, even the poor have something worth confiscating.' He looked up wistfully as he spoke of his days as Torturer-Judge Extraordinary when his father-in-law was Emperor.

'Well, fancy that!' I said, changing the subject. Having been very nearly one of his victims, my own recollection of the dungeons under the Ministry were less rosy. I held up a half sheet of papyrus. It had stuck itself to the underside of one of the denunciation letters, and had stayed there during our first sort through of the pages. Now, it had suddenly dropped free on to the desk. It was dated four years after the closing of the case. The Child should then have been about seven.

'It's a request from Joseph for a passport to settle in Soteropolis. There had been a plague there,' I summarised, squinting at the writing too small for Priscus to follow in the light we had now the windows were beginning to steam up. 'The Jewish community was in need of skilled craftsmen, and was offering to guarantee his support for the first year. The request was refused, but upheld on appeal.'

'Is Soteropolis close by the Pyramids?' Priscus asked. He was all eagerness again. It was obvious what he had in mind.

With a stab of annoyance, I told myself I should have kept my mouth shut.

'It's five, maybe ten miles distant,' I said, trying to sound casual. 'Rather, it may have been, as the city no longer exists, and there is some doubt as to its location. The most certain guess I can make is that the place is somewhere between the Pyramids and Letopolis – where Leontius had his estate.' I hesitated, then explained something of my plans regarding the excavation of the Library's reserve stock.

'Come now, Priscus,' I sighed as he gave me another of his suspicious looks. 'You must accept that, until our agreement of yesterday evening, I hadn't the faintest interest in your piss pot. Until you rolled up here, I really hadn't even heard of the thing.'

'But Soteropolis is surely where we look,' he insisted.

'Perhaps it is,' I agreed; a denial would only have made him worse. 'But we still need more information than we have. Look, Soteropolis may not have been very big. But imagine that Alexandria should one day be in ruins. Imagine even that part of it fell into the sea. It would be very hard for anyone in the future to identify any of the main places.

'Soteropolis was continuously occupied for three hundred years after the Holy Family must have left. It can't ever have had that many Christians. The Jews would have had no reason to preserve any objects left behind by the family of what they regarded as a renegade and traitor. Going up there now with what little we have, we'd need a miracle before we knew exactly where to dig.'

'I would remind you, my dear,' Priscus said with one of his thin smiles, 'that we have had a miracle – two, if you consider what's turned up in this file. And you won't have forgotten the clear directions that slut gave you.'

'They weren't that clear,' I said, emollient again. I fought to suppress that renewed uneasy feeling: you don't let the contents of your mind be arranged on the basis of coincidences. 'But if you want to go off looking for Soteropolis, you're welcome to the workmen I've commandeered. I'll join you there in due course.'

'No good,' he said. 'It's you who found this file, and you who found the hidden sheet about Soteropolis. You were the one the slut was talking to. You are the one who must go looking, because you are the one chosen to find.'

'Priscus,' I said, gathering the pages back into the file, 'let's discuss this again when I've finished with whatever leads I can find here in Alexandria.' I did my best to sound as annoyingly neutral as I normally would have been. A little thought was stirring in my mind. Finding that reference to Soteropolis and then blurting it out might not have been such rotten luck after all.

'For the moment, I'm hungry,' I added. 'And I don't know about you, but I'm ready to melt in this box. It can't be much cooler than the oven you have in mind for Martin and his family.'

'One step closer,' Priscus said defiantly as we were finally signed out of the archives.

'A quarter step, if that,' I replied. Perhaps five whole steps, I thought.

29

I was free. Rather, Priscus had gone off to play with his cat, and there was no immediate claim on my time. I swam for a while in the pool set behind some trees in the Palace gardens. Because it was looking increasingly likely that there'd be another trip into Egypt, I decided to have the canopy taken off so the sun could get at me. Afterwards, I lay in the sun, drowsing while the clerks read to me.

I'd not been away that long from Alexandria. But the administrative mill I'd constructed had continued in my absence to grind out reports and correspondence. There was now a mountain of stuff to be processed. There were the usual survey abstracts, plus all the other matters that had been insensibly diverted to my attention the moment it was realised that I was the only person around able to get Nicetas to listen to anything at all and take any action at all. It didn't help that the posts were in from Constantinople again, and there was a great stack of newsletters and official bulletins to hold back or to let through censored.

Birds twittered in the trees, and slaves rubbed oil on me as often as I shifted position. It was something of the same delicious feeling as when I took just the right dose of opium. The only difference was that the sun was giving me a slight stiffy. I decided it wouldn't do to attend to this with so many relative strangers looking on. I would contain myself until the evening. Then, I'd look to Luella for the usual relief.

'Cut out all reference to the Jewish disturbances in Antioch,' I said lazily as the clerk who was reading finished one of the newsletters. 'Fill up the gap by transferring the story from Ravenna of the stolen jewels and their miraculous return.'

The clerk made a note on one of his waxed tablets. He bowed and took up another newsletter.

The news was generally disastrous. There was nothing on the Persian front. It seemed Priscus had been right about the zone of starvation he'd inflicted on the provincials of Cappadocia; that would keep things quiet until the spring. But it was bad on every other front. Rome was under siege again by the Lombards. There could be no help from the Exarch, as Ravenna was also blockaded by land. The Danubian provinces were effectively lost to the Avars; and the Slavs had now taken everything north of Corinth except Athens. There was renewed piracy in the whole Mediterranean. Communications with Carthage were intermittent, and about a third of the taxable land over which it ruled had been definitely written off as claimed by the desert.

In Constantinople, Heraclius had suspended servicing of the Imperial debt, and the banks were failing one after the other. Money just couldn't be had at the legal rate of interest, and property in even the best parts of the City was going at eighteen months' purchase. In a private letter, my banker, the Jew Baruch, was recommending against buying at any price; he doubted if the falls had reached anything like their bottom, and doubted also if there'd be any meaningful recovery in the next five years. He'd taken the liberty, he explained further, of calling in all the non-political loans I'd made, and would keep the money in plate and coin pending my own instructions.

The one patch of brightness in these narratives was that pirates had landed between Ephesus and Halicarnassus and had devastated two of the smaller cities. But this was an area where my land reforms had been in place for nearly two years. Without any help from the authorities – not that any was available – the locals had taken up arms and routed the pirates. They'd then burned the prisoners alive at a great feast in which they'd also settled a mass of outstanding boundary disputes without reference to the courts. Back in Constantinople, several members of the Council had complained about a 'dangerous spirit of independence among the people' – as if that weren't the intention of the reforms. Happily,

Sergius had flattened their objections with a threat of excommunication, and had got Heraclius to issue what coins he could for the whole of Asia to celebrate the victory.

It was all important – the financial news particularly so: I'd have my Jews in around the midnight hour to discuss its impact on the Alexandrian markets. But it all seemed rather distant as I lay by the pool squinting up at the sun. Uppermost in my thoughts was what to do about the piss pot. This was now the key to everything. Priscus was right: I'd have to do something about Soteropolis. It had been my intention to get the new law implemented, and then go up river with my five hundred diggers. It was plain, however, that I'd never get Nicetas to act, nor the landowners to back down, until we had the piss pot.

Whether and where it might be in Soteropolis, I was increasingly convinced, didn't matter so much as I'd made out to Priscus. The provenance rules applied only to whatever Martin turned up here in Alexandria. In Soteropolis, I'd be in control of all appearances. My first training in Church affairs had been far off in Canterbury, where my employer, Maximin, had taught me the ways of pious fraud. Our 'miracles', had worked there to bring the natives over to the True Faith. I was sure I could produce something really impressive in Soteropolis. We'd dig for a few days here and there. My object, of course, would be the reserve stock. But it wouldn't be hard to plant something in those sands at night for uncovering by day. Let me round up a dozen or so of those desert hermits. Let me spike the filth they ate with hashish or with opium – or just get them singing Hallelujahs together for a day – and they'd swear to any miracle I cared to arrange at the uncovering.

We could arrive in triumph back in Alexandria. The Patriarch would then lay on the biggest service in living memory. Priscus could bugger off in a fog of holiness. I'd get everything I wanted, and those beastly landowners could kiss my feet in gratitude for what I'd left in their possession.

Naturally, after my last trip into Egypt, security would be an issue. But that I could leave to Priscus. He needed me to find the relic. It would never do to have me other than back safely in

Alexandria with him afterwards. His interests being calculated, keeping Lucas and Company away from me in Soteropolis was well within his competence.

Things weren't turning out that badly, I thought. There may be no such thing as miracles. Even so, there are happy circumstances that, rightly used, can bring on happy outcomes. Finding that reference to Soteropolis – and with Priscus looking on – might have been one such happy circumstance. Having him around was never good news. On this occasion, though, his arrival might have complicated matters, but might well have become a means of breaking the stalemate over the land law.

I did think of sending straight off and telling him to get ready for a trip to Soteropolis. But no – this had to be done properly. If there was to be a miraculous finding of the piss pot, he'd have to be among those deceived. That required a continued show of reluctance to leave Alexandria until I'd done with following every other lead. I'd string him along until the flood waters were at their height, and until I'd got more out of Hermogenes about the probable location of Soteropolis and the reserve stock. By the time I gave in to his nagging, he'd be ready to believe anything, and disinclined to suspect I was ready to feed it to him.

I thought of the Mistress – where was she? It was over a day now since she'd vanished from the canal docks. It was surely time for the message she'd suggested would be sent. She'd come down the Nile with minimal baggage. She couldn't have brought much cash with her. She evidently knew nothing of Alexandria, and I doubted she had any relationship with the bankers. Whatever independence she'd shown in the wilds of Egypt, she was now on my territory. If she wanted to go about as a grand lady, she'd surely have need of at least a few letters from me. Once his other business was arranged, I'd send Macarius off on a search. If anyone could find her, it was him.

I rolled over on my stomach. Thinking of the Mistress had brought on a very proud stiffy, and those clerks were still droning on beside me. A quick suck from one of the slaves was wholly out of the question. I tried to redirect myself from thoughts of those naked black bodies in her cabin and what she might look like under that veil.

'The wife of My Lord's secretary approaches,' one of the clerks sang out, breaking his colleague's flow of grain inventories. I sat up and shaded my eyes. Sveta it was, crunching loud on the gravel path, a slave holding a parasol to keep her milky skin from dropping off in the sun. Beside her, Maximin was skipping happily along, a bunch of flowers in his hand.

'Get me dressed,' I muttered to the slaves. It was time to do *something* for his birthday. 'And bring wine and a dish of honeyed figs.' I looked again at Sveta. 'Make that two dishes,' I added.

30

It wouldn't have been hard, but the Egyptian quarter by day was decidedly less forbidding than by night. It was still a sprawl of mostly falling-down slums. Here and there, though, you could see properties that wouldn't have been out of place in the smarter parts of the Greek centre. I could see now that the potty man had been right. The Egyptian quarter had a decidedly alien feel about it. Even so, there was a fair bit of money this side of the Wall.

There was a stiff breeze coming in from the south. Though nothing could wholly take off the smell I'd now come across all through the Delta – of Egyptians huddled together without means of washing, or inclination to wash – I didn't need to be so prodigal with my essence of roses. All round me, there was a sound of banging and shouting as the Egyptians went about their business. As in the centre, the streets were crowded. The guards surrounded my chair, swords drawn as they pushed our way through.

'Oh, the care is for you, my dear boy,' Priscus had said the day before as I settled myself for the first time into the armoured chair. 'I've never been one for bodyguards myself. As you know, if there are enemies to be killed, I've always believed in doing it myself.'

I hadn't bothered so far myself with guards. Even in Constantinople, after word had got round that I was the one behind cutting the bread distribution, I'd never done more than go about the streets with my sword on show and one of my larger slaves for support. Now, as I looked down from the chair at the sea of jabbering, slightly yellow faces, I was glad of the dozen guards. I was still more glad that half of them were Slavonic mercenaries. They were roughly my size and colouring. And if I paid close enough attention, I could just understand what they were saying to each other.

'Sir,' their officer said in the rough Latin still used in some units of the Army, 'can I suggest a detour?' He pointed at the narrowing street ahead. 'I don't like the look of those high buildings. They're ambush territory.'

'We'll have to risk it,' I said. I looked again at the directions Macarius had given me. I agreed those dark, upper windows looked dodgy. A good hail of stones from up there, and we'd be hard put to fight off a determined attack from the ground. But I also knew we'd be lost in a moment once we moved off the path laid down for us. Macarius knew these people and their part of the town. I'd have to trust his judgement of where was and wasn't safe. I drew my own sword and laid it on the table built into the carrying chair. It had a reassuring look as it glittered in the sunlight that streamed down past the canopy over my head.

'My Lord is earlier than expected,' the Deacon said apologetically as the courtyard gate swung shut behind us. With two inches of wood now to muffle the sound, I could barely hear the rush and bustle of the street outside.

I nodded and stepped down from the chair. The Deacon and his secretary bowed low before me. Priests and monks scurried about their business under the colonnade. After the rising uneasiness out in the streets, it was pleasantly quiet and familiar. Except the whispered language around me wasn't Greek or Latin, I might have been within one of the larger Church buildings anywhere in the Empire.

'If My Lord would come this way,' he added, motioning towards a door that led in from the colonnade.

At first, all was dark within. I bowed instinctively to avoid knocking my head on the lintel. As my eyes adjusted, I could see that, after the first two rooms, we were in a longish corridor. It must have run the entire length of the church. Again, it was all much as I'd expected. I really might have been in one of the middling churches in Constantinople. The only difference was that, mingled with the incense was the smell of something foul. It was the sort of thing you came across in hospitals or prisons.

A few yards more and I found out the cause of the smell. About halfway down the corridor, just before an icon of Saint Antony of the Desert, there was a pool of vomit. I could now see quite well in the gloom. Even so, I nearly stepped in it. The Deacon hissed something in Egyptian at one of the church slaves, who was waiting politely for us to pass. The man pulled out a large cloth and fell to his knees by the pool. As he splashed it over himself, the smell drifted up still stronger of stomach juices and rotting fish.

'His Holiness is guarded this month by the Sisters of Saint Artemisia,' the Deacon said as if that explained matters.

I gave him a non-committal look.

'She was the daughter-in-law of an Emperor,' he went on, guessing I hadn't understood the significance. 'It was in the time of darkness before the True Faith was established in the world. She was a beauteous yet abandoned woman, sunk in every vice of the Imperial Court. She put these things behind her when she, with her husband, was converted to the Faith. Thereafter, she grew famous throughout the still forbidden Church for the strictness of her observances. As often as she was compelled to attend the banquets of sinful luxury, she would purge herself out of solidarity with the starving poor of the Empire.

'To this day, the Sisters of Her Order maintain the custom. They are permitted to eat only enough to maintain their efficiency. If inadvertently, or through weakness of the flesh, one morsel above this is permitted to pass their lips, they are required to purge themselves and eat no more for three days. During this time, they must abase themselves with lack of sleep and piercings of the flesh and other holy penances.'

I paid no attention to the rest of his narrative. I'd known the woman by her Latin name, and it was all coming back. She'd died in some overturning of her chair as it was carried too fast down the street. The event itself was unclear, and several mutually exclusive miracle stories had fastened themselves almost at once to it. It was a happy day for the Empire – if not for the Church, which now had to wait for Constantine to come along and convert – that her father-in-law had outlived her equally if differently insane husband.

I was seated and left alone in a small office that I supposed was near the main body of the church. The neat desk and the racks bulging with correspondence reminded me of the Dispensator's office in Rome. Joyous times those had been – I didn't think – when he'd called me in there to charge me with one of his 'little missions'. They were never small, and they'd usually involved me in escapes from death by the skin of my teeth. As often as Martin could be bullied or tricked into joining me, they'd involved me in some very hard moments with Sveta. It was with one of these that he'd tricked us into the journey to Constantinople. That hadn't ended, I thought with a smile, entirely as he'd expected. Recollections of that meeting with him on my last visit to the Lateran Place could cheer me at the lowest moments.

Deep inside the church, there was a late service still taking place. I could hear the chanted responses. They weren't in Greek, but the translation had kept the Greek rhythms well enough for me to follow whereabouts the service had reached. Closer by, there was a Sunday school in progress. In high, clear voices, the boys all together read their lesson from the board. Again, I could just follow what they were reading. The few Greek words placed strategically, and the proper names given at the right intervals, told me it was the trial of Saint Paul from the Acts of the Apostles.

There was no wine on the tray of refreshments left beside me. Most welcome, though – bearing in mind how worn out I was feeling from all that sun – was the very hot, sweetened kava juice. I drank the liquid straight down from the jug. I went back to listening. Yes, the boys had reached what could only be the verse 'Then said Agrippa unto Festus, This man might have been set at liberty, if he had not appealed unto Caesar.' I might not believe a word of it. Even so, I knew my Scripture backwards.

I felt a sudden tremor of interest in learning Egyptian. It might come in handy for the journey to and my stay around Soteropolis. It couldn't be that hard to learn. The hardest language to learn is always the second, and I was now fluent in seven. And if the Egyptian versions of Scripture were as faithful as they seemed, I'd have a wondrously smooth key to the language. I might not even need a tutor.

I drifted into thoughts of how much I could get of the language in private between now and Soteropolis. It might not do to let anyone else know what I was about. If I had to set up a miracle, it would be handy to know something of what the natives were saying to each other under my nose. I could probably get the texts I needed out of Hermogenes. I'd be seeing him anyway in the next day or so.

I twisted round and looked at the icon of Saint Mark hanging above the door. It was in exactly the same style as the one Martin had bought and set up in his office. The only difference was that the text wasn't in Greek. A new and uneasy thought came into my mind. Back in Constantinople, Sergius and I had worked on the assumption that a settlement of the Monophysite dispute would solve most of our troubles with the non-Greek Churches in the Empire. Sitting here, I wasn't so sure. This wasn't like in the West, where orthodox and heretic Churches all worked in Latin, and a switch to orthodoxy meant very little in practice. The native Churches here were in worlds of their own. They didn't know Constantinople. They didn't need Constantinople. They were almost like ripe figs dangling from a tree. They could drop off at any moment. If they rotted where they fell, that was their problem. It might even be good for the tree.

Was Egypt a problem for the Empire, I asked myself, because it was heretical? Or was its heresy part of a deeper problem? Suppose we gave in, and accepted the whole Monophysite case: would that be an end of the matter in Egypt? Or would the Egyptians only find another trifling point of difference to justify their steady drift out of the Greek orbit? I thought of my conversations with Lucas. I'd think more about this when I wrote another of my coded reports to Sergius.

I'd just finished crunching on the residue of the smashed-up beans when the door opened.

'Let the ground be kissed where His Holiness cares to stand,' the Deacon called in his flat Greek.

I stood up and bowed respectfully as Anastasius, Monophysite and so-called Patriarch of Alexandria, walked in. Still dressed in full canonicals, he'd come, I could see, straight from Sunday service.

31

'Do please be seated, My Lord,' the Heretical Patriarch said once the door was closed again and we were alone. He took off the jewelled episcopal crown of a kind I'd only ever seen the Pope wearing – both Sergius and John wore rather modest copes: then again, no one doubted *their* status as patriarchs – and put it heavily on the desk. As he struggled to reach back for the ties securing the immense brocade of his robe, I jumped up and helped. Together, we managed to get him down to something that approached sensible clothing in this climate.

A small, bearded man of about fifty, Anastasius finally took his place behind the desk. He had none of the scowling, broody manner fashionable among priests who looked other than to Rome. His face bordering on the jolly, he might, indeed, have been a Western cleric. Untouched by the sun, his face had no more than the sallow appearance of every Mediterranean race. He looked at the now empty kava jug. Before I could speak, he leaned forward and looked closely at me.

'I had a letter the other day from Constantinople,' he said. 'My dear Brother in Christ Sergius sent what I am happy to regard as friendly greetings to me, and therefore to the whole Church of Egypt.'

I didn't bother saying that I'd been sent a copy of the letter. Certainly, I didn't question his claim to leadership of the national Church. Back in Constantinople, Sergius had assured me – and I'd seen no reason here to correct him – that Anastasius was accepted by somewhere between a third and half of the Egyptian Monophysites. He mattered for our purposes because that included almost everyone in and around Alexandria. The further you went into Egypt, though, the crazier and more independent the heretics became.

'I have not spoken this month with John, the – ah – Imperial Patriarch of Alexandria,' he added. 'But please do convey to him all my brotherly love.'

I nodded faintly in reply. This was an informal visit. But if, for a generation past, the viceroys had left off persecuting the official heretics – and even gave the Heretical Patriarch a degree of recognition – I was still sitting opposite a man who, in strict law, was a criminal. If it was out of the question to treat him as a criminal, it was barely less so to acknowledge the status he was impliedly claiming.

'Your Grace,' I opened – the man was undeniably a valid bishop of the Church, and the form of address was ambiguous enough to cover the more deniable claim – 'I am grateful for your being able to see me at such short notice. I am here on business that you may find surprising, but that has become of considerable importance to the Empire.'

'Your Magnificence,' Anastasius replied – he paused and laughed softly, though at what he laughed was as ambiguous as the form of address I'd used – 'your visit, though welcome, is anything but a surprise. There is very little in Alexandria that escapes my notice. If my dear Brother in Christ John could bring himself to sup with me more often, we two patriarchs could be known, here and throughout Egypt, as the two eyes of the Church.'

He paused again as there was a knock at the door. A monk entered with a pile of letters. I looked up briefly, and then looked again. Even before the guttural conversation opened, I knew there was something odd. Then it hit me: the unmistakable smell of unwashed menstrual discharge. The monk looked male enough. There was even a thoroughly unclerical though empty scabbard on display. But this was a nun.

'The Sisters of Saint Artemisia are a military order,' Anastasius explained to me. 'With the present state of things in Alexandria, I find their term of duty here a great support.' He switched back into Egyptian and was lost for the moment in some kind of directions.

I continued looking at the nun. Her face was turned away from me. For her shape and general bearing, she really might have been a man. Except among the wilder barbarians, I'd never seen armed women, and I did nothing to keep the shocked look off my face.

'I may have the respect of the natives,' Anastasius added with a smile at my face. 'Do not suppose on that account I have their practical leadership.' He spoke again to the woman. She bowed and went silently out.

'You have been in Alexandria just over four months,' he reopened once we were alone. 'You were sent here from Constantinople, without any of our language and without any understanding of our ways. You came to impose a new settlement on the land that has much to commend it in the abstract, and that I can hope will, on the Last Day, set off what I believe to be considerable derelictions elsewhere in your attitude to the Faith. But it is a settlement not suited to the ways of our land.

'I know you have little time for His Imperial Highness the Viceroy. But Nicetas has been here far longer than you have. He may not have the words to tell you all that he knows – he may not be aware of all that he does in fact know. But I assure you that Nicetas has a sounder understanding of Egypt and its ways than is present in your tidy, *philosophical* mind.'

'With all respect, Your Grace,' I began.

He raised a hand for silence as the door opened again. The nun came back in, carrying another tray of refreshments. As she turned to leave, I caught a look at her face inside the hood. It was a flash of screwed-up lunacy and vomit-blackened teeth. It scrambled the reply I'd been about to make.

'I have not received you here,' Anastasius went on, 'to lecture you on the politics of land ownership. I am told you have made yourself as well-acquainted with the relevant facts as anyone could wish. If your judgement of those facts is wrong, that is not a matter I feel competent or inclined to argue. You have, however, been kept, systematically in the dark about other facts. Your ignorance may so far have amused me. It has now become a matter of concern, and I will take this opportunity to make you aware of these facts.

'What do you know about Leontius and the manner of his death?' he asked with a shift of tone. The merry twinkle in his eyes gave way to a look of searching intensity. 'No, let me withdraw that question. I know your answer. You will tell me he was a second-rate politician who got in your way; and in doing so, found himself in matters considerably over his head. Is that what you would tell me, Alaric?'

I nodded.

He leaned forward across the desk. 'What would you say if I told you that Leontius was only incidentally concerned with your land reforms, and that his death was in the only manner by which a creature of his probable kind could be reliably forced out of this world? What would you say if I assured you, my dear son, that your arrival in Alexandria may have opened the way for the return of an ancient and inconceivably powerful evil?'

If he had said that, of course, I'd have had trouble keeping a straight face. But since he was speaking hypothetically, I managed to continue looking more or less respectful. He poured two cups of kava juice. It was hotter than before, and it was worth sipping and savouring.

'If you were to tell me such,' I said at length, 'I might be inclined to ask what you were talking about. The only evils I have encountered in Alexandria or in Egypt are the usual sort proceeding through the ambitions and greed of those who would have what was not rightly their own.'

'The relic you are here to seek my help in finding,' Anastasius answered, 'does not exist. The reason nobody knew of its existence before the arrival here of your friend Priscus is that nobody before then had heard of it. Your belief that it is identical to the object that the Brotherhood was persuaded by Leontius to seek is purely assumption. If the Brotherhood now seems to share your assumption, that does not make it true.

'Leontius approached the Brotherhood with a scheme that fitted its own interests as he explained it. His uncle spent his entire life and fortune on researches into a past that was buried at the triumph of the Faith. He sought an intercourse with demons who, for ages, had masqueraded under the names of the national deities. In return for honours of which they had, in recent ages, been starved, he hoped to receive powers that would extend the natural course of his life – and might even put off his death indefinitely. With this would come a more than human ability to gain and hold dominion over the earth.'

'Yet he died almost penniless,' I observed drily. 'And Leontius, who I imagine succeeded to these researches, still died hardly richer.' I thought again of that old woman outside Richborough. 'You'll be dead within ten days,' she'd croaked when she caught me stealing the eggs I'd been told might keep the pestilence from taking my brothers. My brothers had been taken anyway. But that had all been ten years before, and I was still here. I suppose that had started the train of thought culminating in my discovery in the mission library in Canterbury of those attacks on Epicurus. It wasn't a train of thought to be upset now by yet more sorcery claims. If I could despise an emperor for believing in the incredible, what authority had some unrecognised Patriarch of a religion that, orthodox or heretical, I thought absurd?

'They both perished in the same manner,' Anastasius went on, 'before they had been able to complete the last irrevocable step to worldly dominion. That step requires possession of an object that sleeps somewhere beneath the burning sands of the desert.

'When you arrived last spring, Leontius made himself the connecting point between the landed interest that you knew at once was your opposition, and the Brotherhood, whose support was needed should you grow desperate enough to appeal directly to the children of the soil. The landowners would furnish him with money, the Brotherhood with the human means needed for his excavations.

'The story of the relic is an invention of the present month. It may have been useful for bringing over those elements of the Brotherhood that have some connection with the Faith. In the end, Leontius did overreach himself. But the politics of the Brotherhood are more complex than you realise. The Christian elements never did trust him. They were outweighed by those other elements who thought him a useful idiot for destabilising the government in Alexandria. When he raised the matter of the Philae subsidy, and when you immediately had it cancelled, those in the True Faith appear to have moved – sure there would be no protest now in the higher councils – to end his life in the approved manner for the destruction of such creatures as he was suspected of wanting to become.'

'So, there is no chamber pot of Jesus Christ?' I asked, focusing on one of the points that really mattered, the other one being, of course, the treason of those bastard landowners. 'Not even though much evidence points to its existence in Soteropolis?'

Anastasius sipped long and thoughtfully. Unblinking, his eyes had turned stony cold. 'Alaric,' he said, 'since I plainly have no way of persuading you I am not a superstitious old fool, I see no point in prolonging our conversation. I will simply say that you are guided at present by forces beyond your understanding, and that would be beyond your control even if you did understand them. I beg you to give up the search you have begun. No good can come of it. In particular, I do urge you not to leave Alexandria again. While you remain here, you are safe. So is Egypt. So is the Empire. The moment you leave, you are once more in danger of falling into the hands of the enemies of the Empire – and the enemies of all that is good in this world. If I speak to John, he will speak to Nicetas. Your warrants will be sealed, and you can go back to Constantinople with all necessary evidence of a mission completed. If it eventually gets back that the warrants have been received throughout Egypt as a dead letter, it will be too late for any blame to attach to you.

'But I beg you: give up this search now. Or if your pride really is committed, give up all meaningful activity in the search. I cannot otherwise do more than pray for your safety, and for the continuation of Imperial rule in Egypt – and for the continued existence of the Christian Faith itself in Egypt.'

I put my cup down and looked steadily at the man. I had no doubt he believed everything he was telling me. And it had been useful. Forget all the nonsense about ancient evils – I could now see a way to having those landowners by the balls. I looked round for a question that would bring us back to the politics of the matter.

'You are telling me,' I began slowly, 'that Leontius was a sorcerer. I will not speculate how this corresponds with his known incompetence in other respects. But I will ask if his sorcery was generally known. I am hearing it from you for the first time.'

'It was known, and, where not known for sure, it was suspected,' came the reply. 'You will have heard that John, my brother Patriarch, refused his body burial in consecrated ground, and that his remaining friends had to arrange an interment outside the walls of Alexandria.'

I hadn't heard this. I'd been in the south. No one had bothered telling me on my return. But I pursed my lips knowingly.

'I was consulted by one of your main opponents about a month ago,' Anastasius continued. 'I told him to obey the law made by the Emperor. Heraclius may be ill-advised on theology and on the situation in Egypt. But he is the ruler ordained by God. I told him to avoid the counsels of *any outside power* – a power that has nothing good in mind for Egypt or Alexandria. As I have said, however, I have less influence, even among the better classes, than might be desired.'

'You tell me,' I said, 'that the relic does not exist. Am I right in believing that you are alone in this opinion?'

Anastasius nodded.

More useful knowledge. It meant my planned excavation of Soteropolis could still go ahead. It might no longer be the only way to get the land law implemented, but it was still eminently worth the effort so far as the reserve stock was concerned. As another of the nuns came in with more documents, I fell to thinking what might be and where I could find the minimum evidence needed to have those landlords up for treason or sorcery or both. This had indeed been a productive morning.

I was also thinking of my next conversation with Macarius. I'd been too easy, it seemed, about dropping the matter of the old man and his girl in the Egyptian quarter. His negligence – or his deception by silence – in this matter was far graver. There was also his use of the word 'object', when I'd been discussing the relic with him. Anastasius hadn't been the only one in the know.

As we moved to vague pleasantries in front of the nun, the meeting came to an end. I took my leave of Anastasius out in the courtyard.

'My blessing goes with you,' he called out in a halting Latin that it was sure none around him could understand. 'If you will not hear me in your single-minded pursuit of what is ultimately unimportant, may God in His Mercy keep you from danger.'

I looked back from my chair. He remained where we'd parted, watching me until the gate had closed between us.

32

The web of little streets that surrounded the Heretical Patriarch's residence was surprisingly empty as we passed back through them. On our way here, they'd been never less than busy. I think we now passed more dogs than people. Small, mangy, suspiciously calm in the baking sun, they pawed through the piles of refuse in search of something that wouldn't make even them sick. For a hundred yards at a time, the only sound was often the patter of my slaves as they hurried my chair along, and the more solid tramp of the guards beside me.

At first, the cheers might have been some trick of the breeze on the roof tiles. As we came closer to their source though, there was no mistaking them. It was the sort of massed sound I'd last heard on a trip to the Circus in Constantinople. As we turned back into the square from which we'd get more or less straight back to the Wall, we hit what seemed a solid mass of flesh. It was as if the entire Egyptian quarter had come out and packed itself into one place. Men stood there in work overalls, others in the clothes they'd worn to church. A couple of ladies sat in closed chairs. They were all looking to the middle of the square, to a fountain that no longer worked. Standing in the dry bowl, a man was haranguing them. He was a large, well-dressed man in perhaps his late fifties. I couldn't understand him, but he was putting on an impressive display of bellows and gestures. Standing around him were a handful of lowish thugs – probably his bodyguards – and a couple of priests.

On the steps surrounding the fountain stood some dozen of the native men of quality. They weren't landowners – merchants, more like – and they probably kept to their own side of the Wall.

I didn't know any of them. But I did know of them. I'd never yet heard that they had any time for sedition. They had as much, after all, to lose if the mob ran out of control as anyone of the possessing classes who spoke Greek. Here they were, though, openly supporting what I had no doubt was bitter hostility – at least by implication – to the Imperial government here and in Egypt.

And then – it was the crowning glory on that morning. Lurking just behind those native men of quality was that wretch who'd tried facing me down in the Great Hall of Audience. He had his hat on again, but I'd not have mistaken those Ethiopian lips anywhere, or that look of exalted hate covering the rest of his face. As I watched, he passed up a note to the speaker, and performed a little dance of triumph as it was turned into the appropriate snarling rhetoric. So much for damning the 'wogs'! I thought. The next time I saw Nicetas, it would be with a stack of arrest warrants for him to seal. Inciting the mob to violence was treason in anyone's book. By the time I'd finished with these turds, they'd be begging on bended knees for the deal on their land so lately thrown back in my face. Oh, I'd leave the deal unchanged. Why go for more than you need when it's dropping so nicely into your lap?

I think the landowner saw me as we pushed our way into the square. Certainly, the next time I had a clear view through the crowd, he was no longer in his place. The speaker was still in full flow. If I couldn't understand what he was saying, its burden wasn't at all hard to guess. As he paused and, with a dramatic wave, pointed in the rough direction of the Eastern Harbour, where the grain fleet awaited its orders to depart, the whole mob took up that chant about the Tears of Alexander. By now, I knew that one well enough. Like regular peals of thunder, it rolled again and again from thousands of throats. For disciplined loudness, I really hadn't heard anything to match it since my last Circus attendance. With every repeat, the speaker would throw up his arms and laugh into the sky.

No one was pressing against us. But the chair was beginning to wobble out of control as the carrying slaves panicked. I prodded the two in front with my slave stick and leaned forward with calm words and promises of money. Visibly scared, the guard officer looked at me for instructions. 'No drawn swords,' I mouthed in Latin. I flicked a fold of my robe over my own sword. He was still looking at me. 'No drawn swords,' I mouthed again, this time in Slavonic. He nodded and made the appropriate gesture to his men. Was it worth turning round and trying the back streets? Forcing a way through this seemed about as sensible as shoving your head into a lion's mouth.

But now the two Sisters of Saint Artemisia stepped forward. They'd come with us supposedly as guides. I don't suppose Anastasius had thought it would do with me to explain their real use. They walked straight forward into the mob, calling out something over and over again that included the name of their saint. One of them was waving her arms in the air. The sleeves of her gown fell away, showing thin and hideously scarred, but at the same time muscular, arms.

It was like passing through a night mist that was repelled by torches. As the Sisters advanced, the crowd hollowed out around them. From behind, it closed in again. So, one Sister on each side of us, we passed safely through. The speaker never let up his flow of oratory, other than to give the main crowd room for its increasingly monotonous responses. But if people looked murder at me as I sat still in my chair, with a probably failed attempt at the haughty, no one dared step into the slow-moving void created by the Sisters.

'If you'll pardon the expression, sir, it's fucking chaos all over,' the police officer shouted as we paused at the Egyptian side of the Wall. The mob was now bellowing its guts out in the square, about a quarter-mile back. By the Wall, a smaller mob – or perhaps a grouping of mobile crowds – was striking up the usual chant. Boys darted quickly in and out of the side streets, sometimes screaming abuse, sometimes throwing stones. I wondered why the police didn't pull back to our side of the Wall. There was little enough they could do this side to keep order. And these occasional stone showers had already caused injuries.

'It's the grain ships, you see,' the man explained with a look in the direction of the cheering. 'Both the wogs and our own people think they shouldn't go out. We're stretched thin both sides of the Wall. If the Jews turn nasty, we don't know how we'll manage.' He twisted round and shouted an order to some archers who'd appeared along the top of the Wall. They steadied their bows and let fly. They weren't aiming to kill. It was flesh wounds they inflicted on some of the boys. They fell down screaming. The others backed off. The police moved forward to secure the vacated ground.

It wasn't much better on the Greek side. Just like at night, the mobs were rushing up and down the streets, passing from agitator to agitator. This side of the Wall, I could at least understand what it was all about. As I'd expected, it was the grain fleet. Perhaps worse, it was also claims about the quantity and management of the supplies left in the granaries.

We'd left the Sisters behind as we passed through the gate. Now, if less scary, the streets were more impassable. We moved slowly down Main Street. Its great width served only to contain the so far aimless crowds of the hungry poor and their troublemaking leaders. All the shops were shut up and boarded. I glanced into the streets leading off, where the men of quality had their palaces. Being the richest of all the landowners, Apion took up both sides of one street, which was itself terminated by the high walls of his garden. He'd now barricaded the entry to the street, and armed his larger and more ferocious slaves to hold off any concerted attack.

How much had he known of the conspiracy? I wondered. He must have known something. It was bad enough if I'd been kept in the dark. But I was an outsider, only recently arrived. It would have been impossible for a man in his position to know nothing. If he wanted those preferments, he'd need to work considerably harder in my interest than he so far had.

I thought suddenly of the Mistress. How was she keeping in all this? I dismissed the thought. If she wasn't willing to count on me for her safety, she was on her own – not, I had to admit, that she seemed unable to look after herself.

As we turned into the square before the Palace, the guards came forward to help clear a way through.

'It's bad news, My Lord,' one of them told me as we finally passed through the treble gate into the fortified courtyard. 'A child died of starvation earlier today in one of the poor districts – the one starting behind the Church of the Virgin. As the father carried her body through the streets, a crowd gathered and gathered behind him. It's too big now to break up, and no one knows when it will catch fire.'

I looked up at the high walls of the courtyard. The windows started around sixty feet up. Even if the whole mob – Greek and Egyptian – broke through the front gates, it wouldn't get any deeper into the Palace. The mob ever in their minds, the Ptolemies had built well.

'Has my secretary's chair come back yet?' I asked. It had. I nodded. Martin hadn't needed much encouragement to retreat into his own armoured chair for going about Alexandria. Nevertheless, I didn't want him out on his relic hunt on a day like this.

I walked by myself into the glittering entrance hall of the Palace. It was here that chairs were normally set down, and this was the first view of the Palace that visiting dignitaries would have. At the far back of the hall was a giant mosaic of Alexander putting the Persians to flight. Down the side walls were statues of every emperor from Julius Caesar onwards. Lucky for us only the most Hellenised or loyal of the natives were ever let in. As it was, I was surprised their mob hadn't yet based one of its chants on the fact that, with Heraclius, every available space down the walls was now filled up.

It had taken so long to get across the square that the eunuch greeters had been able to raise my own household. The slaves stood in a group beside the statue of Septimius Severus. Martin – so hastily changed, he was wearing shoes of different colours – stood to their right. He bowed low at the waist. The slaves threw themselves down in a full prostration. This was a public event, and the eunuchs could be severe judges if the formalities weren't respected. Once we were through the door behind the statue, it would be more relaxed. The idea was that I should get into my internal chair and have myself carried sedately up the ramps to the fifth floor, where we had our main accommodation. Without those eunuchs looking on, I'd do no such thing. The kava juice had been having its progressive effect on my bladder since we'd left the Egyptian quarter. I was now bursting for a piss. It would be a quick dash up the stairs provided for the slaves.

'Have you seen Macarius?' I asked as we paused at the fifth flight. It took longer than I wanted for Martin, bent double, to gasp out his negative.

'It doesn't surprise me if he's vanished again,' he wheezed. 'You know that antique chamber pot you gave Maximin last year – the brass one you bought in Cyprus? Well, it's gone missing. Sveta saw it when we came back. Yesterday, she went looking and—'

'Never mind,' I said hurriedly. 'I'm sure it will turn up in time.' Trust Sveta to notice it was gone. I pointed at two of the slaves. They got either side of Martin and readied themselves to propel him the rest of the way. 'I need you to arrange a meeting with the Viceroy,' I said. 'Before then, we've business in my office.'

33

'He went out yesterday evening,' Martin confirmed. 'Since then, I haven't seen him.'

I looked again at the box of documents in Egyptian we'd lifted after Leontius had been murdered. Their content was now of some importance. If only Macarius hadn't decided to vanish again, he'd now be with us in my office and working hard at interpreting them into Greek. He might also be able to have a go at the document in Persian – certainly with its translation in Egyptian.

Before then, though, he'd be explaining himself. The seeds of anger planted in conversation with Anastasius had quickly grown into a mighty tree of rage. His plain job had been to keep me informed of matters that, if not common knowledge, shouldn't have been that hard to uncover. Even a month ago – never mind when he'd first shown up in Alexandria – a set of sorcery charges would have taken Leontius straight out of action. A few quiet hints they might be implicated, and those landowners would have been queuing up to throw their title deeds at my feet. What had Macarius been about?

I hadn't told Martin yet about the Holy Family and Soteropolis – I needed him to keep at his relic hunt with more than a show of determination. But I had told him about the meeting with Anastasius.

'You know my views on the man,' he'd said with one of his sniffs about Macarius. I hadn't argued. On the one hand, I didn't want Martin dwelling too much on the alleged magical side of things. On the other, his words were running along the same course as my thoughts. There are some deficiencies too big to have been made by accident. I didn't go so far as Martin, who was now wondering if Macarius had any tattoos on his body. But I certainly wanted an explanation.

'Am I right that Sekhmet was an Egyptian goddess?' I asked, pulling out the one sheet that we were able to read.

'She *is*' – Martin corrected my tense – 'a demon once known to the Greeks as Sacmis. Her cult was highly regarded among the old kings of Egypt. It was then believed that she was protectress of the whole land, and that the hot winds of the desert were her breath. It was further believed that her breath could strike pestilence into the enemies of Egypt. There is a story that some of her statues could be approached only by those wearing special clothing – that anyone else who laid hands on such statues would be stricken with pestilence.

'When I was in Antinoopolis . . .' He paused.

I tried not to perk up too visibly at this rare mention of his time in slavery. He looked at me. The best I could manage without looking thoroughly unnatural was a weak smile. He swallowed and paused a little longer.

'When I was in Antinoopolis,' he went on at last, 'a statue of the demon was uncovered during the laying of foundations for a church. It was in the form of a woman with a lion's head. It was all of black granite, the head chased with gold. The farm workers who'd been brought in to do the digging set up a wail as the priest himself began prising the gold from its head.

'As he attacked the last piece of gold with his hammer, the granite splintered, and a demon's breath rushed out to kill the priest on the spot. Those who carried the statue to throw it into the Nile later sickened and died. For several days, dead fish came to the surface and floated down river of the spot where it was thrown.'

'And you saw all this?' I asked.

'Not myself,' said Martin with a defensive look. 'But I heard it from a friend of my master as I waited at table. One of his slaves was present when the priest died.'

'But surely,' I asked again, 'you saw the dead fish?'

'No,' he said, a slightly ratty tone coming into his voice. 'My master ordered the household to keep away from the water. But

I was anyway in no position to go and look. It was now that I had my big attack of sunburn. My skin peeled off and I was confined to bed. By the time I was recovered, my master had decided to sell me.'

It was the sort of evidence that would never have held water in an action over a disputed will. But I'd given up for the time being on laws made by and for the sane. For the prosecutions I now had in mind, this would have done very nicely. One day, I'd get the full story of his life from the moment he was sold into slavery to when he turned up in Cyrene as a rather unlikely boy prostitute. Now, though, wasn't the time for prying. It was probably for the best that I'd visibly annoyed him by not believing a word of his wild romance. Anger is a fine corrective for embarrassment.

I took everything out of the box and spread the fifty or so sheets on the big table over against the external wall of my office. The sunlight that streamed in gave me an excellent view of them. A shame it needed rather more than that to understand a word of them.

'These are in the pre-modern alphabet of the Egyptians,' I said, indicating one line of papyrus, each sheet half overlapping the other. 'These are in a script that bears some resemblance to the picture writing of the statues and temple walls, but seems to have been a simplified form used for less ceremonial purposes.

'These two sheets, of course, are in the full picture script. Their somewhat weakened state indicates great age – greater even than the oldest documents in Greek you can see in the archives. These words written here and there in the modern alphabet under some of the picture signs appear to correspond with the fragmentary Greek translation. They do appear also to be in the same hand.'

Martin took up the two sheets of picture writing. They did look old, he agreed, though the freshness of the colouring suggested they had been stored safely for much of the time they had existed. Had they been recovered from a tomb? If so, what about the other sheets in the less ceremonial old script? We moved to a discussion of what Lucas and then Anastasius had said about Leontius. Add that to the items in his house, and it was fair to say that he'd been a skilled excavator of antiquities. Martin pulled out two more of the sheets, one in the old and one in the new script.

'I was thinking that,' I said, comparing the diagrams on each, 'the amount of material may be smaller than it seemed at first. If these diagrams are the same – and the possible copy is just a freehand sketch – everything in the old script may have been transliterated into the new.' I looked at the original diagram. It was something between an astrological chart and a plan of some elaborate machinery.

'From what you now tell me about Leontius,' Martin said firmly, 'these are probably all magical texts. I say we should burn them.'

'Not so fast,' I said. '*Some* of the newer documents might be translations of the older. Some of them, though, might be evidence of treason. The document in Persian almost certainly is such evidence.'

'The danger is too great,' he said. He put down the sheet he'd been holding and wiped its dust off his hands. 'I still say—'

There was a knock on the door. As I called on the Head Clerk to enter, Martin and I moved back to my desk and stared at a survey map of the Upper Delta.

'Put them down here, if you please,' I said to the slaves who entered behind the Head Clerk with yet more baskets of documents for sealing. There were hundreds of them: replies to petitions and reports, letters of instruction, general correspondence. The clerks were working double shifts to keep up with me as I cleared all that had accumulated in my absence. A single 'yes', or 'no', spoken yesterday by the swimming pool could generate a sheet of tightly written papyrus. A marginal scrawl might come back as an entire book roll. Now, it was all coming back. It poured into my office like nothing so much as leaves in a northern autumn through an open door.

I bent down and fished at random through one of the baskets, and then through another. From each, I pulled out three of the still unrolled sheets and put them on top of the map. The first was a conditional remission of taxes to the owner of an estate damaged for the third time in two years by locusts. I checked the wording carefully, making sure it corresponded with the instruction I'd given. I looked at the Head Clerk. He stared impassively back. No one who was on the take ever stood up long to this sort of checking. I turned to the second document, and then the third. I read all the others. All were in order.

I looked into a different basket and pulled out one of the smaller sheets. I knew this would be the grant of something both valuable and highly complex. If ever there was an opportunity for a bribed alteration, this would be it. The Head Clerk was sweating slightly in the heat and slightly from stress – but no more than anyone would with someone of my unbounded power going through work done or checked by him. I dropped it back in uninspected and nodded approval.

There was an aromatic smell as a junior clerk brought in the pot of bubbling wax. I took a key from my belt and opened the cupboard in the wall beside my desk. I lifted out the bag containing the Lesser Seal that let me act as Nicetas in all matters except those that just happened to be vital to my own work. I handed this to Martin, who took out the Seal and heated it.

'In the Name of the Emperor, let it be so!' he cried softly each time I pressed the Seal into the molten wax. Once only we paused. We'd come to the Leontius matter. I looked again at the wording. I held all the evidence. No one could ever dispute the form of what I was doing. I felt the Head Clerk's stare. I looked back at him. Again, he seemed more curious than concerned. I pushed the document across to Martin, who was waiting with his spoon of wax.

'In the Name of the Emperor, let it be so,' he said emphatically. The Head Clerk took the now sealed roll of papyrus and put it carefully with the others for the wax to harden. I still had until the following morning to call it back. But it was now done, and I knew I'd let it go out.

It was all an unwelcome break from what I wanted to be doing. But it wasn't that long before the baskets were filled again.

'Do make sure to leave that one with me,' I said, pointing at the smallest basket. The sheets there were written in purple. 'They must be sealed by the Viceroy in person.' When, of course, Nicetas would set the Great Seal to them was an open question. And I'd not be pushing them at him while my own warrants were still outstanding.

'If you please,' I said of a sudden to the Head Clerk as he was following the slave and baskets from the room. I shut the door after the slave and turned back to face him. He dropped his eyes as I looked again into his face. 'Do please remain with us,' I said. 'I have a matter in which you might be able to assist. Your name is Barnabas, I think.'

He nodded.

'You are also, I think, a native.'

He looked up in surprise.

I checked the protest I could see forming. 'The reason I ask,' I said, 'is that I am in need of someone who can read Egyptian and whom I can trust. If you would come over here.' I led him to the table and waved at the still neatly arranged sheets. On the far side of the room, Martin was mouthing negatives and shaking his head. I ignored him. He'd probably have made the same fuss if it had been Macarius I was getting in on the job.

'What I want you to do,' I said smoothly, 'is to look at this row of newer documents. I don't need you at this stage to do more than explain their contents. It may be that a translation will be needed of some. That being so, I—'

'Don't do this, Aelric,' Martin said in Celtic. He crossed the room and took my arm. 'I beg you to consider the danger of letting those documents be read by this man.'

I looked into Martin's sweaty, troubled face. For the first time, the Head Clerk was showing concern. He couldn't follow the sibilant, aspirated words, but must have understood their sense.

'Have you taken leave of your senses?' I asked, keeping my voice still smooth, though now in Martin's Celtic. You don't show off disagreements in front of underlings. 'Are you going to suggest I have the man hitch his robe up to see if there's a tattoo above his arse?'

'And how do you know if there isn't?' said Martin. 'But these documents may be of immense and uncontrollable power. Just reading them without the right precautions might summon a demon into this room. If you want to know what's in them, you should go back to the Heretical Patriarch. He'll know what to do. But I really think you should let me put them into a fire.'

Demons – yes, demons! And appearing out of a puff of smoke in my office. You know, I dearly loved Martin. Even when we were first brought together in Rome, and I was trying to show who was the master and who the borrowed slave, there had been something about his learned and competent helplessness that appealed to me. He was now the closest thing I had in the world to a friend. And there were still times when I had to resist the urge to give him a good hard punch in the stomach. But I kept my temper and continued looking calmly into his face. As I thought to turn back to Barnabas, the door opened and Priscus walked in.

'Hard at work, are we, on this day of rest?' he said with a nod at the basket of stuff for Nicetas.

Barnabas threw himself down for a grovel. Martin bowed and stood away from me.

'Maximin's birthday was yesterday,' I said, with an impatient glance at the heavy blue silk he was wearing. I let my mind's eye return to those documents, so neatly and so invitingly arranged on the table behind me. All I had to do was get rid of Martin and of Priscus, and then sit down with Barnabas. 'You've missed the celebration,' I said, still looking at Priscus. I'd make sure not to be the only person in that room who was annoyed. 'But let me give his thanks for the little whip and branding irons you sent him. He can have them when he's older.'

Together with all other movements, scowling is something to avoid when your face is a mask of white lead with banks of gold leaf for your eyebrows. Instead, Priscus twitched his nose, which it was clear he'd been using to sniff up whatever passed with him for lunch.

'I take it, then, you haven't noticed how no one can get into or out of this place?' he drawled. He looked at the window. 'I suppose not. Your office is on the far side of the building. The Egyptians are being held on their side of the Wall. But the Greek trash has turned up in force outside the Palace, and won't go away. Apparently, some child died of starvation, and everyone's demanding the grain ships be unloaded.

'It's at times like this that a massacre can really calm things. Sadly, Nicetas has agreed instead to meet the leaders of the mob, and he wants the pair of us on hand for moral support. Since he's got the few slaves on duty running round like blue-arsed flies on other business, he asked me to drop in and summon you.

'Any chance we could pull you away from what I'm sure is work for the highest benefit of the Empire?'

'You may leave us,' I said to Barnabas. As he scurried out, visibly glad to be off the hook, I turned to Martin. 'Get all this packed away,' I said, pointing at the Lesser Seal. I took the whole ring of keys from my belt and handed them to him. I might give him a good talking to later in the day. Then again, I might not. He'd only insist he'd been doing me a favour. This being Sunday, he might even call in one of his conversations with God as a defence.

'If you'll come back with me,' I said to Priscus, 'you might care to fill me in on what's happening while I get myself changed.'

As we left the room, I looked back. Martin had gathered up the whole two rows of documents and was stuffing them into the cupboard along with the Seal.

34

Nicetas and most of his Council were already in place when we arrived at the Great Hall of Audience. I thought the eunuch would have a stroke as he took hold of Priscus and me and led us to our own golden stools in the gathering. This not being one of his days for secular business, Patriarch John was absent, so the pair of us were sitting beside each other just behind Nicetas. I heard the scrape as the golden easel was set up behind us for the icon of the Emperor. The eunuch gave one last pull on the wig of gold and silver threads that Nicetas was wearing. From where I sat, the shaft of sunlight sent down on us from the mirrors in the dome made his head look as if it had caught fire. I wondered if that was how it appeared from the front.

But there was no time for wondering anything – let alone for conversation. Once we were all seated, our faces set into required expressions, the eunuch nodded to the guards at the far end of the Hall. With a loud drawing back of bolts and a whoosh of air and a flood of bright sunshine, the twin gates leading out into the square swung open, and the great unwashed of the poor districts poured in. They flowed through the gates in their hundreds and thousands, and those first through were pushed closer and closer to the front of our platform.

I let my eyes wander over the sea of pinched, desperate faces that stretched from the double row of armed guards just below our platform right down the six hundred feet of the Hall. All that separated these creatures from the natives was a smattering of Greek and a more heterogeneous look when it came to size and colouring. But whatever their size, whatever their colouring, the urban poor are always repulsive. The reason they live in cities and are poor is because they're trash. They're too lazy to dig for themselves on the land, and too stupid to take advantage of the city as a market for useful services. All they contribute to city life is crime and rioting. Take that away, and the respectable can step over them as they starve in the street. But the moment they transform themselves from gathered trash into the mob, they become something professional armies might tremble to confront.

Our trouble here was that these weren't transforming themselves into anything. Even without the revelation I'd had in the Egyptian quarter, this was plainly a directed crowd. I could see the directing agents. They took care not to stand together at the front, but were dispersed among the crowd. Even so, they were dead easy to spot – taller, cleaner, better dressed. Leontius might be dead. His idea of 'Success in Unity', brought about by a coalition of both sides of the mob and the possessing classes lived on. And why not? Use the grain fleet to raise the mob: scare Nicetas enough – and I could wait like a poor litigant in court for those warrants.

With three loud blows on a gong behind us, the Hall fell silent. The herald stood forward. He turned and bowed to Nicetas and the whole Council. As the local custom required, we made no acknowledgement of his bow, but sat still and silent as statues. Except we existed in three dimensions, we might as well have merged into the frieze of Augustus that stretched all round us on the walls. The herald turned away from us again to face the main body of the Hall and took in a deep breath.

'You have been called into the presence of His Imperial Highness Nicetas,' he began in his measured, impossibly loud voice, 'Viceroy to His Imperial Majesty Heraclius, Caesar, Augustus, Ever-Victorious Apostle of God, that your grievances may be discussed, and that you cease to disturb the order of our city.'

As the herald finished his greeting, and a single blow on a gong confirmed its ending, there was a general coughing and shuffling at the front as the crowd parted. At the apex of the resulting gap, a big man stood, his bearded head pressed tragically down on to a bundle that he held against his chest. There was a gentle push from behind and what might have been a muttered order. Slowly, he walked forward, stopping just short of the guards. He raised his head and looked round, and then looked straight at Nicetas.

'O Cousin of Our Lord Augustus,' he began woodenly in an accent that wasn't local, but might have been Cretan or even Cypriotic, 'Most Noble Viceroy, I come before you holding the body of my only child, who has been taken from me by want of bread.' As he spoke, he held out the bundle, and an arm with about the thickness of a broomstick hung suddenly loose. It was a dramatic effect, and gasps of horror and pity rippled backward through the crowd. Assuming it wasn't accidental, it showed the man had been well rehearsed.

'Oh, my dear,' Priscus had whispered as they were all allowed in to see us, 'if only they might have one throat!' I'd not have put it so uncharitably myself. For all I knew, some child had died. The price of bread had risen again, and the free distribution was only enough for a whole family if the parents didn't scoff it all them-selves. Looking at this man, he could have eaten his whole family to death, plus his neighbours. But children were always dying. It didn't need to be starvation. There was accident. There was pesti-lence. There was murder. There was rape and murder. The death bins hadn't been emptied for a while, and suitable bodies could be pulled straight off the top. If this little bundle was from a bin, we'd never have noticed. The smell of the living would have masked the rotting of the dead. Priscus had made sure to deaden his nose before coming in. I almost wished I'd accepted a pinch of the blue powder.

But the allegedly grieving father had made his speech, and was now awaiting a reply. You expect a certain pause after someone of his quality has spoken. Immediate replies are demeaning. But this long silence was pushing things. There was a rising chatter towards the back of the Hall. Someone laughed. The herald looked nerv-ously round again. The white paint somehow transferring itself to the lower strands of his wig, Nicetas might have been turned to stone. I could feel the nerves of the slaves behind us, as the ostrich feathers shook in their hands.

There was a sudden commotion far over to my left. I moved my eyes to see what it was. A woman was pushing her way through the crowd.

'Bread,' she cried, 'in the Name of God, give us bread!' Someone behind her joined in. Over to my right, some utterly disgusting creature with one eye now pushed his way to the front and began howling about the grain fleet. There it still was in the docks, he shrilled, stuffed with food that could keep Alexandria from going without right up to the next harvest. Other voices joined in. The grain fleet! The grain fleet! No one wanted it to leave. No one would settle for less than its immediate unloading.

This was all unscripted, and the directing agents did their best to jolly the proles back into line. But I could see from the confused looks they were darting at the platform that they'd counted on our playing along. The crowd was fast becoming a shouting, rippling thing beyond control. The line of guards that stood between it and us was more for display than use; and the doorway back into the Palace was twenty yards behind us, with stairs down from the platform. And still Nicetas sat, silent and unmoving. If we'd been sitting instead before some vast bonfire, ready to collapse and spill super-heated ashes right over us, it would have been less scary.

'I hope you will one day find it possible, my love, to forgive me,' Priscus said softly without moving his lips. He'd taken advantage of a relative lull the directing agents had managed, though I still had to listen hard to follow him. 'But I seem to have forgotten to say that it wasn't just to show off your pretty face that you were called down here. Since you've made yourself the expert on food supplies, Nicetas thought you might care to speak for him.'

Oh, fuck! I froze with horror. For the first time, I realised that every pair of eyes on the platform was swivelled in my direction. If this was how Priscus wanted his revenge for that birthday sneer, he was excelling himself. I could see from the corner of my eye that he was allowing one of his nostrils to twitch. If he'd been splitting his sides with laughter, it wouldn't have shown his mood to better effect.

241

I swallowed and forced all thought of the Leontius documents out of my head. There was no point, though, even trying to loosen the knots in my stomach. I kept my face rigid and thought quickly. In Constantinople, I'd sat any number of times below Heraclius in the Circus, and watched him debate with the people. It could while away much of a dull afternoon to hear his whispered instructions to the herald, and see how close he was sticking to the line agreed in advance. However, if I'd done as much as anyone alive to set these lines, I'd never yet been called on to whisper the instructions myself. I looked again over the expectant mob, trying desperately to pull together the main facts of a report that hadn't got half my attention as I drowsed by the swimming pool.

'Tell them,' I muttered uncertainly to the herald, 'there is grain aplenty in storage. So long as no one demands extravagance, there is no reason why anyone should starve.' I don't know how the man heard me, but he did. I swallowed again and waited for him to finish. At least I didn't need to get up and speak. The resulting stammer would have brought on disaster straight away.

'Tell them,' I added at last, 'we'll pay for the child's funeral as an act of grace.'

And so we were in business. As often as the herald translated my words into the appropriately slow and ceremonious phrases, and the gong sounded to confirm the reply was ended, so another of the two-legged vermin before us would be put up to a reply or further demand. This was the main difference with Constantinople. There, the Circus Factions had their ritual chants to mix and match as their leaders found appropriate. Here, it was individual voices. But there was, I soon discovered, a limiting etiquette. If it was obvious a prole was using his own initiative to call out a protest or question, no one would make a fuss if it was ignored.

'It is the Will of Caesar,' the herald explained as we got to the matter uppermost in the thoughts of every mob, Greek or Egyptian, 'that the grain be transported to the Imperial City that sits on the waves between Europe and Asia. As the Great King Xerxes had those waves scourged for the destruction of his boats,

242

so equally in vain shall we contest the decision of the Lord's Anointed. The grain ships must go. They will go.'

'And how, then, shall the finest seed of Alexander be fed?' someone called out from about twenty feet into the crowd. He stumbled over the unfamiliar words he'd had whispered into his ear. And 'finest seed of Alexander'! Even now, that shrivelled husk in the Library basement could have fathered better semblances of the human race than this gathering of lice. But I'd finally got my facts and figures straight. By doubling every number in that report, and counting as already present what could be moved in from the smaller cities, I was able to create an impression of plenty in the public granaries. I'd rather have stuck to the more likely bare adequacy – more likely, that was, assuming the black fungus didn't spread too much further. But with those ships on show to anyone who could get through the cordon into the Harbour, we needed more than claims of adequacy.

Someone came back with a detailed question about grain requisitions in the Eastern Delta. It was the sort of question that required inside knowledge. But what could surprise anyone about that? I had an answer to this that was almost the truth. Certainly, no one had the means to doubt it. We moved to another detailed question, and then to another. They came in almost logical order. My impression was that very little was said in this debate. That's an impression, though, that every public speaker seems to have. Even taking into account how everything went through the herald, we did cover a lot. Every so often, there was a tremor in the lighting as the sun moved from one mirror to another. And a mood that had started out as at least belligerent had moved through the sceptical to the barely discontented.

'His Highness the Viceroy will be thirty this coming Wednesday,' I whispered. I lowered my voice still further in the new silence of the Hall. 'Be vague about quantities, but announce a free distribution of flour – no, of fresh bread – for that day.'

That got us our first cheer of the afternoon. With every pause in the herald's ritualised description of the grinding and kneading and baking of the corn, the acclamations rang out. I breathed an involuntary prayer that no one would ask what was on offer once the Christmas distribution had been eaten up.

No one quite did – but the meeting wasn't yet ended. Someone over by the statue of Alexander asked if the natives were to get the same. A tricky question, this. If I said yes, there'd certainly be nothing left for later distribution. And this might lead to the question I wanted to avoid. If I said no – I thought of what I'd seen earlier in the Egyptian quarter. It felt as if every pair of eyes in the Hall that could see past the herald was focused on me.

'Tell them the natives get whatever is theirs by custom,' I breathed so softly, the herald had to sway back a little to catch the words. The exact meaning of what I'd said could depend on circumstances. 'But announce a three-seventh subsidy on the price of beer to go with the free bread.

'Oh' – I thought quickly about another of the reports I'd had read out to me: we needed something to focus attention on the absolute present – 'and announce a distribution of one pitcher of oil to every man who presents himself today at dusk before the Church of the Virgin.' If I worked the warehouse slaves through the night, the natives could have theirs first thing in the morning. For the moment, though, it could be made to seem a Greek privilege.

And that swung them round. As the cheers died away and the gates at the far end of the Hall were pulled open, the herald was crying out in a voice of bright cheerfulness that everyone should go and get ready for the Evening Service, where he could give thanks for the ever-flowing bounty of the Imperial government.

'Well,' said Nicetas, stretching his arms as he moved for the first time that afternoon, 'I think that went rather better than expected.'

The Master of the Works agreed. Another Council member praised my mastery of the relevant facts. Another began some turgid paean to my 'matchless eloquence'. No one bothered asking what might have happened if the landowners had really wanted a riot. Without turning, I could hear Priscus sniffing up one of his milder powders.

We were alone in the Hall. The herald had jollied nearly everyone out, and the guards had pushed the few lingerers into the street. It had been a fine sound as they locked and barred the gates. I loosened my sweaty clothes and allowed what passed for fresh air to get at my body.

'Oh, Alaric,' Nicetas continued with a look away from me, 'you will be pleased to know that I am minded to seal the orders for the grain fleet to depart. His Holiness the Patriarch has finally decided that the day after tomorrow will be our time of greatest blessing. It will be the day of Saint Lupus. He was very good to Heraclius and me when we set out from Carthage. I still have the relic with me that we used to calm the storm on our second day.'

He stretched out his right leg and groaned. As if from nowhere, one of his monks appeared with a box of something I doubted was medicinal by any reasonable definition. Was it worth raising the matter of the redistribution warrants? I asked myself. Best not, I answered. With Nicetas, it was one thing at a time at best, or nothing. I sipped at the wine cup someone had put into my hand.

'No point, I suggest,' Nicetas said again, 'getting out of these fine clothes. I invite everyone to attend Evening Service in my own chapel, and then dinner afterwards. No dancing girls, in view of what day it is. But the new priest who'll read from Saint Basil between the courses has a most beautiful voice.

'What is that still doing here?' he asked, breaking off and looking down the Hall.

It was the child's body. It had served its purpose, and, in the rush to get out, had been dumped. There was other debris left behind. But that little bundle in the stained cloth, its blue-spotted arm still poking out, must have been contributing most to the smell that lingered in the air.

'Get this place cleaned up,' the Master of the Works said to one of the senior slaves. 'We've a presentation here from the schoolchildren of Naucratis.'

As he spoke, the light from overhead suddenly gave out. I looked up at the mirrors. Every one of them was now dull. I looked back

245

down and blinked in the gloom. There was a peal of distant thunder. I felt a draught on my bare chest.

'Ah, that was our reserve plan,' said Nicetas, still jolly though his monk was massaging relic oil into the raw flesh of his leg. 'I did ask His Holiness the Patriarch to pray for rain. If you couldn't persuade the mob to go away, the weather would disperse it. I think you'll agree the storm is right on time.'

35

I followed Hermogenes into the inner parts of the Library. In these corridors, narrowed in places to just a few feet by jumbled racks and cupboards, his predecessors had arranged what fragments were suffered to remain of the old stock. There was no access here for the public. Few visitors to the public areas could have known this place existed. Only those who knew their way by heart through the often unlit galleries and seams of this book mine would venture alone through the little door set into the wall a few yards down from the statues of Ptolemy and his friend Alexander.

Hermogenes strained to lift the door to his office out of its hinges. It was a heavy door, and his strength was long into its decline. But he managed to lift it high enough to open without too much scraping of the floor. It would have been a large room, but for yet more of the book racks. One of these had collapsed, spilling its contents on to the floor. From the dust covering the jumbled mass of papyrus, I could see it hadn't been touched in years. There was a small glazed window behind his desk that drew light from another room that had a skylight. Otherwise, it was an array of six lamps on a bronze stand beside the desk.

The smell of old papyrus was so overpowering, I sneezed a few of the lamps out. While Hermogenes fussed over relighting them, I squinted to try to see the titles of the book rolls he saw fit to keep around him.

'You will forgive me, My Lord, if I bring you here,' he repeated for the third time, 'but all the relevant information is now concentrated in this room.' He gave a nervous look at the ruined white silk of my tunic.

I made what I hoped was a careless grunt and continued looking at the parchment tag on one of the more visible book sheaths. It was what must have been a very old edition of Sappho, with a commentary by what may have been *the* Callimachus. *Impressive!* I thought, taking my place on the chair Hermogenes had finished dusting for me.

'I must thank – and, indeed, commend – you for the amount of effort you've put into this,' I opened. 'But you really will need to persuade me that I was at any time, on my journey through the desert, within several miles of Soteropolis. We know that the town was only abandoned in the time of Diocletian, three hundred years ago. I have some evidence, confirmed by the tax records, that it was a flourishing municipality in the time of Augustus, six hundred years ago. Yet almost exactly between these two reigns, Hadrian turned up and caused to be inscribed on what you tell me was its most famous monument a poem indicating that the whole area was desert. It doesn't fit together.'

'That is, My Lord, because you have assumed that there was just *one* town called Soteropolis, or that it remained throughout its history in the same place.' Hermogenes smiled and opened one of the files that lay on his desk. He'd done his work since our last meeting, and was feeling obviously pleased with himself. 'We both thought, from its name, that Soteropolis was likely to be a foundation of the early Ptolemies. What I have found is that it predates not merely the Greek settlement of Egypt, but also the native kingdom.

'Manetho was not the only native who, under the various Ptolemies wrote the history of his land. A much longer, if less popular, work was produced by one Archilochus, a priest of Horus, who turned Greek and was made Chancellor of the University of Naucratis. I have only been able to locate fragments of the first seven books. But what I have gives our fullest information about the early times.'

He paused as he unrolled a book. It was the skilled movement of one who hadn't been brought up on the more convenient modern books of bound parchment, and the aged papyrus bent in his hands without cracking. His finger hovered over one of the columns of text. I leaned forward and tried to see upside down what he was showing. The columns were only two inches wide, and the ancient semi-shorthand would have been hard in any light. Hermogenes moved his watery eyes close to the text. Then he gave up on citation and gathered his thoughts.

'The earliest mention of Soteropolis comes during the reign of the first King of all Egypt, whose name is rendered in Greek as Menes. This was many thousands of years ago. Soteropolis then was already very old. Its inhabitants were of conspicuously lighter appearance than the Egyptians, and they spoke a different language. No one knows their origin, but they were noted for their warlike pride and technical ingenuity, and it was only with much effort that they were reconciled to external authority.

'Menes besieged Soteropolis for seven years, during which every effort to subdue its inhabitants was made in vain. Only after a pestilence that destroyed most of them, without communicating itself to the besiegers, did they agree to terms. These terms were that they would abandon their town and take up service directly under the King and his successors.

'Settled by Egyptians, its name translated to their own language as "City of Salvation", Soteropolis continued to be a place of troubles. It was said that the ghosts of the original inhabitants would venture forth when the Nile flood was below its normal level. At those times, there would be further outbreaks of pestilence. The Greeks, for whom the town was emptied of natives in the time of the third Ptolemy and renamed again, coined the phrase: "When the Nile is low, death will walk the streets of Soteropolis".

'The most deadly attack of pestilence occurred in the reign of Nero, when the Nile failed to rise properly for two years together. Then the people of Soteropolis, together with all their household goods, were transferred to a new foundation about five miles to the south. That was the Soteropolis that was finally abandoned in the time of Diocletian, when it was clear that the pestilence had followed the inhabitants.'

'If it was that deadly,' I asked, 'why hold the Library's reserve stock there?'

'It was the decision,' Hermogenes said with a shrug, 'of Eratosthenes, the third in the line of Head Librarians. He specialised in natural philosophy, and was noted for his calculations to establish the size of the earth and to attempt to fix the distance from us of the heavenly bodies. He said an oracle had assured him that Soteropolis was a propitious location for his continued researches. It is reported that he went mad in extreme old age after digging in the foundations of a ruined temple there. To be sure, his claim that the sun is ninety-three million miles distant from us can be taken as the product of a disordered mind.

'Whether he died of his illness, or returned to Alexandria, I cannot say. But he spent the entire annual budget of the Library seven times over in Soteropolis, and it was never thought financially possible thereafter to undo his establishment there of the reserve stock holding.'

I'd come across how Eratosthenes measured the earth a few months earlier in the writings of another mathematician. It was a brilliantly simple application of Euclid. The data from which he'd reasoned might be questioned. But the method itself was beyond dispute. The claim about the sun was another matter. A few hundred miles made more sense. Still, I decided I'd like to go myself through the man's no doubt voluminous writings. If they rested beneath the desert I'd seen around Soteropolis, that was another reason for getting back there as soon as possible with my little army of diggers.

'All this being so,' Hermogenes continued, 'the Emperor would have seen nothing on his visit but the monument that you saw some way off, whatever lavish buildings housed the reserve stock. Assuming that his poem had been written for that occasion, and not reused from somewhere else, his words about the desolation around him were not wholly inaccurate.'

'Very well,' I said. 'I can have everything ready within ten days. Would you care to accompany me on the excavation?'

'No, My Lord,' came the answer with a sad smile. 'I am an old man. I have never yet left Alexandria for a journey into Egypt. I do not think now is the time to travel anywhere. Nevertheless, I think I can provide you with a better map than the one I gave you on your last visit.'

He'd given me a map? I looked blankly at him.

'You will, My Lord, surely remember the package of documents I prepared just before you left for the south?' He raised his eyebrows and looked slightly hurt that the days of work he'd put in hadn't been appreciated.

I did remember them now. I'd skimmed a few of them and left the others for my return. After my adventures with Lucas, they'd slipped my mind. They were still somewhere in my office.

'You gave me a map of Soteropolis?' I asked.

'Not a good one,' he conceded. 'It gave a few of the main locations. But I think I can turn up a much better map that will give the location of the reserve stock. I hope the distances will all be relative from the monument. This being so, you will know roughly where to dig.'

'Then I do ask for your best efforts in finding this map,' I said. I'd have liked to spend the entire day in and around that office. Forget Soteropolis – there was no telling what treasures might be crumbling quietly away in those racks. But I had business with Nicetas that wouldn't wait. I rose.

'Hermogenes,' I said, 'I want to thank you for all the work you've done so far, and all that you will continue to do in the service of the Empire. I will ask again if there is any reward I can give for all this – if not for you, then for the Library.'

He smiled, and repeated not for the first time that his only reward was the knowledge that able scholars still existed elsewhere in the Empire. If he could assist their efforts to the best of his own ability, he was content.

'Your bribe of oil has certainly *lubricated* the mob,' Nicetas had said at dinner the previous evening. Everyone had laughed politely at the witticism. But he was right. For the moment, I had soothed things. My chair was carried through streets as crowded and apparently as cheerful as ever. The shops and exchanges had all reopened. I came across a couple of my Jews as I passed by the Law Courts.

They touched their foreheads and bowed in their Eastern manner as I was carried past. Since we were in full public, I ignored them. I represented the Emperor himself, and there was nothing strange if people prostrated themselves in the dust before my chair.

There were still double guards on duty outside the Palace. But this was the result of orders given the previous day, not of present necessity. As usual, people were coming and going with minimal inspection of their documents.

Outside his office, the eunuchs tried to make a fuss about the book dust still clinging to me. But I was almost late, and the business I had with Nicetas was too important for delay.

I sat at my desk with a warm glow of satisfaction.

'So he sealed the dispatch orders?' Martin asked with a look at the leather packets neatly piled up on my left.

I thought to glower at him, but gave up at once. There was no point reopening the matter of the Leontius documents. I'd never shake his lunatic convictions. Besides, they couldn't be that important. If they had contained evidence of treason, would they really have been left behind? At best, they might be a listing of tomb contents that stopped short of anything valuable. Tomb robbers had already seen to that back in the days of the native kings. Why else had the man been counting so much on that mysterious draft from the Saracens?

'The fleet sails at first light tomorrow,' I said. The grain would be with Heraclius well before the shipping lanes closed down for the winter months. I'd be in Constantinople to receive his thanks in person. No luck with the arrest and search warrants, though. I'd explained what I knew over dinner. Priscus had listened in and had joined me in urging the need for immediate action. Sadly, any mention of 'immediate action', always had a bad effect on Nicetas. Against our advice, he'd then raised the matter in the meeting, just ended, of his full Council – only to explain why nothing could or should be done for the time being.

But I had the dispatch orders. First things first. The landowners could wait.

'Sveta still hasn't found that chamber pot,' Martin said. 'It was a valuable object, and we think it was taken by Macarius.'

I nodded. If they thought Macarius would throw up a nice position with me for the proceeds of five pounds of antique bronze, more fool them. But if that's what they thought, I had no reason to defend the man, and every reason to leave things alone.

'While looking in your own dressing room, though,' he added apologetically, 'I found this.' He held up a sheet of papyrus, a line of Hebrew written again and again all over the good side. 'It was concealed in the cloak you wear when you visit the – ah, the house of prostitution that you frequent. Would you like me to get it translated?'

I resisted the urge to get up and tear the sheet from his hand. I checked the sharp accusation already formed in my throat. It was Martin's duty to go through my private things. Anger really was out of the question – and it would only have drawn attention to what I was planning. Isaac had given me a very queer look when I'd asked him for the words 'A present to Jesus from Cousin Simon'. But he could be trusted to keep his mouth shut. All else aside, Jews had long since learned to keep out of disputes involving the Faith. But I needed Martin to remain as much in the dark as everyone else. This was troublesome, as, though I'd got the Hebrew characters well enough for what was needed, I hadn't yet worked out how to transfer the words to hardened bronze and make it all look old.

'Never mind that piss pot,' I said with an easy wave. 'Have you found the important one?' That set Martin off on a long description of the glories he'd found that weren't in the Patriarch's catalogue of relics. One of these was the very pen with which Saint John the Divine had written his Revelation.

'Excellent!' I said, cutting off the flow of credulity. 'Keep looking. Before I give in to Priscus and arrange his digging expedition, we need to make quite sure the relic isn't here in Alexandria.' Doubtless, Martin still had another fifty places to visit and inspect. But I'd tell Priscus the thing wasn't to be found here once the grain fleet was under way. I took the sheet of papyrus from Martin and put it into one of the files regarding the canal clearance.

'I have business tonight in the Jewish quarter,' I said. I ignored Martin's frown. 'Do let it be known to anyone who asks for me that I'm visiting that brothel.'

36

'Wake up, Aelric – oh, for God's sake, please wake up!'

I drew my knees instinctively up to my chin and rolled away. I'd been dreaming, and I wasn't sure that I still wasn't. Martin struggled again with the netting to get at me. In the dim light he'd set on the table beside my bed, I could see his ghastly face.

'Aelric, Aelric,' he cried despairingly, 'get up! All the ships are on fire.'

I was aware of a faint acrid smell. There was a dim flickering against the blind pulled down on the far windows. I jumped out of the bed before gathering my thoughts. I concentrated and tried to push the heavy, delicious velvet of the opium pill from my mind. I ripped the linen of the blind from its housing and let the air play on my face. The windows all faced east – away from the Harbour. But I could see the reflected glare flickering on the higher walls of the Palace far across the central garden.

I finished pulling myself together. Now dumb, his face still terrified, Martin passed me a gown. I threw it on. We hurried out into the dim corridors and ran silently on the carpets to the stairs leading up to the roof.

There was a small crowd already gathered there. It stood on the Harbour side, silent and still, watching the horrors unfolding a quarter of a mile away.

'Fireboats,' Priscus said as he drew me to one side and pointed towards the Lighthouse. I followed his outstretched arm. It was light enough with the towers of flame shooting upwards in the Harbour. But it all appeared to me one great chaos of sparks and drifting smoke.

'Someone's had the clever idea,' he explained, 'of getting across to the Lighthouse island and floating boats filled with burning pitch into the Harbour. The wind has blown them straight into the grain fleet. I think only one ship is afire, but it's a question of time before the bastards get lucky again.'

'Nicetas!' I said. 'Where is he?'

'Oh, he left just before you arrived,' Priscus said with a cold laugh. 'You'll find him in his chapel praying for another downpour.'

'I must get down there,' I cried. This was a disaster. Those ships had sat there an age, waiting for the dispatch orders to be sealed. Now it was all arranged. Come the dawn, they should be away. This couldn't be happening.

'Not so fast, my lad,' Priscus sneered, clamping an iron grip on my shoulder. 'If you're going anywhere, it will be with me in front of you. This is a matter for soldiers, and your military experience, I don't like to rub it in, amounts to fuck-all. I am, I *will* remind you, the Empire's most senior commander. If Heraclius has his grain fleet burned while I'm in Alexandria, I might pick up just a fragment of the blame. You leave this to me.'

As he spoke, slaves rushed puffing towards him with his sword and body armour. A eunuch turned round and started babbling something about unauthorised weapons in the Palace. If he got out a dozen words, I'd be surprised.

'You're lucky I'm not fully in charge here,' Priscus hissed down at him. The creature squirmed and squealed, clutching at his smashed nose. Priscus gave him a hard kick in the stomach and stepped back to avoid the fountain of bloody vomit that gushed in the flickering light from the Harbour.

'Well, come on, my pretty boy,' he said, turning back to me. 'Or do you propose to go back to bed and leave this to the professionals?'

When I'd made the exchange, earlier that night, from the chair provided by Isaac back to my own, the streets had been quiet as the grave. With their promise of food to come, it seemed the protesters had kept to their beds. No one saw me as I'd gone in through the side entrance to the brothel, and been shown out at the front to my own carrying slaves. I'd even stopped and got down from the chair on my way back to the Palace for the inspection I'd been promising myself of the obelisk. I hadn't seen much in the light from the street lamps. But it had been nice to be able to walk again in Alexandria without having to keep looking over my shoulder.

Down by the Harbour, though, it was complete uproar. The police were doing their best to hold back the gathering crowds. They were already through the dockyard gates, and there wasn't the manpower to force them out again. On the dockside, men ran frantically back and forth, trying to unload sacks of grain from the stricken ship, while others tried just as frantically to put out the flames. This wasn't easy. The fireboat had been provided with long iron spikes that had fastened themselves hard to the ship, and whatever combustible material had been used burned even under water.

'Where's the Harbour Master?' Priscus roared as he strode purposefully out of the crowd. 'You!' – he pointed at one twittery official – 'I want whoever's in charge here. Get him now.'

The official dropped his writing tablets and swallowed. He allowed himself one look into that terrible face and was off.

'Still only one ship, thank God,' Priscus shouted after a glance at the brightly lit lunacy of the dockside. And it still was only one ship – though showers of sparks were raining down unattended on the decks of the neighbouring ships. How none of them had yet caught fire was a mystery. 'A piece of silver, from the Viceroy,' he yelled at the dockyard slaves, 'for every sack piled up safe over here. One piece of silver!' The slaves had been flagging. They'd been gazing at the roaring, bubbling flames that looked set to burn the ship to the waterline. Now they rushed back into the flames, pulling frantically at the hatches to get at the deeper sacks.

'Silver from the Viceroy,' Priscus shouted at the watching crowd. He took out a purse and emptied it in his hand. He held up the shining pile and, with a theatrical gesture, threw the coins into the crowd. As the cowed, silent onlookers turned into a scrambling mob, he shouted the promise again and stood back to let them past.

The Harbour Master was a fat, bleary-looking creature. He rushed up still in his nightgown and threw himself at my feet.

'I want those ships out of the Harbour,' Priscus shouted above the noise. He pointed over at the opening to the sea. The wind was steady in our faces. He was ordering those slow, wide-bellied ships into the wind at night. And they'd be going past the point from where the boats had been launched.

'The Food Control Office building's on fire,' a police officer shouted from behind me.

I turned. He looked ready to drop with exhaustion. It was only the panic that kept him going. That building was a mile back inside the city.

'Those old women back in the Palace can witter all they like about how the mob has risen,' Priscus rasped at me. 'We both know better. This is treason – and coordinated treason too.' He looked at the Harbour exit. 'The ships must go out now. They must go that way.' He pointed again at the northern exit.

'With all respect, My Lord,' the Captain of the Fleet said, now beside me as if from nowhere, 'I can't risk going out that way. Without light, and into the wind—'

'Orders,' the Harbour Master cried, looking up from his prostration, 'the orders are—'

'Your orders are to get these ships out,' Priscus shouted. I say he shouted. Looking at him, he seemed barely to raise his voice. But it cut straight through the surrounding noise as if he'd got hold of a speaking trumpet. He dragged the Harbour Master to his feet and pushed him against one of the growing piles of grain sacks. 'Your orders are to do whatever you must to get those ships out to sea,' he said, now menacing. He turned and fixed the Captain with his eye. 'You do as I tell you, or your seconds in command get immediate promotion the moment I've had you bound and thrown into that burning hold. Do you understand me?'

You don't argue with that sort of order – not when given by Priscus. Dressed in his favourite black, he seemed to have grown a foot taller in the emergency. Where everyone else was in or bordering on panic, he was all calm authority. The two men shrank back as if in unison. They looked at each other. They nodded. Priscus turned back to me.

'Come with me,' he said curtly. He didn't look round as I followed him to the water's edge. 'This isn't the mob's work,' he repeated, pointing across at the exit to the Harbour. 'The easiest way on to that island is from the Egyptian quarter. The building on fire is deep inside the centre. Either the two mobs have joined forces – something that I don't think has happened in living memory – or this is a coordinated attack. If the latter, your suspicions are right that someone in the Council is leaking to the opposition. The moment Nicetas raised the matter of your arrest warrants in Council, this became inevitable. If both mobs aren't already on the streets, it can only be because it's harder to call them out at short notice than to arrange a few terror attacks.'

Someone came over and asked Priscus for instructions. He gave them, calmly and briefly, never taking his eyes off the dark waters of the Harbour. This wasn't Priscus the effeminate fop, Priscus the superstitious dupe I'd been planning to lead up river to Soteropolis. But you don't rise high under a competent soldier like the Emperor Maurice unless you know what you're doing in the heat of battle. You don't get as close as he'd come to smashing up the Persians with Heraclius breathing down your neck unless you have some of the qualities of Alexander he was always fancying for himself. I turned and looked back at the burning ship. Men on the other ships were now running desperately about, putting out the sparks that continued to rain on their decks.

'Look,' said Priscus. I followed his pointed finger as it traced a path right, along the Lighthouse island to the causeway and beyond into the Western Harbour. When the wind blew so steadily from the north, I knew that ships came into the Eastern Harbour, but were sent out through the Western. 'The plan is to panic us into launching the ships that don't get fired. They'll then be cut off with another attack of fireboats. If we can get them straight out to sea, there will be something at least to send off come the dawn.'

'But what about the wind?' I asked, holding up my sweaty hands. It blew soft but steady on them from the Harbour exit. I knew little enough of ships and sailing. But I knew ships couldn't set sail into the wind – not in a crowded harbour, nor towards a point held by an enemy that might have another fleet of fireboats to send against them.

Well, I thought I knew these things. But Priscus, it was soon obvious, knew more than I did. By threats and bribes and sheer force of personality, he was imposing order on the chaos. The ship that had taken fire was burning beyond hope. Much of the grain might be pulled out of its hold, but it would burn and burn down to the waterline. But the other ships, after an age of yelling and pulling on ropes, were moving away from the dock. Somehow, the Harbour Master had found boats to pull them towards the exit. One of them positioned itself a few hundred yards from the exit, a dozen archers ready to let fly at anyone on shore who dared break cover to send out more fireboats at the other ships. The Lighthouse and the calm seas would help the grain fleet to pull itself into some order out there as it waited for the light and then some kind of formal orders to depart.

If I'd been the centre of attention when we arrived, I was now forgotten. Everyone looked to Priscus as he strode purposefully about the docks, his dark cloak flapping in the breeze, the dying flames glinting on the breastplate of his armour. Several times, I saw him laugh. Once, I even saw him clapping the Harbour Master on the back. There was no point standing where he'd left me. I was beginning to get in the way, as every square foot of dockyard space was rapidly taken up by more or less smoke-damaged sacks of grain. I found a little brick building and sat on a pile of ropes on the land side. After a while, I gave up trying to look dignified for the few people who bothered staring in my direction.

The dawn was now up, and Martin with his satchel of bread and wine had found me. Coward though he was, he hadn't been happy with my orders to stay behind in the Palace. Now, the emergency past, he'd taken my orders as applying only to the night.

'I saw some prisoners taken out under guard,' he said, nodding his head back towards the dockyard gates. 'They were young men – natives, I think. One of them was wounded.'

That would have been Priscus as well. I'd seen him barking orders at two boatloads of police officers as they set out across the Harbour for the island shore. One had made straight for the point from where the fireboats had come, another for a jetty about three hundred yards to the left.

'I heard that only one ship was damaged in the end,' he said.

I nodded and reached for the satchel of bread. I got up and looked uncertainly at the Harbour. The sun was rising fast in the sky, and it lit up the dimpled waters of the now empty Harbour. Far out, beyond the exit, the grain fleet rode safely at anchor. The wreckage of the burned ship was being methodically broken up and cleared away. A few men lay on the dockside, where they'd collapsed from exhaustion. Officials stepped over them as they counted and recorded the saved cargo.

Of course, I hadn't been able to count the sacks carried off. Still, the impression I had was that most of the cargo had been saved. It was spoiled, and would never do for transporting all the way to Constantinople. One sniff at the bread made from it, and the mob there would start a riot of its own. Any but the most desperate barbarians would throw it back in our faces, and probably burn a few more cities out of wounded pride. But, washed and dried, it would fetch something on the local market.

'But, little Martin, how delightful of you to remember breakfast,' Priscus crooned, suddenly beside me. He took the unstopped flask from my hands and took a long pull from it. Face and hands black from the smoke, his armour discarded somewhere among the grain sacks, he still seemed to loom over the pair of us. He glowed, though exhausted. It was as if he'd taken the entire contents of his drug satchel – and had got the relative doses exactly right. He fell onto the pile of ropes that I'd vacated and mopped happily at his face. The wound he'd picked up on the road towards Siwa had opened up again, and the cloth came away covered in blood as well as sweaty soot.

261

'Any news of events further inland?' he asked.

I looked at Martin. He looked back, plainly confused.

'Never mind,' Priscus said. He turned his attention for the moment to the bread, and tore ravenously at the loaf.

'I imagine there will be an emergency meeting of the Council once we get back,' I said.

'Not if what I've seen of Nicetas is representative of his behaviour in a crisis,' Priscus grunted. 'No, not if he's anything like his dear and Imperial cousin.' He put the bread down and laughed. I thought I might like some of the wine. But Priscus had the flask again.

'You didn't see him as I did outside Caesarea,' he said, laughter giving way to bitterness. 'The Persians had smashed through the wafer-thin front of our best troops. They'd found we had no reserves. Even so, I might have scared them back inside the gates if only I'd been able to pull the two wings in tight.' He looked at me and Martin. I struggled to imagine what I now realise was an obvious tactic. Priscus noticed I wasn't really following and shrugged. 'But you'll hear it all from the poor bloody veterans when Heraclius commissions you to write up the history of his reign,' he said. 'All you'll have to do to make him shine like another Belisarius is to cut out the time he spent puking up his breakfast, and transfer to him my own part in organising the skirmish around his travelling chapel that kept the Persians from swallowing up the whole wreckage of his army.

'No, my dearest boy, if Nicetas is anything like Heraclius, you'll not want an emergency meeting this morning of his Council or with him.' He sprawled back on the pile of ropes and stretched his trousered legs.

I chewed on the crust of bread he'd left me and tried to look more like the Emperor's Legate than I felt. Priscus ignored my efforts and turned to Martin.

'Well, my little secretary,' he asked, 'how goes your trawl of all the churches in Alexandria?'

'We've so far come up with nothing,' I said, cutting short the mumbled response. This was a good time to announce I'd given in and was planning a digging trip to Soteropolis. That would recover some of my lost equality with him. I got no further, though. I as good as had the words in my mouth when one of the junior police officers came in sight round the brick building.

Priscus took his message and read it. He gave me an amused look and bent the sheet back into its containing band.

'I would send you back to the Palace to recover yourself after this most stressful night,' he said, just the right touch of irony in his voice to remind me of my own uselessness when it came to organised force. 'However, something's come up where it would be most valuable to have the pair of you as witnesses. I might also find Martin's famed scribal skills of more than passing use.'

37

The police officer bowed and stood back as he pushed the door open. One smell of what lay beyond, and the breath caught in my throat. It was like a butcher's market at the end of a hot day. I'd been in the City Prefecture building any number of times. But it was never on police business, and never in the cellars, which were sealed from the main building by doors at each end of the narrow, winding stairs that led down from a room just off one of the side entrances.

I must have known this place existed. I'd been twice in the dungeons under the building in Constantinople that had served much the same purpose before the revolution. But these are places normally considered only when brought undeniably into mind.

As if he'd been going there every day for a lifetime, Priscus went up to the crabbed, pasty-faced official who sat in the first room of the City Prison. An underground room, about fifteen feet by fifteen, it would have been normal enough but for the smell. It was a place of filing racks and keys on numbered hooks. We'd entered through the door that led directly from the bottom of the stairs. Immediately opposite this, and to the right of the reception desk, another door led to what I could easily guess lay beyond.

'I take it you have the investigation room prepared,' Priscus said easily, dropping his message on to the desk.

The official looked closely at the unrolled sheet and nodded. He got up and bowed to Priscus and to me, and motioned us towards the other door.

Some of the more imaginative – or perverted – divines have written about Hell as a series of levels, beginning with the moderately unpleasant and finishing with the indescribably awful. I suppose the long, dimly lit corridor that ran from that door under the whole length of the Prefecture would rank about halfway down the scale of horror. Imagine cells five feet square and barely that high, each one crammed with half a dozen naked wretches beside whom the lowest trash of the mob in the streets above was clean and well fed. Imagine the smell of putrid excrements and sores burst open and left to fester. Imagine those desperate faces pressed against the bars of their cell doors. Imagine the whispered, hopeless cries for justice or simply for mercy, and you have the smallest gears of the machinery with which such order as Alexandria normally enjoyed was maintained.

If Priscus had seemed to have grown physically larger from the joy to setting things to right in the dockyard, he now almost filled the passageway separating those two lines of dehuman-ised horror. I heard a continual whispering of prayers behind me from Martin. For myself, if I could have squeezed my eyes shut and stopped up my ears and nose, I'd have done so. I wanted to be through this as quickly as possible. I wanted to get back to the Palace and soak myself in a bath until the afternoon, and stupefy myself with opium and with wine. If no fragmen-tary recollection of this ever came back to haunt my dreams, I told myself, I'd die content. But Priscus walked ahead of me exactly as if he'd been inspecting some guard of honour. He stopped once – I could scarce believe it – and actually pushed his arm through one of those grilles to stroke the bowed head of one of the prisoners.

'Like Christ Himself,' he whispered exultantly, 'we must bear whatever cross Our Heavenly Father makes for us. Let His Will be done!'

'Let His Will be done,' came the response in cracked unison from the few voices that still could be understood at all.

We stood at last in a room deeper beneath the Prefecture. If low enough for the ceiling to brush my topmost hair, it was otherwise too large for the one lamp set into a recess by the door to do more than throw vague shadows beyond its pool of light. I could hear the gurgling rush of the flood waters through the stone grilles in the floor. With the waters came a chill breeze that made the smell almost bearable by comparison with what had been so far.

'Do you know why I've had you separated from your companions and brought here?' Priscus opened in conversational tone. He sat himself carefully on a small table that shifted under his weight, and looked at the three tightly bound figures who lay on the floor about a yard from his crossed feet. They could move their heads for looking around. Otherwise, they could do no more than shuffle like serpents on that cold and damp and sick-makingly dirty floor.

They were young men, I could see as my eyes adjusted to the still deeper gloom of this place – very young men. They certainly weren't my age. If any of them had seen seventeen, I'd have been surprised. Obviously natives, they had the good build and clean look of the higher classes in any nation. Except for the different cut of their clothes, they might have been Greek. One of them looked away as Priscus leaned forward. His mouth moved wordlessly as if revealing some chant or prayer going again and again through his mind.

'Your companions are low creatures,' Priscus said again. 'Their usefulness to me was limited. Before I have my afternoon shit, some of them will be dead. The others will be praying for death. This they might receive today. Or it might be tomorrow, depending on the mood of the assistants who have been set to work on them.'

Priscus stopped and recrossed his legs. He looked at his fingernails. He spoke with the calm authority of a man giving instructions to his secretary. Unblinking, the young men stared back. I wanted to take Martin by the hand and run away as quickly as our legs would carry us. I'd recognised some of the dim shapes outside the pool of light. All that kept me there was the knowledge of what I'd have to pass through before regaining the light of day – and, I suppose, the knowledge that Priscus would never let me forget what, if I remained, I might yet contrive to blot out.

'You, however, are persons of far greater quality,' he went on, his voice still bordering on the friendly. 'You were not intended to fall into my hands. But you have, and you must accept that the Divine Providence has frowned on the plot conceived against the Empire by your elders – a plot of which I am assured you have far better knowledge than your companions.

'Let me tell you now that you can make this easy for us all. Do you see that fat man over there by the door?'

I heard Martin drop something from his shaking hands.

'If you give what I think are truthful answers to my questions, he will write them down. You will then be transferred to a more salubrious confinement than this until your evidence has been considered in court. You will then be released unhurt. If you incriminate any persons under whose will you would normally have inherited, your rights will be respected despite any confiscations that are made.

'You have my word in this. You may not know me, but I am a person with full authority to make this promise. And I am sure you know the Senator Alaric. You will surely know that he is always good for his word.' He broke off and looked at me.

I looked down at the young men. I was sure I'd seen one of them in a shop somewhere. It was hard to tell in these surroundings. I swallowed and tried to get some moisture into my throat.

'Do as he says,' I said, keeping my voice as steady as I could. 'Answer his questions and I promise you your lives. I promise this in the name of the Emperor.'

Silence. One of the young men looked up at me. His dark eyes glittered scared in the lamplight. I stared back and pleaded in silence for him not to be so stupid. Priscus had involved me in his promise. That meant I could enforce it on him, should he feel inclined to break it. The young man looked away. The other two didn't so much as move their heads in my direction.

Priscus stood up and stretched his arms. He stood over the young man who'd looked at me. His voice echoed oddly in that low but extended room as he spoke slowly and with exaggerated clarity.

'I will give you one final chance before we start some Greek lessons of my own. I must warn you, though, I am running out of time even before I run out of patience.' He went to the door and tapped three times on the inside. He stood back as it opened. It was like watching slaves bring in the dining things for a banquet. There were lamps. There was a brazier, well heaped with glowing charcoals. There was even one of those little travelling desks that officials would carry about on their errands. Its inner compartment was stocked with waxed tablets and pens. Priscus pointed to it and looked at Martin.

The light and heat excepted, nothing more was needed. I'd been right about the dim shapes. When you've seen one set of torture instruments, you don't fail to recognise more of the same. There were the spiked cabinets, the tables with their leather restraints and man-shaped depressions, the kettles for heating oil or water, or containing the corrosive fluids. On the walls were the usual racks of knives and pincers and hooked gloves.

I hardly need mention the rack. None of these places would be complete without one. Here, it had what amounted to pride of place. In all, it was about ten feet long, a fixed bar at one end with leather thongs attached, an elaborately geared roller at the other, also with leather thongs attached. I looked away from the instruments. I found myself looking instead at the two craftsmen of pain who'd stayed when the lamp bearers had withdrawn. They might have been brothers. Both were short creatures with heavily muscled arms and shaven heads, both obscenely fat, both with faces that flitted from moment to moment between the ecstatic and the totally blank. But if they had been brothers, I knew well enough they'd have had to be part of a family that had its members in every city of the Empire. Whatever your appearance when you take on that job, that is how in no time at all you end up looking. Naked apart from their stained loincloths, they stood bowed and respectful before Priscus.

'It is my custom,' he opened again – still calm, still bordering on the friendly – 'to give those whom I must question a tour of these places. An explanation of how these various instruments work can have a most loosening effect on the tongue. You will appreciate, however, that time grows ever shorter. I will therefore ask you once more and once only – *do as I ask of you.*'

'The tears of Alexander shall flow, giving bread and freedom!' From what may have been the oldest of the three, the familiar slogan rang out in Egyptian. 'The tears of Alexander shall flow, giving bread and freedom!' he said again, now louder. The other two joined in, defiant in unity. They varied this with something I hadn't heard before, but contained the Egyptian word for Greeks.

Priscus stood looking down at them, waiting for them to run out of energy or defiance. He waited in the silence that followed. The silence continued. He shrugged. He turned to the torturers.

'We'll start with the rack,' he said quietly.

The torturers bowed.

'I want' – his finger moved uncertainly over the three – 'that one.' His finger stopped and pointed firmly at the one who'd been looking up at me.

38

'Priscus,' I said, breaking the tension in that torture chamber. I took a step forward. He turned his head towards me. I wasn't sure what I'd wanted to say. Before I could think of anything, he'd raised his arm.

'Don't get involved, Alaric,' he said in Latin. He smiled and pointed at me to stand back against the wall. 'You know the formalities of lawful authority don't count in treason cases. Whatever I do now I do with the full weight of the Empire behind me. That one,' he repeated to the torturers.

They'd already got him to his feet. Now, they didn't bother untying him, but just cut him out of the ropes. They cut him out of his clothes and even his shoes, dumping the ruined things in a heap.

'The tears of Alexander,' he began with a squeak that trailed off with the dawning of genuine fear.

Naked, he looked even younger than I'd thought. He tried turning his head towards the others. But naked and glistening in the now more than adequate light, his body was arched backward over the rack. They were all stupid, spoiled brats. They'd spent what little time they'd lived among fawning slaves and tradesmen. Their fathers' money had bought their way through every scrape and problem. They'd somehow got themselves mixed up in the firing of the grain fleet without once thinking through what they were doing. Everything so far since their arrest had been just an elaborate game. I was sure they expected their fathers to arrive any moment in that dungeon, purseloads of gold to scatter about and turn Priscus jolly with its magic touch.

But you didn't play with Priscus – not when he had you in his power; not perhaps ever.

'Such freshness, such youth, such perfection of form!' Priscus crooned softly as he leaned over the tethered boy. He ran a finger lightly down the line of the chest, over the stomach, to rest just above the groin. The boy was fastened by his ankles to the fixed bar at one end of the rack, by his wrists to the geared roller at the other end. He'd started babbling and pleading as the roller had gone round to its first click, lifting his taut body off the table.

'Too late, my beauty, too late,' Priscus said. 'Oh, had you only taken my offer – such golden times we might have had. But say farewell now to beauty and freshness. Say farewell to all that might have been. Say farewell to hope itself.' He turned to one of the torturers. 'Take it up to number seven,' he said.

'But, My Lord,' the man began.

'I know the working of your machine as well as you do,' Priscus replied. 'When I say number seven, I mean number seven. Now do it – and take it straight there.'

I don't like the rack. I've always hated it. But you don't normally see it taken far up. For actual punishment, there are the more visual and diverse torments. The idea of racking is to get information. The first few clicks of its geared roller are frightening. The next is painful if prolonged. The next is immediately excruciating as joints, mostly in the arms and legs, are pulled to separating point. After that, it's the popping of dislocated joints, and the ripping of ligaments, and then the snapping of the weaker bones. Long before the flesh tears and limbs are pulled loose from the body, long before the splashing of blood and the partial recoil of stretched limbs, there's no recovery from the damage. It's then a matter of swollen, jellied limbs that never move again, or of paralysis if the weakest point under pressure turns out to be the spine.

But I'd never seen the rack taken beyond the second or third clicks. I say that I watched. In truth, I shut my eyes the moment the poles were inserted into the slotted wheel and those sweaty, chattering creatures leaned forward. What I couldn't blot out was the transformation of a human scream into something like the squeal of a butchered pig. It gave out when all the air had been forced out of the lungs, and nothing could be taken in.

It was a quieter, more sobbing, but still animalistic cry as the straps were suddenly relaxed, and now, at the beginning of his living death, the boy was thrown back on to the floor. He landed with his arms and legs at impossible angles. I forced myself to shift position without falling over, and turned to Martin. Eyes screwed shut, he'd pushed his head down on to his chest. He was praying under his breath in Celtic. I reached out to bring him back to the present and get his writing materials ready.

'Not yet,' Priscus said gently. He stepped away from the rack and looked down at what he'd created. He pointed at the fatter of the torturers. 'We both know the custom,' he said. He looked down at the boy. 'But let's have none of this modern coyness. Do it here and do it now.'

I'd thought we'd already neared the bottom of the scale of horror. As I stood, watching this gross and monstrously prolonged rape, I realised that Priscus had got us so far only halfway down the scale. I won't try describing what I had to witness. Even after seventy-four years, it's enough to freeze the blood. Martin continued praying throughout. I wished I could have joined him. As it was, I made myself think about my price ratios, and how these might correlate in turn with solar eclipses, until I could almost see the numbers dance together.

'Get that thing out of here,' Priscus said at last. He kicked hard at the smaller of those obese monsters, who wasn't happy with first helpings, but was again thrusting into and pulverising the now unconscious boy. He rolled off on to his back, and looked dreamily at the deflating, bloody thing between his legs. Then, like a bow that springs back to its original shape, his face took on its normal, moronic blankness. 'Take it from cell to cell outside,' Priscus added, 'and let the prisoners have their pleasure. If it still breathes after two days, throw it to the dogs.

'Oh, and do take out the teeth,' he added as the door was about to close. 'Don't bother with it here. But do make sure no one in the cells is inconvenienced.'

The door was closed. The babble from outside of expectant grunts and shrill cries could no longer be heard. Priscus stared down at the two remaining boys. They'd sobbed and screamed at the opening of the horrors. They'd rolled about in a kind of frenzy. I could smell that they'd shat themselves. Since then, they'd lain, shocked and exhausted, on their backs. Now Priscus was giving them his full attention. He pointed at the larger one who'd started the defiant chanting.

'Get that one on his knees,' he rapped at the one torturer left in the room. 'I want his tongue pulled out.'

'No – please, sir, no!' the boy screamed. He shuffled desperately forward. He licked at the boot Priscus had planted on the ground nearest his face.

'But do tell me, what use is there in a tongue that doesn't speak as directed?' Priscus asked, pulling his foot sharply back and bending so low his face was almost level with the boy's. 'Is it possible that you might now remember a little of the Greek you surely learned at school?'

It was possible their Greek was among the best Alexandria had to offer. Unable to keep their voices below a bubbling screech, they competed at denouncing everyone and everything in their minds. They denounced their parents. They denounced each other. They denounced the wretch who'd just been broken on the rack. They'd have denounced Christ himself if Priscus hadn't silenced them.

'I want the truth,' he said, now friendly again, 'and I want nothing but the truth. Anything more will only slow me, and I haven't time to be slowed. Now, my dear young things, I know the truth when I hear it. And I do know how to check what I'm told. Anything less than the truth – anything more than the truth – and I'll have the pair of you on that rack.'

Martin snapped his pen several times as he scratched at the tablets. Try as he might, Priscus couldn't impose any order of time on the new denunciations. But I couldn't doubt they were true. When Martin had finished copying it all into the right form, the conspiracy and its authors would be revealed plain enough even for a fair trial.

★　　★　　★

Back in the sunlight of the street, I gave way to nature and vomited against one of the Prefecture columns. The single guard who was on duty by the main entrance twisted his face as if to scowl at me. But he saw the purple border on my robe, and went back to his duties, which seemed to involve looking ferocious at everyone walking too close by the building.

Priscus still hadn't washed off the smoke and dirt of the night. But he was rubbing at his face in the reflection of a glazed window.

'Do feel free with my blue pills,' he said, nodding down at the satchel he'd dumped on the pavement. 'They can work miracles on the promptings of a tender heart.'

I ignored him and leaned forward again. There was another splatter of thin liquid on to the marble. We'd already sent Martin on ahead to the Palace. Prayer, and the certainty that – however it might have been in my own case – there was nothing in the world he could have done to prevent anything he'd witnessed, had brought back his composure almost at once. I was the one who was slowing things.

'Do I disgust you that much?' Priscus asked. From his tone, he could have been asking if the gash on his forehead might frighten passers-by. I stood against the pillar and looked at the crowds. There were fewer persons of quality carried past than was normal for the district and the time of day. The middling people still about were unusually subdued. Most of the shops were open, but with fewer goods stacked up outside them.

'I don't expect thanks,' Priscus said with a change of tone. His voice was now all quiet, if defensive, reason. 'But you'll not deny it was a useful morning down there. You'd have spent days – admit it – in genteel questioning. You'd have teased out contradictions and impossibilities in the answers. You'd have tested hypotheses against facts. You'd have been finishing your report just as the main riots were subsiding. I got the truth in less time than it takes to paint my face. And it won't just be a dozen arrest warrants you'll get Nicetas to sign when he's shown Martin's formal account of those confessions. There will be no one left to oppose your land law.

'There it is, my darling. I'll bet you never thought I'd be the one to unblock four months of prevarication. Even without the Great

Augustus there to get in your way, you'd have done worse than I could against the Persians. For all I opposed it in Constantinople, I could have got your land law through before I'd found my way about the Palace.' He took up his satchel and waved it under my nose.

I looked away, still unable to speak.

'Alaric,' he said again. I thought for a moment he'd pat me on the back. Luckily, he decided against. 'Alaric, I know you don't like my methods. But I gave that boy more chances than the law requires. And I may have got information that will snuff out this planned insurrection before it has time to start. I may have saved countless lives. Bearing in mind the unexpected scale of this conspiracy, even you might agree that I've saved the Empire.'

Still unable to speak, I stared at him.

'Do ask yourself how an empire survives without men like me,' he said with a smile. 'It needs heroes to found it, and poets and artists and philosophers to make it noble. And it needs someone to direct the rack if it's to be kept in order.'

'I think there are certain formalities to be completed before we take ourselves off to Nicetas,' I said, now I was sure of a steady voice. I stood upright and took a step back towards the Prefecture entrance. 'However they were got, you have truths that must be used fast if they are to be useful.'

39

'If you won't let the doctors in, my poor young fellow,' Priscus drawled as my own so far unpersuasive flow of reasoning came to another halt, 'that will soon need to come off.'

Nicetas groaned feebly as he shifted position again. Since our last meeting his leg had swelled up to twice its normal size, and there was no end to the pus now oozing from the sores.

'The head of Saint Mark is being taken specially from its golden case,' he said in Latin, the pain having taken his Greek away. 'Prayers are being ordered in every church for the moment when I feel its healing touch.'

'All the more reason, then, Nicetas dear,' Priscus added as he went back to the matter in hand, 'not to interfere with the arrests. I do assure you that, if we don't have everyone under lock and key by tonight at the latest, Alexandria will go up in flames, and then we lose Egypt. Even if this latter doesn't worry you, the former might get in the way of your church services.'

'Let me repeat,' I added, 'we have five hundred men under arms to control a city of five hundred thousand. I've taken the liberty of sending for reinforcements to every place within a two-day return journey. Even so, I'm not sure it will be enough to put down an insurrection.' I looked again at the warrants sealed earlier at the Prefecture. They were scattered loosely on a table Nicetas had beside his daybed. Every one of them had been heavily scored through in purple ink.

Nicetas followed my glance and frowned at me. 'You had no authority,' he said with an attempt at sternness. 'All security matters that touch the higher classes of any community are for me and for me alone.' He beckoned one of his monks over again. He cried out with pain as the man lifted his leg and dropped it down like a slab of butcher's meat.

'With all respect, Nicetas,' I said, 'my commission gives me full authority to take such actions as I deem necessary for implementation—'

'Your commission,' he snarled back at me, 'gives you no right to take men from their houses when I've spent two years buttering them up. It certainly gives you no right to put their sons on the fucking rack. Can the pair of you begin to understand what you've done?'

He winced and his whole body shook as the monk poked a finger into one of the larger sores and clapped on what looked like a shrivelled scalp. Priscus and I fell silent during the prayers and application of holy water.

'I think you need to understand,' Priscus opened again, 'that this is a matter of treason. What you call possible rioting Alaric and I know is planned insurrection. We are to lose Alexandria to a coalition of the possessing classes and the joined mob. At the same time, there is to be a Persian attack on Egypt from across the Red Sea. If we lose Egypt, the Empire starves. Before then, Syria will be attacked on two fronts. Do you want to go down in the history books as the man who wrecked the Empire?' He held up the two sets of confessions that Martin had neatly copied out. 'We also have the evidence of your own secretary. He confessed without any pressure. He confirmed—'

He stood back as Nicetas picked up a case of waxed writing tablets. He howled something that wasn't in Greek or even Latin, but might have been Berber, and swung round viciously with them and caught the monk straight in the face. The man took his hands off the leg and stood calmly back to continue his praying.

'Now look what you've made me do!' Nicetas cried accusingly. He called the monk forward for an embrace and apologies. He'd do penance, he swore, for this. In the meantime, he'd bear up under the healing ministrations of the Church.

Ignoring the trickle of blood down his cheek, the monk looked pleased with himself and went back to his probing and kneading of the sores.

'I've already had my secretary released,' Nicetas gasped with a nasty look at Priscus. 'Do you know how difficult it is to find trilingual secretaries in Alexandria?'

'I believe the first one you had was poisoned,' I said. 'I think that is a matter that bears reopening.'

'And I suppose you are the expert,' Nicetas jeered, 'when it comes to finding an assistant isn't all you thought he was.'

I fell silent at the reference to Macarius and looked at the icon of Heraclius hung where everyone coming into the office could see it glowering down. It was one of the lush productions we'd ordered for sending out to the provinces. It showed Heraclius in full regalia, Christ and the Virgin standing behind him. I'd wondered for a while which of the two cousins was worse when it came to getting anything done. Nicetas had won the contest within my first month. This was just the presentation of the olive garland.

'My dear fellow,' Priscus said, his face turning darker and darker with suppressed rage, 'I will remind you once again that we have a city of five hundred thousand ready to go off beneath us like a volcano, not to mention a Persian attack by sea. We need those traitors out of circulation, and we need an immediate show of force using the men we have.'

'But it won't be five hundred thousand all rioting together,' Nicetas replied. He covered his eyes as he tried to blot out the pain of the latest ministrations. 'If it's five thousand who riot, that will be the limit,' he said at last. 'And I won't remind you that the Greek and Egyptian mobs are just as likely to turn on each other as on us.'

'We're looking at mobs, each one five or ten times that size,' Priscus said. He was breathing heavily as he repeated the obvious for perhaps the third time. 'The Greek trash is already gathered on our side of the Wall. The Palace approaches are all blocked. Alaric and I pushed our way through on foot with drawn swords. There's an unverified report that the Master of the Works was torn from his chair and disembowelled as he tried to get in to the Palace.'

'And the mobs are being directed,' I said. 'They are being directed on both sides of the Wall. If they are allowed to come within sight of each other, they will combine.'

'If you were that concerned about the mob,' Nicetas asked suddenly, 'why did you let the grain fleet go? Everything was fine before you bullied me into sealing those orders. Are you trying to tell me that if I don't seal everything else you push under my nose, things will get worse?'

I thought Priscus might explode. But if I still hadn't discovered any infallible way of making this bloody Viceroy take action, I did know how to make him not act at all.

'We have clear proof,' I said, pointing at the confessions that Priscus was still clutching, 'that fourteen of the lesser land-owners have been engaged in a treasonable correspondence with the Brotherhood, which is, in turn, allied with the Persians. We know further that the traitors have sent hired agitators to stir up sedition among both main communities in Alexandria. And we know that all the deliberations of your Council have been passed to these people by your own secretary. Where treason is concerned, we have an overriding duty of care to the Emperor. I know that he will be most concerned if Alexandria and Egypt are endangered by any conspiracy that might have been avoided.'

'And why has everyone turned traitor?' Nicetas howled. As if he were now being threatened with the rack, his voice echoed about the high room. 'If you hadn't come here, demanding what I'm sure Heraclius, given proper advice, would never have intended for Egypt, would there have been this "treasonable correspondence"? If you hadn't discovered it and insisted on arrests, would there now be paid incitements to rioting? I don't think so. All my troubles began that day when you showed up here with your schemes of "improvement".

'I even think you brought on my bad leg. I was ever so healthy before you began making trouble. I think you're just jealous because you're a barbarian and I'm not.'

'Alaric and I are both members of the Imperial Council,' Priscus said through gritted teeth. 'If, in our joint written opinion, you are unfit to perform your duties, it is within our power to—'

'Don't you presume to threaten me!' Nicetas roared.

I shuffled a little to my right so he had his back to me. I tried mouthing warnings to Priscus to drop this line at once. It was too late.

'Don't you dare threaten me,' he went on, his voice cracking into a scream. 'I don't like to remind you, Priscus, but, whatever your actual reason for being here, you are out of your area without permission. You have only so much position in Alexandria as I allow you. As for you, Alaric, you may represent the Emperor. But I *am* the Emperor here in every sense that matters. Your power of deposition applies to provincial governors, not the Viceroy of Egypt.'

He shut up and gave us both fierce looks. I glanced at the window. Though shuttered, and though positioned away from the sun, there was that slight change in the colour of the light creeping through that indicated the afternoon was almost over. Nicetas looked down at his leg. As his face had grown redder, this seemed to have taken on a blueish tinge. Managing somehow not to move his leg, he twisted round and thrust his face into a cushion. As the slaves redoubled their fanning, he began to sob bitterly.

'I won't seal *anything* more,' he said indistinctly. 'You can't make me do anything against my will. All we have to do is sit quiet, and the conspirators will send round for an amnesty. This is what always happens. If we do nothing, the trouble will go away. As for the Persians, the Red Sea tides won't let them across. The way you both talk about them, anyone would think they were led by Moses.'

'In ancient times, the poor understood their place in the order of things,' some old fool in a cloth wig intoned for the third time. 'They starved without involving themselves in the affairs of their betters.' For the third time, there was a burst of appreciative comment about him. Someone else stamped hard and called on the Judgement of Heaven.

'I hear the perimeter about the Harbour has gone down,' I said, leaning on the rail that went round the roof of the Palace. 'We'll know soon enough if the incense warehouses take fire.'

'My dearest boy,' Priscus sniffed, 'even now, I could stop all this with three hundred men. Give me the right seal on wax, and I could pacify Alexandria for a century to come.' He went back to looking over the rail. 'Has Martin turned up my relic?' he asked with a sudden change of subject.

It was coming towards the midnight hour. The Viceroy's belief now that doing nothing would help settle things down hadn't turned out yet to be right. Seen from the Palace roof, Alexandria was beginning to look like the constellation of lights on a fresh grave. As yet, most of them might only have been bonfires in the public squares. But here and there, it was plain that public buildings were being fired. Every so often, as the breeze shifted from the north, snatches of wild shouting and a smell of burning were carried up from the city. The one large exception to the rising tide of chaos was a district bounded by the Library, the Wall and the sea. From here on the Palace roof, it showed up as an oval of unbroken darkness against the scattering of flares all around. I tried to remember what district this was, but I was too fixed on other matters. I looked round again at Priscus.

'I think we need to speak about your piss pot,' I began.

I got no further, as it was now that the Master of the Works came on to the roof. Reports of his murder, he assured us, had been exaggerated. Even so, he'd had a close escape. Everyone gathered round as he described how the mob had seized and cut the throats of his carrying slaves. Luckily for him, he'd managed to get into a public toilet, where he'd hidden until a Syrian banker had taken the mob's fancy. It had been his entrails wrapped about the statue of Julius Caesar.

A crowd now formed round Priscus, who began his lecture about the need for a show of force before the mob ran out of all control. Except our meeting with Nicetas hadn't gone as hoped, he'd had a wonderful day: crisis management, and torture that had actually worked. The cup in his hand ever refilled, he was sliding into his confident military hero act that had so pissed me off in Constantinople. How he didn't drop from exhaustion was testimony to a superb constitution – or advertisement for the powders he was alternating with the wine.

'We are quite safe in here, though, aren't we?' Martin asked. We'd moved across the roof and were now looking over the Egyptian quarter. As yet, this was less brightly lit than the centre. I had no doubt, however, things were running out of control there as well.

'The Palace was built with this sort of thing in mind,' I said reassuringly. 'I did read that one of the Ptolemies was torn to pieces by the mob when it broke in. However, he had just raped and murdered his sister, and the guards may have been on strike. I'm not sure of the details, but I believe the Palace defences were strengthened after that. I really doubt if we are in any danger.'

Martin gave me the scared look he kept in reserve for my reassuring tone.

I thought of our families, huddled together in my quarters down below.

'That bloody Jewboy's here again,' the man in the cloth wig shouted behind me. 'Is there *no* security in this place?'

Martin looked even more scared. I turned and looked at the youth. He bowed low.

'So it's arranged?' I asked softly.

He nodded.

'Excellent,' I said. 'Do tell Isaac I'm in his debt – not that he doesn't know that already.' I'd set up my lamp at dusk. Unregarded by all on the roof, it was still burning away in the inspection room. I turned to Martin. I ignored the question on his face.

'Now,' I said, 'unless you fancy the entertainment of watching Alexandria begin to go up in flames, with Priscus to provide the commentary, I suggest there are better uses of our time.'

'You'll not be knocking yourself out on opium?' he asked.

I smiled and shook my head. After what I'd seen today, who would blame me for seeking oblivion in two brown pills and a jug of wine? Bearing in mind what I was about to try, who could forgive me?

Priscus, I could see, had been pretending not to glance in my direction ever since Isaac's clerk had shown his face. But the crowd about him of nervous, twittering eunuchs and the few persons of quality who'd managed to take refuge in the Palace was too large and too appreciative of his own proposals for settling matters with a massacre. He now looked openly at me, and seemed inclined to come over.

'Come downstairs with me,' I said hurriedly to Martin. 'There's business where you might be of use.'

In my office, the lamps were turned up full. The two hooded figures who sat together on the sofa got up and bowed to me as we walked in. The men who stood behind them went down on their knees. I nodded briefly and pulled out the chair from behind my desk.

'I must thank you, My Lords,' I began, 'for your goodness in coming out on this most dangerous of nights.' I stopped and turned to Martin.

'Get up off the floor,' I said gently. 'This is an informal meeting. Even so, I need you to take a full record.'

40

Next morning, we went up to the roof and then climbed into the inspection room. Seen from up here, Alexandria looked much the same as ever. The early mist was joined by smoke from the fires that continued to burn. But there had as yet been no general conflagration. The great buildings were all still in place. The shops wouldn't be opening today. But Alexandria was a city big enough to absorb a few nights of rioting. Ignorant or uncaring of purely human events, the birds still whirled and circled above Lake Mareotis. Nicetas had summoned a meeting of his Council for just after morning prayers. There, we'd learn exactly what the damage had been overnight. We'd also discuss my plan of pacification.

'Are those bodies down there?' Martin asked, pointing at the square in front of the Palace.

I followed his finger and squinted. 'I rather think they are,' I said. I looked harder. 'Some of them may be dead. But look – that one's sitting up. I don't believe the Office of Supply would fall straight away. It's nearly as well fortified as the Palace itself. More likely, the wine shops have been plundered.'

'It's all so peaceful,' Martin said. 'Do you suppose the rioting is over?'

'Hard to say,' I said. 'Alexandria isn't Constantinople. Whatever experience we have of things there doesn't seem to apply here.'

'Priscus is coming up,' Martin said.

I turned from my inspection of the still sleepy city and looked down to the roof. Priscus was indeed coming. Bathed and dressed and painted, he'd put aside some of his military swagger. But, even at a dozen yards – even under the paint – I knew him well enough to recognise the expression on his face. He paused as he looked at the steep flight of stairs to where we were standing. I sighed as I saw him take firm hold of the rail and heard the rasp of his boots on the bronze of the lower stairs.

'So who's been the slippery shit overnight?' he barked as he walked in. He left the glass door open behind him. There was a sudden cooling of the air inside the room, and I could hear the distant calling of the birds. 'Who's been selling out the honour of the Empire for the sake of a little peace?'

'We'll need all the Schedule D maps in one box,' I said to Martin.

He nodded gratefully and took the hint. With a small bow to Priscus, who paid him no attention, he was off. I felt him close the door and the heavy thud of his feet as he scampered down to the Palace roof. Priscus had no right to be upset. But I knew he was, and it was probably for the best if I didn't stand on my own rights in front of Martin and tell him to get stuffed.

'I've just seen Nicetas seal the general amnesty,' he said accusingly.

'Good,' I said firmly. My arms loosely folded, I turned back to look over Lake Mareotis. The distant line of Egypt was beginning to loom into view, now the mist was clearing. I'd done it, I thought. And it was a job well done. Dragging Nicetas from his bed, and waiting for the stimulants and painkillers I'd fed him to have effect, had been the hardest part of the night's business. But having two patriarchs with me to explain the deal had kept him from the usual dithering fit. Still, there was always some doubt where Nicetas was concerned whether he would take the smallest action required of him. Though I'd have preferred it from someone else, Priscus had brought me good news. 'Did he tell you what's been agreed?' I asked.

'He was busy fixing up the surrender meeting,' Priscus said, now bitter. 'But I did gather that you've brokered a complete sellout.'

'Not a sellout, Priscus,' I said, now mildly. 'It was a compromise.'

Taking care not to crack the film of white lead, he twisted his face into a sneer. 'You don't hold an empire together by compromise,' he snapped. 'At least, if you do compromise, you do it from a position of strength. You then don't call it compromise, but clemency. Compromise from weakness, as we did in the West – give to your enemies in the hope they'll be appeased – and you'll soon find it would have been better to stand and fight. You were with me yesterday. You saw what weakness brought about. I meant what I said last night. Hit these shitbags with concentrated force, and—'

'We haven't the forces to concentrate,' I said, interrupting the steady rise of his voice. 'Whatever Nicetas cares to believe, you know as well as I do that there are no tides in the Red Sea – nor many storms at this time of year. Assuming the Persians can hire ships on the Saracen side, they can land at any one of a dozen points. You said yourself that, if Alexandria goes up in smoke, the Persians will certainly try for a landing. There was no choice but to compromise. Without the landowners to glue the mob together with silver, there'll be no rising. Without that, and without loss of Alexandria, there'll be no Persian attack.

'And there will be no massacre.' I paused. 'That's what you really came here to arrange, isn't it?' I asked of Priscus.

He sniffed and looked out of the window.

'I knew there was something odd about your turning up here, and latching straight on to that cock and bull story about the piss pot. You might as well admit that you picked up something on the Cappadocian front about an attempt on Egypt. You hurried here to try to stop it. Well, I've stopped it for you – and without the cataract of blood you had in mind!

'And your presence here was useful for the avoidance of more force. It's only because you are here that we could make any agreement at all.' I clamped a moderately friendly smile on my face and waited for the irony to sink in. I thought of reaching out to pat Priscus on the shoulder. But that was more than I could manage. 'With you around, there was no doubt that we could eventually restore order. This being so, we could have a full investigation, followed by trials and exemplary punishments and confiscations. The opposition leaders knew this, and were as eager for a compromise as we were. Their change of heart, we agreed last night, was the news of Persian involvement. But it was your presence that made everyone think again.

'The deal is that the rioting is called off while it still can be. In return for this, we pardon everyone in sight. There will be special church services both sides of the Wall, and the bread distribution will go ahead as planned, if a few days late.'

'And the new law – what about that?' Priscus asked. 'Have you given up at last? Will you go back and tell Heraclius that you've failed?' So far as he dared through the paint, he'd twisted his lips into a bitter smile.

I smiled back and thought fast about how little I needed to say to take from him even that consolation.

'The opposition has capitulated,' I said. 'Calling off the rioters wasn't enough for the amnesty I was offering. The warrants will be sealed later today.' This was the minimum I needed to say – and the minimum I wanted to say. What we'd agreed was more than the repeated suggestion by His Heretical Holiness of warrants that would never be executed. But it was the barest scheme of implementation I'd prepared with Martin. Leaving the landowners with more than half their best land, it had been a scheme we'd prepared as an absolute last resort. It hadn't been a defeat. Still less had it been a victory. Yes, Priscus had helped terrify the landowners into a better view of their interests. And if I'd never confess it to anyone – not even to Martin – what I'd seen of Priscus in action under the Prefecture had robbed me of all desire to press on through perhaps still more blood for total victory.

A slave was making his way up the stairs. We composed our features and moved to stand arm-in-arm as he opened the door. We read the message together. Not bothering to hide our confusion, we looked at each other.

'Not your suggestion?' Priscus breathed. 'It certainly wouldn't have been mine. If I didn't know him better by now, I'd say he'd gone mad.'

'My place is by your side,' Martin said when I'd shown him the message. It probably was, and he could be insistent when all his loyalty required was letting himself be dragged into passive danger. But I had other ideas for him.

'No,' he said firmly when I'd shut up. 'We both know the Palace is the safest place anyone can be in Alexandria. Sveta will look after the children. My place is by your side.'

And so it was the pair of us who, as the trumpeter sounded the hour, joined the silent and apprehensive crowd in the main hall of the Palace. They'd all been dressed for the Council meeting, and getting them assembled at short notice for what Nicetas had now planned instead of the meeting had been easy enough. Getting them into a better mood hadn't been thought worth the trying. Priscus alone was looking cheerful. He seemed to have got over the lost chance of a massacre, and now had his cat with him. He was showing it the statue of Domitian beside which his own chair was being made ready.

'From the unusual lack of grace about your movements, dear boy,' he said as I came up beside him, 'do I gather you've had the forethought to put on protection? For myself, I'd never dream of going to these events without.'

Back in my dressing room, Martin had bullied the slaves into getting all my clothes off again so he could pack me into a mailed shirt. He'd then stood for an age, breathing in with his hands above his head, while they'd strained to get another one around him. It was a deadweight on me. Just from walking downstairs to the hall, I'd sweated so much the silk lining was soaked.

'But how will you protect Pussy?' I asked with a nod at the cat. It gave me a hateful look, then nestled closer to Priscus as he stroked the fur.

'Oh, Margarita will stay behind,' he said carelessly. 'She's had such a disturbed few nights,' he added. 'Have you never marvelled at the places these creatures can squeeze themselves behind and shit?

'Will Maximin be putting in an appearance down here?'

I shook my head. There was much I wanted to discuss with Priscus. But Nicetas had now arrived in his internal chair, and was being carefully transferred into his outgoing chair. I thought of trying again to speak with him. By the time I'd decided it wasn't worth the risk of a public rebuff, the twittering eunuchs were thick about him. I turned back to Priscus, but he was now strolling off to look at another of the more worthless emperors.

My own chair was ready, and it was a matter of squeezing Martin in beside me. Hard luck on the carrying slaves, I thought. But the instructions were one chair only per member of the Council. Mine wasn't the only chair sagging below the usual height of eighteen inches above the ground. In one or two cases, secretaries had actually to be left behind. No doubt, their masters would have preferred to swap. Tempers were short in that hall.

At last, though, we were all carried out into the courtyard. There, a couple of eunuchs arranged our chairs into a short cluster, two abreast. The curtains twitched on the single chair right at the front, and a greyish, Viceregal hand gave the signal. With a loud crash of bolts and the pulling back of armoured wood, the gates swung open, and we moved out into the square.

'Make way for His Imperial Highness the Viceroy!' the herald cried in a loud voice. What effect his words might have had on the crowd now packed into the square wasn't something we had to find out. First through the gate were about a hundred heavily mailed guards, all with drawn swords. The crowd backed away before them. With a shouted command in Latin – whatever else could be held against him, at least Nicetas was using the Slavs – they formed into a hollow square within which the chairs now huddled, and we were off.

Though the heat was headed again towards the sweltering, Martin insisted on keeping the curtains pulled. With those plumed helmets all around at eye height, there wouldn't have been much to see in any event. But, from the steady crunch of their boots on broken glass, and muttering of the slaves as they skirted the larger debris of the night's rioting, I had the impression of moderate to considerable damage. All around was the smell of stale wood smoke. From beyond the steel square that encased us, I could hear the continual but low murmuring of the crowd. It was a resentful, short-tempered sound, coming from throats that must have been numbered in the tens of thousands. But it was only a crowd, I kept telling Martin and myself. It wasn't yet worth calling a mob.

In the chair beside us was one of the Council members who dealt with finance. He was complaining – I think to his secretary – that the Patriarch wasn't with us.

'Where is John?' he asked peevishly over and again. 'With His Holiness among us, we'd be in no danger at all. Where is John?'

'Isn't the crowd coming with us?' Martin asked nervously. 'If there's to be a native delegation allowed on to our side of the Wall, what's to keep everyone apart?'

'I imagine that has already been considered,' I said. There was no point even trying to sound reassuring. Martin was right. Even if it wasn't moving with us, the crowd was immense enough to stretch far in the streets beyond the Palace square. We must have covered half a mile, and still that murmur wasn't letting up.

'Make way for His Imperial Highness the Viceroy!' the herald continued crying. And it wasn't just for show. Once or twice, our chair wobbled as the guard was unable to push its way through at uniform speed, and the carrying slaves had to vary our own speed. My hand trembled as I squeezed quietly on my sword. I had a knife in my belt. Neither would be of much use if our outer steel casing were breached. But if not so much as the cruciform relic box Martin was clutching and unclutching, it gave a little comfort.

41

One of the larger churches in Alexandria, the Church of the Apostles was in the early style of ecclesiastical building. With not a dome in sight, nor any elaborate patterning of brickwork, it had the plain look of a courthouse. There was a wide flight of steps leading up to an unadorned portico. A large door, plated with bronze, led into the church. The only variation from its overall plainness was two large bronze torch brackets set equidistant between the door and each end of the portico. They were so incongruous, it would have taken a want of taste not visible in any other feature of his design for the original architect to have put them there. More likely, they'd been transferred at some time following the closure and demolition of the temples. I'd seen the church often enough from the outside, though had never thought it worth the effort of looking inside.

I hadn't missed anything, I realised as I got out of the chair and looked around. We'd all been carried inside the church and set down before the altar. There was the usual jumble of paintings on the wall, and the usual memorial plaques. There was the usual smell of incense, and the usual smell of unwashed bodies that lingers in these places even when the active cause is absent. And there was the usual morose, bearded priest. I grunted and turned back to the chair to help untangle Martin from the curtains.

'This is a most auspicious choice of His Highness,' Martin said in his first normal tone of voice since we'd left the Palace. He stepped forward and fell heavily into my arms. With the extra weight of his armour, he almost had the pair of us on the floor. But I recovered my balance. Martin waved at the priest, who was beginning to look alarmed at the number and quality of the persons invading his church.

'Do you realise,' Martin asked, 'that this building contains the chastity belt with which Saint Eulalia held off the forty thousand soldiers commanded to take her virginity?'

'My compliments to the locksmith,' I said. But I dropped the matter. This wasn't the time or the place for entertainment. Directed by one of the eunuchs we'd brought along, the slaves were getting everything as ready for the audience as it could be made at this notice. This was a matter of getting the paint touched up on our faces and our clothes rearranged. We'd managed to pack only one chair, and this would be for Nicetas. After endless fussing arguments between the eunuch and the slaves, it was placed on the far right of the portico outside. Once he was lifted on to it, Nicetas would be looking down the side flight of steps. This, I gathered, would be convenient, if not so completely dignified in its effect as the eunuch had at first wanted.

'Any trouble,' I whispered to Martin as I let myself be arranged in my place behind Nicetas, a foot or so to the left, 'not, of course, that there will be any, and I want you in the topmost gallery. If the doors swing shut, you don't argue for them to be opened. Those are my instructions as Imperial Legate,' I added. Despite this, Martin would have answered. But Priscus was now standing beside me, and was drifting in a snarling row with the eunuch, who wanted him to twist slightly on his hips and lean in my direction. By swivelling my eyes right from where I'd been placed, I could just see the church door. Once Martin was back inside, I gave up on the strain and looked forward again.

Once we were all in position, the makeshift curtains were pulled aside and I stood blinking in the sun. I looked around as well as could be done without moving my head. The church had sat originally on the central island of a vast circular junction. Then the Wall had been built to keep Greeks and Egyptians apart, and the junction was now more or less bisected. The back side of the church formed part of the Wall. The front of the church looked over what was now the semicircular confluence of three wide streets that led back to the absolute centre of Alexandria. Still impressive, if dilapidated, the buildings that stared back at the church had once been palaces of the commercial aristocracy. Most of them, I think, were now monasteries.

I could see most of this if I turned my eyes sharp left. In front of me and to my right, the Wall stretched high and blank. Looming over it from the other side was the weather-beaten façade of what had once been the Baths of Hadrian. What else, if anything, was still there I couldn't see.

The police and the guards had cleared the hundred yards in front of the church. Beyond that, though, it was an unbroken sea of faces that filled the semicircle and stretched as far back along the three streets as I could strain to see. They were all the usual urban trash. I was too far away and standing at the wrong angle to see the directors this time, but had no doubt they were lurking somewhere in that mass of gawping, unwashed humanity.

With a few grunts and hisses of pain, the Viceroy shifted ever so slightly on his chair. Otherwise, it was the statue act again for us all. Our clothes fluttered freely in the breeze. Our bodies were locked into poses of careless elegance.

There was a shouted command over on our right, and the gate to the Egyptian quarter opened a couple of feet. The police officers squeezed wedges under the gate, and stood ready to push it shut again. The herald went forward and called out in a stiffly ceremonious Egyptian. His words seemed to stick in his throat, and he stood a moment looking through the partly opened gate. Then, with a scared look in our direction, he was moving quickly back to stand on the church steps a few feet below Nicetas.

I'd not been able to speak with him. But the impression Nicetas had given me in his message was that he'd arranged a conference with the leaders of the Egyptian mob. These would be allowed through to state their case and then make their submission. Otherwise, the Egyptians would be kept to their own side of the Wall. If that was what had been arranged, it wasn't going to plan.

Even as the herald took his place, the first Egyptians began pouring through the gate. They came at first in their dozens. For all they pushed to cut off the flow of bodies, the police officers might as well not have been there. The wedges scraped on the hard granite of the pavements and gave way. The gate now swung fully open, and – the police scattering with a sudden panic – the pouring of dozens became a flood of hundreds and then of thousands. The slight difference of their smell aside, they were mostly the same refuse as on our side of the Wall. Perhaps a quarter of them, though, had the smaller – often much darker – appearance of recent arrivals from the south. Between them and the Greeks, the guards formed a thin but, I hoped, an impenetrable line. Between us and the Egyptians, who'd flowed forward right to the foot of the steps up to the portico, there wasn't so much as a eunuch with a cane. Keeping still, we looked uneasily back at those hungry, desperate faces.

'Ask for their spokesmen to come forward,' Nicetas said without moving his lips.

The herald climbed on to a lectern that had been brought out of the church. He was perhaps two yards away from Nicetas, and stood a yard higher. He gripped hard on the rail of the lectern to steady his hands.

'No,' Nicetas said again, 'start with the recitation of titles and promise of redress.' He broke off and quickly pulled a fold of his robe over the still swollen bulk of his leg. 'Oh, and do you have the promise of amnesty rehearsed?'

'Yes, My Lord,' the herald said softly without turning his eyes. With a muttered prayer and then a great sucking of air into his lungs, he opened his mouth to call the meeting to order. Except it was now in a language I didn't understand, it followed the same pattern as the meeting in the Hall of Audience. Our clothes billowed or hung loose as the breeze took them. Otherwise, we were still and silent as the custom required. All communication was through the herald, who, now his nerves were under control, was managing the same sonorous rhythms in Egyptian as he had in Greek.

It was as he fell silent – I suppose having asked about the spokesmen – that the pattern took its next variation from the intended. There was a ripple of giggling through the crowd, followed by silence. It was a silence that seemed prolonged beyond the few moments it must have lasted. I heard Priscus breathe in sharply. I darted a look at the now impassive faces at the front of the crowd. What were they waiting for? I asked myself. It was worse than if they'd been shouting and edging forward. At least that wouldn't have involved this dreadful wait.

'Ask their spokesmen to come forward,' Nicetas whispered again. 'Tell them they can stand before us on the lower steps. But stop them if they come too far up towards me.'

The herald got as far as another intake of breath, when we had our answer. Here and there in what was now the mob, long poles were suddenly pushed upright. On each one of them was a severed head. It isn't easy to recognise heads – not separated from their bodies, nor at a distance, nor when their features are still contorted with their dying agonies. But I did think I could make out the speaker at the demonstration I'd seen the previous Sunday. There too might well have been that scum landowner. I stared harder, and my stomach did a little jump. Undeniably, that was a priest's head on the pole nearest the Wall. I could see it clearly against the smooth background of the rendering.

'I think we can take it as read, my darling,' Priscus drawled without moving his lips, 'that the wog lower orders haven't accepted your settlement. They've dismissed the leaders who brought them together and appointed new ones. I don't suppose my rack nor your concessions will mean much now. I hope that sword so clumsily hidden under your clothes is your favourite one.'

'I take it you have a plan of escape?' I muttered back.

'Not really,' he said. 'A word of advice, though. Don't try getting into the church. You won't believe how these places can be made to burn with a little effort. I don't see any shame in running away.'

'Flight from this lot?' I hissed. 'We'd never outrun them.' I might also have asked where to run. The wall was in front of us, and the mob between us and it. To the left was the mob. Turn right, and there was a long wedge, bounded by the wall of the church and the Wall of Separation as it joined the back of the church. Behind didn't seem much better.

Priscus laughed gently. 'No experience of retreat!' he said, now obviously enjoying himself. 'Such a warlike race of barbarians, your people must be. To stay alive, you only need to outrun Nicetas and these toads who advise him.

'But – oh, for a brigade of cavalry. With these tight-packed masses, it would be like scything corn. And oh, for another of my red powders!'

I ignored him. The herald was now interpreting what I took to be the less chaotic shouts from the mob.

'They ask, My Lord,' he said with a growing tremor, 'when you are planning to evacuate Egypt.'

There was a long pause while Nicetas digested this question and cast round for some kind of answer. Standing a few steps down from me, the Master of the Works didn't seem to move so much as a hair, while somehow getting himself visibly ready for a dash inside the church.

'Tell them that bit about my leg,' Nicetas finally said. 'Tell them it's my birthday. Also, remind them of the bread distribution that was supposed to be today, and still might be. Yes, promise the amnesty if they'll all go peacefully home.'

The herald did a fine job on the leg. Even without understanding the words, the tragic tone and gestures carried all the meaning anyone could have needed. He paused for a response. The mob looked up at us in stony silence. He might have suppressed the birthday notice. If so, his next comment about the bread was followed by a burst of satiric laughter. Whatever he said next was drowned out in a massive roar of displeasure. It sounded like the Circus protests in Constantinople over the cut in the bread ration. Then, we'd had to face the mob from an Imperial Box thirty feet above anyone else, and with an escape behind straight back into a fortified palace. Here, the screaming and shaking of fists and waving of severed heads began three paces in front of us.

It was a massive roar. As yet, though, it was the overall effect of individual cries. Then, imperceptibly – as gusting breezes give way to a settled wind – the shouting resolved itself into an orderly and repeated chanting. What this was at first I didn't know, and the herald had given up on interpreting. But I did recognise the Tears of Alexander chant. As ever, it was the mob's favourite. Again and again, it rolled towards us, like thunder across water. It was deafening. It flattened all intention of reply with its massive loudness. The mob – and it was now worth regarding it as that – rippled forward, pushing its closest members up the first couple of steps towards us. Those shining, hate-contorted faces now almost within touching distance, I reached slowly under my cloak and gripped my sword.

They had ignored their part of the agenda. It was now our turn. With a cry of pain and annoyance and a clutching at his walking stick, it was now that Nicetas stood up. He heaved himself to his feet, and, his stick wobbling as it held him up, he looked out over the sea of faces.

All of a sudden, there was silence. Every movement ceased. If Christ Himself, surrounded by Angels, had stepped out of the sky, I'm not sure if the effect would have been greater than Nicetas produced by standing up. He raised his arms for a hearing. There was a collective gasp of shock. It rippled back through the Egyptians, and was taken up by the Greeks. It wouldn't have surprised me if it was fifty thousand jaws that fell open and a hundred thousand eyes that widened. The Viceroy had moved. Worse, the Viceroy had stood up and was now continuing to move. From far out in the hush came the occasional cry of astonishment and even horror. For the first time in living memory – for the first time, perhaps, in centuries – the people were seeing their ruler move in the execution of his duties. Someone a few yards along from me sat hurriedly down on the steps. Someone else appeared to be struggling with a fainting attack.

'This has all gone too far,' Nicetas shouted in Latin. 'Tell these people that the Empire is ordained of God, and will never – not until the Last Day – evacuate Egypt or anywhere else. The Empire will – and must – last until the end of time. Tell them to go home before God smites them all with a pestilence to add to the other sufferings their disloyalty has brought upon them.'

The herald looked back confused. He knew Greek, and he knew Egyptian. Latin wasn't a language he'd been taken on to handle. From some parts of the mob, there was what sounded like an attempt at interpreting what had just been said. I relayed the words to the herald in Greek, pausing at each phrase so he could shout them in Egyptian in the appropriate form.

'Alexander cannot weep,' Nicetas went on, his voice cracking with the unaccustomed strain. 'To say otherwise is treason against the Emperor, and blasphemy against the Decrees of God – who will never work a miracle through any object dear to the Old Faith.

'Behold! I will show you these "Tears of Alexander".' Again taking care not to move his bad leg, he wheeled round to face the open door of the church. He beckoned wildly. From somewhere far inside the darkness of the church there was a scraping and then the banging of something heavy that had been dropped.

42

'Oh fuck!' I said, realising what he was about. Nicetas hadn't just moved – he'd also planned ahead. And as the horror grew within me of what he'd planned, I nearly shat myself.

Since the Viceroy himself had given up on playing at statues, I saw no reason why I should stand rooted to my spot under the portico. I'd turned sharp right and was watching the wooden box as it was carried out into the light. Like the moon against the darkest night sky, Martin's face peered out from the interior of the church. To say it looked scared gives no fresh information. I pulled a face at him, mouthing that he should get back inside. He ignored me and came fully out and took up a position just to the right of the doorway. I turned back to Nicetas.

'Please,' I said quietly, 'this really isn't a good idea.'

'I think I shall be the best judge of that,' he snapped back at me. He motioned the four slaves forward with their burden and pointed at a spot a yard away from the front line of the still hushed mob. Incredulity and outrage blazing through the paint on his face, Priscus watched the unfolding of this new lunacy.

For me, it was very like that afternoon at the Circus in Constantinople. I'd been chewing dried *ganjika* resin to support myself through the tedium of an epic poem Heraclius had commissioned about himself and then ordered to be read out before the races. I'd mistimed the dose, however, and had sat wincing through every inflated image and false quantity. It had hit me during the races, just as two chariots crashed into each other on the final lap. Time had suddenly slowed down, and it was an age for me within which the splintering of wood and upward motion of the thrown racers played itself out to the inevitable end.

So it almost was now. The box seemed smaller and more faded than it had in the basements under the Library. Its colour was bleached out by the sun. Its handles gleamed as it was carried slowly past me. The mob shrinking back to make room, the slaves put it carefully down at the foot of the steps. They stood back from it and bowed low before it.

'You're bloody mad, Nicetas,' Priscus rasped in Latin. 'You'll get us all killed.'

Nicetas must have heard, though he paid no attention. He turned back to face the mob. Then, doing his best to keep the pain from his face, hobbled, one step at a time, down to stand beside the box. There was another small commotion as the mob tried to shrink still further back. Nevertheless, if I couldn't see properly from where I was standing, I believe the hem of his robe was close enough to brush against some of those now scared faces.

'Get it open,' he said to the slaves.

Unfamiliar with the locking mechanism, they struggled a while with the lid. Eventually, by twisting, and partly by main force, they pulled it loose. As it came off, there was a strange, collective sigh from the mob. Several people at the front fell to their knees. With his back to the mob, Nicetas ordered the slaves to get the mummy out and hold it up for all to see. With hands shaking but infinite tenderness, they did as they were told. Slowly, the stiffened, black remains were lifted out of their box. Turned upright, they were held up for all to see.

All notion of protocol forgotten, Priscus and I hurried down the steps to look at the Great Alexander in the full light of day.

Except he looked smaller and still more frail, he was as we'd left him. His eyes stared sightlessly forward. The gold ring still shone where it had stuck in the depression between his ribs. The scars shone lighter than they had under the lamps. It was hard to say with any surety after so long. But I thought I could see a faint patterning of tattoos on his upper right arm. It made sense. For all his boasting about Greek culture and Greek blood, Alexander was a Macedonian. That placed him barely two generations from the semi-barbarian.

Now, a thousand years after his death, the remote posterity of those he had conquered looked down at his body, within the city he had founded though never seen, and that had ever since then borne his name.

'Behold the Great Alexander,' Nicetas shouted again. This time, his voice gave out under the strain.

The herald took up the theme for himself, improvising loudly and at great length. Whatever he said was having its effect. With a slow wave, spreading ever further back among the mob, people were falling to their knees and then forward in full prostration, and calling out in reverent tones the glorious name of Alexander in Egyptian. The cries fell to whispers, and then to silence – and still the prostration continued.

It was as if someone had flown overhead and scattered some sleeping potion that had rapid effect. One moment, I was ready to pull out my sword and make a fighting retreat. Another, and it was like staring over a carpet of sleeping woodlice. I could have stepped forward and walked, passing from sloping back to sloping back, all the way over to the guards and to the Greeks beyond – the Greeks who were themselves standing silent with arms upraised as if in prayer.

'I think he's done it,' I whispered to Priscus. Incredulous, we looked at each other and then out again across the concourse. The herald never let up his sonorous improvising. Though I could hear it was beginning to fray, his voice had taken on an almost musical quality.

Nicetas pointed at the slaves, who, with equal tenderness, replaced the mummy in its box. Then, each arm supported by one of the slaves, Nicetas moved back to take his place on the golden chair.

It was a matter of getting ourselves back into position before everyone looked up again. And then of jollying them along a while longer. We'd mention the bread distribution again. We might throw in a few prayers. After that, the Egyptians could be shepherded back through the gate. So long as the Greeks gave us no trouble, it would be back to the Library for Alexander, and back for the rest of us to the Palace – where I, for one, was intending to get quickly and totally drunk.

'Hello, Alaric. We do seem to meet in the strangest circumstances.'

I looked to my left. Lucas was dressed in the white, elaborately folded linen the ancient kings of Egypt wore in some of the friezes I'd seen. His beard had been oiled and plaited into a further imitation of the ancient kings. He must so far have been standing round the corner, where he'd have been facing the main flight of steps up to the portico. Now, he'd been able to take advantage of the sudden peace to move round to where things were happening.

'You'd surely not attack an unarmed man?' he asked, nodding to where my sword hand had moved. He smiled as he threaded his way closer through the motionless, prostrated mass of his people. 'You are the first who would call it unfair,' he said. 'Besides, it would break the mood none of us believed His Highness the Viceroy would ever be able to manage. Now, you'd not want that – would you?'

There was a lot I might have said back to the man. But he was right. I didn't want to break the mood of that crowd. Once all this was over, I told myself, I'd put up his weight in silver as prize to have him delivered to me in chains. For the moment, I did my best to ignore him.

'Who, in God's name, is *this*?' Priscus asked. He'd let go of his own sword. Now, just as helpless, he stood beside me, clenching and unclenching his fists. I tried to think of an answer. It would have to wait.

'I thought you'd see reason,' Lucas added with a smile any onlooker would have thought friendly. You'd never have believed what a raving lunatic he was behind that bright, casual exterior. 'I, of course, feel no obligation to see reason,' he said.

Before even finishing his words, he leaned forward under my very nose. I nearly retched at the sudden smell of his breath. I stepped back out of his way. He reached into the box containing Alexander's mummy. He put one hand each side of the head. With a smooth, practised motion, he twisted. As of dried twigs, there was a gentle snapping of bones. Before I could move forward again a single step – before I could so much as lift a finger – he'd raised the withered head above his own and was walking calmly back into the crowd.

'I'm going to tell them how it weeps,' he called happily back. 'Just you see how they believe me.'

'You'll fucking bring that back!' Priscus shouted as he recovered from the shock of what we'd just seen. 'You'll show some bloody respect.' He jumped off the lowest step and moved between the prostrate bodies.

Still smiling, Lucas moved further back. He began calling out in Egyptian. It was a high-pitched, sneering sound, the name of Alexander in every burst of the calling. He waved the head and twisted it in his hands. All around, the slumbering mob was coming back to life. Men were looking up. At first uncomprehending of what had been done, then terrified by it, then with a range of emotions that lay between relief and exultation, every face was turned to Lucas and the head of Alexander. With every repetition of his words, Lucas was raising more men to their feet. Radiating outward from him, and soft at first, the chanting had started up again: 'The tears of Alexander shall flow, giving bread and freedom.'

'Give it back, you wog fucker!' Priscus cried above the regathering storm of noise as he moved deeper into the mob. No longer angry, his was a desperate, horrified cry. 'Give it back! Give it back!' he cried over and again. He kicked and punched at the men who were getting up to block the few yards of distance that lay between him and Lucas.

'Priscus, come back,' I shouted in Latin. 'You'll get yourself torn apart.'

He stopped and looked back. He was perhaps only a dozen yards from the foot of the steps. Already, it would have been impossible to turn and recross the distance. Men plucked at his clothing. His hat of office was knocked from his head. Before he was lost within the screaming, jostling crowd, I saw him pull out his sword and stab at someone who'd raised a cudgel to him.

It was now chaos all around. In front of us, to the left of us, all the way behind us on the other side of the portico, the Egyptian mass surged and screamed. Further back, the rising chant was taking on a tone less of hatred than of triumph. As yet, most had their backs to us – they were more interested in straining to catch sight of the head of Alexander than in turning back to face the living.

'It weeps! It weeps!' someone shouted up at us in Greek. He was turned towards us. He was a brown, runtish creature, with open sores on his face. 'The day of deliverance is at hand,' he went on. He reached into the box and pulled at what remained of Alexander. One of the arms came away. He turned away from us and waved it overhead. He turned back to us and bit into the shrivelled, crumbling flesh. He chewed and spat and tried to shout something. Like dust, though, the ancient flesh stuck in his mouth. He spat again and poked at me with the arm. I drew my sword and smashed hard with the hilt into his face. I could feel his lips splash and the crunching of teeth under them. He screamed and fell backwards into the boiling mass of humanity.

'The Greek mob's broken through,' someone behind me cried as a new shout rose far behind us. 'Oh dear!' he added philosophically. 'I don't suppose our people will be pleased with us now. Still, they'll have to fight their way through the wogs before they can get to us.'

'Nicetas, get back inside the church,' I shouted. He'd been trying to stand up again, but his walking stick had given way. He now sat awkwardly on one of the lower steps. His face had the grey, tense look of a gambler who knows but still can't feel that he's just been broken. It was only a matter of time before the mob turned round and decided to rip us all apart. It was almost a miracle only one Egyptian so far had ventured on to the steps. 'Come on,' I said to the herald, 'help me get him up the steps.'

As I spoke, something heavy crashed into my back. The chainmail spread the force of its impact, but it knocked me forward. I looked round. Something else landed a few feet from me.

'Shit! They've started on the cobblestones,' I said. I pulled at Nicetas. I kicked at his leg, and pulled him again as he jerked upwards in agony. For someone who hadn't run noticeably to flesh, and hadn't even thought to come out in armour, he still managed to weigh surprisingly heavy. Getting him up those steps under a growing hail of stones and other projectiles seemed to take an age. But I shoved him at last through the doorway into the church. He sprawled on to the mosaic floor and began a sobbing fit as the eunuch took over and pulled him deeper inside.

I turned back. The mob was now coming up the steps. It wasn't yet a rush, so much as the creeping forward of a tide. A few other members of the Council had drawn their swords and were backing slowly up to the church doors. I pulled my own out again and waved it at the now anticipatory, gloating faces. I could see no blades of any kind on the other side. The worst to show against us was cudgels. But it was a question of numbers. Dozens to one against us, they came slowly up the steps – dozens to one, and with hundreds and thousands pressing from behind. The chair on which Nicetas had recently been sitting, and around which we'd clustered, was already lost within the advancing mob. If Priscus was right, we were about to lock ourselves into our own funeral pyre. Much longer out here, though, and we'd go the way of the Great Alexander.

'Get the doors shut,' I called back. It was now just me outside and the Master of the Works. We slashed and poked at the oncoming mob. As if by prior agreement, we'd hold the mob back while the bronze doors could be swung into place. I could feel the massive click behind me as terrified, dithering hands got them loose and pushed them outward.

'You first,' I shouted at the Master of the Works. I blocked a stone with my left arm. Another crashed into my chest, almost knocking the breath out of me. I knew my arm would ache horribly later. At the time, I felt nothing. I lunged forward again with my sword. I think I did catch someone this time, though it would only have been a minor wound.

Far over on my left – far beyond the other side of the portico – there was a great scream of rage and terror. What could be happening I had no idea. But it drew attention away from me

305

for the moment. I prepared to dart backward through the closing doors. Then I heard the despairing wail on my right. It was a familiar sound, quavering above the snarling of the mob. I glanced right.

43

Shit and bugger! What was Martin doing up there? I'd seen him come outside the church when Alexander was carried out. I hadn't seen him go in. I couldn't now imagine how he'd managed to climb on to one of the bronze torch brackets. However he'd done it, though, he had his arms clamped round the top of the bracket, and one of his legs hooked over the bar securing the whole thing to the wall. With his free leg, he kicked ineffectually at the hands reaching up to pull at him. He was a good eight feet up, and no hands had yet been able to catch hold of him.

'Martin!' I shouted. The doors were swinging shut behind me. Someone inside was shouting at me to get through them. Another volley of stones thudded against the doors or crashed on to the pavements around me. Still wary of my sword's glittering blade, the few members of the mob who'd not turned to face the scream-ing hung back. Martin got one of his hands free. He raised it despairingly to heaven, and then – his face suddenly determined – waved at me to get inside the church.

'Martin!' I shouted again. 'Martin!' There was another shout behind me. 'Get it shut,' I cried at no one in particular, turning half round. As I jumped rightwards, I heard the door crash shut and the thudding of bolts drawn into place.

I could see what Martin had been trying to do. A few feet up from the torch bracket, and a few feet further along, there was a series of metal rods poking from the wall. These formed something best described as a ladder with only one arm. So far as I could tell, they led diagonally up the wall, going beyond the portico to the roof of the church. They must have been there for cleaning or repair purposes. Little had ever made sense with him when he was in a panic. But it made sense that if he was too scared to cross the few yards back to the door, Martin should be trying for the roof. How he'd got as far up as he had was a mystery. But he was now too scared – or physically unable – to make the further leap and get to the roof.

I filled my lungs and managed a passable imitation of an English battle cry. I lunged forward and got someone in the guts with my sword. That cleared a larger space around me. Any moment now, and the full mob would turn back to face me. I rammed the sword into its scabbard and jumped up at the torch bracket. The armour adding about twenty pounds to my weight, I nearly jumped short. But nearly jumping short isn't the same as nearly catching hold. I did catch hold. I dragged myself up to perch on the top of the bracket.

'Come on, Martin,' I shouted, grabbing at him and pulling him fully up. I felt the bracket shudder under our combined weight. It was coming away from the wall. Below us, men were poking up with sticks. The bracket was an elaborate thing. Its bottom bar was about six feet above the ground. Its top was another few feet up, and we were safe from being pulled down – though only so long as no one else tried jumping up, or went at us with sticks, or so long as the whole thing didn't just collapse under us.

Holding on to Martin to steady myself, I stood upright and reached across to catch hold of one of the rods. I clamped my left hand on to it and pulled. It seemed firmly set into the bricks. The lowest rod of all was another four feet down. I got my left foot on to it. I took hold of Martin by the collar of his mail shirt, and swung his presently gigantic weight clean off the torch bracket and nearly bashed his face in on another of the rods.

'Take hold and climb,' I gasped. I felt like that boy must have on the rack. More than a moment longer of this, and I'd drop Martin, or fall with him on to the mob below. But the strain relaxed as he took hold by himself. One hand over the other, I climbed upwards. Behind me, calling out prayers and imprecations in Celtic, Martin followed. It wasn't far to the lower part of the roof. But it felt easily as if it were hundreds of feet rather than the few dozen that it was. At last, though, with a soft ripping of silk, I twisted right and heaved myself on to the rain-pitted lead. As soon as I'd rolled myself stable on the sloping roof, I scrabbled forward and pulled Martin up the last few rods until he could lie there beside me.

'Shut up!' I snapped, cutting off the babble of thanks and apologies that had begun and might otherwise last all day. 'We need to find a way down from here.' I knew I should have been straight up on my feet and running across the roof to find some escape. Instead, I sat up and rested on the hot lead. I rubbed at my sore arm and shoulder.

I had a good view of things from up here. For the first time that morning, I could form a reasonably synoptic view of what was happening about me. I couldn't see now under the portico. But I could hear the banging of fists and cudgels on the bronze doors of the church. So long as no one brought up a battering ram – not an easy matter through these densely packed thousands – or started heaping up kindling in front of the door, Nicetas and everyone else was safe enough. But the wide space of the concourse really was packed. It was like looking down on aroused ants outside their nest. I could see that the guards had given up all effort to keep the two mobs apart. Where I guessed the border had been, they now merged insensibly into one mob, or fought viciously. It was as the local inclination took them. The guards themselves had gathered again into a hollow square, and were slowly pushing and cutting their way towards the church. How they'd get here – or how, once here, they'd manage to do any good – wasn't a question I could answer. What I did know was that there was no point looking for any way back down to ground level that would take us into this bubbling sea of hate.

'Oh, Sweet Jesus!' Martin screamed. I looked sharply down to the edge of the roof. We'd been followed up from the portico. I drew my sword and poked at the head that had now reached the level of the roof. As, with a bubbling shriek, it vanished, I leaned forward and looked over the edge. Sure enough, there were men climbing up those rods. I managed to cut the fingers off the one who was now closest to us, and he fell back on to the others.

That was the end of this attack. There was no point asking what had prompted anyone to try following an armed man upward to a place of stability. It was enough that the effort had been made once. If there were other ways up, they too might soon be found and used. I reached down and pulled hard on the last of the metal poles. My left arm was beginning to seize up, and the pole seemed too hard set into the brickwork for me to have pulled it loose even with my full strength. I sat back. I gave up on the vague plan I'd been considering, of staying out of sight up here until the trouble was over. We were in a place of at best relative safety. Besides, there wasn't an inch of shade to be seen, and thirst can be a terrible thing in that sun.

'Take this,' I said to Martin, pushing my sword into his hand. It trembled there, then dropped with a dull thud on to the lead. 'Take it up,' I repeated, now angry. 'If anyone tries coming up again, cut at his fingers, or just poke him hard.

'Do you understand?'

He nodded.

I pulled myself unsteadily to my feet and looked up at the wide central vault of the roof.

'Do you think Priscus is dead?' he asked.

I looked at the surging, screaming crowds below and laughed grimly. 'If he's managed to survive in that lot,' I said, 'we can count this day as an utter disaster. Now, keep a lookout for anyone stupid enough to try climbing after us. I'll be back as quickly as I can.'

There shouldn't be any way down at the back of the church, I told myself. After all, this was where it had been made part of the Wall of Separation, and would have been made secure long ago. But over on the other side, towards the back – there we might find some way down. And it might even take us down to a place where the mob was at least thin on the ground.

However it might have gone for Priscus, our luck seemed to be holding. Over where I was hoping to find something, I did find a rope ladder. Still connected to a set of hooks projecting from the roof, it was coiled up and left beside an uncompleted repair to the lead. It might have been there for months, and most colour had been bleached out of the ropes. I pulled part of it loose and tested the ropes. Hope was dashed as they came apart in my hands. The sun had bleached out their colour and their strength. But I pulled feverishly at the coil to get it undone. Some part of the ladder might still be sound – if not part of the ladder, perhaps some part of one of the ropes. There might be something else to get us down, I thought.

I got no further. With a yell of terror, Martin was running towards me. There was no point asking how he'd abandoned a position from which a crippled child couldn't have been dislodged. No point, either, in asking about the sword. I ran over to the edge of the roof and looked down. It must have been a forty-foot drop. Jumping would simply have saved anyone the trouble of throwing us down.

But no, there was a bronze downpipe to carry water from the roof. Like others in the more unsafe parts of Alexandria, it would have stopped eight or even ten feet above the ground. But it was a way off the roof.

'This way,' I shouted as I dragged Martin over and pointed at the downpipe.

He shook his head and shouted something back that I somehow couldn't understand.

'I don't care,' I shouted again. 'Get down – just go!' Shaking and twitching with the accumulated strain of at least that morning, I waited while Martin finished his dithering fit and climbed slowly over the parapet.

I snatched up what looked like a long broom handle and ran at the one man who'd come in sight over the vaulting. He opened his mouth to shout something, but I had him over before he could get anything out. Some twenty yards behind him, other men were climbing on to the roof. As yet, they had their backs to me, and I managed to jump back before anyone could see me. I skipped down to the edge of the roof and heaved myself over on to the downpipe. It creaked and shuddered. With a snapping of the aged spikes that held it against the wall, it moved a foot backwards.

For a moment, I swung helplessly, my feet treading on air alone. Then, with a fraying of skin, my hands were dragged by my enhanced weight diagonally down the pipe until I felt my knees crash against the wall. I got myself against the still firm next stretch and slithered down.

'Let go,' I snarled as my feet knocked against Martin's head. He'd reached the bottom of the downpipe, and had both hands clamped hard about the thing. How he managed to hold his weight up was another mystery. There was no doubt he was in my way.

'Jump, for God's sake,' I roared down at him. 'Jump!' I looked up. About twenty feet above me, a single face, framed against the perfect blue of the sky above, grinned down at me. Another joined it. The downpipe was too damaged at the top for anyone to follow us. But there was plenty of loose junk up there to throw down on us. First came part of the rope ladder. It missed. Another part followed. That gave me a glancing but unimportant blow to the head. It was only a question of waiting there for more substantial objects to come our way.

I kicked savagely at Martin's hands. They might have been iron clamps. I'd have to get down to his level and somehow make him let go. I swung out and prepared to hold him in an embrace as I got level. I may have got my knees level with his chest. Just then, a very long stretch of the rope ladder hooked itself about my neck, and we fell with a tremendous, bruising thud the last three or four yards on to the pavement.

At least no one could follow us down, I remember thinking. I rolled over and prodded at Martin, whose face had gone a pale shade of green. I looked round. From above, this part of the church surroundings hadn't been empty. As I've said, the whole concourse was packed. But there's a difference between active troublemakers and those who come along to a riot to watch or for a bit of looting. The first were still making a tremendous racket over on our right. But that was now a good hundred yards away. Here, it was spectators and looters.

A few scrawny creatures hurried up to us as we rolled about on the dusty pavements. One of them spoke to me in a language that wasn't Greek and that didn't sound Egyptian. But I had my knife out, and he went back sharpish about his own business. I stood up and prepared to drag Martin to his feet. I fell straight down, white flashes of agony blanking out all thought of what to do next.

44

'Fuck! Fuck! Fuck!' I gasped, clutching at my ankle. I'd twisted the sodding thing as I fell, and somehow hadn't noticed until trying to stand on it. For all I knew, I'd broken it. I rocked back and forth, cradling it as I tried to force the pain to the back of my mind. The last thing I needed was to show weakness. Looters and even spectators can be dangerous to the injured. We needed to get away. That meant getting as quickly as possible out of this vast semicircular junction with its lack of cover, and into the streets and side streets beyond.

'Let me help you,' Martin said. He'd got up, apparently uninjured, and was pulling at me. 'We can't stay here,' he added. As he spoke, the rest of the rope ladder landed beside us. It was followed by a selection of objects taken from the roof. I looked up. There were more faces looking down. To be sure, the top of the downpipe was bent too far back from the wall, and was too loose, to let anyone follow us down. Sooner or later, though, they'd start throwing down heavier stuff and to better effect.

Carrying himself in armour, and supporting something like half my own weight, wasn't something I'd expected Martin could do at all without a heart attack. In the event, he got the pair of us across the concourse with surprising speed and without more than the occasional glance from the moderately dense crowds that moved back and forth. A hundred yards over on the right, there was what – with the wild shouting and clash of weapons – sounded a regular battle. Back here, it might have been a market day. We dodged round a thicker than usual cluster of what may have been Greeks or Egyptians – it was hard to tell, and made no present difference to us – and got ourselves into one of those wide streets leading back to the centre.

I hadn't discussed with Martin where we were going. At first, it had been enough to get away from the church, and then as far away as we could from the main action of the rioting. I'd picked up a wooden spar, and this was letting me move forward at a reasonable speed. The pain in my ankle was getting steadily worse, and my breath was beginning to come in ragged gasps. But I was moving. We were heading in the general direction of the Palace. There might be some effort there to keep order. We might be able to get in through the main gates. If not, it wasn't far to the Harbour or to the wooded central parks. We needed to get out of sight and stay out of sight.

On a casual glance, if choked with rubbish and piles of booty, the street seemed pretty well empty. In fact, it was so long and so densely packed with shops and other businesses that it had absorbed a mob and a half like water into a sponge. The shop-keepers had based their defences on the assumption that the police would be round before things turned really nasty. But there were no police any more, and these competing groups of Greeks and Egyptians amounted to a plundering army. They'd managed to pull all the wooden screens off those shops that had windows. Some of the buildings were already on fire. All along, we could hear breaking glass and the screams of those who'd made their homes behind or above their shops. The looters were mostly interested in laying hands on whatever might be valuable and could be carried away. But any living creature they stumbled over in their search was fair game for them. Then, it was a matter of maiming and dismemberment, of roasting and of rape. The lucky ones died soon. The bodies and parts of bodies that littered the carriage tracks and the paved area under the central colonnade were a grim sight.

'Keep going,' I'd said several times to Martin. 'We can't afford more trouble.' He'd nodded. He only slowed down when it was a matter of helping me over the more chaotic piles of smoking rubble and pieces of smashed furniture.

Over on my left, a woman screamed. It was close, and it stood out from the background cries of pain and terror. I tried hard to follow my own advice. But the scream came again and was closer. I heard a broken sob and looked left. I should have looked away at once and pressed on along the street. Instead – for just a moment – I stopped. A woman had broken free from whatever place of horror had been her home. Naked, her body a mass of cuts and burns, the place between her legs visibly a swollen mush, she staggered towards me. I didn't think at first she'd seen me or anyone or anything else. It was the fixed stare about her eyes. She screamed not at me, it seemed, but to take her own attention from what she'd seen or experienced. I was wrong.

She caught me as I tried to hurry past. She took hold of my arm and almost had me over. She pushed the bag at me she'd been carrying. It was a large thing, and heavy. There was something in it that moved feebly. She pushed it firmly and even desperately into my hands. I tried to think of words. I couldn't think of anything to say. Perhaps there was nothing I could say that would have made sense to her, let alone have brought the comfort I felt I was expected to give. I looked round for some piece of cloth or other covering among the rubbish.

'Oho, running off, eh?' a voice called from behind her. He was a big man, with a face too scarred to carry much of a beard. For what it mattered, he was probably a Greek. There were five or six other men still further behind. They swayed drunkenly on the threshold of the smashed-up building the woman had just left. They laughed noiselessly, pointing at the woman as she fell down and then avoided me as I tried to help her to her feet. The big man had straightened up on seeing me. Now, he had a sword in his hand. He waved it at me and laughed loudly.

'Get behind me,' I said to the woman. I put the bag carefully down beside me and reached for my knife.

'Take him!' she screamed at me. 'Take him!'

I felt the bag pushed back into my hand. I tried to grab her again, but she lurched out of reach, and I was in no position to dance after her. With a wild, chilling wail, she was rushing back at the big man. She picked her way over the heaps of rubbish, and ran unsteadily across the clear stretches of pavement. She opened her arms as she got close. But for that nightmarish cry, it was as if she were rushing to meet her lover.

He cut her down with an incompetent slashing stroke at her neck. Still screaming, she fell to the ground. She tried to clutch hold of his legs as he advanced. He finished her with another blow to the neck that did more to smash the vertebrae than separate them. Waving his sword again, he ran at me. He turned once to call his friends into the battle. For the moment, they chose to watch things from where they were. I had my knife out. I held it at waist level and tried to look able-bodied.

'Not so fast, my fine little lord!' he rasped. He jumped off a heap of stones dug out of the road and smiled and went at me.

If you can imagine it, I held fast to my walking staff while going into some kind of fighting position. In the normal course of things, this scarred, shambling item of trash wouldn't have dared give someone like me a second look. Now, it was as if he'd smelled blood. I barked at Martin to keep moving on.

As he came at me, he discovered to his cost that there was more to fighting with a sword than waving it like a cudgel. Watching more of his incompetent slashing, I gave up on the knife and went at him with my staff. He did succeed in dodging back. But I got him now with a lunge hard forward into his crotch. He fell screeching backwards on to the cobblestones.

That would have been the end of him, if I hadn't fallen as well. I'd put my full weight on to the bad ankle, and I went straight down with the agony. I breathed deep in and out, and fought to regain control. It was only a few moments before I had my eyes open again and was pulling at my knife. But it was already over for him. Martin had finished the creature for me. He'd done it from behind with a cobblestone the size and shape of a loaf. Looking at the splashed red and grey all over his face, Martin had no need of a second blow.

The big man hadn't meant much, it seemed, to his friends. By the time I'd got his sword in my own hand, and was testing its weight, they'd vanished back inside the building.

'What is it?' I asked, pushing the sword clumsily into my scabbard, where it was a very bad fit. It was a redundant question. Martin had already tugged at the restraining straps of the bag. So far as I could tell, the baby was about six months old. He should normally have been screaming his head off. But if somewhat bashed about, he seemed to be in good shape.

'Oh, bring him along,' I groaned. The mother – assuming that had been her – was dead. It was an easy guess what had become of the rest of the family. We couldn't stop here much longer. Nor could we leave the boy behind. If we got through this, I could see, I'd have another adopted child. But there was no time for the formalities of acceptance. We had to keep moving. Already, we were attracting more than passing looks. Half-cut, bleary-eyed men were staggering together in the street as if from nowhere. There were still things to steal, and rapes and murders to be committed. But we looked interesting, and might not be able to run away. Though ragged and filthy, my clothes put me obviously into the higher classes. Though I had a sword again, it was plain I was injured.

We got another fifty yards along the street, then swung left into a side turning. I was desperate for water and any kind of a rest. And further on, there was what we agreed was an unpleasantly tight grouping of men sitting under the colonnade. Most of them lounged in the shade. A few of them were standing. They were all staring in our direction with what struck me as more than passing interest. We turned in, and then turned again, and then again. We were now in one of the narrow, airless streets common to poor districts in every city. The differences between this and what I'd seen of the Egyptian quarter would have been hard to list. I'd never been here in any of my wanderings through Alexandria. The sunlight was blocked by the upper storey of the buildings on either side, and it was impossible to know which way we were going. But we were alone. And this was the last place mobs bent on blood and plunder were likely to frequent.

For the first time, I was able to sit down and have a proper look at my ankle. It was horribly swollen. I was glad I'd put on shoes, rather than the jewelled sandals the slaves had tried getting

me to wear. Even touching it was painful, and it wasn't possible to say if it really was broken or just badly sprained. I cut
the tattered remnant of my cloak into strips and had Martin bind
them as tightly as he could around the ankle. Afterwards, I stood
up. Running was still out of the question. But movement would
be easier. I might even be able for a half-dozen steps at a time not
to look so disabled.

'Keep him in the bag,' I said, nodding at the baby. 'He'll come
to no harm in there – and it mutes the crying.' Food was something we'd consider later. That would be for all three of us. Of
course, this was a district without running water and there were
butts placed on every corner. With all the hard work of rioting,
these hadn't been filled for at least a day. But they had moderately
clean water for anyone willing to risk falling in as he stretched
over to get it. Martin cupped some in his hands for the child, who
now became somewhat quieter. All we needed after this was some
place of safety, preferably inside the Palace, or in some place from
where we could get to the Palace.

I looked around me. It was a poor district. Yet the mean, crumbling buildings were also well-secured. A few old women and
children were darting glances from upstairs windows. But the
streets were empty, and there was no chance, it was soon made
clear to us, of being let in anywhere.

'Which way do you suppose to the Palace district?' I asked.
Even if we couldn't get all the way, there were some churches
where Martin might be recognised.

'I think that way is east,' he said with an uncertain wave back
the way we'd come. He listened closely. 'But surely there's a main
street not far off,' he said.

I also could hear the faint commotion. It was an annoyance,
showing, as it did, that the rioting wasn't confined around the
Church of the Apostles. But it wasn't surprising. Every poor
district borders eventually on to somewhere richer, and we knew
that we were only in the first few streets. This particular mob might
be a few hundred yards away as it went about some mischief that,
given luck, would keep it from any place we wanted to be.

'Did you bring any money with you?' I asked, pulling him back to the matter in hand.

Martin shook his head.

Nor had I. The golden slide for my hair hadn't survived the climb to the church roof. Beyond that, I'd deliberately not put on any jewellery. The knife was valuable – but much more at present for its blade of Damascus steel than for the weight of its hilt. I didn't suppose anyone here would accept a promise to pay. For food and for shelter, then, we might have been beggars in the city that I helped rule.

'Do you think it's getting closer?' Martin asked anxiously.

I would have told him to shut up. But I listened again. I looked at Martin. He looked at me. The baby was beginning to cry piteously.

45

'They *are* coming closer,' Martin said.

I nodded. There was no point in denying the obvious. The street around us was as still and quiet as in one of the abandoned suburbs of Constantinople. But the distant noise of rioting was growing louder. It wasn't the rushing about and screaming of the mob back outside the church. That sort of rioting soon burns itself out. This was the tramp of perhaps hundreds of feet, and that rhythmical – and, in my view, that increasingly tiresome – chant about the Tears of Alexander. Add to this the regular thumping of cudgels against wood when people are marching past close-packed properties and checking to see which, if any, are not locked and barred.

It was Egyptians. And they weren't marching by this poor district, on their way to rob and murder more Greeks of quality. They were inside the poor district. And they were getting closer.

'It's fair to assume they're after us,' I said flatly. 'They were waiting for us and hoping to cut us off as we approached the Palace district. Who wants us and why, and what's to be done with us – search me. If only we could find somewhere to hide . . .'

But where to hide? As I said, every place worth entering was already secured. The streets, though filthy as any pigsty, had no shelter. Unless we could find an open door, the best we could hope for was to keep out of sight, and wait for the mob to give up whatever search had brought it our way, or for the Greek residents to come back from their own rioting to deal with these invaders. Yes, with all this noise, there must soon be a Greek mob on the scene. That would complicate matters nicely.

With a muffled crying, much heavy breathing and the scrape of my staff on the dried mud of the street, we started off again. Even as we covered the distance to the corner of the street, the chanting grew louder.

'But where is it coming from?' Martin asked.

Good question. The sound was bouncing from every wall. It was impossible to tell what was original and what its echo. How Martin was avoiding one of his fits of the vapours was another mystery of the day. To be sure, I was increasingly rattled by this hunt with us as the quarry. For all the usual reasons of nationality, there was no chance of cooperation between invading mob and those residents here not of rioting age. What we most likely had was a methodical search of one slum by dwellers of another who knew the ways of all. But it seemed to me, as I hobbled painfully on, as if someone were watching us from the sky and somehow advertising our position to the mob. It didn't matter which way we moved. We could hurry as best we could along the full length of a street. We could make turns at random and double back on ourselves. No matter what we did, the joyous chanting grew steadily louder.

Or it grew louder while it continued. Every so often, it would fall silent. Then it would be the soft tramp of many feet. Or it would be total silence. Then it would start all over with a burst of sound. It was the silences that were most unnerving. Why, if they were hunting us, these people advertised their presence at all was beyond me. Why the silences was equally so. Whether we tried to get away from the chanting, or worried we'd come face to face with the silent hunters, we pressed on deeper into the labyrinthine slum.

'They're coming from down that way,' I said, pointing along one of the wider and less winding streets. And they were. I turned back and began to stump heavily towards one of the smaller turnings. I wanted to stop and rest. I should have taken the armour off while we were resting. It had started as a minor inconvenience. It was now dragging me down. Martin put his free arm round my back and began pulling me forward. It got us moving faster. But where were we going? There was no point complaining we were lost. That was a problem to be sorted out later. For the moment, it was enough that we couldn't find a scrap of cover. There wasn't so much as a doorway for squeezing into. It didn't help that I'd come out dressed as brightly as a songbird.

There was an alley leading into a courtyard. I saw the dark opening as Martin hurried us past. I managed to stop him and push him towards it. We threw ourselves into it. I stood leaning against a wall, wheezing and gasping as I tried to catch my breath. No one had come yet round any of the corners. If we could get ourselves into the courtyard, and stay there, the mob could look to its own affairs.

'Get out of here!' It was a man in late middle age. A stained leather apron covered his belly. One of his massive hands was wrapped round a hammer. In the other was what looked like a sharpened iron pole.

'In the name of God,' I cried softly, 'give us shelter. There are wogs in this quarter, killing every Greek of whatever condition. Ask what you will of me. But give us shelter.'

Martin held up the twitching bag, as if the muffled crying from within wasn't enough. I thought of offering my knife with the golden hilt. Another man, equally big, appeared. This one had the sort of metal saw you normally see two slaves working. He raised it threateningly.

'Get out,' the first man repeated. He jabbed the metal spike in our direction.

I'd have had trouble taking on the pair of them in the best circumstances. These weren't anything like the best circumstances. Even the sword I'd picked up was a cheap thing I'd not have trusted to stay in one piece for a serious fight. I pointed at the bag.

'Then at least take the child,' I begged. All else aside, the poor thing was slowing us down.

'Get out or I'll kill you both,' he replied. He jabbed viciously forward, and caught me in the stomach. The armour stopped the blow from doing any actual harm. Even so, I was knocked to the ground, and I was sure the spike had forced a small gap in the chainmail. I groaned and clutched at the probable if minor stab wound. As I pulled myself back up, the man's friend lashed out with the saw and got Martin in the face with one of its wooden handles. Martin dropped the bag and pointed to it as we retreated backwards from the alley. I looked behind. The chanting had started again, and was loud and close But the street was clear. We could still make a run for it.

'Take it with you,' the man snarled. 'Take it up – or I'll cut it in pieces and throw it after you down the street.' He stabbed at the bag, pinning one of its hems to the packed earth.

'Bring him with us,' I said to Martin. Leaning heavily on my staff, I followed Martin towards the light of the open street.

Once in Constantinople, I saw some lunatic jump on to the Circus racetrack. I think his idea was to hold up the race while he addressed us on its sinfulness. I saw him stand and hold up his arms for attention. I saw him take in breath. Then he was simply gone. He'd been struck by one of the racing chariots that had been going too fast to veer aside. What was left of him was eventually carried away from a spot fifty yards from where he'd been alive.

That's how it seemed to be with Martin. As he emerged into the light, the mob reached us. No longer marching, it was breaking into a stampede. It crashed straight into Martin. He vanished, propelled forward by the unstoppable rush of hundreds of tightly packed bodies.

'Martin,' I screamed. I pulled out my sword and hobbled forward. I'd dropped my staff and fell into the mob as it rushed past. For a moment, I was caught up in that surging, cheering mass. Then I'd fallen. Now I was dragged forward on the ground. Feet trampled and kicked at me. I tried to roll out of their way. But now arms reached down and pulled me on to my back and dragged me down the road. I tried to kick on the ground to get myself upright as I was pulled backwards. I was going too fast, and my ankle didn't allow more than a notional effort. I screamed and screamed again with the pain and the terror.

I was dropped down at one of the junctions of the streets. I lay in the middle of a circle of men. The sun was directly overhead, and I couldn't see their faces. I tried to sit up. I did begin babbling for mercy. But someone struck hard at me from behind.

The blow glanced off the armour, but knocked me over on my side. Someone kicked me hard in the stomach. Again, the harm was limited, but I was winded. Hands reached down and began ripping at my clothes. I was rolled on to my front as someone began pulling at the leather straps holding the armour to my body. Still wearing it, I was rolled on to my back again. Someone struck at my good leg. I heard the dull sound of wood on bone before I felt the pain.

Men were kneeling beside me, pulling at me and striking and jabbering incomprehensibly in an ecstasy of joyous hate. I was pulled into a sitting position. Someone had found the child. He dragged the poor creature from the bag – writhing and crying in the sudden light. He held up my knife – how he'd got it from my belt I didn't know. He slit the stomach across and pushed his face close to catch the splashing of the blood. He pulled out the little entrails. They came out in tight coils. All round me, there was a great cry of triumph, so I didn't hear the wailing. But I vomited as the dead or dying body was rubbed hard into my face. I got my hands over my face and tried to turn away. I think someone kicked me in the head. I know someone hit me very hard across the shoulders. As I jerked round to avoid going over on my face, I dropped my hands. I couldn't see from my left eye. I panicked again and screamed.

I was pulled straight. My arms and legs were stretched out as if I were on the Prefecture rack. I felt a sharp pain and then numbness in my hands as if a vice had closed over my wrists. I felt hands reach under my tunic. I screamed again. I screamed and screamed. The faces all around me pressed in closer and closer. From my good eye, I could see the leering grins. One of the mouths was stopped with a tiny hand and wrist. I could see how it was sucked and chewed as if it had been a child's comforter. I could smell the garlic and the rotting teeth. I began to black out with the horror.

I heard a sudden roaring, and the breath was stopped in my throat. The ground beneath me began to ripple and convulse as if in an earthquake. I felt a still greater tremor in the air around me. There was wailing from the back of the crowd. I heard one man scream, and then be cut off in mid-flow. The faces twisted again – now into fear and then outright terror. All around me was a pandemonium of screams and wild threshing. Someone collapsed forward on top of me. Then he was lifted off me as if by some vast but invisible force.

No one was pulling on my limbs, and I was able to roll myself into a ball of liberated agony. As the waves of blackness grew shorter and shorter, and sound and vision faded, I had the impression of being absolutely alone in a sunlight that was no longer hot. All pain and all fear slipped away from me. My last feeling that I recall was an immensely serene calm.

46

I was in a tunnel lined with glass blocks that shone with some inner light. I was moving rapidly towards one of its ends. I tried to see what was there, but was dazzled by the warm light that flooded in from whatever lay beyond. I looked harder. But whatever I did see was so indefinite, and so changed from moment to moment, that I was no more certain than if I hadn't looked at all.

I say that I was moving. I wasn't walking, though. Instead, I floated, as if carried on some invisible chair. I tried to shift position, but seemed to have no control over my body. Indeed, it was hard to tell if I had a body at all.

I felt that I was coming to a moment of understanding. The shapes within the light were beginning to resolve themselves into something definite and perceptible. Even as I focused, however, I was moving back the way I'd come. The light still dazzled, though from a growing distance. The distance stretched and stretched as I flew back at a now incredible speed. The tunnel was miles long – hundreds of miles long – and still I moved back along it, away from a light that may have been more distant, though it shone with undiminished brightness.

My speed was increasing. The glass blocks were merging into a single blur, and still I was going faster. I had no sense of hearing. I couldn't feel any resistance of the air about me. I felt none of the forward rush you get when a chariot or a fast ship accelerates. It was enough to know that I was moving. I don't think I was falling – though it was hard to know if concepts of up and down had any meaning here. I was sure I wasn't falling. That couldn't have accounted for the speed I was moving. I was like one of the atoms that Epicurus conjectured – small and unimportant by itself, and moving at inconceivable speed through a universe infinite in space and time.

I was no longer moving. I lay still on a soft surface. I opened my eyes and looked round. I was in a strange room. It was crowded with furniture of immense elaboration. There was a window of glazed panes looking out into blackness. The walls were hung with silk and with paintings in a realistic style of men in clothes I'd never seen before. There was an open fire in a grate against the wall. I heard its steady crackling and smelled the clean vapour of the sea coals. On a shelf above this was a machine with a dial set round with numbers in the Roman style. From it I could hear a slow, steady clicking of its works.

As I looked about in the candlelight, I saw a man dozing in a chair. A fat, dumpy creature, dressed in the silk brocade of the men in the paintings, he had a book in his lap. It was a book in our own modern style – folded and bound in sections – but surprisingly small. Other books of the same kind were heaped about him on the carpeted floor. Beside him, on a table of polished wood, was a glass bottle containing something dark. There was a glass drinking cup beside this, about a third full.

I climbed to my feet. I saw that I was dressed in the plain white and purple-bordered robe of a senator. The fat man shifted back deeper into his chair and snored. I stood over the fat man. He'd drunk himself into a doze that meant I was quite alone in the room. I took up the drinking cup and raised it to my lips. Its taste was sweet and much more powerful than any wine I knew. I drained the cup and refilled it.

Cup in hand, I moved towards the desk and reached for one of the crumpled balls of what looked like very white parchment. I smoothed it out and squinted at the neat but unknown writing. It made no sense to me. I saw there was ink in a silver pot. There were no pens, though, of the usual reed or wood. For writing, there was a collection of bird feathers, cut and split at the ends into the right shape. I picked one up and rolled it between my fingers. It didn't strike me as at all a convenient sort of pen. I looked again at the neat writing. It was all, I supposed, a matter of custom. So too the idea of filling a room with expensive objects, and spoiling it with an open fire.

I was picking up sheet after sheet and still trying to see if I could understand any of it, when I heard a noise behind me. I looked round. The fat man was stretching his arms. He grunted and opened his eyes. I looked full at him. He looked back at me and rubbed his eyes. He reached for his drinking cup. He looked round in some confusion before staring at the cup, now empty on his desk.

He said something nasty in a language I'd never heard before and tried to stand. The effort was too much and he fell back into his chair. He reached for a silver bell, but then looked at me again. I smiled nervously back. He raised his voice and spoke again in the unknown language. I shook my head. He spoke once more in a language that sounded different from the first, but that I still couldn't understand.

'Do you know Greek?' I asked in that language.

He smiled, and with an evident collecting of thought, replied in Latin.

'There are those who stand between us,' he said in a slow and oddly accented manner, 'who say you served a higher purpose. We, of course, know otherwise.'

He laughed gently and repeated himself: 'We both know better than those monks and barbarians.'

With that, his eyes closed again and he drifted back into his doze. As he did so, the room began to darken and its various objects took on a weirdly translucent quality.

I snatched up the book from his lap. It fell straight through my hands as if they didn't exist. It fell open on the floor. I dropped to my knees and tried to see what was on the pages. Written on the left page in very small and neat characters that looked like a variant on the Greek script, and on the other in something equally small and neat that contained Roman letters and might have been Latin, I wanted to look at it in better light. Particularly interesting was that the words appeared to be separated by spaces between, and there were obvious punctuation marks. But the darkness was spreading around me like a mist.

I grabbed again at the book to try to lift it. Again, my hands went through it. All I could see before the darkness became total was the separated words written in Roman letters at the head of each page:

SANCTI AELRICI DE UITA SUA DECEM LIBRI

As everything around me faded into nothingness, I could hear the faint chiming of a bell in that machine above the fireplace.

Then it was all gone.

I woke with a simultaneous contraction of every muscle. I lay naked on a bed in a room hung with yellow silk. Just out of sight, I could feel the breeze from a window, and hear the calling and fluttering of little birds. A black hand was mopping at my face with a sponge soaked in something that smelled of lemon. I sat up, but fell back again with the sudden effort. I tried to put my thoughts in order.

'Where's Martin?' I cried. I tried to sit up again, but was pushed gently back by the black maidservant. She looked across me and began a twittering call to someone on the far side of the room.

'I thought you would wake around this time,' the Mistress said. She was perched on a little table, and had been reading from a book that she was scrolling in both hands with practised elegance. She placed a bone clip in the book to hold her place and rolled it shut. She clapped her hands, and more of the maidservants came into the room, carrying dishes.

I was still trying to get my thoughts working. Questions were pouring into my head, and I couldn't think which ones to ask at all, and which ones first. I looked down at myself and reached feebly for the sheet that was folded away from me.

'Dear me, Alaric.' She laughed so that her veil shook – she was wearing one of the loose but shapely robes that covered her whole body. 'You may be unusually pretty. But I do assure you that you have nothing I haven't seen many times before.' She crossed the room and sat beside me. She motioned to one of the women, who began spooning broth into me. It had a taste of menthol and of fish, over something else I couldn't even begin to recognise.

'Do you know what has become of Martin?' I asked when the feeding was over.

The Mistress sat back a little and stared carefully into my face. 'No,' she said. 'You made keeping up with you difficult even for me. By the time I did find you, it was only you who could be rescued.' She put a hand up to silence me. 'No, let me be as clear as I can be. I had a search made of the whole area. Martin was not among any of the animals who failed to get away. If your poor secretary is dead, he was not killed where he was taken.'

'Where is this?' I now asked. If this was another dream, I was at least with someone who seemed inclined to answer some questions. And if this wasn't a dream, there were questions that had to be asked.

I now had an increasingly clear recall of my time in the poor district. It seemed she had turned up in time to save me from being torn apart by the mob. But how had she done that? And – I looked again at myself. I had a few superficial bruises on my chest and legs. I could move my left arm without pain. The swelling had gone from my ankle. I moved the foot. There was a slight stiffness, but nothing to stop me from walking and even running. I know that fear can magnify injuries. But the impression I'd had of those last few moments was of a brutal smashing to every part of my body not protected by the chainmail.

I did now sit up. I was weak – no doubt of that – but there was no sense of internal bruising, still less of breakages.

'What happened back there?' I asked. 'How long have I been here?'

'Taking into account the day you came here, you have been with me five days,' the Mistress answered. 'That makes today the festival you celebrate every seven days of Christ your Prophet and Deity.' She'd answered my second question. The first she was unlikely to have forgotten, but showed no inclination to answer.

'How have you escaped the rioting?' I asked. I looked about me. 'You've armed your male slaves?'

She laughed again very softly. 'Male slaves?' she said. 'I have none. They displeased me shortly after my arrival in Alexandria. I had them sold to a Saracen for export to his own country. There, they will be castrated and set to guarding the harems of the great. I have no male slaves – nor desire for any.'

I sat back again and closed my eyes. I *was* awake. It wasn't a matter of the surrounding normality – there was precious little of that for the moment. Nor was there much sense of continuity of space and time with what I knew had been real. But self-awareness carried the whole burden of assuring me that, somehow, I was alive and well, and still in Alexandria.

I swung round and sat on the edge of the bed. My feet brushed the cool tiles of the floor. What I wanted to ask was how the Mistress had got herself about Alexandria in the middle of a gigantic riot, without male slaves, and had rescued me from a baying mob. And since I didn't doubt her assurance, how had she also been able to have the area searched for Martin? I'd have to do better than I had.

'When we first met,' she went on, 'I reminded you of the old truth: that those who rescue strays take on further duties for their welfare. I remain firmly convinced of that truth. I only wish I could have helped Martin. To have you both here safe and well would be delightful indeed.'

She got up and motioned to the maidservants. They darted noiselessly around, clearing away various pots and boxes. Two of them went over to a cupboard and pulled out a robe of white silk. I stood carefully up as they brought it to me. Yes, the ankle was a little stiff, but I could walk on it without pain. What I'd looked like when brought here was hard to say. Since then, though, I'd been washed and shaved and anointed. I could feel that my hair would be in need of further attention. Apart from this, I was soon about as respectable to behold as anyone might have wished.

I thanked the Mistress. I'd learn more later, I resolved, about the details of how she'd saved me. The firmer my recollection, the odder it all seemed. For the moment, though, it was enough to give thanks. She acknowledged these with a nod of her veiled head. I went over to the window and looked out. So far as I could tell, we were on the upper floor of one of the palaces overlooking the Harbour. This was no longer the fashionable district it had been when the palaces were built. But it was one of the quieter parts of the centre, and it caught the sea breezes very nicely. My window looked away from the sea – it looked out over the city, or would have but for other buildings that prevented a full view. I could see one public street. It seemed completely untouched by the rioting. Slaves carried messages along it from one palace to another. I saw a fine lady being carried past in her chair – with guards, certainly, but no apparent sense of danger.

Looking up, into the distance, showed a different picture. The smoke rose in an almost continuous haze above the higher buildings. With Priscus dead, and Nicetas possibly still holed up in the Church of the Apostles, I tried to think what might have happened in the past few days. Had the rioting burned itself out? Even urban mobs eventually grow tired of murder and rape. Or had some coalition of interests formed to use what force and persuasion might be available? How much damage was there to the buildings of Alexandria? How many had died?

Above all, had the Palace remained safe throughout? I thought of Maximin. I thought of Sveta. The mob was a beast without conscience and without mercy. It chilled me to think of the baby I'd seen killed. The Palace was easily the strongest point in the city. But Nicetas had gone out with much of its garrison. I wanted to be polite to the Mistress. She had saved me. She had nursed me back to health. There was much I wanted to discuss with her. At the same time, I wanted to be back in the Palace.

I turned back to face the Mistress. She had already moved beside me.

'You will find that the rioting is at an end,' she said, pre-empting my question. 'Much as I am amused by your company, I see no point in seeking to detain you under my roof. You will find you are fully rested and in no further need of my attentions. The streets are safe enough for persons of quality, and I am sure you have duties that require your attention. If you wish to accept any further help from me, please be advised to go back to the Royal Palace and stay there. No harm can attend you there. Nor can you be made a source of harm to others. Stay there and await such time as you can return to the Imperial City.' She went back to where I'd seen her on first waking. She reached again for her book.

'You will forgive me if I do not accompany you back to the Royal Palace,' she said. 'All else aside, you and I together would be an unreasonable burden to my maidservants, whose job it is for the moment to carry my chair.'

47

I was carried back from the western end of the Embankment Road. On my right, the shops and restaurants were opening late because of the Sunday service. There were hardly any customers. Still, the effort was being made. Slaves had set out the tables and chairs. Shopkeepers were gently crying up their goods. Every so often, the few passers-by would stop and watch the oddity of a blonde man carried past on an obviously feminine chair, and by some very young black women. I paid them no attention. I set my gaze eventually to the left, where stretched the immense crescent of acacia trees and the docks beyond. Not much could be seen of these through the heavy boughs. Every so often, though, there was the sight of lifting machinery and of the sea that sparkled far out in the sun. It all looked so normal. But I couldn't escape the smell, whenever the breeze let up from the north, of death and of burned-out buildings.

I saw the scale of the devastation as we turned right into the wide street that led from the docks to the Central Forum. Buildings – whole blocks of buildings – had been razed to piles of smoking rubble. Banks, exchanges, warehouse buildings, shops, palaces, churches, schools, baths, monasteries: they had gone. Street frontages that had shown a thousand years of continuous development were now swept away. The fires still burned in places. Front elevations still leaned inwards, not yet pulled down or ready by themselves to collapse. But the work of ruin was done. When it came to ruination, Alexandria didn't compare with Rome – still less with Ephesus or Corinth. But a good third of the centre was gone. And how, in the straitened circumstances of the present, it was ever to be rebuilt as other than a patched-up slum wasn't something I could say.

The destruction had barely started when I was taken out of things. There could be no doubt, though, that it was over. The impaling stakes removed any doubt that order had been fully restored. A section of the better classes in Alexandria, assisted by the mob, had challenged the might of the Empire. Now, after a struggle that I had largely missed but that gave every appearance of the colossal, the Empire had triumphed, and the impaling stakes were an outward symbol of the restoration of order.

About eight feet high and twenty yards apart along both sides of the street, each of the stakes had been set into one of the stone gratings beneath which the flood waters rushed and gurgled. Each of them carried at least two bodies. The two lower bodies had been impaled through their stomachs. Blackened, already putrefying in the sun, they hung as they'd died, the lower one brushing arms and legs on the pavement. Flies buzzed and swarmed and settled on the dead. Carrion birds perched along the tops of every high place, calling out and fluttering their wings. Some of them – not vultures: I was surprised by how pretty they often were – were braving the crowds of onlookers to fly down and peck at the eyes. Stray dogs licked at the pools of blood, or slaves outside the better class of shops that remained fussed about with brushes and buckets of water.

Where a third body had been added, the impaling was generally, though not universally, done upright – through the anus. Those were a ghastly sight. The faces looked straight back at any onlooker, twisted with agony beyond describing and with eyes pecked out. Flies crawled in and out of the slack mouths. The sun had already brought the faces out in black patches.

I watched one of these executions. My chair had reached a pile of rubble that blocked half the width of the street. There was no way through the crowd, and I had no means of giving precise instructions to the chair carriers. I started at the back of the crowd. One further sign, though, of restored order was that everyone else no sooner saw me seated than they got smartly out of my way, and the women moved me forward right to the front. Bound and already naked, the victim was twisting about and squealing for mercy even before he was pulled from the closed, slave-drawn carriage. I saw the crazed look on his face and the glistening of tears. I saw him clutch and unclutch his hands in supplication. It took three men, all wearing Prefecture uniforms, to heave him up into position, the sharpened tip of the stake between his legs. A fourth stood before him, quietly and rapidly reading something off a sheet of papyrus.

With a start, I realised that he was the potty man. I hadn't recognised him at first because he was naked. The pinched, wiry look of the lower classes has little individuality. But the face I'd have recognised anywhere. 'Me – I don't never mix with wogs,' he'd said, which seemed so very long ago, while wiping Martin's bum. Perhaps he'd broken his rule. More likely, it didn't really matter what he'd done or not done.

At last, the reading finished. The jabbered supplication didn't let up. It was a waste of breath, and – so far as it mattered at this late stage – it showed a want of dignity. No one paid attention. The fourth Prefecture man nodded to the others. With a count of 'One, two, three!' they let go of him, and then held him again as his weight took the stake deeper into his body. Once he was firmly on, they cut his bonds and stood back. The crowd had let up a great cheer as he was dropped on to the stake. Now, it was fallen silent, and nothing covered the shrill, incredulous screaming as the man took the stake into his body. I had thought it would be a quick slide down and then silence. However, the stake was of a thickness, and was so notched at intervals, that the descent was agonisingly slow. He reached down with his arms, desperately trying to hold himself up. He hugged himself, and covered his eyes. He pressed on his stomach. He waved about like one of the more inebriated dancing girls. It all had no effect on the slow progression of the stake through his body – tearing or displacing organs, snapping bones, making every moment an infinity of pain and horror-stricken fear.

At last, his legs straddled the lower bodies, and the tip of the stake emerged from his mouth. There was another cheer from the crowd, and men held up their little children to see the bloody froth dribble off his chin. No longer jerking about, he twitched for longer than I'd have thought possible. His eyes fluttered in little spasms. Clouds of flies buzzed madly about, waiting for all to be still again.

Their faces showing utter exhaustion, the men from the Prefecture sat down in a clean patch beside the stake and called across the road for a jug of wine. They leaned forward to stretch their tired muscles, then sat back to rest in the sun. As the crowd parted and let me through, I was carried close by the carriage. I heard the desperate, terrified cries of those still waiting for their end. Maddened eyes stared out from behind the closely set bars. A hand was pushed through and raised as if for mercy as I was carried past. I raised a cloth soaked in lemon scent to block the sudden smell of shit and vomit from within.

I wasn't able to count how many other carriages were being trundled up and down the road. Nor could I count the number of bodies, already swollen by the gases of their internal corruption, that had been stacked out of the way in side streets. Their faces covered by spiced cloths, slaves struggled with the carrion birds and ravening dogs to pull the bodies out and pile them into carts for carrying away. Much longer, I knew, and the internal corruption would generate the seeds of a pestilence to sweep away further multitudes.

The Palace square was a forest of the dead and dying. The sudden shock of seeing it stopped my breath. I wanted to poke at the maidservants and have them carry me round to one of the other entrances. But I sagged back in my place, unable to move, and those women carried me steadily forward with no more feeling than if we were entering a garden. Every stone grating had been put to use, and I could see for the first time why they had been placed in their otherwise inexplicable pattern. Longer stakes had been used here, and each one held up to six bodies, all impaled with some of ingenuity. I saw men impaled through their stomachs and out through their bottoms. I saw men impaled in the other way. I saw men impaled in ways that may have let them stay alive all morning, and that might not kill them until after darkness had fallen. All around me, the cries of those who still lived mingled with the calling of the carrion birds and the swarming of the flies.

'Where's your ticket?' a voice screamed beside me.

I looked round. It was an armed man. He had the look of a cavalry soldier, though he had no horse. So, the reinforcements I'd ordered in had eventually arrived, I thought.

'Where's your fucking ticket?' he screamed again. He waved a long cavalry sword at me.

The chair shook as every one of its female carriers cried out in a unison of terror.

'I am,' I replied, 'the Senator Alaric, Legate Extraordinary from His Imperial Majesty to His Imperial Highness the Viceroy.' I stepped unsteadily down from the chair and tried to breathe through my mouth. I didn't know how to tell the women to go back to the Mistress, but expected they'd get the idea. 'Do not presume to ask me for identification,' I said with a look down my nose.

The soldier opened his mouth for what I had no doubt would be a stream of very ripe abuse. Before he could spew any of it my way, however, someone else came running over.

'My Lord! My Lord!' he cried happily in Latin. 'We'd heard you were dead. It is a true delight to see you in such good health.' He was one of the Slavonic guards. He had a bandage round his left arm, and didn't look as if he'd shaved or even washed in days. He waved the cavalry soldier away and led me through the Palace gates.

As I walked into the entrance hall, I could hear my name passing from voice to voice. There was a crowd about me before I'd got halfway across the floor. Faces bobbed in and out of my sight, calling my name. Hands stretched out to touch my robe. I'd never thought I was so popular. Even the eunuchs looked happy. I had no choice but to stop and give a little speech of thanks to God for my preservation, and of thanks to everyone else for being pleased

339

I had been preserved. There's a big difference between a cheering crowd and one that wants to rip you apart. But, if the Mistress assured me I was well, I could feel my legs trembling. All I wanted now was a long drink and maybe an opium pill or two.

48

'So how *did* you get out alive?' I asked Priscus a second time.

He looked up from the list of names placed before him on the Viceroy's desk and laughed. 'My dearest Alaric,' he said, 'did you really think I could be killed by a handful of wogs? I don't think I ever told you about my part in the loss of Serdica. That was back in the early days of Maurice, when I was just a staff officer. It was all rather boring at first. Then, one night, ten thousand savages – every one of them as big and blonde as you, and every one of them fighting mad – came pouring over the wall. The whole garrison was put to the sword. I was the only one not to be—'

He broke off as a secretary knocked and came in with a sheaf of documents. As Priscus arranged them on the desk, I saw that every sheet was another list of names. Priscus looked briefly down the columns. A couple of times, he took up a pen and crossed out some of the names. Once or twice, he added others from memory.

'These ones,' he said, holding up one of the more crowded sheets, 'I want impaled. For all these' – he signed his name on one of the smaller sheets – 'the punishment is blinding and confiscation of property. For all the others, it's burning. Do make sure to tell me if we run short of timber from the demolished buildings. In view of the Patriarch's message, we'll hold all further executions over till tomorrow. As for the blindings' . . . He paused and measured out a spoonful of one of his powders. He tapped the shaft of the pen on his teeth and thought. 'As for the blindings, cancel them. I hereby degrade everyone on that list to the class of the freeborn poor and sentence them all to the galleys.'

'How is Nicetas?' I asked when we were alone again. I had thought of asking about Alexander. But then I'd seen the splintered box lying in a corner of the office. It still contained an entire leg and some larger fragments of the trunk. Of the head I saw no sign.

Priscus refilled my cup and pulled over a candle to heat his powder. 'Resting,' he said after another long pause.

I'd not expected any other answer from the moment I saw Priscus sitting so firmly at his desk. 'Once I found the mob couldn't get in,' he went on, 'and wasn't doing much to cut through the lead on the roof, I decided to leave him for a day and a half in the Church of the Apostles. When I did eventually have him let out, he was more dead than alive. All that had kept him going, I am told, was repeated cups of communion wine. He had the priest bless every mouthful.' He paused again, and breathed in the fumes of his evaporated powder. He pitched forward, banging his head up and down on the desk.

Nothing could kill Priscus. Nothing could harm Priscus. I'd known him too long now even to hope otherwise. I refilled my cup and drank deeply.

Getting sense out of the clerks in my office had taken an age. In the end, though, I'd heard how Priscus had somehow made his way back to the Palace and taken charge of affairs. No one could accuse him of irresolution. He hadn't waited for the rein-forcements. Instead, he'd lined up all that remained of the Palace garrison and led it out in person to a massacre of everyone who didn't run for cover. He'd cut his way to the Prefecture and recruited every one of the quaking officers to his little army. With them puffing up his numbers, he'd slaughtered until the streets ran with blood and until every one of the rioters lucky enough to survive had burrowed his way back into the filthy slums from which he had issued. Now, order was fully restored, and it was time to punish all those who'd called the mobs into being before losing control of them.

'Have you ever seen a man eaten to death by maggots?' Priscus asked heavily. He looked up at me, tears carrying the mascara down his face in green rivulets.

I shook my head.

342

'Then remind me in six days' time, and I'll take you back under the Prefecture. You'll find the Viceroy's secretary in a cell of his own. He came the high and mighty official when I staggered in here more dead than alive. Of course, I beat him to pulp when he tried to stop me from laying hands on the Great Seal. His death sentence was for treason. The manner of his death is for pissing me off.'

He sat up again, his mood brightening. He reached into a drawer and pulled out the Great Seal. Every one of my own intrigues since arriving here had been connected with getting Nicetas to use this as I desired. I'd never thought of just taking it. So long as Nicetas lay sobbing in his bed, surrounded by priests, Priscus was the supreme power in Alexandria and for as deep into Egypt as Imperial rule might still reach.

'My darling Alaric,' he said with one of his more charming smiles, 'if I seemed less than overjoyed when you walked in, that is because I already knew that you were still alive.' He reached into another drawer and took out a leather packet. From this he took out a folded sheet of papyrus. 'This was waiting for you two evenings ago, when I got back from burning the poorer half of the Egyptian quarter. I hope you'll not mind that I opened it in your absence. It does answer a question I know has been hanging on your lips ever since you walked in here.' He pushed the folded sheet across the desk.

I took it up and unfolded it.

'From the second and greater Pharaoh Meriamen Usermaatre Setepenre,' it began, 'to Alaric, Legate of the Greek Emperor – greetings and congratulations.'

'I assume he's the wog fucker who took Alexander's head,' Priscus broke in.

I nodded. He scowled and went back to scanning his death lists. I looked closely at the sheet. It had a few crossings-out and changes that made it pretty clear Lucas had written this by himself. It was good Greek and in a good hand. He must once have had the choice to be Greek or Egyptian. Why he'd not chosen the Greeks continued to astonish me.

Anyway, the congratulations were on my escape from his people. Apparently, they'd exceeded their instructions, and those 'still in need of punishment', would receive it from his own hands. He explained how the purpose of the attack had merely been to take me prisoner, 'so that we might continue the business you cut so painfully short last month'. After much elaborations on his admiration for me, and his personal desire to continue 'our most interesting discussions', – I shuddered at that one – he got to the point:

> You have, or are in a position to obtain, a relic of the Faith that we regard as of the highest value to the freedom of the Egyptian people. You will hand this to us – together with attestation from the appropriate religious authorities – at the midnight hour on the twenty-seventh day of the month of Mechir. For this purpose, you will attend on us in the market square of the town that sits in the shadow of the Great Pyramid.
>
> You may bring armed men sufficient for your protection, and these will guarantee your safety when you meet with us. Do not presume to think your forces will be sufficient to overwhelm us. You will be on our territory. Do not presume to think we shall not observe your every move from the moment you leave the Royal Palace in Alexandria.
>
> If you fail to attend on us in the place and at the time specified, I regret that we shall need to kill your servant Martin in a most unpleasant and prolonged manner. I have no doubt – bearing in mind your opinion of Martin and of the Faith – that you will do your utmost to comply with our wishes. The relic is as worthless to you as it is valuable to us. My only doubt is that you will believe Martin still to be alive. Since he has refused to write in his own hand to confirm this, I enclose evidence that you will surely regard as final.

The letter continued in a recitation of his praises for me, and of repeated promises for my own safety. I looked across the desk to Priscus, who'd gone back to chewing his pen.

'Quite mad,' he said. 'Quite mad in all respects. By the way, dear boy, I've had the Egyptian date explained to me. Their calendar, I'm told, has no leap year, and so their dates and ours never line up in the same way. But this year, the date given is the 15th September.'

'That's twelve days from now,' I said. 'What is this "evidence" that Martin is still alive?' I kept my voice neutral. I didn't want it seen how my heart had leapt at the mere claim that Martin was still alive. Of course, I'd get him back. But it wouldn't do to have this out with anyone – certainly not with present company.

Priscus smiled again, and reached back into the leather packet. He took out something rolled into a linen cloth, and passed it across to me.

'You can trust me without hesitation, Alaric, that this was cut from a living body. You should know that I'm an expert in these matters.'

I unrolled the cloth. Within it, still reddened by exposure of northern flesh to the sun, was a left ear.

49

The sun was fully up. The wind had fallen. The smell of death in the Palace square was omnipresent and oppressive. Priscus breathed in with an appreciative sigh and held the breath.

'How many do you think you've killed?' I asked with a change of subject. Priscus had pressed me to an early and liquid lunch. Now, we were outside, and free to take our conversation up again.

'I'll have the full report once all the bodies have been cleared away,' he said. 'My experience tells me, though, that it won't be under twenty thousand. That will include the three thousand executions I've warranted. I think on our side we lost thirty men. If I could be left to manage that sort of proportionality against the Persians, I'd have Chosroes under siege in Ctesiphon.' He breathed in again, and smacked his lips.

We fell silent as we made our way through the elaborately spaced avenues of the dead. They spread out before and around us. Wherever I looked was the blank look of death on faces still twisted in their final agonies. Like the sighing of winds in a forest was the soft groaning of the nearly dead. It sounded clear when the flies weren't rising up in great buzzing swarms. You need a lot of opium and a bad night for dreams to produce the same horrors as Priscus had managed here. I resisted the urge to run back inside the Palace. I forced myself not to shudder.

'There was no other way of settling the riots,' he said, starting again. He must have seen something on my face of what I felt. 'If Nicetas had taken my advice *before* the rioting began in earnest, the body count would have been closer to a thousand. But when you've lost control of a city as totally as he did, and when you have limited forces, promiscuous massacre becomes the only option. If you're as disgusted as you seem to be trying not to show, I'll tell you bluntly that you are partly to blame for the whole thing.'

I looked at him. Had the scale of killing embarrassed even Priscus?

'Until you rolled into town with your notions of reform and improvement,' he said, warming to his argument, 'Nicetas was doing a good job – given the circumstances he'd allowed to come into being – of keeping Alexandria quiet. It's a question of keeping the national groupings within the mob more at odds with each other than with us, and of neutralising dissent within the higher classes. What you did was to drive the higher classes to an alliance with this wog Brotherhood, and then into a desperate attempt to use the combined mob to put pressure on Nicetas. Even when they heard the Persians were sniffing about, they were so scared of what you were trying that they weren't willing to back out until it was too late. Your "compromise" with the bastards came just a few days late. By the time you got that deal brokered in your office, the Brotherhood was already here in force, and had taken control of the Egyptian mob.

'Oh, he could have handled things better than he did – and I look to you to countersign the letter of protest I'm drafting to Heraclius. But if you hadn't presented Nicetas with a situation beyond his abilities to manage, he'd not have failed so completely.'

'The land reforms have already been a success in Asia Minor,' I said firmly. I thought round for a better argument to get me off the hook. You can't argue with success, and Priscus had regained control in Alexandria with minimal forces. But if I could put up with accusations from fools like Nicetas, I didn't like to hear them repeated and fleshed out by Priscus. Before I could find the words I wanted, Priscus stopped to admire one of the more inventive impalings. Here, the victim had been driven on to the stake through his collarbone. All vital organs had been avoided, and there were still remnants of life in the twisted body. The lips

347

moved in some silent prayer. Priscus called to one of the police officers.

'Wine for the malefactor,' he ordered curtly. 'Bring him back so that he knows he is dying.' He turned back to me. 'I'll grant your scheme has been working out better in the Asian provinces than I expected,' he said. 'Indeed, I'm convinced enough by it to have had the law implemented in the areas I recovered from Persian control. But Egypt is different – as you'd have quickly noticed had you paid more attention to people than to ideas. The wogs are slaves by nature. They are slaves for us or for someone else. Between enslavements, they are dangerous animals. You don't get the same system of control, replicated century after century, with every variant of foreign and domestic rule, without a very good cause.

'I want to tell you, however, that we both deserve a better master than Heraclius. I represent order. You represent hope. Within the space that we together create, there can be civilisation. Let us somehow work together, and we can save this Empire.'

'You can try all you will for a soldierly ring to your argument,' I said, looking at the dying face while trying not to see it. 'But you came here already knowing that the Persians were in the plot. I'll grant you got names and details from that racking that you didn't already have. But you'd been lecturing Nicetas for ages on the need to guard the Red Sea ports. You were doing that two mornings after you first announced your arrival to me. I'm not sure how long before then you'd been lurking out of sight. So why wait for the rising? Did you come here to keep Egypt from the Persians? Or was it to win a battle in Alexandria that you couldn't win outside Caesarea?'

'The answer to your question, dear boy,' Priscus said, 'is Nicetas. If he'd taken my advice, I'd have had half a dozen landowners into the Prefecture dungeons. A day later, none of this killing would have been necessary. As it is, however, Alexandria is pacified, and Egypt cannot be taken from us.'

We watched awhile in silence as a sponge soaked in wine was applied to the victim's lips. The eyes fell open for a moment. Then life faded rapidly away. The police officer stood back apologetically, waiting further orders.

'Dear me,' said Priscus, poking at the now still body. 'I could have sworn the creature had more capacity to bear pain.' He sniffed and looked up at the burning sun. 'Carry on about your business,' he said to the police officer. We moved into another avenue of stakes. A few yards further down this one, and we'd bumped into a group of relatives weeping and praying over someone they'd eventually found.

'What do you think about Martin's chances?' I asked. I could see no point in letting Priscus think other than that I wanted Martin back to the exclusion of all else.

He smiled and stopped his inspection. 'You've been given twelve days to save him,' Priscus said. 'Let us assume you can get a digging party together and up to Soteropolis, and let us assume you can find the relic on your first dig – both rather unlikely assumptions, I must say. Let us then assume you can get it authenticated by whatever counts with these people as the appropriate religious authority. That doesn't give you long to hurry over to the Great Pyramid and make the exchange. I'll also ask what reason you have to trust a mad wog like your friend Lucas. Martin was alive when that ear was cut off. That doesn't mean he's alive now. It also doesn't mean that either of you will be alive once the relic is in his hands.'

I steadied my features. Priscus knew what I was thinking. I knew he knew, and he knew that I knew he knew. But I'd not give him the satisfaction of seeing what I thought.

'And if it were that I could lay hands on the relic and get there in time,' I said, 'and if I were sure I could get away with me and Martin in one piece – would the effective power in Alexandria allow me out through the city gates?'

'He wouldn't,' Priscus said with a bright smile. 'We can agree among ourselves that I'd sooner have a month's rations for an army than some piss pot to send before them into battle. But now I'm here, and now that everyone else appears to want it, I do rather fancy having the thing for myself. Certainly, I'd not be

349

keen to know it was in Brotherhood hands. And do bear in mind it would be high treason to give the Brotherhood anything that could make our position in Egypt more uncertain than it already is. The reinforcements you brought in are enough to hold Alexandria. If we send them away too soon, we risk losing Alexandria again. Even given time, there are no other forces available in the Empire to send out here. Here, as elsewhere, we rule by custom and by threats of violence we dare not allow to be tested.'

'And if I were to go up river alone for the purpose of getting Martin back?' I asked.

'Then you'd be mad,' he said. 'I'll not bother arguing about Martin's actual value as a human being. He's a good draughts-man, I'll not deny. But he really is neither your equal nor intrinsically worth the risk of your own life. And I do think you'd be running straight into a trap. Your absence from Alexandria would be noted at once. I've had a few names out of the fucking snake Nicetas nursed in the bower of his secretariat. But you can be sure the whole government is riddled with traitors. Order a passport, have horses saddled or a boat readied, and there would be a messenger speeding off to Lucas before you could set eyes on the city walls.

'We agree you can't lay hands on the piss pot in the time specified. That means Lucas is using Martin as bait to get you into his hands, when you can be kept alive just long enough to supervise the digging in Soteropolis. For that reason alone, I'll not allow you out of Alexandria. Besides, I need you here to help manage Nicetas when he eventually does come out from under his bed.'

'Priscus,' I said, speaking low. I led him into one of the denser thickets of the dead and dying. I wanted to avoid more of those shocked, silent groups of relatives. If there was anyone here able to pick up my words, he'd be in no position to pass them on. 'You know that I'll do whatever I must to get Martin back. You know that I can't lay hands on the piss pot in anything like the time specified. You also know where it is, and you do have sufficient forces to stop anyone but you from having it dug out.'

'I know what you're saying,' he broke in, savouring the mastery I'd given up trying not to acknowledge. If Lucas had me by the balls, so, in his own way, had Priscus. 'But why are you saying it? Can't you see that you've won? You've got the widest scheme of land reform even you could have wanted. You don't need to argue with the landowners over every acre of land you want to hand over to the wogs. We've just confiscated half the private estates in Egypt. The only landowner you'll be depriving is Heraclius himself. Are you seriously proposing to risk all this for some fat Celt who doesn't know when and when not it's permissible to fart in public?'

'Supposing I were to die – and die perhaps in disgraceful circumstances,' I said, ignoring an argument I could answer, though not to Priscus. 'You wouldn't get the piss pot, and the Brotherhood might. But my loss would change the whole balance of power in Constantinople. Heraclius, we know, is so short of anything approaching talent, that . . .' I trailed off. I could tell from the smile on his face that Priscus had got there first. He'd give me what I wanted. He'd give it to me because, either way, he won.

'If you do leave Alexandria,' he said, 'it will be with the full knowledge of Lucas. I could make Nicetas regard it as desertion of your post. He'll be looking for scapegoats to cover himself, and I might not stand up for you with him, or with Heraclius. I could then be waiting to arrest you in Soteropolis, assuming you ever got there. And I can be there after the date set by Lucas. If I can't leave now, I do expect to hand control back to the Prefecture within the next few days. If you didn't make it there, so much the worse for you. And without you to back Sergius up, I'm sure I could get the True Cross out of the authorities in Jerusalem.

'On the other hand, I could announce a fever brought on by exertions too soon after your escape from the mob, and I could have prayers laid on in all the churches for your recovery. That might give you a couple of days before the truth leaked out. If you got a move on, that might be enough. I could then wait for you in Soteropolis, though this time not to arrest you. If you rolled in with

Martin, you'd be the hero of the day. You know what Heraclius would make of that – one of his key men, willing to risk all for a person of no consequence. That's exactly the spirit he wants to encourage in his new Empire of Love and Justice.

'In that case, of course, I'd regard you as duty bound to start digging with your own hands if need be to get my relic out of those sands. Can you object to that?'

We were back at the gates to the Palace. We stood on the steps up to the gate and looked back over that gigantic and level Calvary.

'We have a deal,' I said.

'Then you're a bigger fool than I ever thought you.' He laughed. 'I did once try telling Heraclius you were an atheist. Sadly, though he knows about heresy and apostasy to the Old Faith, he can't get his head round the idea of belief in nothing. Watching you sweat over that flabby little Celt, anyone would think you believed all those teachings about the absolute value of every life.

'But if God has made you a fool, who am I not to take advantage?'

It was late evening. Maximin was on my lap. Sveta had heard me out in calm silence.

'If you are the man he's always told me you are,' she said, 'you'll get him back.' She looked at her child and then at Maximin. 'If you fail, though, what then?' Good question.

'What I've arranged for your safety isn't something I'd ever consider in normal circumstances,' I said bluntly. 'Patriarch John cannot protect you or the child. Don't even ask about Nicetas. We need to trust other forces or no one. If I fail in what I'm about to try and then in what I've arranged, you and your child will need to face Priscus. Maximin, of course, he'll take back and corrupt in no time at all into a younger version of himself.'

The boy looked up at me with his big, scared eyes. He couldn't understand the details of what was happening. But he knew something was wrong.

'What I need you to tell me is that you are willing to take that risk. If I do nothing, Martin dies for certain. But he may already be dead. If I try and fail, you and the child may die. If I do nothing, we all go back to Constantinople, where you and the child can stay in my household, or from where you can retire to some other place of comfort. I will risk myself for Martin. I must risk having Maximin grow into something evil. But I need to know what you are willing to risk. You also have a child.'

Sveta looked at the severed ear. I hadn't wanted to show it to her. But she told me that Priscus had already been round waving it under her nose. The only reason, he'd assured her, she wasn't already among the impaled masses outside was that he took this as evidence I was still alive. She got up and walked about the room. She seemed to be stopping by and touching every stick of furniture and every other object she and Martin had bought for themselves. She paused before the icon of Saint Mark she'd had from his office. She turned back to me.

'God tells me you are the man Martin says you are,' she assured me.

At any other time, I'd have laughed in her face. It was obvious that Martin's lunacies were contagious. But I put on a solemn face and looked back.

'You will not fail. But if you don't come back – both of you – with Priscus from Soteropolis, neither I nor the child will be taken alive. Will you resign Maximin to me on the same terms?'

I thought hard. 'No,' I said. 'Whatever Priscus tries to make of him, Maximin stays alive.'

And that was it. No tears. No recriminations. Just a calm exchange of risk assessments. Underneath her ungovernable wife act, I'd always known Sveta was made of steel. Martin had chosen well back in Rome. And I'd done well to spare him and free him and pay for the wedding.

But that wasn't quite the end of matters. As I was kissing Maximin and preparing to leave, Sveta got up again.

'Take this,' she said, holding out a silver medal of Saint Peter. 'It was blessed by the Pope himself. Martin is sure it saved the pair of you from the Lombards. It may save you now.'

It hadn't been blessed by anyone. I'd lied about that to Martin when getting him to agree to the Lombard mission. But I took it anyway and put it round my neck. I left her with the two children. They sat silent together in the light of a single lamp.

50

'I want these copied by morning,' I said to the exhausted clerks. 'I have business with the Lord Priscus all night. Bring them to us in the Viceroy's office. We will both seal them there.'

They bowed low and left my office. I sat alone behind my desk.

'The Empire can't take effective possession of it,' Priscus had told me earlier. 'So what if it all now goes to the wogs? I've told you it won't work in Egypt. But *someone* has to own the land.' He'd shrugged at my further suggestion and gone back to scanning his lists.

The minimal scheme of redistribution I'd agreed with the two patriarchs had lapsed, no one could dispute, outside the Church of the Apostles. Priscus was right. I could now have something like the maximal scheme. It was simply a matter of racing through the various drafts I'd prepared with Martin, and making sure that the innocent interests were exempted. It was easy in principle. Doing it all by myself, and at breakneck speed, had been a dreadful job. Then there had been all the supplemental work that Priscus had taken on himself when he'd lifted the Great Seal but not had ability or inclination to discharge. The loss of the only trilingual secretary in Alexandria had only made things worse.

But it was all done. Priscus would have the warrants before breakfast. I had no reason not to trust his promise to seal them without delay, nor very much to doubt that he'd tell the clerks I had been taken ill in his company. I hadn't asked him to promise much because he'd only deliver on what struck him at the time as in his interest to deliver. But on the warrants he would deliver.

'I shall be grateful, Barnabas, if you could stay a moment,' I said as the Head Clerk was about to close the doors. He came back and stood before my desk. Was that a little dart of his eyes to the cupboard where Martin had locked all those documents? So what if it was?

'Barnabas,' I said, looking closely into his face, 'there are some letters in this bag that I want you – and only you – to deliver. I cannot stop you from opening them and reading their contents. I cannot stop you from frustrating my intentions. But I feel that you are a man who believes in obedience, where possible, to lawful authority, and otherwise to what is right.'

He looked back in silence. I didn't insult him with offers of gold or of preferments. I'd known the man, in a very limited degree, four months. In all this time, we'd exchanged barely a word that wasn't connected with some aspect of official business. But I had to trust *someone* in this place. Isaac might be good for many things. But I'd now exhausted every possible favour with him, and the contents of those letters might easily get whoever was caught carrying them a place all by himself on an impaling stake. I had to trust someone. Without that, this whole risky scheme – risky even with that someone beyond the verge of lunacy – would fall straight to the ground. This really was one of those times when you have to step into that barrel and push yourself into the current that leads over the waterfall.

'My Lord's devotion to the people of Egypt,' Barnabas said softly, 'has been appreciated in very few quarters. Be assured, however, that the Brotherhood speaks not for the whole of Egypt.' He took up the bag and stuffed it into his satchel of writing materials. He left without looking back.

I took up the bag of clothes and other items I'd packed earlier and looked out of my office. The junior clerks were in their copying room. Barnabas was standing by the window, looking out over the still glowing embers of Alexandria. If he had heard the gentle click of the door catch, he didn't turn to me. I quietly crossed the room and looked out into the corridor. As usual, the lamps burned low in the silence of a Palace that – the passing visit aside of some bad Emperor – hadn't been a place of riotous pleasure since Antony and Cleopatra had killed themselves. In bare feet, I padded across the carpeted floors to the slave staircase located in a turning-off that led nowhere.

The entrance hall had a few eunuchs fluttering about on whatever duties they had that continued by night. I evaded their attention by keeping to the wall behind the rows of statues. From behind, the statues tended to look alike – all in the same triumphant style brought in by Alexander and taken up by every ruler since then influenced by Greece and its artistic traditions. The statue of Anastasius was a wretched thing; because he'd been regarded here and in Egypt as a fellow Monophysite, it deliberately owed something to the last gasp of the native tradition. After his came Justin, and then the Great Justinian, and then another Justin, and then Tiberius, and then Maurice. Phocas was still there, though the head was broken off. Squeezed in beside him, with barely a foot between it and the gate, was Heraclius. There could have been room for another. But Nicetas had ordered something in a full return to the ancient style.

There were guards outside the Palace gates. Now the rioting was over, though, they were back to huddling in a corner with dice and wine. I stood behind the statue of Heraclius and listened to their conversation.

'Came back here more dead than alive,' I heard one of the Slavonics say in Latin. 'Sure enough, though, the bawd comes knocking with a whole bloody troupe of whores swathed in black. Signed them in, signed them out, I did. Me – I'd not be up to wanking in his position.' He giggled and went back to shaking his dice.

There was a slow reply by one of the locals in Latin. He'd picked up something about my afternoon in the poor district, and didn't like it.

'Oh, shut the fuck up, dark eyes,' came the dismissive reply. 'You'll be saying next it was Saint George's big toe protected the Palace, not the swords in our own hands. As for numbers, you didn't say nothing at the time. And what would it matter – one tart more or less?'

The exchange merged into an argument over the odds some-one had failed to make clear. I dodged through the open gate, and then into a dark recess.

There was a moon very dim in the sky. It was enough – the street lighting was still not back in order – to show the outline of those thousands of still bodies in the square. It was just a few yards of open square. Then I was lost within their cover, and could change quickly into my going-out clothes. Now it was night, and there was no one even to think of asking for identification, the forest of dead held quiet multitudes of the living. They darted about with dimmed lanterns and stepladders, looking for some-one they'd loved. There were bodies pulled off stakes and dumped by the side, so lower bodies could be lifted off and taken away for burial. There was a continuous whisper of argument between the living over identification of the dead, and of soft weeping by women and the old.

'Have you seen my husband Nicodemus?' some old woman asked.

I looked up from tying my bootlaces. I told her to come back in the daylight. She'd never find anyone by herself tonight, except by a miracle.

'He didn't come back from buying bread,' she added. 'I was told that men arrested him in the street and brought him here.' She spoke now in the confused, wandering tone of those who are beginning to outlive their faculties.

I took her gently by the shoulder and led her to the far side of the square. I told her to go home and look to her family. It was hard to read anything for sure from the silence that followed.

'Go home at once,' I said again. 'Take this with you and don't linger on the streets. Come back here if you must in the morning. But go home now.' I pressed one of my purses into her hand and hurried past. I tried to put her sense of total helplessness out of mind. On a night like this, it wasn't hard.

Before we'd gone back inside the Palace earlier, Priscus had stood on the highest step and reached out his arms to the dead.

> If I perceive some mischievous design
> To sap the State, I will not hold my tongue,

he'd intoned, quoting Creon from the *Antigone* of Sophocles. Then he'd filled his lungs, and to the accompaniment of flapping wings and that endless buzzing of the feasting flies, he'd continued:

> But for the miscreant exile who returned
> Minded in flames and ashes to blot out
> His father's city and his father's gods,
> And glut his vengeance with his kinsmen's blood,
> Or drag them captive at his chariot wheels—
> For Polyneices 'tis ordained that none
> Shall give him burial or make mourn for him,
> But leave his corpse unburied, to be meat
> For dogs and carrion crows, a ghastly sight.
> So am I purposed; never by my will
> Shall miscreants take precedence of true men,
> But all good patriots, alive or dead,
> Shall be by me preferred and honoured.

Some of the police officers had looked up at him, unable to follow the complexities of the ancient grammar. The Slavs, for whom any Greek was a trial, had continued about their business of keeping the death lanes clear of sightseers and relatives.

'I think I'll publish an amnesty tomorrow,' he'd giggled once we were back inside. 'And I'll levy a charge for the return of bodies. After all, if I don't charge, the police certainly will!' He'd tripped off, saying it was time for his cat to be fed.

I'd tried not to look back. It was impossible not to.

Now it was over. All were dead. Tomorrow, the bodies would have been cleared away and the stakes would be taken back into storage, ready for the next time they'd be required. Alexandria could go back to such business as might still continue. We'd even go ahead with the promised bread distribution. So would the Empire temper Justice with Mercy.

The streets too were unlit this night. But the Prefecture slaves were working day and night to clear away the bodies; and their torches flared in every central street. Evidently high on something powerful, they shouted cheerfully to each other as they worked deeper and deeper into the heaps of putrid, rat-infested flesh. Their voices bounced oddly from the walls of the buildings that still stood undamaged. The smell was now overpowering, and it was not just to avoid being recognised that I hurried past with my face buried in my cloak.

The embanked road took the breeze straight off the sea, and it blew without shifting. It was a blessing to breathe clean air again. Though the street, so far as I could tell in the unlit gloom, was empty, I kept to the shade of the acacia trees. The curfew was mostly unpoliced, but it would never do to be stopped. Every so often, I stopped and looked back the way I'd come. I made all the usual checks, and unless there was a really skilled agent on my tail, I was unfollowed. I could hear the lapping of the sea over on my right. Far ahead of me, I heard the barking and howling of what might have been a pack of wolves, for all the noise the dogs were making.

The little palace was in darkness; and though the gates were open and unguarded, I thought at first I'd misremembered the location, or got lost in the dark. But the starlight shone down bright enough in the central courtyard to which the gate opened for me to know I was in the right place. I crossed the courtyard, passing the little statue of Niobe that adorned the fountain. I walked in through the open door to the main wing of the palace. At first, it was all in darkness. There was a glazed window near the top of the entrance hall, but only enough light came through to show where it was and to reflect on the polished stone of the floor. I stopped and looked up. If I went left, I remembered, there was another doorway. Beyond this lay a staircase leading up.

There was a little sound a few yards to my right. I reached for my sword, but never got there. I heard the nonsensical twittering before the maidservant emerged from behind a screen. She'd been waiting there with a covered lamp. Balancing the now uncovered lamp in her hand, she bowed and set up a regular stream of greetings in her own language. I didn't understand what she was saying. But I did understand the outstretched arm. It motioned me towards a double column on the other side of the hall. Behind this, I could just see the glint of what seemed a silver door handle.

Still reading, the Mistress was in her library now. She sat within a ring of lamps that made the room, by comparison with where I'd been, as bright as day. She put her book down as I was ushered in and stood up. She'd changed her clothes since I'd parted from her in the late morning. Otherwise, she was still veiled and wrapped up as if for a visit. The maidservant bowed and left. I stood looking at the Mistress.

'Do you want to go through the motions of asking what brings me here so late at night?' I asked.

'Not really,' she said. 'Shall I bother asking why you think I will help you – or why you should trust me, of all people, to help you? Did I not make it sufficiently clear that you should remain in the Palace?'

I shrugged.

She got up and moved to a table by the wall. 'Am I right in believing your favourite wine is red?' she asked. She poured me a cup and turned back to face me.

'Do you think I'm a sorceress?' she asked.

I took a second and then a third mouthful of the good Syrian wine. I thought of that bizarre evening in the Egyptian quarter. I thought of the knuckles on my left hand. Forget anything else that might have happened that day. I clearly recalled how I'd scraped them to the bone when sliding down from the church roof. That had been five days earlier. They weren't now even scabbed. I thought of many things between these events. But there was no doubt of my answer.

'Mistress,' I said, 'if by magic you mean possession of knowledge that is not yet, or is no longer, generally available, you are perhaps a sorceress. If you ask if I believe you to be in contact with powerful but invisible spirits that can divert the normal courses of nature, my answer is no.'

She smiled.

I put my cup down and moved to the other side of the large central table in the room. I took up the leather sheath for the book she'd been reading and looked at its tag.

'You are familiar with Zosimus?' she asked.

'As an historian,' I said, 'he's highly derivative. He's often obscure. His judgements of character verge on the extreme. But if you want a narrative in one place of Imperial history from Augustus to Anastasius, you'll not do better. How far back do you need to start in order to bring yourself up to date?'

She laughed and sat down again in front of the book. I stood hastily back from her place. I looked at the book racks lining the walls. Every niche contained its leather sheath, each one containing its tightly rolled book. I stepped towards one of the racks and scanned the book tags. There was a certain amount of history and geography. Most of it, though, was poetry and romances – all from the modern period. Not having read much of this stuff, I was in no position to judge it individually. But the Mistress would need to be very lonely wherever it was she lived to be collecting this as reading material.

'Sit down, Alaric,' she said. 'Before I have you put to bed, there are several questions I need to ask you about the things I have read. I do not welcome comments on the nature of my questions, nor on whatever their tendency may seem to show. We shall speak for a while in this bright room. Then you will be put to bed. In the morning, we will leave Alexandria. Do you understand?'

I nodded.

'Good,' she went on. 'Let us begin with this concept of the Trinity.'

51

The gates of Alexandria had been open all night for the passing and repassing of the burial carts. The dogs, the rats, the flies, the carrion birds – these were annoyances. The real enemy was a sun that could turn the twenty thousand corpses stacked up in the side streets into mountains of pestilential slime. I'd sealed the order myself to override all the normal security measures. Everything had to be in burial pits outside the walls by noon. There was a shortage of quicklime, but officials from the Cleansing Department had assured me that three feet of packed earth should keep the miasma from seeping out. If it rained, they added, we were stuffed. Otherwise, we could find a little comfort in having reduced the number of idle mouths to be filled.

We arrived at the Southern Gate shortly after dawn. As I'd guessed, it was crowded with carts. There were also hundreds of women and the old, come out to see if there would be one last chance of identifying loved ones. They clustered round the gate, annoying the guards, who puffed and shouted to keep hands off those cloth-covered carts.

'Passport, if you please,' someone snapped from just outside the curtains on the chair.

I groaned inwardly. I'd hoped that going out through the busiest gate would avoid this. If this carried on, it would put a block on the other movements I'd arranged.

'Get down,' the Mistress whispered. She pulled a silk shawl over me and opened the curtains fully.

'The rule is, My Lady, that passports are needed for all but walking out and without luggage,' the guard explained. 'Passport – and you'll need to step down so we can search the chair.'

'I need no passport,' the Mistress said softly. 'I need no passport, and you will soon forget that I was ever here.'

'She needs no passport,' the guard repeated to one of his juniors. He spoke in a strange tone.

I heard the creak of the wooden bar placed across the gate to stop all but pedestrians. It lifted and guards stood back, dreamy looks clouding their faces. Soon, the maidservants were clipping along the road at a surprising speed, bearing in mind their double burden. The smell of death still followed us on the breeze from the sea. But the cracking of whips over the slaves of the digging parties and the disorganised shouting of the overseers and guards was fading quickly away. The Mistress had hung her bells along the chair again, and their merry jingle was soon the only sound I could easily hear.

'How did you do that?' I asked. I knew I shouldn't have asked, but it was one of those questions that pops out from pure astonishment. I'd pulled off my covering. Now, the curtains were open wide, and I was glad of the cooling breeze to take the sweat off my face.

The Mistress arranged her clothes to keep them from fluttering too much in the breeze. She reached under the seat and took out a small book. 'Yours is the empire of the sword and the tax gatherer,' she explained. 'My empire is of the imagination.' She fell silent and began reading from what looked like a tale of dazzling stupidity.

I wanted to ask how we were expected to make any time at all in this chair. It made sense that taking the road to Canopus, or going directly by barge along the canal, would have invited Brotherhood spies. But a chair, carried by women, along even a good road would take us days and days to get anywhere close to where we needed to be. This time, though, I didn't ask. I'd agreed not to plague the Mistress with questions over her methods, and it was too soon to start bending the agreement.

It goes without saying that I would bend it. Martin and Nicetas and Priscus – indeed, everyone I knew – would have accepted the Mistress as a sorceress. Even if they had sought her help, they'd never have dared to question, considering how she achieved her effects. But I'd told her the truth the previous night. I didn't think there was anything in the least supernatural about her. There comes a time when the accumulation of evidence is such that you have to change some opinions. The odd message given to me in the Egyptian quarter I'd firmly dismissed as nothing at all. Coming then upon the Mistress 'between the dead palms and the monument to human folly', I'd also dismissed as coincidence. But if the pursuit of knowledge requires a certain blinkering, wilful blindness is another matter.

No – things had been happening during the past twenty-five days that couldn't be explained in everyday terms. But I had no doubt that they could be explained. And if I'd not made it obvious what I was about, I'd have my explanatory hypotheses formed and tested long before I saw the walls of Alexandria again.

Alexandria lies on the far western tip of the Nile Delta, and the floods had turned the land either side of the road to marsh. We were on higher ground than further into the Delta, and the land wouldn't disappear. And I knew from my survey maps that the road going due south was embanked. It would be passable at all times of the year, even if the floods were catastrophic. The Mistress, though, had other ideas. We weren't going south. Instead, we were taking the western road into the desert. This began about five miles further along. At our present speed, we might be there come nightfall. I say 'at our present speed'. But if those women didn't seem particularly tired yet as they carried us briskly along the paved road, I didn't see how they could keep this speed up once the sun rose higher in the sky.

I looked right over the dreary expanse of marsh to the sea that shone in the distance. Large birds of various kinds flew over-head, or burrowed into the clumps of reeds that rose out of the mud. Every so often, I heard the splash of something in the larger puddles. The road itself was absolutely empty. It was entirely a military road, and all our mobile forces had been sucked into Alexandria. There was no cause for any but the occasional group of pilgrims to use it otherwise.

'What does this word mean?' the Mistress asked suddenly.

I looked away from the increasingly distant line of the sea and pulled my thoughts into order. I focused on the narrow column of text in the place where her finger pointed.

'That's a corruption of the Latin word *hospitium*,' I said. 'It is used by the more careless modern writers to mean a house.' She sniffed – and well she might. From what I saw of the surrounding text, the whole style was atrocious. 'I suppose you are familiar with Latin?' I added, trying to keep too much of a questioning tone from my voice.

'Even where not of collapse,' she replied, 'most ages are times of decadence and stagnation. I did wonder, even so, if the Greeks had avoided the common lot of humanity.'

There was no answer to that. I reached between my feet and pulled up a flask of wine. No point offering any to the Mistress. I tried, nevertheless, not to drink it all.

The sun was growing hotter. There was nothing to see and nothing to do. The Mistress continued reading with evident – and, in my view, embarrassing – enjoyment. The bells that jingled with every swaying of the chair seemed to sound louder and louder in the surrounding silence. I leaned back and pulled my hat over my eyes. I drifted off into a world of luxurious warmth.

The sun told me it was around noon when the Mistress prodded me awake.

'Come along, Alaric,' she said. 'It's time for you to make a contribution to the journey.'

I blinked in the brightness and looked ahead. We were approaching the first post station outside Alexandria. It was of standard design: two storeys of mud brick around a central courtyard. With only slits for windows – and these on the upper floor – the outer wall doubled as fortification. We must have been seen from a long way out. By the time we were approaching the station, the bar had been lowered across the road, and a single guard was lounging wearily in the shade.

'You can show your passport here,' the Mistress said. 'This far out of Alexandria, I don't think we need worry about leaving *some* footprint in the records.'

I looked at her. While I was asleep, she'd changed out of the elegant dress in which she'd started the journey. Now, she was dressed in the black riding clothes of the desert nomads. With a scarf wound about her head, it was hard to tell that she was a woman.

'You can change once our business is complete,' she said. 'If these people have camels to give us, so much the better. If not, we'll settle for their best horses.'

I took out the passport I'd prepared for myself back in the Palace. I'd done my best to copy out not just the words of the sample I'd found in Martin's files, but also the smooth penmanship. It still appeared rather crude. Then again, it carried the Lesser Seal. That would have covered up many worse defects in its form.

Lips moving, the guard squinted over the passport. He handed it back with a stiff salute, and then a bow. He went back inside, and came out with his commanding officer. They'd both made an effort to brush themselves down, and we were ushered straight through the gate into the colourless, dusty courtyard.

After wine and dates and a brief account from me of the rioting, we were led back out from the coolest room in the building for an inspection of the stables. The pair of camels on the far side of the block seemed decidedly inferior to the horses. They were big, surly-looking creatures. They were mangy. Their smell brought back unpleasant memories of my last ride through the desert. But the Mistress pointed straight at them, ignoring the horses, and watched closely as they were saddled and provided with the usuals.

'Would His Magnificence care to state destination and reason for his journey?' the senior officer asked with another bow. He sat back down at his desk and scratched with his reed pen on a blank page in his ledger. Nothing came out. He squeezed the spongy length of the pen and scratched again. He muttered an apology and looked at the congealing mass at the bottom of his ink well.

'There is no need for any record to be kept,' the Mistress said. She stretched nonchalantly back in her chair. Except for the two slight bumps on her chest, she might have been a younger male companion of the Lord Senator.

'There is no need for any record,' the man repeated in the low pitch of one who talks in his sleep. He dropped his pen on the desk, and went right back to commenting on the account I'd long since finished of the rioting.

Back out on the road, the Mistress looked at me in my own nomad clothes.

'With your height, you'd never pass,' she said. 'Still, the clothes aren't so much for disguise as for convenience.'

'What about the chair?' I asked. If those women had been fed and watered, it must have been while I was asleep. Though in the shade, they'd stood quietly by the chair the whole time we were inside the station.

'They go back to Alexandria,' she said. 'How they get back in is of no importance to you. They will come out again as and when I see fit to summon them.' She continued loading her things into the saddlebag. She dithered briefly over her book. Though small, it would take up valuable space. She took out a bag of dried dates and pushed it hard in.

I may have ridden a quarter of a mile before I fell off. Mine was a bigger and nastier beast than the one Lucas had tied me to. Rather than swear myself blue in the face, I suppose I should have been surprised I got that far.

'Should I take off the saddle so His Magnificence can ride on his belly?' the Mistress sneered. She wheeled her own camel round with the merest touch on its reins.

I glanced back to see if anyone was still watching us from the station. We were alone. 'Where I come from,' I groaned, 'we ride horses. These things are wholly different.' This was true – though I might have given the impression that I was very much better on horseback.

'Oh, my poor little stray.' She laughed. 'Such duties I must assume for your welfare!' She made a clucking noise, and her own camel immediately knelt. She swung off the saddle and began showing me the basics of riding a camel.

'Remember,' she finished as I climbed on for the fourth time, 'don't overcompensate for the motion. And do try not to pull hard on the reins. Camels are more intelligent than horses. They don't appreciate instructions that go beyond the polite request. Now, let us be moving, my blonde barbarian from the West. We have much ground to cover if we are to have any element of surprise.'

Once you overcome the queasiness from the motion, riding a camel isn't so bad. Just as we reached the limit of the black land, and as the road swung definitely west, we turned off to the south. For a while, there was the same scrubby, rocky terrain that I've already described. Then this merged insensibly into the desert proper. I thought of how much water we'd had packed for us on the camels, and felt nervous to be heading straight into this burning waste again. But the Mistress seemed to know exactly where she was going, and seemed – or so I thought from ten yards behind her – to be thoroughly pleased with herself.

52

We rode on through the day. Until late in the afternoon, the sun beat down savagely. The camels pressed on across the firm sands, indifferent to the heat. I lost all track of time and fell into a kind of waking doze. I was conscious enough to keep myself on the camel, but not enough to feel worse than moderate discomfort. By now, I thought, it would be out that I'd left Alexandria, though not how or in what precise direction. The Mistress had asked the night before why I should trust her to help get Martin back. I hadn't asked. I wouldn't ask. But to have just the two of us, moving at whatever speed through this boundless desert, on our way to challenge a conspiracy that had come close to taking Alexandria from the Empire – and might yet succeed with Egypt – in the flashes when my thoughts moved in this direction, I was glad not to be fully awake.

At last, the sun lost its power as it sank low on our right, and the rocks on the desert floor threw longer and longer shadows.

'We shall rest tonight over there,' the Mistress called back.

I looked up and followed her pointed finger ahead to our left. How I hadn't noticed the temple surprised me once I'd seen it. Built of sandstone, it was the same colour, near enough, as the desert, and the air all about was growing dark. But it was a gigantic structure. It was hard to get its proper scale out here in the middle of nowhere. But it must have been a couple of hundred feet high and five or six times that in length. At the centre of the colonnade that made up the whole of the front elevation, two colossal statues of seated kings or gods towered above the whole structure and framed the entrance.

Once you get off the black land, which is needed for growing food, Egypt is full of these things. The native kings of every generation competed with each other across thousands of years to heap up piles of sandstone more solid and more elaborate than any other. The Ptolemies had joined in the competition as often as they needed to draw notice from the fact of Greek domination. Even the early emperors had made the occasional gesture. Since the abolition of the Old Faith, of course, the temples had all been shut – excepting, that is, the temple at Philae in the south that I had closed. Some of them had been cut up into monasteries. Most had been abandoned. That doesn't mean they were empty. The less fanatical desert hermits needed somewhere to live. There were wild animals and the rural poor if the floods completely swept their homes away. For months now, I'd been reading complaints to Nicetas about gangs of bandits and runaway slaves who were terrorising the countryside from these places.

'Are we going inside?' I asked.

'Do you propose that we spend the night in the open?' she replied. 'You have been once in the desert. You will surely have noticed how cold it can get at night. Or are you thinking of the ghosts and other spirits that are said to haunt the temples of the formerly established religion of this country?'

That wasn't a challenge I was inclined to refuse. I slid off the kneeling camel to get a light going. I found myself writhing and crying out on the ground. I'd noticed on the saddle how much I ached. Once I was off, my arse felt like I'd been in some brothel game gone wrong.

The Mistress stood over me, laughing cruelly. 'Poor little Alaric!' she said in mock sympathy. 'A fine, young barbarian from the West, sent to put the corrupted Greeks and Egyptians of this land into order, and how sore his bottom must be from the look on his face! Lie on this,' she added, spreading a blanket on the ground. 'You'll feel a little better by and by. But don't wriggle so on the ground. You will only get sand inside your clothes. And that might bring you out in a rash.'

Burning with shame and annoyance, I made myself sit up. The Mistress turned away and took out the horn lanterns we'd got earlier from the station. She turned immediately back to me with both of them lit. Sore as I was, I had almost to bite my tongue not to ask the obvious question.

'If you can possibly bring yourself to walk a few steps, shall we go in?' she asked.

I ground my teeth and stood up. We led our camels through the gateway into what turned out to be the first of the courtyards. Much of the temple, indeed, turned out to be courtyards of various kinds. There was this outer courtyard. Through another massive gateway was an inner courtyard. There were smaller courtyards as well – or these were large rooms from which the roofs had at some time been removed. The covered spaces took up about a third of the total area. Most of them smelled damp; it does rain in the desert, and the rain does collect where no sun ever shines. Most had been used at various times, and put to various uses. For the moment, all that I looked into were empty. I think we looked in every part of the complex. This said, it was very large, and the light was going.

It was hard to see how much of the original colour remained in the fading light. But I could see the reliefs that covered every wall of the courtyards. Every inner wall was covered with paintings in the same style, though the damp had brought down most of the plaster from the walls. Inside or out, it was all in the standard native style: giant kings killing midgety foes, or offering pots and other objects to various gods with animal heads or green faces. Inscriptions in the old picture writing covered every patch of wall not taken up by the reliefs.

It really is hard to look at all this stuff without disgust. What I'd said to Lucas about his old civilisation I really did believe. Having read so much by the Greeks about the grandeur and antiquity of the Egyptians, I'd been shocked in Alexandria at the crude ugliness of their arts. I'd now seen enough outside Alexandria to be impressed by the scale of some of their architecture. But that broken-down Greek building just off the road to Canopus was worth more than all this stuff taken together. With her approving nods as she wandered about inspecting the reliefs, the Mistress appeared to think otherwise. But given her choice of reading matter, I had no respect for her taste. Still, I hadn't put myself into her hands on account of her judgement as a critic.

'Can you read Egyptian?' I asked.

She looked away from an inscription made up more than usually of bugs and crouching women.

'Do you know how this temple was built?' she asked. 'Do you see how these columns are in sections? They were once covered in plaster to hide their method of erection. But the plaster is long gone, and the method of erection is plain to see. Tens of thousands of workers toiled through the flood season to raise the outer walls. Then the column bases were laid out, and the first sections of the columns set on top. Sand was then brought in to fill the whole area. With every new level of columns, the level of the sand was raised. That is how the massive stone blocks of the roof were set in place. Once building was over, the sand was evacuated. Can you conceive anything more simple and more elegant?'

'Very impressive,' I said. No point asking again if she could read any of this writing. If she could, it probably told nothing of any value. I thought of the Great Church in Constantinople. Granted, it was a Christian building, and it was smaller than this pile of stone. But I doubted the Mistress could step inside there and not realise the true place of Egypt in the scale of civilisations.

'Where shall I prepare dinner?' I asked.

She turned back to her inscription. 'Do it where you please,' she said. She straightened up and pointed through one of the inner gateways. 'Do it in there,' she added. 'There is a small room first on the left as you go down the corridor. It still has a roof over it. You will find it convenient in size and position.'

It was a cold dinner of bread and dried fruit. Then again, I didn't need to share the wine. And at the end of this very long day, I made sure to drink deeply. I looked at the Mistress, who sat on the other side of the fire of dried reeds I'd managed eventually to get alight.

'No doubt, you have a plan for getting Martin back from the Brotherhood,' I said. 'Might it be time to ask what is to be my own part in this?'

'We have a while yet to go before these matters need to be discussed,' she said airily. 'I will prepare you when the time is right.' She pushed another sliver of dried apple between the folds of cloth that covered her face.

'I do accept,' I said – I was beginning to feel decidedly ratty from the pain in my backside and the lack of information about anything at all – 'that modesty has an eminent place among the feminine virtues. But do you not think this disinclination to show your face begins to border on the excessive?'

'No man may see my face and live,' she said, now coldly. She changed the subject to the fitness of Latin as a legal and administrative language. Since she gave no sign of understanding a word of Latin, what she made of my answers was rather hard to say. At length, as the fires burned low, and the sound of the desert winds outside the temple took on a mournful tone, she stood up.

'It is time for you to sleep, Alaric,' she said. She motioned inside the temple. In the little room she'd chosen for us, there was a pile of sand in the corner. If I patted it into shape and put my blanket over it, I'd make a fair mattress of it all.

'Should I suggest taking turns to keep guard?' I asked. I tried to avoid any note of satire. I probably succeeded. At any rate, the pointed finger didn't waver. I had thought of asking the Mistress where she would be sleeping. Instead, I went inside and made a bed of sorts.

'You will sleep,' she said firmly once she'd followed me in. She lowered her voice and repeated herself: 'You will sleep.' It was the tone she'd used to get us out of Alexandria without showing passports and again in the post station.

If it had worked a treat back then, it had bugger-all effect on me now. Sooner or later, I'd have to nod off – and I had packed a box of opium pills, just in case I felt the need of one. On the other hand, I was lying on a heap of damp sand, in a pretty well ruined temple in the middle of a desert, with a being of ambiguous nature, and with a nagging doubt regarding what might be left of Martin. Add to this the increasingly unpleasant moaning of the wind outside, and you'll appreciate I'd sooner have read that ghastly romance the Mistress had brought along than just fall asleep. I wasn't at all sleepy. Still, I lay down as ordered and closed my eyes. The fire was burning low just outside the door, and it was soon quite black around me.

I heard her come deeper into the room. Her sandals grated on the sand that covered the stone floor. She stood over me. I lay still and kept my breathing regular. I sensed that she was bending low over me. I grunted softly and shifted position as if I were asleep. She straightened up and stood back. She laughed softly.

'What a silly little man you are,' she said. 'If only you knew what I know, would you be here with me? Or would you put your worthless Martin from your mind and be on the first ship back to your Constantinople?' She paused. Then: 'But we must get Martin back – and we will get him. We will get him and much else besides.'

She laughed again, now bitter. Bearing in mind I was still wide awake, her confidence in her powers to command sleep was beginning to worry me. It was one thing to be here with a being of possibly immense power. It was another to be with someone whose confidence in her power was so misplaced. I was relying on her to help do over the Brotherhood. It was beginning to look as if her best contribution would be her choice of fast camels for running away.

'You are not the one,' she continued. 'You are not the one for whom I wait. Yet I have been forced from my solitude to assist in your purpose. Oh, my dear and pretty little man – if only you knew what I know!'

I heard the slow scraping of her feet as she recrossed the floor. I listened and guessed that she was going back out into one of the courtyards. There I supposed she'd be making her own bed for the night. I kept my eyes shut and commanded sleep. I've never had much faith in my own power in this respect, and I was more annoyed than disappointed when nothing happened. I lay there a while longer. Then I got up and pulled off the cloak I was using as a blanket. We were safe enough in here, I told myself, and I'd need to get some sleep if tomorrow were to be as hard on the body as today had been. I fished around in my satchel for the lead box of pills. I thought again, but made my mind up. I washed one down with a mouthful of wine. I lay back down and waited to see which would be first to hurry me into an oblivion that would last out the remaining hours of darkness.

Still nothing. I lay there for what seemed an age, calculating price ratios. I felt warmer from the opium, but hardly sleepy. I'd not risk taking a second pill. Instead, I sat up again. I felt round for my shoes, then decided it would be better to do without them. I'd had time for my eyes to adjust to the darkness. There was a tiny sliver of moonlight somewhere overhead. And there were the stars. In the desert, these shone dense and bright. I crept to the doorway, and then out into the inner courtyard. The ground was dark, and I made sure to keep against the walls. I was still dressed in black, and the Mistress, if awake, would need unusual powers of sight to see me as I skulked round the abandoned temple. I shivered in the night chill of the desert. I was glad I hadn't bothered undressing.

I thought for a while I was making a fool of myself. It was a big temple, with many rooms and courtyards. The most I might do was get lost – that would be embarrassing. Perhaps I should go back to that little room and wait for the opium to do its work. It wasn't that hard, however, to find the Mistress. She plainly thought I was dead to the world, and was doing nothing to silence her own motions. I heard the rhythmical scrape of sandals on the loose sand. It came from the other side of the entrance to what I'd earlier discovered was the innermost courtyard. I heard the scraping of her feet and a low chanting in what sounded like the language I'd heard her speak on the boat to Canopus. I crept over to the stone doorway and looked carefully round. I pulled back and rubbed my eyes. I wished at that moment I hadn't bothered with the opium. Was this some waking dream? I thought hard about who I was and where I was. There were no oddities about the situation – other, that is, than the inherent oddity of what I was seeing. I wasn't dreaming. This being so, what my senses told me must be taken as reliable beyond reasonable doubt. I looked up at the bright carpet of stars that threw an uncertain light, and looked once more.

As on the boat to Canopus, the Mistress was dancing. This time, though, she danced alone and unaccompanied. And this time, she was naked. Her clothes were piled up in a dark heap not two yards from where I was standing. In a slow, circling motion, she danced round the courtyard. She barely moved her head from looking at some part of the reliefs that I couldn't see in the gloom. But I could see her well enough. The starlight was enough to show that slender white body as it went round and round in its slow, unaccompanied motions.

It was a splendid body. For seeing that alone, it would, in other circumstances, have been worth the risk of discovery. She had good legs, a firm belly and breasts, and a really glorious neck. But I'd been able to guess that already. As I said, she covered up, but did nothing to hide the shape of what she was covering. It was the face that I strained to see in the starlight. I could see every inch of that white and, so far as I could tell, completely hairless body. It almost shone with its own inner light. But her face was either fixed on that patch of relief work, or was covered by the waving of her arms when she did occasionally turn in my direction.

Once and once only I did see her face. It was a brief flash as she turned in my direction, this time with her arms fully outstretched. It really was the briefest of flashes. But that serene and utterly terrifying beauty didn't need more than an instant to burn itself for ever into my mind. It has never left me. Certainly, if I close my eyes now, I can see it. I see no point in trying to describe what I saw. Words are useful for describing what others can see for themselves, or reasonable compounds of these things. But I do assure you, what I saw has nothing in the common run of things that compares to it. You can turn to some of the more imaginative ravings of the desert saints. If you can find any of these, and understand their language, good luck to you. I'll not try competing.

I could have hung around, waiting for another look in my direction. But I'd seen all I needed to – and rather more than I'd been intended to. 'No man may see my face and live,' she'd said. Well, I

377

had seen it, and I was still alive. I now planned to keep it that way by not hanging around to be discovered. I'm not saying I'd changed my mind about any supposed supernatural abilities. A wise man proportions his belief to the evidence. And I hadn't seen anything – not this night, nor the day before, nor any of the preceding days – that couldn't *somehow* be explained in naturalistic terms. But that face had been supremely mad or wicked. Having her round me day and night with a grudge simply wouldn't do at all. And the opium was now reaching out in earnest with fingers of delicious warmth. It was time to be getting back.

With some going wrong in the darkness, and then going back on myself, I found my way to where I'd made my bed. As I waited to be carried out of this world on a litter of black velvet, I heard the faint scraping of sandals on sand. How long she stood over me I can't tell. I suppose she was now fully dressed, though I heard her still breathing hard from her endless if slow dancing. She may have whispered my name. She may have prodded me. She may even have rolled me over. But I was too far gone to notice.

53

The Mistress threw her book across the weeds with a howl of rage. I reached instinctively for my sword and looked round. The camels were making their usual noise as they continued drinking from the pool. There was no reason to suppose we weren't wholly alone in the oasis. She pointed accusingly at the book that had come unrolled where it landed.

'That bookseller will beg for death before I release him,' she snarled. She trailed off and looked towards the setting sun.

I got up and retrieved the book. It had bounced off one of the stunted trees and had now become completely unrolled. I took it up and smiled to myself. The Mistress had been had good and proper. At some point during its lifetime, the book had come apart and been repaired. The long roll of papyrus had been glued back to the inner spine minus at least one sheet. The final sentence read: 'And thus spake Apelles, saying . . .'

'How shall I ever know,' she cried almost tearfully, 'if he escapes from the pirates and is reunited with his Penelope before her uncle marries her to the false Antiochus?'

One of the camels looked up at her.

'I'm sure it all works out well in the end,' I said reassuringly. 'These things always do. Let us imagine that he escapes from the pirates by leaping into the sea. He is then saved by a friendly dolphin, who just happens to be passing by, and is taken to the very spot where Penelope is to be married. There needs to be an argument, and perhaps even a duel. At last, though, Apelles convinces the uncle that he really is whatever the Reader knows him to be, and the wedding feast goes ahead with another groom. Everyone, then, including – and I'm only guessing here, not having read the preceding adventures – Penelope's ever faithful slave, lives happily ever after. There, does that ring true?'

I could feel the suspicion radiating towards me from that well-wrapped face.

Then the Mistress relaxed and laughed. 'Am I become so contemptible because I sometimes act as a woman?'

I put on my emollient look and assured her of my deepest respect for her abilities and my deepest gratitude for all she had done to help. But she wasn't interested.

'Can you imagine how it is to sit absolutely alone as long as I have?' she asked. 'Can you imagine how it is to have read and reread every outstanding work of the Greek mind? Do that and you may begin to appreciate how welcome the trashiest new writings can seem.'

'I can try to imagine,' I said. 'Even so, the Greeks since their very best age have produced much that is considerably better than *The Trials of Penelope*. There is, for example, Plutarch, and there is Lucian, and there is—'

She grunted and snatched at the book that I'd just finished rolling back up. She was now more angry than disappointed.

We'd covered an immense distance since leaving the temple. That was the morning of the day before. The desert border was far behind, and we were deep into the limitless waste of sand where only the sun told the direction. All day, whenever we'd stopped for me to piss or shit or have a sip of our now indifferent water – the Mistress herself didn't seem to need any of these things – she'd been hurrying with heightened excitement through the last stages of the romance. Now that we were comfortably seated within the little oasis we'd reached just as the sun was beginning to go down, there was nothing for her to do but talk to me. There was nothing else to do, that is, unless she wanted to go back to the beginning and read more slowly to where it broke off – this time stopping to search for any incidental beauties of language or construction of the plot.

'It was in surroundings rather like these that we first met,' I opened. 'I now believe we were above the ruins of Soteropolis.

Back in Alexandria, I took the trouble to learn something of the place.'

'So you know about Soteropolis?' she asked. 'I wonder how much of what you know is true and how much childish legend?'

I kept silent. For a while, I thought I'd have to try again. But she reached for her cup of fresh water and sipped through the hollow tube that let her drink without uncovering her face. She put the cup down and stretched her legs.

'You will surely be aware of its anomalous position in the Kingdom of Egypt,' she continued. 'Unlike the Egyptians, its people did not originate in this land. Like you, they were people of the lightest colouring from an island in the West. Their island was about the same shape and size as your own, but was much further out in the great sea that terminates the world as it is known to the geographers.'

Ireland? I thought. But I said nothing. The Mistress was telling me something that might be of value. I didn't wish to break the flow.

'They rose but slowly from the barbarous state. But, undisturbed in the remote fastness of their island, they had time, and they were persistent. They took no interest in philosophical matters. Without ever seeking to learn the underlying nature of things, or the connections between things, they were satisfied if they could fashion devices to enrich and glorify their rulers. At last, they brought on themselves a disaster involving the complete loss of their home and its works. The survivors – a pitiful remnant of what had been – came for refuge to Egypt and still further south. Long before the beginning of time as recorded even by the Egyptians, they built their cities and set about the recovery of what they had lost.

'It was in vain. Those who survived were the least of their race. They had only fragments of the ancient knowledge, and no grasp of the method by which it all might be regained. After a long stagnation, they were overcome – either by pestilence or by the incursions of the lower but more numerous men of these regions. So it was with Soteropolis. So it was with the larger settlements far south beyond the origins of the Nile.' She fell silent and watched as I made my best efforts with steel and flint to get a fire lit. My efforts amused her, but also took her from her theme.

'I believe the people of Soteropolis contributed much to the Egyptians,' I said, prompting her to start again. 'And I suppose their learning passed in some measure through the Egyptians to the Greeks.'

'No,' came the reply. 'The Greeks took certain things from other peoples. But the essentials of the Greek genius owed nothing to. any but the Greeks themselves. Unlike the people I have described, there was nothing slow about the Greeks. What they sought in the first instance was abstract understanding. And it is from this that practical knowledge most surely and swiftly follows. They were like a comet that suddenly appears in the sky, and, as if from nothing, outblazes every other object. I doubt I need say more to you of how different the Greeks were from every other people – how everything good that men have since achieved owes something to their legacy.

'But it is only a legacy. The Greeks gave the world a new beginning. But like a comet in the sky, they dazzled only to fade away as quickly as they had emerged. In destroying themselves, they destroyed all hopes for mankind. There will be unbalanced recoveries, and men will boast of how they have exceeded the Greeks. There will be no full recovery. It will at best be Soteropolis again.'

Well, that was a mournful end to the day. Beside the inherent gloom, it brought back memories of the poem Hadrian had caused to be set up on the statue in Soteropolis. But I'd got the fire going, and the water would soon be boiled in which we could soak some of the dried fruit and soften the now hardened bread we still had. Though not so much as before, I was stiff again after a day on my camel. I was tired. I'd not be in need of assistance tonight for sleep.

'You should bathe before it grows cold,' she said with a change of tone.

I looked over at the little pool in the middle of the oasis. It would soon be warmer than the surrounding air, and I was beginning to smell. It was three days since my last bath, and not far off that since I'd changed clothes. If I got in at the other end from where the camels were spitting and showing their teeth, I might also wash my clothes. Would they dry, though, once the night was here and it turned cold again? Or would we have a while in the morning? I also thought about the blanket I'd have to use for drying myself – it might be sandy. Above all, of course, was the matter of seemliness. Having a bath was all very well. Having one with her looking calmly on was not so well.

I'd pretty well decided to make my excuses. But the Mistress was now pulling at her own boots and then unwinding her leggings. I slumped back in confusion. I tried to think of something to say.

'Cleanliness, my dear Alaric, is our duty as well as our pleasure,' she said, with a slight lingering on 'pleasure'.

You might, if you are a person with limited opportunities, think ill of me if I decline to say in detail what happened next. However, while pain is easily described – in yourself as well as in others – pleasure is something as hard to describe as beauty. The mingling of limbs and the repeated bursts of ecstasy are things that can be imagined without any close narrative. I will only say that, throughout that night of continuous and unrestrained passion, the Mistress never once thought it appropriate to uncover her face.

'You are not the one,' she whispered softly in my ear as I finally drifted asleep. 'But you have pleased me.'

I woke with a start. The sun was already rising high in the east. It would soon be on my face. It was already on my body. I tried to sit up, but found I was wrapped in my blanket as tightly as an embalmed corpse. I lay down and wriggled free. I stood up and stretched. My back was sore. From the red scratches all over my belly and thighs, it wasn't hard to guess the cause. Whatever she'd done for me after the rioting, it was plain that these would have to heal by themselves. The only part of me to escape her mauling was where I had the medal of Saint Peter hung round my neck.

'Surely, we ought to be moving,' I began to cry out. I looked at the single camel tethered to the biggest of the trees and fell silent. The oasis was only about sixty feet across at its widest point, and there was no need to do more than glance round. Just for the avoidance of doubt, I wandered about its perimeter, looking in all directions at the sands stretching endlessly around me.

She'd gone. When she had gone I couldn't tell. Where wasn't worth asking. But she had gone. And I didn't believe she'd be back. Naked, I went over and washed myself by the pool. The water had been warm enough last night. Now, it felt chilly. My clothes had been hung up where they'd catch the first rays of the sun. They were completely dry. I dressed with slow deliberation. The tunic had shrunk a little, and some of its colour had gone in the wash. But it was good to be clean and to wear clean clothes.

Finally, I went over to my camel and picked up the folded sheet of papyrus I'd seen even before realising I was alone. It was taken from *The Trials of Penelope*, cut carefully from the front of the roll to avoid any further loss of the main text. She'd written on the rather stained outer side with a burned twig from the fire.

'I have brought you as far as is required of me,' the message went. 'The Brotherhood camp where Martin was taken is twenty miles due south of here. You will know what to do.'

You will know what to do, she was telling me! It was a good joke, and I made sure to sit down and have a good laugh over it. But the camel looked back at me, and the sun was rising higher. Oh, I'd conceived a general plan of action back in Alexandria. When it came to details, though, I hadn't the foggiest what I was supposed to do. I'd have to start rather earlier than expected on settling the details as and when required.

I went and stood on the outer edge of the oasis – right on the eighteen-inch border within which the tangled green sustained by the pool and shaded by itself gave way to the yellow sand. I looked out over the sands that stretched like the sea on and on up to the horizon. Had the Mistress run off, I asked myself, because we'd spent half the night fucking? Or had we spent half the night fucking so she could be sure I'd sleep through her getaway? The latter struck me as more likely – even if it supposed that she'd seen me watching her in the temple. Why, then, had she run off? Was she punishing me for having watched her? Was she working with the

Brotherhood, and was this the trap from which I'd be collected? Was she a fraud? She might have certain healing and persuasive abilities. But going against the Brotherhood on its own territory might be far outside those abilities.

I asked these and other questions. I didn't get very far with answering them. I regretted saying goodbye to the fraud theory. But – with all the reservations already made – I had no doubt she could avoid any direct confrontation with the Brotherhood, and could win in any confrontation that she cared to allow. Her decision to clear out was part of some design that I hadn't means of explaining.

Still keeping to the green side of the border, I sat and thought, and I thought harder, and I went back on my thoughts, and I thought again from fresh. I can't say I reached any conclusions that advanced beyond any that I'd already formed in Alexandria. But it was reassuring that, after all I'd been expecting, whatever I now did would be at my own direction. Whether it would work was another matter that might best be left unconsidered.

I had a late breakfast. I refilled the water skins. I attended as best I could to the camel. I sat down in the shade and commanded myself to sleep. My body obeyed me this time. I woke again as the sun was heading into the west. I felt rested and relaxed. If the Brotherhood really were twenty miles due south, now seemed a fine time to be setting out.

54

At least I'd got my timings right. I arrived at the Brotherhood camp just as the sun was dipping below the western horizon. The sandy ocean was at my back, and I was once more in one of the rocky zones separating this from the black land. I got the camel to kneel down at the far side of a cluster of rocks behind a small hill that overlooked the camp. Tethering it to anything that would keep it from running off like the last one had was out of the question. Leaving it there was yet another risk I'd have to take.

I had rather expected this to be the main Brotherhood camp. I'd hurried through the last miles of desert with another old temple in mind – something high and solid, with a continual stream of animal and human traffic. Banners and rebuilding works had also featured in my imagination. What I'd found was a disappointment. If it held more than a few dozen men, I'd have been surprised. It was just a collection of tents made from woven papyrus, grouped round a couple of mud-brick buildings that looked about to fall down. There was no outer wall or other protection. The only men I saw had on the loincloths of the lowest grade of Egyptian. Nothing had kept the sun off their upper bodies all through the day. I didn't suppose they'd have anything to put on against the cold of the night. With no appearance of urgency, they slouched between the tents and the buildings with various jars and packages.

I'd almost missed it at first. Having seen it, I'd come close to dismissing it as the place I was looking for. It was only because there was nothing else in sight for miles around that I'd bothered with a second look. It was then, however, that I'd seen the covered pen filled with camels, and the heaps of spears and shields between the buildings.

This couldn't be the main camp of the Brotherhood. But it was the place where the Mistress had wanted to send me. The closer I'd approached, the more I'd been thinking about whether I was going straight into a trap. After all, who was the Mistress? What was her interest in me and my concerns? Questions it had been so easy to settle or dismiss back in the oasis wouldn't stop coming into my head. But I could see that no one here was expecting to be disturbed. It made sense. It would take days longer to get a body of armed men through the desert, and they'd surely be seen long in advance. As for the Nile approach, all landing places would be covered as a matter of course.

The last time I'd done anything like this was with the Lombards, back in Italy. Then, it had meant getting close to King Agilulf in the middle of his army. And I'd known Agilulf was on to me, and had put the managers of his torture garden on alert. But Pavia was nothing compared with this. Then, I was on terrain that I understood. I could dress as a Lombard and, so long as I didn't try for extended conversations, be taken for one. Above all, I'd known what I was looking for and where to get it.

Keeping my head low, I looked down again at the camp and watched until the darkness had thickened and a few fires were lit. This was nothing compared to the Lombards – except it seemed impossibly harder. But here I was, and the quicker I was about my business, the better it might be. I looked up at the brightening stars to get some bearings. It would be at least an embarrassment if I somehow managed to lift Martin out of there, only to have mislaid the bloody camel.

I crept down to the outer limits of the camp. I crouched suddenly behind one of the larger rocks as two men wandered by. It wasn't a big rock, and if they'd taken the trouble to look in the right direction, they might have seen me. But they were lost in some animated conversation. I listened hard, but could hear nothing I recognised. If only they'd been Lombards, or from some other race of Germanics, I could have tried jumping them. Armed, and with all the surprise of darkness, I could have killed one and pulled the other one over somewhere quiet for questioning at leisure. But these really were Egyptians of the lowest class. If those settled in Alexandria didn't learn Greek, what reason had I to hope better of these? I let them go, and hurried forward to take more shelter from what looked and smelled like a low shithouse.

Sure enough, a shithouse it was. There were more men inside, straining and gasping as they squatted low together on the ground. What they said in between made about as much sense as anything else I'd heard. I can't have been above ten yards from the nearest of the brick buildings. If Martin was here at all, shut inside one of these places seemed his most likely whereabouts. Between me and the building, though, a fire was being lit. The lighter had his back to me, and wasn't having the best of luck with his dried reeds. But he would get there in the end. If I didn't hurry forward, I might as well dart back to the outer limits. Soon, the moment I stepped beyond the shadow of the shithouse, I'd be in full view.

I looked left and right. No one was about or looking this way. The firelighter was still cursing away with his back turned. I took a risk and raced across to the building. In dark clothes, facing outwards, I pressed against a dark wall. If I now went left, I'd leave the firelighter far over on my right. There was no entrance on the wall where I was pressed. It might be on any of the other three. I might as well start by looking round the corner to my left.

I was about to put my head round the corner to see if all was clear, when I heard more voices. They were loud, and they were coming my way. Another moment and they'd be level with me from round the corner. I looked back along the wall. It wasn't far to get round the other corner. But the firelighter was getting up to turn, and he'd be less likely to see me still against the wall than running along it. Uncertain, I froze. I could see the approaching glare of torches. They made the corner of the building throw a diminishing shadow as the torchbearers came on ahead of the voices.

With a shock, I suddenly realised that the voices were in Greek.

'I must confess, Your Majesty,' one of them was saying in good if accented Greek, 'that I have been impressed by all you have shown me so far. I think I can accurately predict that my cousin will be highly pleased by the report I will make to him on my return to Ctesiphon.'

The torchbearers came level with the corner. One of them stopped and turned and then stepped backwards. He now stood just in front of me and was looking forward. He had his left side to me. If I'd wanted to reach out and touch his shoulder, I'd not have needed to bend forward. If he so much as glanced left, he'd see me. At least this hid me from the firelighter, who'd now come forward to prostrate himself on the ground. All I had to do was not breathe or make any other movement. Given luck, he'd wait for the two speakers to catch up with him, and then move on. Without moving my head, I looked left at the two men, who'd now come into sight and also stopped.

It was Lucas and the man who'd been speaking. I paid no attention to the second of these. He would normally have been uppermost in my thoughts: what was a kinsmen of the Persian King doing so deep within the Empire? But there was nothing remarkable about his appearance. He had the beard and slightly fussy dress of a rich Syrian, or perhaps an Armenian. Like every diplomat, he'd have passed anywhere without remark. My whole attention went to Lucas. He was now done up in the complete finery of the old kings of Egypt. As in Alexandria, he was wearing the crinkled linen robe. But he now had a false beard tied over his real one, and a headdress so elaborate it almost put to shame those I'd seen in the ancient reliefs. Indeed, the reason he and everyone else had stopped right next to me was that parts of the thing kept falling off at every turn of his head, and one of his flunkies was fully employed in keeping it in place.

'My dear Siroes, you will surely not object if I ask when more substantial help will be forthcoming,' he said. 'If we are now to finish the work of clearing the Greeks out of Egypt, we shall need more than fine words. My letter did specify arms and military advisers.'

'Your Majesty's letter did specify these,' the Persian Envoy said, now in the friendly tone used by diplomats who are about to say no. 'However, Alexandria is the key to Egypt, and I deeply regret

389

the failure of your uprising there. You told me yourself that your whole organisation there has been torn up by the roots.'

'A purely temporary reverse,' said Lucas. He stopped and swore as the big white crown right on top of his headdress pitched over into the dirt. He squatted down so it could be put back on. He raised his own hand to hold it in place as he stood again. His massive collar of gold and lapis lazuli glittered in the torchlight – not ten feet from where I was standing. I breathed softly in and tried to disappear into the wall.

'One useful outcome of the rising, however,' he continued, trying to keep his head absolutely level as he spoke, 'was that the other leaders of my Brotherhood were caught up in the reprisals. I do not know if anyone escaped. If any did, it doesn't alter the fact that I am now the supreme power in the Brotherhood.'

'That is most useful, I agree,' the Envoy said, still friendly. 'You will appreciate, though, that now the rising has failed no invasion across the Red Sea can be considered. All effort, then, must be devoted to the march on Syria. Once we are in Antioch and the Empire is cut in half, we shall be better placed to open a second front in Egypt. I might also touch on the matter we have been discussing for much of today. Whether or not we arrive in Antioch within the year, there is very substantial assistance that *you* can provide.

'And I can assure you that His Majesty is entirely of one mind with you as regards the future settlement of the world. We have no territorial demands that go beyond the core territories snatched from us by Alexander. This means the whole of Asia Minor, but no more than that. The Greeks may keep the territories they so ably defended from the invasion by Xerxes. Since it is their modern capital, they may even keep Constantinople – though whatever emperor it pleases Chosroes to place there will be required to swear fealty to him and to his successors for ever.

'And Egypt will be absolutely free – on that you have my unforced word. It was a mistake of Cambyses to try incorporating Egypt the last time we were powerful in this region. Once we have succeeded in placing you on your rightful throne – in Memphis or perhaps in Alexandria – we shall, of course, withdraw all our advisers and such other persons as we may send for the purpose of your liberation.

'Be assured, Your Majesty, we are determined that the age of universal empire is past. Darius and Alexander and Caesar are all dead. There will be no other. Our new order of things will be based on justice among peoples freely covenanting together.'

I say I was trying not to breathe. After all this, it was hard not to gasp – or just burst out laughing. Here was someone talking, at the end of a thousand years, about repeating the work, while avoiding the mistakes, of Cambyses, Darius and Xerxes. And he was doing it in Greek to someone who should have thought himself a Greek, but was instead prancing about in stuff that could only have been snatched by Leontius in one of his tomb-raiding sprees.

'Your words fall on my ears like music,' Lucas said earnestly. 'You will be aware of the treason of the National Church of Egypt, which has objected to my coronation in Memphis next month. If you could prolong your stay, it would be highly symbolic of the new order that we both ardently desire if you were the one to place the double crown formally upon my head.'

'Oh, Your Majesty,' the Envoy cried, 'nothing would do me greater honour. And, of course, I will prolong my stay with you. There is, after all – and do forgive my raising this yet again – the matter of the object that is part of the reason why the Great King sent me to you.'

'Yes, the object,' Lucas said with a hint of impatience. 'You shall have your object. That I can promise. But we both know the prophecy. Until the One Who Shall Find can himself be found, we have a probem.'

'That, Your Majesty, is most regrettable,' Siroes drawled. 'When I took ship from Jedda, I left seven hundred men behind me. There was no point in bringing them to Egypt. But they were sorely pressed by a tribe of Saracens Nicetas had bribed into hostility. I came here myself at great personal risk. It would be most helpful if I could have *some* indication of when I can at least set my hands on the object.'

I'd put myself in the barrel. I'd pushed myself into the right current. It was now simply a matter of shutting my eyes as I was carried straight over the waterfall. I tried to look nonchalant as I stepped out of the shadow.

'Hello again, Lucas!' I said with a warm smile. 'I see you've done rather well for yourself since our last meeting.

'Oh dear, is that camel dung in which the double crown of Egypt has just landed?'

55

There are meetings on which the books of etiquette give little advice. But I did my best in the circumstances. I stepped past Lucas, who was now kicking viciously at the man who'd failed to catch his crown in time, and held my hand out to the Persian Envoy.

'Greetings, Siroes,' I said as easily as I could. 'I am Alaric, Legate Extraordinary from His Imperial Majesty in Constantinople. It may please you that the Imperial Council is aware of your name and your many achievements on behalf of the Great King.'

One of the nice things about a beard for a diplomat is how it can help in moments of utter confusion. But Siroes was good. His eyes barely widened as he looked back. He smiled and took my hand.

'And greetings to you, Alaric,' he said. 'We in Ctesiphon have heard much about you. Together with Priscus and Sergius, you are nearly at the top of our list of dignitaries to be handed over for execution when we dictate peace to the Empire. It may please you to know that if Priscus is before you on the list, you are before Sergius. It goes without saying that the usurper Heraclius comes right at the head of the list.'

'Funny you should call him that,' I said. We both ignored Lucas, whose crown was still covered in camel shit. 'There's no doubt Phocas was an usurper. He killed poor old Maurice and all his family, and then ruled as a tyrant. You might have had a case for not recognising him. Heraclius, on the other hand, was freely accepted by the Senate, the army and the people. He was crowned by the Patriarch of Constantinople; and he has the full

393

endorsement of the Universal Bishop, His Holiness in Rome. It can be argued whether the constitution requires an emperor to have the Church on his side. There's no doubt, however, that the opinion of some foreign prince is of no account whatever.

'You are, by the way, on one of our lists. Only we aren't thinking of your execution. We'll need a candidate for the Persian throne once Chosroes has been put out of the way.'

Siroes touched his knuckles to his head in a gesture of respect. Lucas opened his mouth to say something, but one of those big men he'd had with him on our first trip through the desert came in sight. He took one look at me and screamed like a stricken bull. Straight down on his knees he went, crossing himself and babbling away in Egyptian. Whatever he was saying was taken up by a few others who'd been following Lucas and Siroes. As it spread to the low-grade Egyptians, Lucas had to start a screamed lecture of his own. He wheeled about, hitting out with his rod of Kingly Office and kicking anyone within reach. His crown was off again, and his wig was slipping down the back of his head. I looked at him and did my best not to laugh at the crudely applied make-up on his face. He was supposed to look majestic. The best his people had managed was to make him remind me of the Circus buffoons in Constantinople.

'You join us at a most opportune moment,' Siroes said, speaking loud above the incomprehensible shouts and squeals of the debate in progress. I think he also was trying not to laugh at Lucas. 'There is immediate business of which you may be aware. If you serve me well enough in that, I may see fit to put in a word for you with the Great King. You see, our Christian minority speaks well of you for the tolerance of their heresy you have urged within the Empire. We might spare you as a token of our mercy in victory.'

'Your goodness of heart robs me of normal speech,' I said.

Siroes touched his forehead again. He even smiled. It was now that Lucas, who'd restored a sullen order among his men, butted in with a gloating and self-important speech about my function as finder of the piss pot of Jesus Christ. It seemed this really had been on the agenda the last time I was taken. This time, he said, I'd be under closer watch.

'No one will save you now,' he said. 'Not the Greeks in Alexandria, nor, I think, the sorceress whose concern for your safety has surely not outlived her better acquaintance with you.'

'That's all very well,' I said. I paused and waited while the whole headdress was stabilised again. 'However, I do represent His Majesty the Emperor, and I think that entitles me to supper.'

We set out from the camp just after dawn, and were soon headed south-east along a rough trail through this borderland of the desert. There was no camel for me now. Instead, I was tied into the chair that I supposed had been made available to the Persian Envoy. Muttering away in his own language, Siroes looked on.

'With the deepest respect, Your Majesty,' he said once Lucas had come over, 'I do suggest that, as a person of quality, His Magnificence should not be bound – not, at least, with common rope.'

'You will understand, my dear Lucas,' I added, 'if I agree with the Lord Siroes. If you were the low bandit that I at first took you for, common rope would be appropriate. However, you are in rebellion – even if not with much success – against the Empire, and I do represent His Imperial Majesty. I would suggest golden fetters or nothing at all.'

Siroes nodded gravely and seemed inclined to add another of his own protests. More to the point, some of the Brotherhood men who'd survived the rising in Alexandria were drifting over and looking mutinous again. Lucas swore softly and twisted with rage, but came forward and shouted for the procession to stop. He took out a knife and cut the ropes.

'If you so much as move from this chair,' he hissed into my face, 'I will personally cut off your feet at the ankles.'

'God's tits!' I gasped, pulling myself back from the filthy gust of his breath. 'I know your rules demand celibacy after you've produced two sons. If you won't take a little guidance on oral hygiene, you'll remain celibate before then as well.'

Lucas gave up trying to look majestic. 'I will also tell you this,' he continued, keeping his face close. 'If you do somehow manage to escape again, I will lay hold of your secretary and personally stitch his testicles into his mouth. Don't deny any interest in his fate. There is no other reason for your being here – and so many days before anyone would have thought it possible for you to get here from Alexandria.'

'Is it true,' I asked loudly, 'that the old kings of Egypt used to strip off once a year and have a public wank into the Nile?'

He stared at me a moment. He swallowed, plainly thinking of some response that would crush me. Then, with a scowl, he was off, shouting at everyone to get under way again.

'Not like a horse, is it?' I said brightly.

Siroes stared down at me. He'd put off the fussy robes of the night before. Now, he was in the local riding costume. Like all Persians, he was probably an accomplished horseman. Camels, as I don't need to keep saying, are not the same as horses.

'The less time I spend seated on this beast,' came the reply, 'the happier I shall be. I am assured that, if all goes as planned, I shall require neither chair nor camel for my return.'

I shifted position. The chair was big and comfortable. Even if the sun hadn't yet acquired its full power, I was glad of the shade from the canopy overhead. I yawned and stretched my legs.

'Oh, you expect me to dig out your piss pot,' I said. 'Do you suppose it will let you grow wings and fly back? If so, it must be *ever* so powerful.'

Siroes gave me a sour look and twisted in his saddle.

'Do tell me, though, Siroes,' I said with a change of subject, 'you really can't be serious about leaving Egypt to the wogs. Whoever controls Egypt and its corn is in a position to control the world.'

'We are perfectly determined,' he said with a shade too much emphasis, 'to reorder the world on a basis of equality between peoples.'

'And you really mean to set up Lucas here as Pharaoh?' I asked. I could hear him far off, close to the front of our procession.

Something or someone had upset him, and he was screaming again like a steward over a broken vase.

'Our mutual friend,' he answered '– let us call him Lucas: it is less of a mouthful than the other name he has tried to teach me – is a man of just the qualities we need in a ruler of Egypt. However, let us discuss your own interesting position. When I spoke last night about your death, I think we should take that as a statement of possibility rather than of intention.

'We are expecting to bring an end to the war between our two empires some time in the next six months. It will be an unconditional surrender on the Greek side. I am already considering how what remains of the Greek Empire is to be ruled. I could speak at great length of nothing very important. But I will avoid doing so and simply ask if you would like to be the next emperor? You would, I must clearly state, be an emperor under our complete protection. We would even station forces in Constantinople to ensure the safety of your reign.'

'Once more, your goodness of heart astonishes me,' I said with a little nod. 'But let us leave aside the question of how someone like me could rule the Empire except as a Persian satrap. What interests me more is how you can be so certain the war will soon end. Granted, it's been going on for the past ten years, and hasn't gone our way. But you've not yet made a breakthrough. Cappadocia was hardly a catastrophic loss. And we are aware in Constantinople of the strain the war has put on your own resources. What makes you suppose we are anywhere close to suing for peace – let alone on the terms you mention?'

Siroes smiled and turned his attention to the camel. I thought he'd be diplomatic about this. Not so. He looked back at me, his smile now become a broad grin.

'My dear young Alaric,' he said, 'how right you are when you say that whoever controls Egypt is in a position to control the world. If only we had known properly a thousand years ago what we think we know today, Alexander would never have taken Egypt from us. Nor would he have conquered us. Our archives earlier than some four hundred years ago are fragmentary. Indeed, we must often rely on Greek sources for our history before then. But some records have survived. The Great King is advised that Egypt contains a prize that brings control of the whole world. I am here to ensure that he gets it.'

'You know about this prize from records that predate the conquests of Alexander?' I asked.

Siroes nodded.

'Yet Alexander died some three hundred and twenty years before the birth of Christ.'

'I fail to see what the Jewish Carpenter has to do with this,' he said, giving me a funny look.

'And what does the Great Pharaoh up ahead think of this prize?' I asked after a moment's thinking. 'If he knows about it what you claim to know, why should he be so willing to hand it over to the Great King?'

'I think this conversation has continued long enough,' Siroes said with a grave nod. 'We shall speak again when the time is right.' He eased his camel out of the procession and stopped while the sweating, almost naked carriers took my chair past him.

We continued on our slow but steady way. The sun rose higher in the sky and I began to swelter in my chair. I could see the trail of camels in front of me and hear them behind me. I could hear the tramp of feet following. My carriers grew sweatier and were taking regular drinks from bottles strapped to their waists. How, in that heat, they didn't die from exertion might have been worth asking if I hadn't already known the limitless capacity of their sort to do as they were told and only die later on. They staggered a few times, but never let up their pace. Once or twice a young man pulled up beside me on his camel and made elaborate gestures that always ended with the sign of the Cross. As often as he began some whining chant, I'd bare my teeth and claw at him like a cat. That would get rid of him for a while. If the natives chose to think I was some kind of monster, that might have its uses.

At last, Lucas came beside me and tried for a conversation. He'd put away his regal finery for a huge black robe that must have been still hotter for him than the chair was for me. Since

I had nothing I wanted to say to him, I pretended to doze off. And that, after a long swig of the local finest, plus another mile of swaying about in the heat, is what I eventually did. Whatever was coming next, a good rest would do me no harm at all.

56

I've only seen the Pyramids twice. My first view of them, I'll assure you, was from exactly the right direction at exactly the right time of day. It was coming on for late afternoon, and the shadows cast by every jagged rock and every pile of sand were lengthening around me. We were coming out of the desert from the north-west. They must have been about five miles off when I drifted awake, and I didn't notice them at first. I was thirsty and my wrists were hurting. Looking ahead, I seemed only to see more of the endless heat haze that obscured the horizon.

Then I saw them: three vast and regular mountains that shone a dazzling white as they caught the rays of the sun. I didn't know where Siroes had gone. But no one around me paid the slightest attention. They'd seen it all so often, they hardly noticed how wonderful it was. My carriers didn't once look up as they trudged ever onwards. Of course, Lucas had to be different. He bounced up again beside me, pointing and jabbering about his 'ten thousand years'. I did think of starting another argument over his beloved Egypt, this time sneering at his idea of its antiquity. But I grunted at him and pretended to be still half asleep.

In truth, I was privately willing those carriers to go faster. I badly wanted to get as close alongside the Pyramids as I could before night fell. They were a wonderful sight. Nothing I'd read in Herodotus or Strabo or the other historians had prepared me for how they actually were. According to Herodotus, the biggest of the three took a hundred thousand workers twenty-six years to complete, and its function was to serve as the tomb for some megalomaniacal king. Manetho gives a different account, more flattering to its builder. But no one disagrees on its size. It is seven hundred and fifty feet long on each of its four sides, and around five hundred high. It is a huge structure. You could pack the Great Church inside it several times over, and still have room for some of the other sights of Constantinople. The two pyramids beside this one are also very big, but are dwarfed in comparison.

We came at last to the flat expanse of rock on which the Pyramids are built. In or out of flood, this is far above the level of the Nile, and there are still miles to go before the edge of the black land is reached. Even so, the plateau is crowded with buildings. At this time of year, it was naturally the home of those displaced by the floods. But there is a dense network there of ruined and semi-ruined temple buildings. And there may be dozens of monasteries dotted about, these obviously in continuous occupation.

There had been some kind of market all day when we arrived at a small town. But I paid no attention to the mud-brick buildings and the brown, shouting lower orders of Egypt. I'd long since given up concealing my interest in the Pyramids. The Great Pyramid must still have been a good mile distant. But it loomed over everything. The light around us was fading fast away, but the Pyramid still shone white as if it had been a mountain of snow. I believe the inner part is of granite blocks arranged round a core of rock. But the exterior of each of the pyramids is one smoothness of white limestone.

'So, Alaric,' Lucas said as he came yet again beside me, 'are you willing to agree now that the Greeks have nothing to set beside this?'

'Get enough men together,' I sniffed, 'and work them long enough, with just the right touch of the whip when they get uppity, and I've no doubt anyone could put up this sort of thing. The question is who else would have thought it worth the effort?

'Any chance of another drink?' I asked, cutting short my paraphrase of Herodotus. The wine flask he'd reluctantly handed over was long since empty, and my tongue was getting ready to stick to the roof of my mouth. I pretended not to notice the flies, which, with the fading light, had begun buzzing about in predatory manner.

Lucas got off his camel and began walking beside me. I was in no mood for a laugh, but the long account he began of the Pyramids as a love gift from the people of Egypt to their kings was absurd both in itself and in its earnest narrating. In its own way, it was more absurd than any miracle of the Church. Those usually involve a deviation from the normal course of things as a result of God's commanding. This farrago didn't so much deviate from as suspend the normal course of things. But I did get a full cup of water pushed at me. It was now evening, and we were approaching the centre of this town that huddled so inconsequentially at the foot of the Great Pyramid.

We stopped in a central square that served during the day as a market. I stumbled from the chair and stretched my arms and legs. I looked round. It was rather like Letopolis, but without the appearance of better days past. It might have been far older as a settlement. It might have dated back to the building of the Pyramids. But the jumble of narrow streets that led off from the square in which we'd come to rest looked about as tempting as turd pie.

Lucas snarled something at the carriers that didn't sound particularly worthy of any love gift at all. They bowed and padded off somewhere.

'If your people haven't stolen all the cash I brought with me,' I said, 'I think I could stand you a dinner somewhere. I don't suppose you'll find anywhere about that's fit for a king – not even a pretend king like you. But you might care to point me in the direction of an inn that won't give us the shits.'

Avoiding a pile of rotting filth that I could more smell than see, I walked away from him and stood looking up at the Great Pyramid. Its lower parts were now buried in the advancing gloom of evening. Its topmost twenty or thirty feet, though – just below the stained apex, where some ornamentation of bronze, or perhaps even of gold, had once been – still shone bright in the rays of the departing sun. Even as I looked, the line of shadow moved rapidly higher, until only the very apex remained. For a moment, the apex alone glowed. It was as small and as bright as some object in the darkening sky. Then it too was gone. As a result, there was no longer any contrast in the light, and I could now see the whole bulk of the Pyramid outlined against the ever darkening sky.

I turned back to face Lucas. His torchbearers were picking their way towards him. Until they got closer, I'd not be able to see his face. But I could feel the disapproval radiating from him. And my perception of his mood was as cheering as a cup of really good wine.

'So which establishment in this probably nameless dump is up to serving persons of our quality?' I asked, taking up the last subject.

'Are your bodily needs all that concern you?' Lucas hissed at me.

The torchbearers had now arrived, and I could see the insanity blazing from his eyes.

'Do you expect a visit to the town brothel once you've stuffed your belly?'

'Oh, not at all, dear Lucas,' I said, speaking brightly and loud. Several passers-by stopped and looked in my direction. I doubted if they understood me, but I carried on as if I had an audience. 'If Egyptian women smell anything like the men, I'd have vomited on them long before I'd lost any mess inside them. Dinner will be quite enough – oh, and a little wine.'

I watched Lucas while various passions battled for control of his mind. There was outrage at the affront I'd offered him. There was his evident need to keep me in one piece and undamaged until further notice. As his fists unclenched and his face relaxed, he smiled and motioned me towards a large building almost next door to the main church.

I stopped for a moment at the open gate. I put a smile on my face and turned to Lucas with another witticism. But for the first time, I was seriously scared. Of course, I'd been in his power an entire day. At any time since I'd stepped out of the shadows, he could have had me strung up on hooks, or staked out naked under the burning sun. He could have done as he pleased. His people wouldn't have lifted a finger. Siroes was rather stuffy about the proprieties and needed me alive until I'd turned up his piss pot. But unless he was serious about putting me up for emperor, we might be talking of days. And how much control did he really have over Lucas? Now, as I looked through that black entrance to who knows what, my stomach turned over. I stopped at the threshold and found I couldn't go further.

'Come now, Alaric – do you need a formal invitation?' Lucas breathed behind me. He'd perked up since our last exchange. Worse, he was beginning to sound horribly gloaty again.

'Not at all, Your Majesty,' I jeered. 'I'm just wondering how much nastier the inside of this place smells than the street.' I thought I'd get a push from behind if I didn't move soon. That was too much. Lucas might play at being Pharaoh. I *was* the Emperor's Legate. If I was now to be put out of the way, blubbing at the doorway wasn't likely to change matters. I might as well go out with a 'Fuck you, arsehole!'. I bit my lip and stepped forward.

As we went through the usual gateway leading to a central garden, there was a left turn into the building. All was dark at first, though not smelly in the least. If anything, the place was rather pleasant. With Lucas to guide me, though without any lamp, I passed through a series of interconnecting rooms, each unlit and stuffed with furniture. We turned right into another stretch of the building. There were more rooms, again all in darkness. In still more complete darkness, we went up a staircase, our feet scraping on the rough brick of the stairs. There was a short corridor at the top. This terminated in a door, light pouring out from underneath to show the dull roughness of the floor.

'You go in alone,' Lucas whispered with what sounded like a suppressed snigger. I said nothing. He knocked briefly, then pushed the door open and stood back for me to go in. I stepped forward, my mind a deliberate blank, and rubbed my eyes in the sudden brightness. Except for a couple of chairs and a little table over by one of the walls, the room was unfurnished. In one of these chairs, his back to me, a man was sitting. He twisted round and looked at me.

'Ah, Alaric,' he said, 'I've been expecting you.'

Priscus stood up and advanced towards me across the room. He had that bastard cat of his in his arms. As he got within a few feet of me, the thing hissed and raised one of its paws at me.

57

'Oh go on, my blonde little darling,' Priscus said, returning to his theme, 'just admit you've been had.' He rocked back on his chair and raised his cup in a mock toast. He hadn't bothered in this heat with cosmetics, but he did have on the robe of an Imperial Council member. 'Yes, it is the piss pot. I was telling the truth when we first spoke in Alexandria, and a lie when we last spoke. You may have given our friend the Pharaoh the slip more than once. But when Uncle Priscus sets his trap, no one escapes.'

'So tell me, Priscus,' I asked with a sneer, 'when did you turn traitor and throw in your lot with a bunch of wog rebels? Was it on your trip to Siwa? Or was it as late as your improbably lucky escape from the mob?'

He put his cup down and rubbed his face into the cat's fur. 'I don't think I need explain the details of what I'm about,' he said. 'Besides, the story is both long and a touch improbable.' He now put the cat down and reached for his satchel of drugs. He was about to make a selection when Lucas grew tired of lurking and walked into the room.

'Lucas, how delightful to see you again,' he said. 'Would you be a dear and arrange for another jug of wine? You might also care to bring a cup for young Alaric here. I'm sure he could do with refreshments after his dash here through the desert.'

'My name is not Lucas,' came the chilly reply. 'You call me "Your Majesty" or by the name my people have urged upon me.'

Priscus sighed. 'My dear boy,' he said with a tired wave, 'this night is far too hot for unpronounceable and unmemorable wog names. Your real name is Gregory. You are the son of a customs clerk in Naucratis. You have a warrant still pending there for defacing a statue of Septimius Severus while drunk and disorderly. Unless you really want me to call you Gregory, you'll have to settle for Lucas. Let's face it, if you don't like the name, you should have found a better one when you introduced yourself to Alaric. It's too late now to change things. Now, go and get more wine – and be quick about it.' Priscus mopped at his face and motioned me into the one other chair in the room.

Looking several inches shorter than when he'd come in, Lucas turned and went out.

Priscus waited until the door was pulled to. 'You left Alexandria almost before I'd noticed,' he said. 'How you got here so fast is quite beyond me. You will surely rejoice when I tell you, though, that Nicetas remains out of action, and Alexandria is in most capable hands of my own choosing.'

'You're feeling sure of yourself,' I said. 'Where is Martin? I suppose you told me the truth in Alexandria about his being alive.'

'I told you, my love,' Priscus said, 'that he was alive when the ear was sliced away from his head. I made no warranties regarding his continuation in this world. However, he is alive, and you will see him soon enough.' He switched into Latin and dropped his voice. 'It goes without saying that you will do exactly as I tell you if the pair of you want any chance of getting out of this in one piece.'

The door opened again. Lucas walked in, a slave carrying wine behind him. Priscus smiled and waved at the table against the wall.

'I think His Magnificence the Legate may feel obliged to give up his chair,' Lucas said in a tone that hovered between the mad and the plain nasty. 'We do have another guest whose status may be taken as higher than that of a mere commoner.'

There was a long moment of silence as Priscus and Siroes looked at each other. Their faces would have been a scream in better circumstances. But persons of quality don't allow their composure to slip in front of people like Lucas. After the first shock of recognition, and the first apparent realisation that things were not as they'd agreed, they both recomposed their faces.

407

'Siroes, what a delightful surprise, and after so many years,' Priscus cried. He got up and hurried across the room.

Siroes opened his arms, and there was a most convincing reunion of old friends.

'And do tell me,' Priscus asked after some endless reminiscing over a work of nastiness they'd played on a barbarian king back in the days of Maurice, when the two empires had been at peace, 'how is Roxana doing? And the children?'

From the brief answer, I gathered the woman had been taken as one of the Great King's concubines, and the children had been smothered. Priscus squeezed his face into an expression of sympathy, and the conversation moved to less personal matters. I noticed that Siroes continued looking downcast.

'Since when,' Lucas broke in loudly, 'has a Pharaoh been host to supplicant representatives of such great rulers?' He struck a pose, showing his chest and shoulders while twisting his legs and head into profile.

I don't suppose it was other than incompetence that led Egyptian artists into painting their kings in this pose. But Lucas appeared to think otherwise. Siroes looked at him, a thoughtful look just visible on the strip of his face not covered in hair. Priscus smiled politely.

'It may be that I have called you here with a slight element of deceit,' Lucas continued. 'But you are here, and I will state my demands of you both.'

No chair was now free, and I wasn't inclined to sit on the floor. It was as clean as anywhere else I'd sat this day, and there were some rugs that had a comfy look about them. But this wasn't the time for putting aside dignity. I leaned against the wall and waited for this little comedy to play itself out. Priscus was first to speak.

'I don't know about Siroes, but I haven't found it hard to guess what you have in mind. Let us consider. We made a deal. I would deliver Alaric. He would find the relic. I would then use this for my own purposes, granting Egypt full autonomy within the Empire and recognising you as its lawful King. You appear to have made a similar deal with Siroes – or with Chosroes directly. Now that we're all gathered here, you are about to announce that all deals are off, and that you will keep the relic for yourself. Is that it?' Priscus waited for Lucas to puff his chest out before continuing. 'Well, my dear Lucas – and I still can't speak for Siroes – do you really think I'd deliver myself into your hands, here in the back of beyond, without some precautions?' He held out his cup for a refill.

Lucas scowled and muttered an order to the slave.

'If I don't return to Alexandria,' Priscus went on, 'or if I do return without what I came here to get, a series of letters in your own hand will be passed over to the Monophysite Patriarch. These are most incriminating, and you should recall that they are conclusively incriminating. In particular, you will recall your promise to Leontius to establish Isis as the tutelary deity of Egypt. I got these from poor foolish Leontius after I'd killed him. While he was still alive and able to speak, I got a mass of circumstantial information that only blackens your name further.'

'How the fuck did you kill Leontius?' I blurted out. I thought back and tried to reconcile the times. They didn't fit. He'd been with me all evening. Priscus gave me a look of cold power. It was as if I were in one of his dungeons, awaiting his pleasure. I fell silent and leaned back against the wall.

'All very good, Priscus – and I expected nothing less of you,' Lucas replied, sounding more troubled than he wanted to appear, 'but what should I care about the opinion of a Christian priest? You know that my first act as Pharaoh will be to reopen all the temples, not merely the one at Philae.'

'Don't give me any of that, you silly little man!' Priscus said. As he stretched his legs out, his robe fell back slightly, showing a patch of varicose blue. 'You know as well as I do that Egypt is a Christian country. The wogs will humour your taste in dress, so long as you can kick out all the foreigners. They won't stand by you for a moment if you lay hands on the Faith. I haven't made enquiries among the common wogs, but I had a real heart-to-heart with all the other leaders of your Brotherhood. Get a man close enough to an impaling stake, and he'll scream the name of the God in which he truly believes. Not one of those fuckers you betrayed to me called on Isis. When it comes to the Old Faith of Egypt, I'll wager you're in a decided minority.

'But this isn't the end of it. I have some of the letters you wrote to the Brotherhood leadership, getting them to Alexandria. The Intelligence Bureau broke your code years ago. I have the most damning evidence that you sold out the whole upper leadership of your movement. Those who might be inclined to overlook your theology will never forgive you for that. Let those letters be published, and you're in the shit good and proper.' He put his cup down again and beckoned to his cat. It jumped straight up. He stroked it with his free hand. Its back arched as it purred. It still found time to twist round and give me a horrid look.

'Now, Lucas,' he added, 'you just have my dear friend Siroes taken out and hanged, and we'll proceed with our business.' With a flash of his riddled teeth, he smiled broadly at Siroes, who got up from his chair and bowed to Lucas before sitting back down.

'I don't think that would be wholly sensible,' Siroes said with one of his diplomatic smiles. 'You may agree that Priscus has a controlling hold over you. But what makes you think he'll give up this hold once he has what he wants? I think he will cheat you – just as he tries to do with everyone. I can give you the names of a dozen fools who trusted him and are now dead.

'With all respect, Your Majesty, I suggest you have my thrice-sworn brother Priscus taken out and hanged. You just put yourself in our hands, and we guarantee you the throne of Egypt. We may have a Christian minority. But our army is true to the Faith of Zoroaster.'

The room fell silent. The window out to the courtyard was shuttered and bolted. With five people there, and all those lamps, the air was growing uncomfortably stuffy. Priscus rubbed noses with his cat. Siroes drank steadily. Lucas tried to put on a brave face in front of the slave. He failed miserably.

'But I am now in a position to get the relic for myself,' he said at last. He straightened up and began to look as chirpy as he'd been when Siroes had first come in. 'I must remind the pair of you that I command every armed man within a day's ride of this place – perhaps more. Neither of you has so much as a bodyguard. We all agree that whoever has the relic becomes unapproachably power-ful. Why should I listen to either of you? Now that Alaric is here, I can take what I please.'

'Dear me, no!' said Priscus with an easy smile. 'We all agree that the relic confers great power, but it does so only once it's been authenticated as what it's claimed to be. If your Patriarch declines the authentication, you might as well piss in it yourself. And your Patriarch won't support someone like you against the Empire – not when there's a deal on the table to settle the whole Monophysite controversy and get him back in full communion with Constantinople and with Rome. You could ask Alaric here about that. He's the scholar, and can lecture you black in the face about these things. But I don't think you'll need to do that.'

The room fell silent. The three protagonists of the little play acted out under my eyes looked at each other and then at no one in particular.

'You all seem agreed,' I said, breaking the long silence that followed, 'that only I can lead you to this powerful object.' Since there appeared to be at least two opinions about the nature of what was sought, I clung to the ambiguous phrasing I'd had from Siroes. 'You all assume that I will do this for whichever of you is still alive tomorrow morning. Well, I want to see my secretary before I make any commitments. I also want to know what guar-antees you can provide that either of us will survive its finding.'

'Please keep out of this, Alaric,' Priscus said wearily. 'You will see Martin when I see fit to have him produced. If you refuse to do exactly as told, you know what I can and will do to him. If that fails to persuade you, bear in mind what I will certainly then do to you. If I tell you that you will both return safely with me to Alexandria, that is just something you'll have to make yourself believe. You have little choice, after all. You gave up all freedom of action in this matter the moment you fell in again with Lucas.'

'Not good enough, Priscus,' I said. I stared at Lucas and pointed at the wine.

He spat an order to the slave, then went back to a morose inspection of the floorboards.

'You see, if I don't choose to believe you, I remain as free an agent as the three of you. When I've seen Martin and the nature of your joint guarantees, I will consider what steps may be required to secure the object. One way or another, let me observe, everything you have and everything you want is staked on getting this object. Either you give me what I want, or you might as well kill me now, and then see how well you can sort out the resulting mess among yourselves.' I drained my cup and sat on the third chair a slave had just brought in and set before Lucas.

There was another long silence. Then Siroes got up. He brushed away more of the dust that still clung to his riding clothes and looked round.

'Do you not agree how fine a place this world would be if only there were a little more trust among equals?' he asked with a sigh. 'However, it does appear that not one person in this room trusts any other person. This being so, I can only propose that we proceed as if we did trust one another. His Magnificence must be given what he demands. Once he has done what the prophecy says that only he can do, we can proceed to a discussion of what should be done next. I already feel a suggestion for compromise may be in the air. But I do beseech you all to put everything out of mind for the moment except the finding of what we are all gathered to find.'

'Agreed,' said Priscus. He and Siroes smiled at each other.

Lucas appeared set to speak again. But the slave was looking at him. If he hadn't understood a word of the conversation, it couldn't be hard to guess that Lucas had been worsted. All else aside, he was the only one of us still standing. The anger on his face was visibly giving way to dejection. Priscus put his cat down. It went and sat on one of the rugs. It looked up at me with the sort of face even his master hadn't been able to match – not even after a lifetime of practising in front of a mirror.

'That leaves the matter of our late supper,' Priscus said. 'Let us pretend it is out of friendship alone that the four of us will drink from the same cup.'

58

We set out again at dawn, this time for Soteropolis. Priscus and Siroes rode together. Watching them talk, anyone would have thought they were bosom friends. I rode with Lucas.

'I hope I shan't need to remind you,' Priscus had said as we were mounting up, 'that His Magnificence Alaric is not a prisoner. It should be enough that we have his secretary.' Lucas had scowled into his beard. But Priscus had started to border on the nasty, and that was the end of the matter.

It was a ride of about twenty miles through the edge of the desert. The Nile rolled by sluggishly far down on our right. I did see a few boats, though nothing that could have been useful to me, even if the wish had been there. The journey was completely without event. Lucas had put off all his antique finery and was now dressed in normal riding clothes for the desert. This meant we attracted no more attention from the few lowly travellers on the road than twenty mostly armed men always would.

Martin and I had been coming from the north when, a month earlier, we first saw the monument marking the centre of the old Soteropolis. We'd then had to go over a sand dune before we could see the Mistress and beyond her to the dead palm trees. We were now approaching from the south. The whole expanse of sand that had then seemed so desolate was now crowded with tents. They stretched all the way to the dune, and spread out right and left before then. Was this where the Brotherhood had pitched its camp? I asked myself. There could easily have been a thousand men in this temporary city. This was almost everything the camp I'd found had not been. But, no. I squinted to see better in the bright sunshine. Most of the figures darting between the tents were locals of the lowest class. As usual, burned a dark red by the sun, they ran about almost naked. These weren't the five hundred workmen drilled and well fed I'd been thinking to divert from work on the old canal. But they would do very well for the excavations I had evidently been brought here to oversee.

As we rode into the camp, someone came running over to Lucas. He saluted and shouted something. There was a brief conversation. Lucas sounded mighty pleased with everything. He got down from his camel and disappeared among some of the minor players in the Brotherhood who had escaped the purge laid on by Priscus in Alexandria.

'I think you'll find everything in order, my dear,' said Priscus as he helped me down from my camel.

I wanted to say that the tents might be covering the area under which the Library reserve stock was buried. Sadly, even a twenty-mile ride had left me bruised and stiff again. I pulled my hood back, and let the breeze rustle my hair. A few of the locals stared with dull interest at my unusual colouring. The Brotherhood people, however, let up a terrified clamour. Those who'd seen me the night before last had got almost used to the idea of having in their midst what they took for a corpse brought back to life by a sorceress. These evidently hadn't been given prior warning. Pointing at me, and calling out an unfamiliar phrase over and over again, they shrank back. 'My empire is of the imagination,' the Mistress had said. I was beginning to see there might be advantages in being one of her provincial governors. I smiled back at the scared, jabbering throng.

No one could claim Priscus had been brought back from the dead. Still, he was able to cause a big commotion of his own. Here, among them, was the Hammer of the Brotherhood, the man who'd skewered so many of their Grand Masters through arse or belly and had saved Alexandria from what might otherwise have been their most spectacular success in a thousand years. I was almost forgotten in the now threatening buzz. Lucas had to come out of the tent he'd been inspecting and work hard to keep his people from butchering at least Priscus on the spot.

But the commotion was eventually settled. I still got any number of funny looks, and Priscus got worse. But the Brotherhood was again following the orders of its leaders, who now set in earnest about doing the bidding of the one Grand Master who'd not come to an end in Alexandria.

'I was serious when I told you last night to follow my instructions,' Priscus said softly to me in Latin as we found ourselves together in the jostling crowds.

'No Latin!' Lucas shouted from nowhere. He pushed his way past a couple of grooms and stood before us. 'You will not be alone together,' he said firmly. 'All you have to say to each other will be in front of me and in Greek. I must remind you, Priscus, of how little loved you are among the Brotherhood. Without my protection, your safety cannot be guaranteed.'

'Oh, Lucas, Lucas!' Priscus said, rolling the hated name in his mouth with cheerful satisfaction. 'I've given you Alaric. I've given you the one man all the prophecies say is the One. And I'm not the only one needing to remember that it's thanks to me that anyone up to challenging you is now rotting in one of my mass graves. Don't presume, Lucas dear, the pair of us to be in anything together. That would need to be a very deep plot.'

Lucas wasn't impressed. He took me by the hand and led me up the dune to look over the monument.

'We'll eat,' he said. 'Then you will supervise the digging.'

I looked across the still clear expanse of sand that covered the centre of Soteropolis. From what I knew of his way with his beloved people, he'd have a few flogged to death if they slacked. The rest would dig as if someone had buried gold coins for them to find. Even so, it was a large area, and there was nothing at surface level to indicate street plans or other buildings. I heard Priscus following behind me.

'I don't think, Alaric, introductions will be in order,' he said.

I turned. Martin stood beside him. He was manacled with eighteen inches of chain between his wrists. There was another manacle about his right leg. This was attached by another length of chain to a large iron ball that needed two hunched brown bodies to lift off the ground. Someone else held a sunshade over him.

For the first time, I lost control. I broke down at the shock of seeing him. I didn't bother trying to hide my sobs as we embraced. He pushed me gently back.

'Aelric, you're a fool for coming,' he said in Celtic. 'I prayed you would simply light a candle for me in church and get everyone out of Alexandria.' He sat down in the sand. The sunshade was moved to keep it in position. 'I prayed for you to use some common sense. But I knew in my heart you wouldn't.'

Martin hadn't shaved, and his red beard was flecked with grey. So far as it wasn't covered in a stained bandage, there was a haunted look on his face. Otherwise, he was in good health. I looked more closely at the bandage. Priscus caught my glance.

'A regrettable but necessary loss,' he said loudly in Greek. 'But I found Martin unusually firm about signing the letter I'd had drafted for you to read. All things considered, though, has the Legate's secretary any complaints about his treatment?'

'No, My Lord,' Martin said. Not bothering to look up, he stared glumly at the heavy manacle round his ankle.

'Then let us keep it that way. Alaric,' Priscus said, still with raised voice, 'I must inform you of these conditions. You will supervise the digging as you see fit. You will lay hands on the relic and pass it immediately to the three other principals in this endeavour. Once you have done so, you and Martin will be taken to Letopolis and sent in a postal boat safely back to Alexandria. Siroes, Lucas and I will swear later this day in public to keep our word. The Bishop of Letopolis will witness our swearing, and you must rely on his influence with virtually the entire Brotherhood and all the local population to ensure that we keep our word.

'If you have not located the relic within fourteen days, you and Martin will be put to death. Be assured that I would give you longer than this. However, Siroes has been privately advised that the only auspicious time for locating the relic will soon pass. I cannot dispute his advice, and so must bow to his insistence.

'There is one further point to these conditions. We are in a hurry, and wish to make it clear that seven days mark the reasonable limit of our patience. Today is nearly half gone, and so does not count.

Tomorrow is a Sunday, and I have already been worsted in an argument over that. I will give you one day beyond that. Three days, I hope, will be sufficient for you to do your work. However, if you have uncovered nothing that I find interesting by noon on Tuesday, I will have Martin's other ear sliced off. If you have uncovered nothing by the noon following, I will have the little finger of his left hand cut off. We shall then proceed by such stages as I think suitable until Friday, which is the twenty-seventh day of the month of Mechir that Lucas specified in his letter. At midnight, I shall have Martin blinded or perhaps castrated. Enough of him will survive the full time specified either to be sent back with you to Alexandria, or to be put to death with you in such manner as we shall find appropriate. Do you understand me?'

I nodded. Forget the fourteen days. We had three. Martin was taken back to wherever he was kept. I sat down to lunch with the other persons of quality. From where I sat between Lucas and someone who kept quietly farting, I could hear Priscus and Siroes toasting each other and refighting the Battle of Daras. They used cups and pieces of bread to show the various dispositions of forces. I ate in silence. I kept wondering if Martin hadn't been right. I'd been so sure of myself in Alexandria. Even since giving myself to Lucas, things hadn't gone so badly. I now realised I was fixed in a timetable over which I had no control and from which there was no obvious escape. Thanks to me, four people might now die instead of one. And what of Maximin? What if Isaac hadn't been able to get him out of Alexandria? At best, he'd be brought up as a cross between Priscus and that bloody cat.

'If you need anything not already provided,' Lucas told me as we stood in the shade of the monument, 'you will ask me. For the simple relaying of orders to the diggers, you will use my assistant. I believe you have already met. This being so, you can trust his skills as an interpreter.' I'd already seen Macarius during lunch. Lucas had got up several times from his place to give instructions. Macarius had taken these with his usual impassive look and bowed. There was no element of surprise when he now stepped forward. I'd long since guessed he was serving more than one master. Still, I went through the motions of showing disgust.

'Fucking wog traitor!' I snarled.

Macarius bowed gravely and looked back as impassively as if I'd been complaining about the flies.

I now put myself to the matter in hand. The more detailed map Hermogenes had promised before the rioting had somehow arrived in my tent. I unrolled it and oriented it with the monument and the sun. The street plan was vague and perhaps even conjectural. Its indication of where the Jewish quarter had been was at best unreliable. Looking straight ahead was the big dune on the other side of which the Brotherhood tents were pitched. Under that may have been the reserve stock. Then again, from what Hermogenes had told me, the place had never been large, and was a building by itself. Digging for it would need, at the very least, to wait. The city centre was around the monument. The most reasonable place to start the digging was about five hundred yards north of the monument.

I paced out the distance. I didn't look round, but I knew Macarius and one of the big armed men would be close behind me. I stopped and again unrolled the map. I looked back at the monument. This was a fairly level expanse of sand, and it may have been only a little higher than the sand around the monument. I waved around me and looked now straight at Macarius.

'I want that lot uncovered,' I said. 'I want it uncovered as far down as it takes.'

'How is it going?' Priscus asked.

I looked up from the ruins of a cook shop. We were moving fast into the evening of the second day. I'd consented to release the whole workforce for a big Sunday service. I could have kept the diggers going in relays. I'd even been thinking how long I could keep them all going until they really did start dropping from exhaustion. I'd been getting increasingly funny looks as I made my rounds. Word had spread, it seemed, from the Brotherhood to the diggers. As hoped, this had kept everyone in awe of my word.

But there is a limit to what even Egyptian muscle can achieve with a spade.

'You will be happy to know that another delivery has just been made of pitch for night digging,' Lucas added.

They stood together in the doorway of the building. I'd now had the whole area excavated down to pavement level, and had spent much of the afternoon having the interiors of the buildings cleared of sand.

'So what have you found?' Priscus asked again.

'Soteropolis is turning out to be larger than expected,' I replied. And so it was. Everything I'd seen about it in Alexandria indicated a smallish city. Now that I'd widened the area of excavation into the centre, I could see how large it had been. It didn't help that digging below the level of the Greek city had turned up foundations of earlier buildings that may have been as massive as anything in Constantinople.

'I've said you can't have any more people,' Lucas said hurriedly. 'I've given you every able-bodied man in the area. You have nearly all the women and children to carry baskets of sand. I'm flooded with complaints about essential work to dykes that has been disrupted.'

'Oh, is *that* what they're all moaning about,' Priscus said satirically. 'I was beginning to think they were frightened of something.'

Lucas scowled and looked away. Priscus stepped in through the doorway and straightened up. He beckoned Lucas in behind him. We all stood for a moment looking at a tiled floor I'd recently had cleared of sand. I'd been hoping there might be a hatchway to a cellar.

'My dear Lucas,' he said, the beginnings of a stern look on his face. 'We are for the moment partners in this venture, and I expect to be kept informed of all relevant circumstances. It isn't because their dykes are crumbling that your wogs have been in and out of the shithouses all day, squirting and jabbering. They're frightened of something. Now they've seen him shitting and being rubbed with oil for his sunburn, it isn't young Alaric who's the cause of their terror. They're frightened of something else – and they're frightened of whatever that thing is almost as much as they are of you. Any chance of telling me what it might be?'

Lucas scowled again and muttered something about tales told to children by the old.

Priscus snorted. 'Then you'd better just make sure your wogs remain more frightened of you than they are of ghosts,' he said flatly. 'So far as I'm concerned, if Alaric asks for women and children to *dig* the sand, I suggest you find more shovels. In the meantime, I suggest you get that Bishop to lay on more services. He might also be persuaded to consider an exorcism.' He turned back to me. 'Now, Alaric, I'll ask again – what have you found?'

The shortest and most truthful answer was nothing. This particular Soteropolis had been vacated with careful deliberation. It wasn't like Richborough, where decline had been gradual, or other cities back in Kent that had been taken by storm and burned with the corpses of all the slain. There, you could dig down a few feet and find any number of treasures: bronze pens, lead cooking pots, even the occasional handful of unlooted cash. Soteropolis had been systematically stripped of everything that could be moved. Even roof tiles from the more expensive buildings had been carefully pulled off.

I'd worked several thousand men through the better part of two days and a night. We'd uncovered two acres of city, bleak and skeletal in its ruination. We'd turned up broken pottery. We'd turned up broken furniture. We'd turned up a few sets of bones – probably of sick, and therefore unwanted, slaves knocked on the head and left behind in the move. Much earlier in the present day, I'd smashed open a large crate, only to find it filled with packets of nails that may have been brought in from Smyrna. In general, we'd exposed enough of the street plan to suggest what I'd said about the size of the city. Beyond that, we'd found nothing.

'I have a feeling that the collapsed wall over there' – I pointed to the edge of the excavated area: it was a length of mud brick that vanished into a sloping cliff of sand – 'is part of the synagogue. If you put some broken stones together, they may show Hebrew writing. If it is, we've found the Jewish quarter. Once I'm sure that is what we've found, I'll have the courtyard gardens dug up as well. There will be objects there concealed or simply lost before the evacuation.' What I didn't say was that the Jewish quarter may have been close to the walls. Outside those, there would be grave-yards and grave goods.

'And you suppose Jews would leave even their toilet scrapings behind?' Lucas asked with a laugh. 'I would remind you,' he said to Priscus, 'that it's only Siroes who says this relic shall be uncov-ered by a blonde man from the West. Before he got in touch with Leontius, the story was very different. If only you hadn't killed Leontius . . .'

'You were pleased enough when I did kill him,' Priscus snapped.

Again, I wanted to ask how he'd done it. He had been with me – so had Macarius – the whole evening of the murder. If Macarius had disappeared for a while, it wasn't anything like long enough to get out of the Egyptian quarter, commit that lovingly slow murder, and then get back to meet us near the Wall of Separation. And it wasn't Macarius, but Priscus who was claiming respon-sibility for the killing. Given time, I'd have sat down and gone through the evidence again. But there was no time. As if he'd read my thoughts, Priscus pointed up at the setting sun.

'You have until the day after tomorrow, Alaric,' he said. 'I may have broken more promises than I can remember, but I've always been punctilious about delivery when it comes to hurting people. You just think on that – and keep digging.'

59

It was dawn the following day. I stood on the top of the sand dune, looking down over the excavated area. The diggers on the morning shift were being pushed away from their earnest conversations with the night diggers. Some of them were looking up at me.

'What do you suppose is frightening them?' I asked.

Martin looked down at the cluster of humanity nearest the foot of the dune. A couple of the Brotherhood guards were clubbing one of the diggers to pulp. He wasn't screaming. No one was intervening on his behalf. Martin swallowed and looked away.

'His Grace the Bishop comes and speaks to me now and again,' he said. 'He's a native and a convinced Monophysite. But his Greek is good, and he means well. He tells me the diggers can feel they are being watched by night. Some have seen things they can't describe. There are stories – stories that I don't think you want to hear . . .'

I sighed. Reports of ghosts were the last thing we needed. For sure, it had been a difficult night. Every time the wind shifted, men had been throwing their shovels down and trying to run away. I had managed some sleep, though only after being kept awake by thoughts of a strike – or even a mass walkout.

I thought of asking Martin about the Bishop. He'd been brought in to supervise a thoroughly shifty oath regarding our safety. If he couldn't lift a finger to save us in the event of failure, I didn't see how he could insist on our release if we did find the thing. Having him turn up with his Gospels in Egyptian and his relic of Saint Antony was the best I could get. But I didn't think it that good. Now, he seemed permanently on call about the camp. If he and Martin were starting up a friendship, it might come in handy.

My trail of thought came to an end. Lucas had now staggered from his tent. He stood about ten yards down from us, straining to watch the clubbing. It didn't seem to concern him that he'd soon be minus yet another of his loving subjects. Since we were at one in wanting these poor buggers to work their guts out, I wasn't inclined to think ill of his methods. I looked again over the excavated area. The sun was behind me to my right, and was still casting long shadows from the ruined walls. Nevertheless, it was possible to see the scale of what had already been achieved. We were nowhere close to uncovering the whole city; even at this frenzied pace, that would take nearly a month. But the whole centre was now exposed, and much of what had undoubtedly been the Jewish quarter.

'You were a fool to come looking for me,' Martin said again, now in Celtic. He was less bitter than sad. 'It should have been obvious you were walking straight into a trap. You had one miracle in Alexandria. Don't suppose you'll get another one out here.'

We turned from looking over the broken ruins of Soteropolis and looked towards the sun. The dead trees were still there in the distance. They marked the limit to the city of tents called into being by the excavation – a city of tents that was now packed with shuffling, unwashed humanity.

'Did you speak with Sveta?' he asked. 'Did she agree to your coming?'

I nodded.

'With all respect, My Lord,' Macarius broke in, 'I have already told you both that Greek is the only language in which you are permitted to communicate. If you cannot keep to His Majesty's rules, I am firmly instructed to have your secretary shown back to his place of confinement.'

'His Majesty, my arse!' I snapped in Greek. His back to me, Lucas stiffened and broke out in the little twitches of someone who wants to join in a conversation, but fears for the loss of dignity. 'Isn't it enough that you come before me again as a traitor? Must you show yourself a fool as well?'

Macarius shrugged and turned to an inspection of Soteropolis. The diggers were now setting to work. I was having them concentrate on the courtyard gardens in the Jewish quarter. He looked back and smiled weakly.

'My Lord is from a place that was removed from the Empire two centuries ago,' Macarius said. 'Your secretary is from a place that was always beyond the frontiers. Let me ask what would be your opinion of the Greeks if their tax gatherers were stripping your people naked, and if their priests were calling your people heretics?'

'That's beside the point,' I sniffed. 'Your loyalty was to me personally, not to the Greeks. I suppose you forged the letter of introduction from my banker?'

'If I might be so bold – Your Lordship has notions of personal duty more fitting to a Western barbarian than to a citizen of the Empire. I might also note that Jews have been given little reason to love the Empire.'

'Fuck you!' I snarled. And that was the only answer he'd get from me. At least Martin had other things on his mind than to glory in having been right all along.

'Martin,' I said, still in Greek, 'I want you to know – and always to know – that friendship is a duty beside which all others are secondary. I believe this is one of those points on which Epicurus and your Gospels are in agreement. You must have known I'd come looking for you – whatever the risks. And if there is a God, there will surely be a miracle.'

I'd said my piece. I've never been one for showing my feelings when they can possibly be controlled. Forget all other evidence. It was their stiff upper lip that showed the old Romans weren't native to the Mediterranean. Like me, they came from the North. Besides, I wasn't giving that swine Lucas the joy of seeing me break down again and weep like Martin – not a man of the North, whatever his complexion said to the contrary.

I'd like to have asked when Martin had been taken out of Alexandria. Had he spoken first with Priscus? Had he any information about when the snake had joined up with Lucas? But there was nothing more to be said in front of Macarius. And the sun was getting stronger. Unlike me, Martin hadn't the right clothes for keeping most of it off his skin.

'It looks, my dear fellow, as if your celebrated luck is still holding,' Priscus said.

We stood just outside the low walls that remained of what might once have been a carpenter's workshop. It was probably within the Jewish quarter, though I was the only one able to comment on the geography of Soteropolis. The diggers held up the shapeless lead container.

'It might have been a piss pot,' he said. He stepped back to avoid contact with it. 'And that is undoubtedly Jewish writing on the side.'

'Don't you think the writing looks rather fresh?' Lucas asked. He wasn't afraid of contact, and he snatched it from the digger. He held it up in the sunlight. His eyes took on their mad look and he raised his voice. 'The Prophetess told me,' he said in a tone of rising triumph, 'that the twenty-third day of Mechir would bring glad tidings for all who fight against subjugation by light-eyed foreigners. This *may* be it.' He looked closely at the lead container.

I couldn't deny that the writing looked very fresh. On the other hand, who was I to argue with the Prophetess?

'Your Majesty will surely know,' the Bishop said in his heavy accent, 'that from the moment it becomes holy, a relic never ages.'

That was a new one to me, but I'd not be the one to correct him. With shaking hands, he took the thing from Lucas. He began a dialogue with the digger who'd pulled it from the loose sand he'd been clearing from the courtyard. I didn't need Macarius to interpret. The holy looks and upstretched arms were enough. I sat on a pile of mud bricks and kept my face non-committal. There was a sneering laugh behind me. I turned. Siroes was looking down from the level of the uncleared sand on the far side of the building.

'I suppose I shall have to tell you till I'm quite black in the face,' he said to Priscus, 'that we are *not* looking for a chamber pot – nor anything else associated with Jesus Christ. I agree that it must be found by someone matching Alaric's description. But I have not travelled all the way here – in considerable discomfort, and at some personal risk, I might add – to be palmed off with a piece of tat fished out of a rubbish dump.'

'But, My Lord,' the Bishop exclaimed, 'you are looking at the first chamber pot of our Lord and Saviour Jesus Christ. It is a relic of the highest—'

'For all I care, it could still be full of his piss,' Siroes said with rising impatience. 'Priscus, if I find that you are trying to swindle me, you know perfectly well that—'

'Oh, shut up!' Priscus groaned. 'This looks just the thing we came to get. We've even had provisional authentication. If you know something that I don't, I really think it would save time to say what you *are* looking for, instead of what you're not.'

'I'll tell you what we need when it's put in front of me,' Siroes said. 'In the meantime, you can throw that thing away and have your people keep digging.'

Lucas looked confused. Unable to think of anything better to show his equality, he raised a hand to strike the Bishop. He suddenly realised what he was doing. The Bishop hadn't flinched. Several of the diggers were looking surly. His own bodyguard was looking on in horror. He turned and padded after Siroes.

'Nice try, Alaric,' Priscus said with another look at the lead container. 'But it does look as if you'll need to work a great deal harder to please Siroes.' He looked up at the sun. 'You still have a whole day. I heard Martin praying as I came over. Shall I get him to pray harder – and this time in Greek? That is, after all, the language in which the Faith was revealed to the world.'

The Bishop looked happy enough with his relic. He was holding it up while every digger in sight grovelled in the sand. I'll not say I felt much affection from the gathering. But I was for the first time feeling a certain lack of hostility. It was all worthless. I fought to control the tears.

'What do you think it is, My Lord Alaric?'

Siroes passed the length of glassy cord to me. Priscus had tossed it back with a contemptuous sniff. Lucas had made up some nonsense about jewellery manufacture for export in the days of the native kings. I hadn't supposed that a serious answer was required. But Siroes wasn't giving up on his question. I reached across the table and took the offered eighteen-inch length of glass strands within a glass sheathing.

These weren't jolly meals the four of us were taking together. It was uncooked food from a common plate, and water from cups allotted by casting dice. I might have insisted on proper food for myself – after all, I was the one person there who had nothing to fear for the moment. But it struck me as a better idea to keep up some pretence of equality. So it was dull food for me as well. Apart from this, there were long silences and funny looks every time the flow of bright chatter dried up between Priscus and Siroes. One friendly meal had been easy to ensure. This was our fourth dinner together, not to mention other meals. The pretence hadn't broken down, and wouldn't be allowed to break down during the time it had to be maintained. But the strain was getting to us all. Discussion of what had been found was something not yet seriously tried.

'I don't think jewellery manufacture explains this stuff,' I said.

Lucas sat up, outrage on his face. No one paid attention. If I was there as a prisoner masquerading as an equal, his own equality was highly notional. Never much in the first place, his royal act was wearing thin. All he had to offer was some diminishing ability to control the diggers – and a continuing monopoly, it had to be said, of armed force.

I twisted the glassy cord, again noting how it moved in my hands as if it had contained bunches of silk rather than of glass. I forced the dull glow of misery to the back of my mind and tried to pretend I was here in more scholarly circumstances. I dipped my cup into the water bowl and drank awhile in the silence.

'So far as I can tell,' I went on, 'Soteropolis exists on three levels. There is the modern city, dating back to the beginning of the Greek settlement. There are the remains of an Egyptian city. These two mostly run into each other, and it may be better to describe them as different periods of the same place. Deep underneath, though, there is something much older and much bigger. This stuff is buried in the foundations of that earlier city. It's now in short lengths. But it seems once to have run in long stretches between the buildings.

'Most likely, it served some religious function – though what it is and how it was made are beyond me.' That wasn't much of an explanation. But it gave me the excuse to ask a few questions of my own. 'More useful to know, Siroes,' I said, 'is what you think is under those sands. It's plain you aren't interested in Christian relics. Indeed, all that seems to connect what the three of you are after is that it's in Soteropolis, and I'm the one to find it.'

'If my sources tell right,' came the reply, 'you will know what I seek when you find it. Beyond that, I am unable to comment. I hope for your sake, though, that my sources are right about who will do the finding. I am told it must be a man of light complexion from the West, who has much learning and great power over the Egyptians. Yes, let us all hope that describes you.'

We fell silent again. A gust of wind moved the leather flaps of the tent where we had our meals, and brought a little shower of sand through the woven papyrus of the roof. I wondered if this would cause problems again. From the wrong direction, a stiff wind could undo the work of half a day.

'Shall I have musicians brought in again?' Lucas asked with an attempt at bright hospitality. 'They've had all day to cut new flutes.'

Siroes pulled a face. Priscus appeared not to have heard. I thought of making an excuse and creeping off again to where Martin was tethered. Doubtless, Macarius would notice and tag along. Certainly, I'd done everything I could, and it had failed. But we could sit together through the night. I'd try to think of some deal – even now – that I could strike with Priscus or anyone else. I might also find time to sit alone in the cold night air. I'd had little time for reflecting on things since leaving the oasis. There was much new material to fit into the hypothesis that was still only half formed in my mind.

'What's that bloody noise?' Priscus asked, slamming his cup down heavily. His now rather bedraggled cat left off pawing at a dung beetle that had been deprived of a few of its legs. 'Can't you give us a single night when the fucking natives aren't restless?'

Looking alarmed, Lucas got up and went to the leather flaps. Given luck, I thought, the diggers had grown sick of being driven day and night like pyramid builders, and had come to string up their latest Pharaoh. That being so, the Bishop would surely intervene for me and Martin. Lucas paused at the entrance to the tent, then went out. I heard his voice raised in some threatening snarls. The wailing started over again, almost blotting out the shouted jabberings to Lucas.

'There has been another accident,' he said as he came back in. He flopped down and looked at his cup. He thought better of daring to drink from it again, and instead stared at the ring of lamps.

'My dear boy,' Priscus sighed, 'we are not so bored we need to be told about another dead wog. What is it this time? Scorpion bite? Falling masonry? Broken back at the bottom of a well shaft?' He took up his fly whisk and flicked around without enthusiasm or success – not that he needed either. The flies were making a proper meal of me. They weren't desperate enough to bite into Priscus.

'This one is different,' Lucas said, gathering himself back into a semblance of leadership. 'I think you should all come.'

60

We made our way through a forest of torches to the larger of the two craters I'd had dug as the light faded. We were outside the foundations of the city wall, and I'd waved at this spot earlier as the likely site of a graveyard. There ought to be bodies here that had been buried with their household goods. Some of these might not have been looted, and I might find something here that wouldn't be rejected out of hand by Siroes. This crater was about forty feet across at the top, though the sand was rather loose, and it sloped gently down to a spot that was only six feet across at its widest.

'Get a light down here,' I said curtly. The moon was waxing strong now in the cloudless sky. But I wanted as much light as I could get. I pointed at the two diggers closest to the edge. Torches in hand, they peered uncertainly at me. If they didn't understand what I was saying, they could guess what I wanted. 'I want those men down here directly,' I said.

Lucas had given up protesting when I used him as an interpreter. He nodded and shouted at the men. They shrank back. There was a general murmur of fear and anger from the crowd. But Lucas shouted again, and snapped his fingers in a gesture that usually brought a couple of his guards forward. The men stepped reluctantly over the edge. They held their torches upright as they slid down the twenty feet of loose sand.

During the day, I thought we'd found a funerary temple, or the tomb of some local person of quality. Soteropolis had been abandoned long before the establishment of the Faith. Graveyards would be in the full ancient style. I was wrong. Now the digging had uncovered more of those ancient foundations, it was plain that they continued outside the walls of the more recent city. I stood at the bottom of the crater on a surface of huge but perfectly cut blocks of granite. The now sobbing wretch who'd made all the noise was still grovelling face down on this platform.

'What is it?' I said, hoping the peremptory tone would save the need of interpreting.

He looked up and pointed waveringly at a stone at the edge of the crater, still half buried in sand, which seemed to rest on the granite floor. I went over and scooped some of the sand away. The stone was about the size and shape of a millstone, but I could now see it was topped in the centre with a granite cone that rose up about a yard. Covered in Egyptian picture writing, its very top was in the shape of what I knew to be the Goddess Sekhmet.

'They say it resembles the creatures seen at night on the fringes of the camp,' Lucas called down, reluctance to explain anything clear in his voice. 'They say that whoever looks first on a demon's image found at night must die before morning.'

One of the torchbearers beside me pointed at the depressions cut into the round stone at regular intervals round its outer edge. As I bent to examine them, the digger who'd found all this went into a renewed screaming fit. He flopped over and jerked about. His eyes mad and staring, he screamed a single phrase over and again. Above us, beyond the edge of the crater, the other diggers took up the phrase. They mixed it in with religious imprecations I could more or less understand.

'I want that Bishop on site now,' I shouted up at Lucas. 'Failing that, get a priest. Go on – we'll have a night riot on our hands if you don't move quickly.'

As quickly as it had started, though, the fit came to an end. One moment, the crater was filled with despairing wails. The next, all was silent and still. There was no point giving instructions for the two men down there with me. I bent down myself and got hold of the now lifeless body. I pulled it into a semblance of normality and flipped the eyes shut. They opened again in an instant, reflecting still the light of the torches. There was another wail of terror overhead. Lucas had to scream what sounded the most horrifying threats to keep the crowd from stampeding. I hoped religious help wouldn't be too long in coming.

'Not a pretty sight,' Priscus said. He stood beside me, looking down at the twisted features. 'You'd think he'd seen straight into the pit of Hell before he died.'

I was glad he spoke quietly, and that almost no one else could understand him. It was a ghastly sight. I swallowed and looked at the jaw still open and locked into that long final scream of horror.

'There's no doubt in my mind, by the way,' he added, 'that the bugger did die of fright. I've seen that look any number of times on the faces of men tied to the rack and who've pegged out before a single click of the wheel.' He smacked his lips appreciatively and looked up at Lucas.

'Do get those torchbearers closer,' he called. 'You did say it was the first to see the wog goddess who was to die. Well, that being so, the curse is surely spent.'

But Lucas was busy keeping order and paid no attention. With a dissatisfied grunt, Priscus reached down for the now extinguished torch the dead man had been carrying. He went over to relight it from the torches of the diggers, who were cowering as far away as they could get without clambering back up the slope.

'Do you suppose those are leverage holes?' I asked, pointing at the depressions around the edge of the stone. 'If so, this may be some kind of opening to a cellar.'

Priscus bent down further to see where I was pointing. He straightened and looked at me. 'I do think they might be,' he said, now cheerful. 'It does look, dear boy, as if you really are lucky this time. Even Siroes would have trouble accusing you of fabricating this.'

'I want six strong men,' I called to Lucas. 'Get them down here with crowbars to use as levers.' Once that was relayed, I had the satisfaction of hearing real terror in the crowd. Lucas had to scream himself hoarse, and set his overseers loose with whips before I got what I wanted. Even with some very strong men to do my bidding, though, it took much of the night before we managed anything at all. Long before the stone began to grate within its granite housing, Lucas had managed to send off most of the onlookers to bed or about their digging elsewhere on the site.

'May the relic of Our Lord and Saviour Jesus Christ preserve us from harm,' the Bishop, now beside me, interpreted himself into Greek. Taking care not to remove it from the linen bag that shielded mere humans from its raw holiness, he waved the lead container I'd earlier arranged to be 'found', and the men sweating over the circular stone looked a little less troubled.

It was nice, I thought, that someone had believed in my relic. If only that bastard Siroes hadn't stuck his nose into the matter, we could already have broken out the wine. I looked up at him. He was standing overhead just beyond the edge of the crater, muttering away in Persian.

The stone grated again. This time, it turned free. Round and round, the men pulled and pushed it with their crowbars. At last, they set their crowbars beneath it and flipped it over on to the granite floor. It fell with a heavy thud that dislodged a rush of sand from the crater wall. The upper cone of the thing crunched as it turned on the loose grains of sand. Priscus and I stood looking down at it in the silence that followed. Several of the torches had been dropped and extinguished in the shock of the noise, and the men who'd been holding them looked stupidly down. One of the men we'd brought to supply heavy muscle fainted clean away. Another turned to bolt back up the sandy slope. He was only stopped by Priscus, who set about him with the little cosh he carried in his clothing.

It was a big piece of stone – about a yard and a half across and eighteen inches deep. On its underside was a threaded projection about a yard across. It was this that had fixed it into the opening that it covered. The stone must have weighed several tons. There was a soft and sinister murmuring from the few onlookers who remained. It was one of those sounds that could easily presage real trouble. But the Bishop was praying loudly again in Egyptian and waving the relic. It really was going down a treat with everyone who didn't matter.

Then it was back to business. We got the torches relit. Lucas had the men threatened back to the job of extending the crater properly so the opening was in its centre, and then of sweeping sand away from the opening. The Bishop now helped no end, with his continual prayers and waving. He even came down and stood beside us. His repeated mentions of Jesus Christ had a perceptibly steadying effect on the men. At last, the work was done. I looked into the round blackness. I'd expected foul or at least stale air from a place sealed for so many thousands of years. Apart from the slight smell that reminded me of dry wood left out in the sun, the air wasn't bad in the least. I coughed and listened for the echo. I took up a pebble and dropped it in. I hadn't counted to one before I heard it fall. I threw another in at an angle. I heard it skip sharply along a flat surface. So far as I could tell, we'd broken into an underground chamber. From the drop and echo of the pebble, it must be a very large chamber, or the entrance to something large. This might be the only entrance If so, this was the sort of find tomb raiders in Egypt had been talking about for ever. Very likely, it was the tomb of someone really important. Leontius would have died for this. Then again, he probably had.

'You are the luckiest man alive, young Alaric,' Siroes called down with another of his laughs. 'I no sooner tell you that you will know what we seek than you find it.'

'God be praised!' Lucas cried, not to be outdone by some Persian. Perhaps mindful of the look on the Bishop's face, he'd lapsed back into Christianity for the moment. 'The twenty-third of Mechir shall be remembered for ever in Egypt as the first day of its liberation. We will rename our capital – in Egyptian, of course – as City of the Twenty-Third Mechir.' He looked at Siroes, who seemed baffled. 'Among the Greeks,' he explained, 'this day is known as the 11th September.'

'I don't think we need lectures on comparative chronology,' Priscus sneered up at him. 'And don't you think we should wait and see what's down there before we start celebrating?' He turned to me. 'But you really are the luckiest,' he repeated softly. 'It doesn't matter how deep the shit you fall into – you still come out smelling of roses. I'll give you until the third hour of the day to get yourself

435

rested. It goes without saying that Martin is under conditional reprieve.' He looked at my face.

'Don't play stupid, my dear fellow,' he said, now laughing. 'Someone has to go down that hole. And you can be perfectly sure it won't be me.'

In broad daylight, the stone was still more curious than it had appeared in the night. Its top, where it had faced outward, was as weathered as if it had been on show for a thousand years in Rome. Its underside, though, and along its thread – which was, by the way, as perfect a spiral as I'd ever seen – it was polished to a high gleam. The hole it had until just now filled was still a yard width of blackness. While men around me chattered and moaned away, and the Bishop raised his voice beside me in prayer, I gripped the edges of the hole in both hands and cautiously dipped my head inside. I shut my eyes and waited for them to grow used to the darkness. When I opened them, I saw the dull roughness, about ten feet below, of granite. Otherwise, I could see nothing at all.

'I'll need lamps and two men to carry them and give general assistance,' I said to Lucas.

He looked round. Macarius was an obvious choice. I'd have asked for him anyway. I didn't see how there could be anything actively nasty down there in a place that had been sealed for thousands of years. But he might have his uses in overcoming more passive difficulties. Who else, though? Martin was out of the question. Even if everyone could be sure the place had only one point of entry, we'd never be allowed together out of sight. But I wanted someone else who knew Greek.

As if he could read my thoughts, the Bishop stood forward. He swung his relic in its bag and swallowed.

'"Yea, though I walk through the valley of the shadow of death,"' he said in Greek, '"I will fear no evil: for thou art with me; thy rod and thy staff they comfort me." This holiest relic of Jesus Christ will keep us secure from all demons,' he added. 'And I am told that the medallion around My Lord's neck was blessed by His Holiness the Patriarch of Rome.' He paused, and then: 'I have the highest regard for His Holiness, of course. I have long prayed that he might see through the false learning of the Greeks that has blinded him to the Unpolluted Truth of—'

I interrupted him with thanks for his goodness and courage, and racked my brains for what I'd been told about the care of slaves in some mining venture I'd joined the previous year.

In all work involving deep tunnels, you see, air is the limiting problem. Men use up its goodness to nourish their bodies, and lamps sensibly diminish its volume. It is gradually replenished from above, but not fast enough to allow unlimited work. I didn't know how deep this place went. But I did know that even three men with lamps would need to move quickly. I knew Macarius was good for the job. The Bishop had the wiry look of a native from the middling classes. So long as we stayed together and kept our nerve – and so long, of course, as our luck was in – we could do our business and get out. I only hoped the place did contain something credible. Doubtless, Siroes would continue to be a harsh judge of progress. Even so, he'd boxed himself in to some extent by allowing that what we'd found did represent progress.

'As I've told you, my dear,' Priscus said to me while good walking shoes were laced to my feet, 'Martin is under conditional reprieve. You just take whatever time down there you think is needed. But this is always governed by what you call the test of reasonableness. If you're down there so long that I have reason to suppose you've found another way out, I shall not be happy.

'Other than that, Alaric dearest, I wish you the best of luck. If there are any spirits down there, I really do hope that relic is as holy as your blackbird friend believes it to be.'

With that, and a friendly slap on my back, Priscus stood aside to make room for the twelve-foot ladder that had now been produced. Further and further into the hole it slowly went. The men holding it sweated and trembled. One of them was obviously beseeching the Bishop not to risk himself down there. His Grace dismissed the warnings and stood forward to see how the ladder was doing. For a moment, I thought I might have misjudged the distance, and that we'd need to send for an even longer ladder, or lash two together. But it came to rest with about eighteen inches above the level of the hole.

'I'll go down first,' I said, pushing Macarius aside. Whatever might be down there, I told myself, let no one suppose Aelric of Kent was a coward. I stepped on to the ladder and scurried down.

61

The moment I was out of the sun, it turned cold. The sounds of men and animals and of the breeze that had just been all around me now came from a single point overhead. I stepped from the bottom rung of the ladder on to a floor that was, as I'd already seen, of levelled granite. I looked round. Macarius and the Bishop were still fussing beyond the entrance with their lamps. Now light was coming through the hole again without blockage, I could see a little around me. I was in a high, circular chamber several dozen feet across. It might originally have been a natural bubble in the rock. If so, it had been heavily remodelled. With its level floor and its curved walls that tapered upwards to the opening, it had the appearance of a small water cistern. It certainly had nothing about it that suggested a tomb. Other than the rubble that had fallen in from above, it was empty. There was no coffin or funeral goods. The walls looked much the same as the floor. They had no paintings or reliefs of the sort I'd read were to be found in the tombs of the Egyptian great. It might have been a cistern. The doorway, four feet or so wide and seven high, that led into complete blackness might have been an access point for water.

I was still down there alone and without light. But my eyes were now adjusted, and the entrance above me shone with an intense, if not very effectual, brightness. Keeping a careful watch on the floor in front of me, and testing each step as I went, I moved towards the doorway. It had no door that I could see, and another loud cough told me that it went off in some direction without blockage. The cistern possibility was reducing by the moment. This was too obviously a doorway.

Now I was standing close to it, I could see that the wall wasn't quite the same as the floor. It was painted all over with a kind of pitch. I ran my hands over the smooth surface. I could feel indentations that might have been consistent with reliefs that had, for some reason, been covered over. I turned my attention back to the doorway. But now Macarius and the Bishop were hurrying down the ladder, and faces looking in from above blocked the light.

'Is all well, My Lord Alaric?' Siroes called down in a voice that might have been satirical – though it was always hard to tell with him. As he set his hands around the edge of the opening, he managed to knock in some loose pebbles. The sound and echo of their fall was shockingly loud.

'I've just been eaten by fucking monsters,' I snarled back, 'and this is my ghost calling out from Hell. What else do you bleeding suppose?' Like the pebbles, my voice echoed loud in the chamber. No reply. Though perfect in Greek, Siroes hadn't shown much taste for badinage. The lamps now with me showed more of the chamber, but revealed nothing more than I'd seen already or supposed to be there. If there had been anything on the wall under that coat of pitch, it wasn't showing in the light from the lamps. Before the smell from the lamps could permeate the room, I breathed in slowly through my nose. Except for that smell of dried wood in the sun, the air about me was sweet though pretty still. I looked at the shaft of light now coming freely again down from the entrance. It was sharp and clear.

'Unless you can suggest anything else,' I said to Macarius, 'we go that way.' I pointed at the still complete blackness of the doorway. There was nowhere else to go.

He bowed silently and offered me the nicer of the two lamps he was holding.

'Jesus God!' the Bishop called softly. 'Is this not indeed the entrance to Hell?'

Too late to worry about that now, I thought. I took the lamp from Macarius and stepped forward into the doorway. I shivered a little from the deepening cold – and perhaps a little from fear of what lay beyond.

I found myself in a corridor that sloped both downward and to the left with moderate sharpness. It kept about the same dimensions as the doorway, but was finished more roughly than the chamber by which we'd entered. The walls had no pitch covering on them, and I could see the reflection of our lamps on the chisel marks that showed how, with what must have been immense effort, the corridor had been carved through the solid granite. And there was little doubt that this was an artificial work. Without knowing yet how far it went, or if it deviated from what I could see, I had the impression of a spiral leading down into the earth.

'We must be quick about this,' I said to the Bishop, who seemed inclined to hang back. I explained about the air.

He nodded. The relic bag was beginning to shake in the tightness of his grip. I put an arm round his shoulder and quoted from Scripture in my reassuring voice. He thanked me in a voice that still shook. But he quickened his pace.

My earlier jitters now behind me, evil spirits were the last thing on my mind as I walked carefully ahead. I'll not deny, though, I was worried. I was worried about how large this place was, about whether its layout became more complex the deeper we went into it, and – above all – about what, if anything, we'd find to take back and show to Siroes. But I could hear Macarius behind me with his usual firm step, and could hear his steady breathing. Except I'd keep a lookout for shafts or subsidence in the floor ahead of me, I didn't plan to show the smallest concern.

That was until we reached what may have been a complete circuit on our downward path. Here, the smooth corridor came to an end. In its place was what looked a natural fissure in the rock. On the left side, it had been cut back to about the width of two men. On the right, it had been left as jagged as it must have been when found. From here, a flight of steps led sharply down into the earth. They may not have been that level when first cut. Now, they were much worn. In places, they had been chipped by the carrying of heavy objects into little more than a very steep incline. We paused. The air was still sweet, our lamps still bright. There might have been the smallest hint of a breeze coming up at us. I peered uncertainly down. The steps seemed to deviate to the left in another spiral. Or perhaps the course moved about to take advantage of the natural shape of the fissure.

'We must press on,' I said to no one in particular. These were the first words any of us had uttered since leaving the upper chamber. Apart from the scraping of our shoes, it was the first sound anyone had made. My words had a flat, echoless quality. I didn't feel inclined to utter that many more of them.

'The Lord Siroes will expect nothing else,' Macarius said, the natural flatness of his voice emphasised by the surroundings.

He was right. Like it or not, we had to press on. If we came to a dead-end, we'd have to reconsider. But this was simply a matter of going down some steps that may already have been a quarter-mile from the entrance hole.

'This is a place of ungodliness,' the Bishop quavered. 'Can you not feel the evil miasma that reaches up to embrace us?'

It was turning colder, I'd grant, and I didn't at all like the shut-in feeling that increased with every step. But evil around us hadn't been something I'd yet noticed. Regardless of the words, though, what I could hear was the voice of a man looking for some reason to put his lamp down and refuse to go a step further.

'If you dissent from Chalcedon, Your Grace,' I said in an attempt at the conversational, 'I suppose direct relics of Christ are still more holy.' I looked at the bag and pursed my lips. 'It was, I think, the Patriarch Nestorius who asked: "How can Jesus Christ, being part man, not be partially a sinner as well, as man is by definition a sinner since the Fall?" Now, the answer that your side in the dispute gives is that His Humanity is wholly absorbed within His Divinity. This being so, the relic was possessed by an almost purely Divine Substance. For us, though they "undergo no confusion, no change, no division, no separation", the Substance of Christ also partakes of the Human.' I looked as far as the flickering light showed into the depths before us. If it weren't for that bloody trio waiting far up in the sunshine for what I'd find down there, I'd have turned back myself. But we had to go further. If that meant rehearsing the debates at and after the Council of Chalcedon, it was a price to be paid.

'That is, My Lord, a most just observation,' came the reply in a suddenly firmer voice.

I took a step forward and asked him to explain. I knew he wouldn't be able to resist.

'Let us begin with a statement from the First Council of Ephesus,' he said, taking a step to keep up with me, 'that I think is accepted equally by both sides of the most unfortunate dispute that has sundered the garment of Holy Mother Church.' He closed his eyes a moment to recall the exact wording, then quoted: '"The Word in an unspeakable, inconceivable manner united to Himself hypostatically Flesh enlivened by a Rational Soul, and so became Man."'

I nodded reverently and, bowing to keep my head from knocking against the uncut granite, took another few steps. He followed. I kept going. So did he in both senses.

'Now, My Lord,' he said, oblivious to where he was, 'the important question is the nature of this Union of God and Man. I do so regret the claim of the Greeks that both Natures remain distinct within the Single Personhood of Christ. This surely raises difficulties; in particular, it renders meaningless the title traditionally given to the Virgin of "God-Bearer". For if Christ has a Double Nature, She can be so described only so far as She gave birth to the Human Nature . . .' So he droned on and on and we continued down the steps. It was crude stuff. His Patriarch, Anastasius, could only have accepted this line of argument with endless reservations that brought him pretty close to the orthodox position of Chalcedon. Still, it was useful to hear what might be a fair sample of opinion outside Alexandria.

Of course, it kept us moving ever down those steps. And they did seem to go on and on – sometimes winding one way, now another; sometimes going down in a straight line. Once or twice, I slipped where the steps had been worn away, and my lamp nearly went out. More often, it was just a matter of keeping my head from knocking against the unsmoothed granite of the ceiling. At last, though, we stood again on level ground. I couldn't say how far down we were, or which way we were now pointed. I gave the job up as useless. It was impossible to estimate anything. The air continued good, the breeze now more noticeable. I forced myself not to speculate on another entrance. Those bastards still had Martin.

62

We were now in another corridor, much higher and wider than the first. Much greater care had been taken with hollowing out and shaping what may also have been a natural fault in the rock. So far as I could see, this followed a more or less straight course, though there was a continued downward slope that prevented us from seeing even as far ahead as the lamps threw their light. How far from the surface were we? I kept asking myself and asking again. How much deeper must we go? No point in asking, I told myself. It went as far as it went. I held my lamp and took a firm step forward.

As said, this was a higher and wider corridor. Its surfaces were more finely chiselled. If wondering how far it went was pointless, I couldn't help but wonder *how* this had been carved. Even assuming there had been some original pathway through the rock, this was granite. The work of hollowing and smoothing with such perfection of finish, and of carrying away the rubbish, must have taken whole armies of men, slaving down here for decades. In its own way, this was no less remarkable than the Pyramids. All else aside, *why* had this been done?

Again, I put the questions out of mind. I looked instead at the reliefs. This time, there was no doubt of them. They stretched along this corridor on both sides. Ugly, depressing things they were, too. They had nothing Egyptian about them. They were in a style more realistic than I'd seen from the Egyptians, though also less varied. Whatever race had produced them showed a partiality for violence and pain unusual by any standards. A recurring theme was the siege and capture of towns. Machines of great ingenuity would be employed to break down or under-mine defensive walls. Once through the walls, the attackers would go into a frenzy, sparing neither children nor women and the aged. They would kill by stabbing and dismembering and cutting to pieces as if in a slaughterhouse. Their male pris-oners they would take pleasure in hanging on low gallows, so that the feet touched the ground. Sometimes, they would pack straw round the feet of their victims, or wrap them entirely in straw, and then light a fire.

For a full quarter-mile the reliefs extended. When their authors tired of siege warfare, they turned to more individual atrocities: pots filled with burning liquid placed on the heads of tied victims; women strapped on to beds of nails and ravished with immense, heated phalluses; children thrown into vats of corrosive fluid. And every few yards, in couples or trios, embracing or delicately reaching out to touch finger to finger, you could see the insanely grinning perpetrators of these horrors. How old the reliefs were I couldn't say. They must have been thousands of years old. They might – if Lucas and his odd chronology were to be taken seri-ously – be tens of thousands. The granite from which they were carved was, of course, unweathered and immortal. But the paint that had once covered the whole in a coat of bright colour was long since faded. In the lamplight, it was barely more in places than a uniform brown. But every one of those mad, evil faces, I could easily see, had once been topped with a mass of golden hair.

Onward along that silent corridor we walked. I say these things went on and on. After a while, though, I stopped looking. After what I'd seen done to living flesh in Alexandria, you might think none of this could have much effect on me. But there is a differ-ence between what is done from some shadow of regard for the public good, and is an admitted deviation from the normal course of government, and what is gloatingly celebrated in what may be the best art of a race manifestly superior in the art of war to those attacked and conquered and eradicated for pleasure. Priscus himself might have learned something from all this. Priscus himself might even have been rattled by the immense iteration and reiteration of horrors.

I tried to start a debate with the Bishop about the orthodox claim that 'at no point was the difference between the Natures taken away from the Union, but rather the property of both Natures is preserved and comes together into a Single Person and a single Subsistent Being.' He made a faint effort, and the mere sound of our voices, as we went over words traded again and again on the surface, brought some cheer in that place of dry and ever colder silence.

We ran into trouble after perhaps half a mile of our twisting downward course. At first, it seemed we were reaching a dead-end. As we got close enough, though, for our lamps to make sense of the dim shapes outside the immediate pool of light, I could see that it was a door. Better described, it was one of those stone slabs you read about that drop from the ceiling and close off all access beyond. In Egypt – elsewhere in the Empire too in the days of the Old Faith – the rich would try endless elaborations of these things to keep their embalmed corpses and their grave goods safe. Fat lot of good it ever seems to have done: if not because of tomb raiders, why else are the antiquities markets so often glutted?

'We could go back and bring down men with tools,' the Bishop suggested.

I shook my head. I had no wish to turn back now. Besides, getting anyone else down here might be more trouble than it was worth. If there was any way through this door, it wasn't to be had by brute force. I leaned against the slab and pushed hard. I took the pressure off, then leaned again. There was no movement.

'There may be some hidden lever,' I said. There was any number of concealed openings in the Imperial Palace back in Constantinople. Three centuries of palace intrigue around emperors, sometimes driven mad by fear of being trapped, had left the place riddled with secret tunnels. Most had been forgotten on the death of the commissioning Emperor. Many led to the least likely places. I'd seen enough of these on my exploratory trips with Heraclius to know the ingenuity with which the rocking levers that opened them could be blended into the surroundings. As said, the decorative scheme here tended to the elaborate, and it was a matter of feeling round for a concealed depression.

Whatever we did next, there was no point in hurrying. By unspoken agreement, this was an opportunity for rest and reflection. We sat down on the floor. We chewed slowly and in silence on some bread and dried dates and drank some of the water the Bishop had been carrying on his back.

'My son,' he said, now looking for words of greater directness than he'd needed for theological dispute, 'for what little comfort it may bring, I will say that, if I had influence over any but the unarmed Sheep of Christ, I would never allow what is happening. As it is, I will, if required, excommunicate the renegade Egyptian and write to the Greek Patriarch in Alexandria about the shameful conduct of the Lord Priscus.'

I nodded. Flowery thanks would have been less convincing. So too would a pretended conversion to the Monophysite heresy. Martin had done good work with the man. We might yet have a way out of this mess. The Bishop prayed awhile in Egyptian, interpreting every line into Greek for my benefit. I tried to look solemn as I thought again how stingy Priscus had been in not having any wine packed for us.

'I am wondering, My Lord' – Macarius spoke for the first time since we'd left the surface – 'if these tunnels might not be an elaborate ruse to throw us off the true path. Might not this doorway be nothing more than a carving into the solid rock? I have heard of such in tombs.'

I continued chewing on the rough bread. I'd been thinking the same. If this were a diversion, it might mean retracing our steps all the way to the surface, and examining every inch along the way. There might be another concealed way from the entrance chamber. There might even be another entrance from the surface, and the function of the one through which we'd entered was to draw attention from this.

'No,' I said after a long silence. I got up and pointed. 'Those torch brackets have been used too often to suggest this is just a dead-end. Look at the soot marks on the ceiling. There must be centuries of deposits there.' I was about to mention the good air: it had to be coming from somewhere. But I found myself staring back along the way we'd come. I was at just the right angle to see. 'Look at the floor,' I cried eagerly. I pointed again, now downward. It was so plain, I could hardly under-stand why we'd not seen it as we came here. The floors nearest the walls were as rough as when first chiselled out of the rock. The central couple of feet, however, were worn smooth, and in places shiny, from the passing and repassing of many feet. This smooth smear on the granite came from as far along the corridor as we could see, but stopped short about six feet from where we were sitting.

'There's a hidden door in the wall!' Macarius hissed. There might be. Or there might have been some hidden entrance in the floor or the ceiling. One thing for certain was that people had come to and gone away from a certain point in that corridor, but then had come no further towards where we were sitting.

It was in the floor. Now that we were looking, the slab in the floor couldn't have been more obvious. Though of the same granite as everything else, the more finished texture of the stone would have shown its nature even without the tiny shadow made by the gap that ran about it. Running my hands over it, I could feel that this was the source of the draught that had kept the air pure around us. Less obvious was how to lift the thing. I must have fumbled my way over every square inch of wall space several yards either way along the corridor. I ran hands over the grosser or more theatrical tortures shown in the reliefs. I tapped on every carved protrusion from the background of burning cities. I found no hidden lever. I had little doubt there was one. If not on the walls, it would be on the ceiling or on the floor. It was a question of looking.

'See – it moves!' the Bishop suddenly cried, stepping back from one of the torch brackets. He'd pulled gently on the ring that was to hold the base of any torch. With a gentle rumble, the slab in the floor had moved upwards a fraction of an inch. This should have been the mostly likely suspect, and I couldn't understand how I'd not thought of it first.

'After so long,' Macarius said as he bent down to look at the slab, 'the mechanism may have perished. I suggest you pull gently. The moment there is a gap opened, I will push in this water flask to stop it from falling back.'

Good idea, I thought. I took a deep breath, then pulled firmly but slowly on the bracket.

With a sudden rush of air, the slab flew upward on powerful hinges, and flipped over on to its back. The crash was deafening. It echoed up and down the way we'd come as if a hundred other doors had smashed all at the same time on to the granite floor. If it hadn't been heard right back at the entrance, it would have been a surprise. As it was, I barely noticed at first how the rush of air had blown our lamps straight out.

'We must go back after all,' the Bishop said mournfully out of the blackness. 'We must go back for more light.'

I felt his hand reach out for me. I took it in the darkness and squeezed – as much to receive as to give reassurance. It felt suddenly colder without the light. I was much more aware of how loud our breathing was in the surrounding silence. Everything seemed suddenly so much more open, but also more oppressive. Until I wasn't able to see them, I hadn't realised how comforting those ghastly reliefs had become. It would be impossible to get lost on the way back. The single corridor led, with whatever twisting, to only one place. However far it might be, the way back was clear and open. Still, I had to fight with all my courage – and all my pride – against the urge to turn and bolt.

'Stand where you are and be silent!' Macarius hissed beside us.

I heard him go through his satchel. He cursed and muttered in Egyptian. I heard things drop on to the floor and then his rummaging among them. Then I heard the striking together of flint and steel, and saw the bright sparks. Four – perhaps five – times, the sparks jumped and went dark again. At last, I saw a comforting glow as the dried weeds caught fire. Another few moments, and he was pushing the horn protector into place on his own relit and now refilled lamp.

63

While Macarius refilled the other two, I pushed the lamp that was now lit down as far as I could reach. It flickered in the upward draught and nearly went out again. What it showed was another flight of steps. Though worn, these were of better workmanship than the first. How far they led I couldn't say. But, four feet wide, they led straight down. On either side of them now were walls of smoothly shaped and mortared stone. As if reading my thoughts, Macarius tugged at the displaced slab. It was enormously heavy. Even with my help, it couldn't be lifted back into place. Of course, we were all alone down here. No one would follow us in. Anyone who might follow us in had no interest in closing the stone over us. But we strained and shuffled and gasped for breath over that slab before we felt confident enough to give our full attention to this new flight of steps. As ever, I went first.

I counted a hundred and seventy-nine steps, and each one had a regular drop of perhaps ten inches. That made near enough another descent of a hundred and fifty feet. I was beginning to shake again with fear. It didn't matter that the air was as fresh as on the surface, or that granite was the least likely of any rock to collapse upon us. It reminded me of the journeys into the Underworld described by the poets of the Old Faith.

We were now in an immense cavern. Even holding up our lamps and straining to see into the gloom didn't give us more than a vague idea of its walls and ceiling. From what I could see, there had been a limited effort to reshape its features. The floor had been smoothed, and there were a few courses of stonework. Otherwise, it was much as nature had left it. Now we'd emerged from the narrowness of the steps, the draught was no longer perceptible. Its only evidence was the continued dry smell of nothing in particular. Had we now reached the level of the Nile? I wondered. If so, there had been no seepage of damp into this cavern. I stepped forward.

'A moment, please, My Lord,' Macarius said.

I stopped and waited while he got out one of the spare lamps, lit it and set it on the fourth step leading up. He was right. We'd need some reference point for getting back. But now, which way? Should we try to hug the walls and trace the limits of the cavern? Or should we strike out for its centre? I chose the latter. My lamp threw a pool of light that was reliable within a six-foot radius. Beyond that was gloom and then darkness. By looking back at the glow on the steps, we were able to navigate a straight path across the floor. This was far less regular in its finish than in the corridors. It was also more cluttered. There were pieces of smashed furniture and scraps of cloth that might once have been clothing.

Perhaps a hundred feet from the bottom of the stairs, we came across a stone block. Of shaped granite, it was about six feet long and three wide. Its top was about a yard above the floor, and had depressions carved into it that reminded me of a bed that the slaves haven't yet had time to pat into shape. Even without the ancient stains that showed dark on the darkness of the stone, it was plain what function the block had served. As the Bishop muttered more of his prayers in Egyptian, I stepped back. I felt something crunch and give underfoot. I bent down and picked up some strips of withered leather. Restraining thongs look the same in all times and places. I dropped them again and wiped my hands on my outer tunic.

'Why bring victims down all this way?' I asked. 'Those reliefs don't indicate any sense of shame about their tastes. Why bother with any secrecy at all?'

The Bishop folded his arms and pushed his head even further onto his chest as he continued praying. Macarius had gone off about twenty feet. He'd set his lamp on the floor and was making scraping sounds nearby. Good idea! I thought. I left the Bishop to his communion with God and joined Macarius in gathering up some of the broken furniture. We arranged it into a tight pile on top of the block. It was so dry that the merest touch from the flame of one of our lamps was enough to set it burning. The ancient wood made almost no sound as the flames consumed it. The slight and pale smoke was carried gently back towards the steps where the lamp still burned. For the first time, we had enough light to see properly round this cavern.

The roof was too high or too dark to be seen. But we could now see the continuation of the reliefs, carved into the stonework that ran in stretches round the walls. At regular spaces, we saw doorways set into the walls. Each of these was flanked by statues of alarming ugliness and ferocity. Our eyes were drawn, though, to what must have been the centre of the cavern. Here, a single statue rose about fifteen feet and glowered down at us from eyeholes cut deep into the stone. It had nothing about it of the smooth serenity the Greeks in their best days gave to their art. Nor had it the dull smoothness of the Egyptians. Instead, the thing radiated an arrogant nastiness that made me want to look away. 'It's your business to know who I am,' it seemed to sneer. 'Who you are is a matter for you alone.' Rising diagonally from the waist was a giant erection that much attention had polished to a gleam. The arms, pressed together, were outstretched slightly downward over a stone tub about the size of an Egyptian sarcophagus. A flight of steps led up to a stone platform about five feet below its shoulders. I swallowed, guessing what I'd find, and went over to climb the steps. I looked down into the tub.

'What do you see?' Macarius asked.

I stared awhile at the deep layer of white ash and the little scraps of bone that still here and there projected from it. I opened my mouth to speak, but found trouble in arranging words to describe the horrors I could see. Instead of my own words, I found myself quoting one of the Greek poems of Claudian:

> First Moloch, horrid King besmear'd with blood
> Of human sacrifice, and parents tears,
> Though for the noyse of Drums and Timbrels loud

Thir childrens cries unheard, that past through fire
To his grim Idol.

'God have mercy upon their souls!' the Bishop cried with a
fresh burst of prayer, now in Greek. It was his duty to believe that,
since they'd died without the Faith, these unfortunate children
were even now writhing in still hotter flames. But the Christian
mind, I've sometimes found – if not often – is gentler in these
things than the more consistent theologians would have it.

Still on the platform, I looked round. It wasn't hard to imagine
this cavern once as a kind of pandemonium. Then, the altar flames
would have burned night and day, and the air would have been
filled with stinking smoke and the shrill cries of the dying. If the
reliefs lining the walls here and above were accurate, there would
also have been music and laughter too, and drug-driven orgies. I
could easily imagine how the floors in that approach corridor had
been worn by the shuffling steps of thousands as they'd queued
there – learning from the reliefs what they could expect when it
was their turn to be dragged screaming down the steps into the
cavern. If I still thought no better of the Egyptians as a race, I
could now see that Menes had done the world a favour by taking
Soteropolis and shutting this place down.

That had all been thousands and thousands of years ago. Now,
the smoke was long since dispersed and the screams fallen silent.
The altar fires were cold and the instruments of torture and death
perished by age. Whatever draught came through had anciently
cleansed this place.

The fire Macarius had lit was dying now, and he was having to
gather fresh wood. I strained harder to see what might lie outside
the contracting pool of light. I focused on the far side of the
cavern. I could see nothing reliably. But perhaps a hundred yards
away, there was a faint glint as if of something metallic. It was too
far – even with a replenished fire – for me to see what it was.

'We must go this way,' I said, pointing. I climbed down, and,
lamp in one hand, burning spar in the other, I hurried across
the floor. I stopped after a few dozen paces. Even with the lamp

alone, I'd not have missed it. But the good light I now had with me showed at once the chasm that ran across the cavern, dividing where we were from where I wanted to be. It could only have been a natural feature, though it might well have been smoothed and tidied in a few places. At the narrowest point, it may have been thirty feet across. About ten yards to my right, there was a bridge of rope and wooden planks.

'After so long, My Lord,' Macarius said, 'I wouldn't trust this.'

I nodded. The three of us stood together just by the bridge. Thick ropes were tied to high bollards carved directly from the granite of the cavern. It looked solid enough. But he was right. This had been here for millennia. I looked round for something solid to throw. The first thing I saw was a skull, grinning though dark from scorching. There was nothing else suitable that I could see, so I reached down and picked it up. I tossed it lightly so that it fell on to the bridge about six feet from the edge. With a soft crack, the plank where it landed gave way and fell, taking the skull with it, into the depths. I listened and listened, but heard no impact of the fall. I took up a fairly substantial piece of broken wood and threw that into the middle point of the chasm. Again, I listened. Again, I heard nothing. The makeshift torch had burned down three-quarters, but was still bright. I held it over my head and looked straight forward. Still, I could see the glint of something on the far side. Still, I could see nothing that made sense.

'We'll find nothing here,' I eventually said. I strained for a final look across the chasm, then turned with reluctance and led the way across the floor towards those doorways into the wall.

They were tombs – that much was certain. And this made some sense of the torture entertainments so far underground. Even the dead of this perverted race were to be comforted by the agony of others. Each tomb had originally been sealed with courses of mortared stone. All had been broken into and carefully looted, which explained the broken furniture scattered about in the main cavern. The normal arrangement within each ten-foot square was a stone bench for the corpse. A few of these were still in place. Not embalmed in the Egyptian manner, they had been set there and allowed to shrivel naturally in the dry air. They'd dried out to the colour and general appearance of old leather. A few scraps of yellow hair still adhered to the scalps. Except they were much shorter, they might have been people of my own race. Whatever gold and jewellery had been placed beside them was long since gone. But, arranged into circlets closed with bronze rings, there were still a few lengths of that flexible glass sheathing in place around necks and ankles. Because worthless, these had been left in place.

'So Lucas was right in something,' I muttered. 'It is jewellery after all.' But the corpses of the great hadn't been the only residents here. Chained together by collars, each a few feet apart, there were other bodies. The more intact tombs showed how the chained ones had been unable to reach the main bench. Their collars were fixed to the wall at a height that allowed only standing. They had been closed in with each lord and left for hunger and thirst or despair to carry them into the greater blackness of death. Most had come apart in the ages following the burial, and, headless, they were fallen into common heaps of desiccated flesh. A few still held together, and gave some idea of final agony.

'God have mercy on them. God have mercy,' the Bishop was muttering as he followed me from tomb to tomb. It was all utterly depressing. Not the least of it was the rising worry that there was nothing we'd found so far that seemed likely to keep Siroes happy. I went back out into the main cavern and sat down for another bite of the rough bread. While Macarius had gone ahead into another tomb, I'd taken a chance and slipped into my clothing a bronze knife no one had bothered stealing. This at least might come in useful. Something portable, with arguably magical powers, would have been really useful. I sat, staring into the lamp – which would soon need another refill – and reflecting again on the lack of wine in our supplies. If Martin himself had been in charge of the packing, more thought wouldn't have gone into that deprivation.

'If you please, My Lord, come in here.'

I looked up. Macarius was calling from the last of the tombs before the end of the built wall. He stood just behind one of the guardian statues. Fangs bared in the fishlike head, it seemed to laugh at me.

'Do come over,' he repeated, a tone of urgency in his voice.

I pulled myself up and stretched tired arms and legs. Perhaps he'd found a relatively unlooted tomb. A few ancient trinkets might inspire me to some lie back on the surface.

But this one too had been looted. Indeed, it had been cleared of everything originally placed there. I looked wearily at the desk made from reused planks and at the chair, salvaged and repaired. There were a few sheets of papyrus on the desk, together with a lamp and some metal pens. I followed the pointed finger to the things stacked on the stone slab.

'What the fuck is this doing here?' I whispered, looking at the wooden crate. It was three feet high and about the same square. Painted neatly on the side facing me were the Greek words *Homeric Apocrypha Box Twenty*.

64

'How the buggery did it get down here?' I asked again, now louder. I rubbed my eyes just in case I was seeing things and leaned against the far wall. Ever since leaving the sunlight, we'd been in a world that seemed untouched since the dawn of our own time. Here at last was something I could recognise. If only I could also understand it. Beside it on the stone bench was a small book rack stuffed with papyrus rolls. It was something else I could recognise. It might also bring understanding.

'What's that?' I said to Macarius, nodding at the glass bottle in his hand.

'It seems to be lamp oil, My Lord,' he said. 'It would be useful if it were. Otherwise, we may have only enough for one lamp on our journey back to the surface.'

The Bishop gasped at these words and, in the manner of all the natives, squatted on the floor. There was nothing to fear, I assured him. I told him to remember that, so long as the lamp on the steps was still alight, we could feel our way back to the surface. But I watched with inward prayer as Macarius sniffed the contents and rubbed some between his fingers. He poured a small amount into the ancient lamp on the desk and set a flame to it. It may have had some other use when bottled. Now, it made a really superb lighting oil. It gave off an intense and bluish flame that consumed almost no wick. In this light, I took up one of the papyrus sheets that had been left on the desk. It went something as follows:

It is with reluctance, though also with the assurance that I do rightly, that I now suspend work on the project that has been the support of my final years. The degraded remnants of a once mighty race who

now rest in these halls were ignorant of writing and skilled only in
terror. But they carried with them images and things that allowed me
to reflect and at length to dread. Call it magic – call it by some other
name that is not similar to wisdom. But there are certain forces that I
do not think it proper for mortals to understand.

It once pained me how little appreciation my work received even
among those whose opinion I valued. I am now glad to be regarded
as a lunatic. If I were to publish my results, they would set a path –
however tentative – that led surely to the displeasure of the One God
who stands above those worshipped by men.

If I were less vain – or if I had no faith whatever in the goodness
and wisdom of my fellow beings – I might destroy all I have written,
rather than hide it away. But hide it away I will. I might hope that
these words will never be read. I can only pray that if they ever are
read, my name shall not become for ever accursed.

I write in the eightieth year of my age, and in the fortieth year since
being made Chief Librarian to His Majesty.

Eratosthenes of Cyrene

What a very queer letter! I thought. I passed it to Macarius, who
read it with his usual impassivity. I got up and went to the book
rack. I pulled out the largest of the book sheaths. The tag on it gave
the title as *On the Fundamental Unity of Matter and Motion.* I took
it out and scanned the first section. It was in a highly compressed
style, and used words that may have been compounded specially
for the use in hand. Generally speaking the work owed something
to the physics of Epicurus, and something to the mathematics of
the Platonic school. They came together in a synthesis that I'd
often urged on Martin as the path to knowledge. It might, indeed,
still make me a boatload of money if I'd got my Nile predictions
right – and, of course, if I lived to see this. Eratosthenes was reasoning in the best Greek manner. He seemed, however, to be moving
from obvious premises to outrageous conclusions. It was something that might make sense if I were to give it more time. As it
was, the ratios of what seemed arbitrary units to each other struck
me as madder than anything Hermogenes had mentioned back

in Alexandria. Imagine the Hypostatic Union with a bit of maths thrown in, and that was how all this struck me on first inspection.

But I was wasting time. I rolled up the book and put it back in its sheath and then replaced it on the rack.

'What makes you suppose,' I asked of Macarius, 'that this box contains the things we came to collect?' I pointed at the crate. Though old, it was still solid, and it was nailed securely shut. It was too heavy for me to lift by myself. If we looked about, we might find something that could be used to force it open. I thought of the knife I'd picked up, but chose to keep that to myself.

'It doesn't contain anything that we were sent to bring back,' Macarius said.

I thought of trying for a hollow laugh, but changed my mind.

'We already have what we came to find,' he said.

What that might be I couldn't guess. Nor did I feel inclined to try. I rapped hard on the crate and then struck my knee against it. There were some firm wooden spars outside we could use.

But Macarius saw what I was thinking and shook his head. 'We have what we came for,' he repeated. 'We carry back nothing tangible.'

There were other tombs that we still hadn't entered. From back in the cavern, I looked at the dark gaps knocked into the stone-work and sighed. Except for the one Eratosthenes had used for his office, they were much of a muchness. There was no point looking in them. I couldn't begin to tell how long I'd been down here. But I could feel a growing weariness. If we really had found what we'd come to find, it wasn't possible to justify staying longer. It was time to go.

From the bottom of the steps, I looked back towards the make-shift office. I couldn't see it, though I knew where it must be. Here, the great Eratosthenes had sat day after day, surrounded by death that must have been as ancient to him as it was to us. Wherever his thoughts had led him marked him out as an equal of the great Epicurus. That – or he'd become the raving lunatic everyone then and since had taken him for.

We left the lamp still burning low on the steps. Since Macarius made it plain there would be another visit here, there was no point in cluttering ourselves. With that mineral oil left behind by Eratosthenes, the reliefs in the corridor showed brighter than before, and gave up still more of their carefully depicted horrors. But I tried not to look. I thought instead of the surface. Whatever awaited me there, this wasn't a place for lingering.

Getting back to the surface was easy in that we knew where we were going, and there was no element of tension. It was also harder in that we were now going steadily uphill. I hadn't fully noticed on the way down how steep the incline was. Now, we were tired, and the going was too hard to complete without longish rests.

'My Lord,' Macarius whispered in Latin as we reached the entrance chamber, 'I suggest that your interests might best be served by setting your weapon down here.'

I stared at him. He continued staring back. I sniffed and took out the knife from under my tunic. For all it had given me some feeling of control, I saw no value in arguing. I put it down and kicked it against one of the walls.

It was dark in that entrance chamber, though noticeably warmer. With a shock of horror, I wondered at first if the granite covering had been screwed shut on us. But the reason we were in darkness, I soon realised, was because it was dark outside.

'Well, hello!' Priscus called down when I'd shouted for the second time. I saw him outlined against the opening by a torch that someone held behind him. 'We were beginning to worry about you. I think some of the wogs were coming to the conclusion that you'd been eaten alive by demons. For myself, I was getting prepared to suggest a search party for the morning. Did you find anything useful down there?'

'Yes,' I lied, waiting for the ladder to come down. 'If the Lord Siroes isn't happy with this, he'll find plenty more to amuse him if he goes down himself.' And with any luck, I thought, the Bishop might prevail on the wogs to seal them all in together.

65

'I think the young barbarian has done us proud,' Siroes said.

We were back in our dining tent. It was a late meal, and the food was as insipid as ever. And I felt a slight annoyance that a bloody Persian was calling me a barbarian. But I was too tired and hungry to care much about either defect. Buckets of cool water had got the dirt off my body. My clothes could dry overnight in the desert wind. For the moment, I sat wrapped in a blanket, finishing a dinner of dates and gritty bread.

'It is,' he went on, 'just as the prophecy led me to suppose. I therefore believe, with more than reasonable assurance, that we in this tent constitute the supreme power in the world.'

'Well, I might agree if he'd at least brought back a piss pot,' Priscus muttered. He looked sourly at the notes Lucas had taken of my narrative. They filled several sheets of papyrus in a hand that showed what a clerk the world had lost when its owner chose to be Pharaoh.

'I don't think, my dear Priscus,' Siroes broke in with a sneer, 'we need concern ourselves with receptacles of human piss. I have told you repeatedly that what I came here to find had no connection with your Jewish Carpenter. I will also tell Lucas that the object we still need to recover serves none of the purposes that your late mutual friend Leontius appears to have conceived for it.

'The object's location and its correct use, I will say, are matters known only to me. My information so far has been absolutely correct. I have no doubt this will continue to be so. Let it be enough for the moment that I have no interest in holy relics. Nor, let me say for the avoidance of doubt, do I care for the ravings of some long dead philosopher. In this, as in so many other concerns, the Greeks have nothing to offer. The object I seek gives access to a power that comes from the ability to inflict death without hope of escape or vengeance.'

'I suppose you could frighten someone to death with it – assuming you ever do lay hands on it,' said Priscus with yet another of his mirthless smiles. He stroked the moulting fur of his cat, then wiped his hand on a napkin. 'Of course, we already have one dead wog. Show a few of those statues Alaric describes, and I've no doubt we could improve on that.'

There was a movement of the tent flaps and Macarius entered the room. It was a hot night, and my clothes had dried faster than expected. He laid them out on an empty chair. He looked briefly at me, and then at the heap of notes. I ignored him. Priscus stopped him as he was about to leave.

'Do have more water sent in,' he sighed. 'And do have the bowl filled to the brim this time. It's been a fucking hot day waiting out there by that opening, you know. A bit of haste on your young friend's part wouldn't have been unwelcome.'

Macarius bowed and went silently out.

Priscus tugged slyly on one of the cat's whiskers. He looked up again. With a faint snort, he pushed the notes across the table in my direction. 'I've heard more profitable narratives in church,' he said.

'I find your lack of faith disturbing,' Siroes replied. 'Sitting round this table, we have a king of Egypt, which is or could be the richest country in the world. We have the cousin and grandson of a great king of Persia. And we have the descendant of at least one Roman emperor. Believe me that we have the means to make ourselves masters in our own right of half the world. And believe me that we shall soon have the means to bring the other half very speedily under our control. It is a matter of one repaired bridge to the unvisited side of that cavern, and of a little willingness to work thereafter as one.'

'There is something over on the other side,' I broke in with a show of eagerness. 'I just couldn't see it in the light we had.' I hadn't for a moment been taken in by all that guff about the 'perfect equality of peoples'. It didn't surprise me now if Siroes had dropped it like a hot brick. But it was at least slighting that his talk of dignitaries had left no room for Legates Extraordinary – still less for England. I'd been well and truly demoted from His Magnificence to barbarian youth. 'We explored perhaps only a fraction of the whole complex,' I added, keeping my face heroically straight. 'Moreover, even if they weren't on your list of things to find, the writings of Eratosthenes were highly suggestive of what might be achieved by following his own lead.'

'So you tell us, dear boy,' Priscus said with another of his smiles. 'So you said. We don't disbelieve a word of your story of the marvels deep underground. Indeed, while you were cleaning up, we – or at least Siroes – decided we were so intrigued that nothing would keep us from making our own inspection first thing tomorrow morning. Because of the great love we bear each other, and as a sign of our complete unity of will, we have decided to go down there together, drawing lots to see who should go first through that hole. We must rely on the popularity Lucas has among his own people that all three of us – plus you, of course – are not sealed in the moment we are at the foot of the ladder.'

The tent flaps opened again and the usual serving man came in with a pitcher of water. While Priscus watched intently, he poured a cup for himself and drank. We waited. Priscus nodded and the man filled the bowl up past the two-thirds mark. I dipped my own cup into the bowl. As I was about to set it to my lips, the tent flaps opened yet again. Macarius entered, now with a jug of wine. Things were looking up. I set my cup on the table and waited. Macarius turned and rasped an order. Through the still open tent flaps Martin now was pushed in among us. His fetters had been taken off, and he'd been allowed a wash – though still not a shave. His bandage had been replaced with something smaller and cleaner.

'Ah, little Martin!' Priscus cried, rising and making an ironic bow. 'You come at a most opportune moment. You will have heard already from His Grace of Letopolis that young Alaric is alive and well. You will surely wish to volunteer for another trip

465

underground with us. I hope Alaric's description of the narrow steps is accurate in its dimensions. It would never do to have you trapped there by your own belly.'

'It is as you wish, sir,' Martin said in a flat voice. He looked at me and swallowed.

I could see how baggy his face had become under the ginger bristles. Well past any desperation, his eyes were dead. I smiled weakly at him. Things might easily be worse. He still had his right ear.

'So we are agreed?' Siroes asked. 'We are agreed on a permanent alliance of our three crowns – an alliance to take what is ours by right, and to take what ought to be ours by means of the force prophesied to us?'

'Let it be as you suggest, my dear Brother in Purple,' said Lucas.

I'd been glancing at his face while Priscus and Siroes were talking. He hadn't yet spoken much. But he was looking at his notes with a mixture of awe and cunning. He was visibly thinking how not to be other than last to go down that hole – and how long before its covering slab might safely be lifted again.

'We may be agreed, my dear fellow,' Priscus said wearily. 'But I'd be grateful for some explanation of how we are to translate possession of this object that so excites you into shared dominion over all the nations. I can't say it wouldn't please me to watch Heraclius devoured by hyenas in the Circus in Constantinople. But the prospect won't excite me until I've been given some indication of the means.'

Siroes smiled. 'I understand that you retain command of all the military forces in and around Alexandria,' he said.

Priscus nodded. If Nicetas really had recovered from his fright, that wouldn't be technically correct. Even so, the men might follow Priscus rather than him. Setting them to an easy massacre, with rape and plunder for dessert, is the quickest way to a soldier's heart.

'Good,' Siroes continued. 'Then we will march on Alexandria just as soon as our business here is finished. From there, we will send letters to Heraclius and to Chosroes. We will invite both to come in person to Daras on what is still more or less the border between our two empires. There, I will recite the words that only I know, thereby combining what I have with what we shall jointly acquire tomorrow into a demonstration of the power that we have. I do not expect any difficulty beyond that. We shall take power by acclamation. If there is any delay, we shall simply have to see one or both capitals go up in a fire that cannot be quenched.'

'Before we both declare ourselves traitors,' Priscus replied, 'and that might well bring on the truce Heraclius has been begging for these past two years, I think it would be best if we could all be sure that the power you promise really is what you believe it to be. I might add that, if this is a power that still requires *some* armed support, it might not be what you would have *us* believe. I suggest a prior demonstration for our own benefit. Whatever you are planning for Daras might be tried first in Alexandria. Nicetas can stand in perfectly well for Heraclius in this as in all other respects.'

Siroes laughed bleakly. 'Then let it be so, Priscus,' he said. 'I did suppose His Majesty the Pharaoh would choose to make his capital in Alexandria, and that this might be taken with conventional force. But if you wish to see Nicetas devoured from within, let fire and pestilence be spread also through the streets of that great and famous city.'

If Priscus still didn't look convinced, there seemed no point in his continuing the interrogation. He shrugged and pointed at the wine. Lucas sat nearest the jug. He pulled a face and stared back. But there were none of his people in the tent to witness any humiliation. Priscus pointed again, then went back to stroking his cat. Putting on what he may have thought an hospitable look, Lucas got up and filled four cups. Siroes took out his dice and Priscus cast them. We took the cups allotted, and then exchanged them one last time at random.

'Come, dear friends,' Priscus called with a semblance of cheer, 'let us drink to Success in Unity.'

Two firm voices, and one with a mutter, repeated the toast. We raised our cups. I drank.

I looked up in the sudden silence. Still full to the brim, three other cups had been set down again on the table. I looked at Priscus, who was now smiling expectantly.

'Oh, Jesus!' I cried. 'I blame myself for this. I should have remembered what a fucking snake you were.' I clutched at my throat and rolled my eyes.

'You were right, Priscus,' Lucas cried exultantly. 'The barbarian drank as greedily as if he'd been a sick slave.' He turned to me. 'You can now look forward to an eternity in Hell for your impertinence to the Chosen One of Isis. You can see there what the demons think of your "State of Nature" and your "Perfect Freedom".' He took up his water cup and refilled it. 'Did I not once tell you,' he asked, 'that I am now a sworn stranger to wine? Did that fact slip your drunkard mind?' He spat in my direction and laughed. 'No witch will save you now,' he gloated. 'You will die choking in pain before our eyes. The very night beasts of the desert will spurn your tainted barbarian flesh.' He drank again and laughed triumphantly.

'Do believe me, Alaric,' Priscus said, now friendly, 'that this was a difficult task. I did argue your case. But I was outvoted. And you will agree that your usefulness as finder of whatever this object may be is now at an end. Siroes is assured we can do the rest together.

'Gentlemen,' he said, now raising his voice again, 'I give you the toast a second time: Success in Unity!'

I fell back and coughed hard. Siroes raised his water cup in another ironic toast and drained it.

'Oh, Aelric! Aelric!' Martin sobbed as he threw himself at me. 'This is all my doing. You should have left me to die at the Church of the Apostles.' He snatched the cup from my hands and drained it to the bitter dregs. He embraced me and slobbered a kiss on my cheek. My blanket fell loose and my nipple stiffened in the slight chill that I now felt around me. 'O God,' he cried in a loud voice, 'let me burn in Hell for my sins. But show mercy on this blessed if foolish barbarian child.' He dropped the cup and clutched at himself. 'I feel death already clawing at my vitals,' he called, now speaking still louder. 'Let the agonies of death be just the prelude to my deserved sufferings in Hell. O God in Thy Mercy, let—'

'Oh, do shut up, Martin!' Priscus said wearily. 'Whatever happens when you're out of it, you really should remember your position in this world, and only speak when spoken to.'

I kicked Martin hard on the shin and pulled a face. That shut him up. I resisted the urge to laugh at the expression on his face. I rearranged my blanket and sat forward again.

'Now, gentlemen,' Priscus said to the whole company, 'because I'm in talkative mood, I'll tell you something not many people know.' He took out one of the black pills he reserved for moments that he was already relishing. 'Tittymilk of Hera is the finest weapon in the poisoner's arsenal. I cannot recall how useful I've found it these past forty years for removing those inconvenient souls who cannot be got at by other means. However – and Alaric should know this – it is completely useless in wine. Never mind the taste, you'd need to be pissy drunk not to notice the smell.

'In water, on the other hand, it has neither smell nor taste.' He put down his own still full water cup and put the black pill on to his yellowish tongue. He washed it down with a long single gulp of his wine. He looked around, bright anticipatory pleasure on his face.

Siroes opened his mouth, his face gone suddenly grey. He looked at his empty cup. Lucas simply looked stupid.

66

'Because I'm still in talkative mood,' Priscus continued with a complacent look round the table, 'I'll tell you what you can expect. In the dose I've just administered, you should already be feeling a paralysis of the speech organs and of the limbs. This should last some while, the stiffness growing progressively more uncomfortable. You should feel the approach of death in some convulsions – convulsions that will be exquisitely painful and, from my point of view, conveniently silent.

'Do have some more of this, Alaric, my dear boy,' he said, leaning forward with the wine jug. 'I'll not grudge a taste to Martin. But it really is too delicious to pass up.'

I drank again and it set my teeth on edge. Martin was still retching and clutching at his stomach. I kicked him again, and followed this with a gentle slap to the unbandaged side of his face. Siroes and Lucas, now speechless, were beginning to tremble and to sweat heavily. Priscus smiled and stretched his arms. He sat back in his chair. He looked round for his cat. It was quietly shitting over in a corner of the tent.

'I must thank you, Alaric,' he said, 'for playing along so well. Do tell me, though, how it was you managed to guess my intentions.'

'I've never known you to trust anyone,' I said. 'I really couldn't imagine you'd play along with these two a moment longer than you needed. It was when you had the water bowl filled right up that I guessed you'd been at work on the brim.'

'Clever lad!' he said appreciatively. 'If I ever need to poison you, I see I'll not be able to pull that one again. But how did you know the wine wasn't poisoned? Three bodies, after all, might be just as useful to me as two.'

I smiled. The truth was that I'd taken a risk. If the wine had been poisoned and I'd refused it, death would have been at best delayed. Playing along, on the other hand, might keep me alive. And Priscus might easily still have some use for me in arranging the getaway. I changed the subject.

'It took me far too long to realise the truth,' I said. 'Don't you think it would have saved a lot of time and effort if you'd told me what you were about?'

Priscus smiled. He leaned across the table and pressed his fingers together. 'Why not tell me, my dear, what it is that I was about?' he asked. He looked at his two victims. His smile broadened.

'I knew that last evening in Alexandria that you were trying to set me up,' I said. 'I didn't yet know why. I knew you were up to something with Lucas, and I assumed it was treason – though I couldn't work out why – even if you were plainly after the piss pot – you'd chosen a duffer like him for accomplice. My only surprise, though, when I saw you again in that scummy town was at your speed in getting up the Nile. I'd already realised, listening to Siroes and Lucas, that you hadn't turned traitor.'

Priscus grinned and waved his cup at me.

I continued: 'I supposed you'd some notice of what Siroes was up to and you came here to stop it. That's why you really had Nicetas combing the Red Sea ports. A few hundred Persians in Jedda could be left even to Nicetas. Siroes, I could see, was another matter.'

'My dear young fellow!' Priscus said with another look at his two victims. 'The Battle of Caesarea wasn't a complete disaster. Heraclius did his best. Even so, we managed to capture one of the senior staff officers. He gave me some very useful information that supplemented our intelligence reports. I was able to learn that Siroes had been sent to Egypt on a mission to get something important, and that he would be able to claim the assistance of a light man from the West. I really couldn't have you blundering into his clutches.'

With a gasp, Siroes moved his right hand in the direction of his sword. The effort was too much, and he fell heavily forward on to

471

the table. Priscus had him back in position directly. He checked the pulse and smiled. He kissed him on the forehead and sat down again.

'I did think at first of going to Heraclius with a treason accusation,' he continued. 'That would have killed two birds with one stone. It would have got you away from Siroes – and removed what I must regard as a general irritant. But the man has too much faith in you for accusations to mean much with the evidence I had. So I decided to come out here myself. You already know I'd been in Alexandria ten days before I rolled up at the Palace. I'd already made contact with the Intelligence Bureau and got a fair bit about the Brotherhood. I made up the piss pot story, and watched it go round Alexandria like fire in a corn field.'

'How did you kill Leontius?' I asked.

'I didn't,' he said. 'I guessed Lucas would want him dead for what he did with the temple subsidy, but was short of time. And I too wanted him dead. His dealings with Siroes were far less open to prediction and control than I could manage through Lucas. Yes, I wanted only Lucas to be at the centre of the web connecting the Brotherhood and landowners and, at whatever remove, the Persians. I wanted Leontius out of the way, but didn't put him there myself. The police did the job for me. They aren't ever good for much, but they can usually manage a moderately inventive murder. They did question him first, but got nothing useful. If I'd thought there was anything to learn, I'd have made sure to be there myself.' He followed my glance at the twisting body of Lucas.

'Oh,' he said carelessly, 'I can't be bothered with the details, but I had already made contact with him through a double agent in the Intelligence Bureau. I called him by his real name at first – that mouthful he took on for the wog trash was never worth learning. Lucas suits him better than Gregory ever did. And it's too late to insist on proper names, especially for such a low sort as this. He fancied himself a king. His breath alone ruled him out for that.' He got up and leaned close over Lucas. 'I would have killed you anyway,' he said, enunciating carefully. 'But do regard this, at least in part, as your punishment for violating the mummy of Alexander. That wasn't on the agenda. Yes, for that alone, the punishment is just.'

'So, you arranged that pantomime in the Egyptian quarter?' I asked, trying not to look at the dying man. 'That was your way of getting me involved?'

The tent flaps opened at this point. I thought of reaching for the sword that was now useless to Siroes. But it was Macarius. He looked at the two victims, and went to stand beside Priscus.

'I got Macarius to arrange that,' Priscus said. 'Fuck knows what went wrong there. You were supposed to be sent to the Pyramids, not this burning waste where you can't get an army from the Nile without being seen a day in advance. But the slut seems to have got carried away. No harm done, though. It fitted in rather well with the details of what Siroes had in mind, and with the accidental discovery of that stuff about Christ. You must know for yourself that a well-planned conspiracy often gets additional and unplanned lubrication. Call it the Mandate of Heaven – not, of course, that you'd call it anything of the sort. But we don't need to argue over your religious inclinations, or lack of them.'

'How did you know I'd go straight south after looking at those documents you left with Leontius?' I asked.

Priscus smiled and shook his head. 'Because I can read you like a book. Macarius had already told me about your spying mission. Leaving all that evidence of your financial corruption was as good as an instruction from Heraclius. I'd already put Lucas in place to lift you in Bolbitine. The idea was that we'd get you up here before Siroes arrived. As it is, I got you here just in time – and I had to treat poor little Martin with a roughness I'd never otherwise have found necessary.' He smiled again and looked at Martin. 'Do forgive me,' he said with a stab at the apologetic. 'You'll get used to the loss in time. Otherwise, I can have you fitted for a nice red wig. And it was all for the higher good of the Empire. If I hadn't been here, who can say what trouble Siroes might have made for us in Egypt and in Syria? As it is, things have worked out rather nicely. Chosroes has lost one of his most able men. The Egyptian

Brotherhood is fucked.' He looked at me again. 'You even get your land reform.

'Let's face it – all's well that ends well. You came up here to get dear Martin back. Uncle Priscus followed on to keep you from harm, and, of course, to foil a dastardly plot. We might tweak the story a little to have you in on foiling the plot. But there's plenty of time for agreeing the details. I think Heraclius will now be inclined to forget any shifting of blame for that little local difficulty in Caesarea.

'Yes, all's well that ends well.'

With a soft thud, Lucas fell to the carpeted floor. Priscus got up and stood over him as the final convulsions took hold. Eyes bulging, his lips twisted back on themselves in a silent scream, Lucas jerked and twisted like a slave under the branding iron. I looked down at him.

'He is still conscious,' Priscus assured me. 'Have you any last words for the Great Pharaoh?'

I shook my head. I'd sooner have continued with questioning Priscus. I had nothing to say to his victims. As I continued staring down at Lucas, his tongue forced itself out. It swelled and swelled, forcing his mouth open as wide as the jaws would stretch. It blackened in the lamplight. I thought it would burst. But it swelled further until both throat and nasal passage were blocked. The ragged breaths became more frantic, then stopped. Still the wild threshing continued, his face ever more contorted. As if from some inner fermentation, his body was now swelling. I heard a gentle ripping and smelled the eruption of shit. I saw a dark stain spreading over the front of his linen tunic. Then – suddenly – it all stopped. Hands now clamped over his face as in some closing gesture of depair, Lucas lay dead.

'The punishment was just,' Priscus softly repeated. He turned to look at Siroes, who still hadn't entered the stage of convulsions.

He looked back at us, rage and hatred blazing from his eyes. I looked away.

'What is your getaway plan?' I asked. Unpopular as Lucas had been for his theological views, I couldn't imagine that his people would be terribly pleased if any of them now chose to walk into the tent.

'Time enough for that, dear fellow,' said Priscus with a casual wave. 'Do be a love and put that eggy tart down,' he said to Martin. 'I saw Lucas fussing round them earlier,' he explained. 'I don't know about you, but I can almost smell the arsenic.'

Martin dropped the thing with a terrified grunt and went back to cowering by the tent flap.

Priscus went over to Siroes and looked closely at him. He reached for the bracelet on his left wrist and unscrewed the tip from one of its ends. He pulled out a two-foot length of fine cord. 'Though somewhat distant,' he said, 'we are cousins. And – as I hope you'll both agree – blood does have its duties.' He stood behind Siroes, arranging the cord around his neck. He bent forward and kissed him on the cheek.

'Goodbye, old friend,' he whispered. 'Be assured that if I ever lay hands on Chosroes, I'll get even for you over the smashing up of your family.' When the work was done, he sat heavily down and reached for his drug satchel.

I listened for any sign of disturbance outside. There was a distant sound from the diggers of something churchy. Otherwise, it was quiet. We might have finished another of our dinners and been getting ready to retire to our sleeping tents.

'We do need to be away from here,' I said again.

Snot and tears running down his face, Priscus smiled blearily back at me. 'I've told you, dear boy – it's all in hand.' He looked at Macarius. 'Have you given the signal?' he asked.

Macarius bowed.

Priscus grunted and pulled himself to his feet. He went back over to the body of Siroes and pulled at the clothing. With skilled hands, he felt over every inch of the three layers of cloth. He grunted and reached for a knife. He slit open one of the seams and pulled out a folded sheet of parchment. 'I guessed it would be here,' he said, speaking more to himself than anyone else in the tent. He unfolded it and squinted hard before handing the sheet to Macarius.

'Do oblige us,' he said. 'I've little doubt your many talents stretch to reading Persian. This, however, is in Greek. I just don't see too well nowadays after one of my black pills. Do let's hear these no doubt magic words. Siroes died in the effort to make them effective. The least we can do, I suppose, is intone them over his body.'

'Would My Lord have me read this?' Macarius asked, looking directly at me.

I listened again. All was still fine outside – why shouldn't it be? Martin was now sitting on the carpet and looking up at me, his face ghastly with shock and continuing strain.

'Is it My Lord's wish to know the contents of this document?'

'Yes, it is,' I said, ignoring the renewed protest I felt sure Martin was trying to form. I might have told him the words only had effect alongside the object. But I didn't. 'We might as well know what it says,' I added. 'Just be quick about it.'

Macarius took the unfolded sheet over to one of the lamps and looked hard at the faded script. From where I sat, it had an aged look about it.

'It is a rather corrupt Greek,' he said. 'I think it might have been written by a Persian, and may be a translation of something from Egyptian. However, it says that, for the destruction of enemies – their destruction as a last resort – an object that is not described should be taken in sight of the enemy. There, its possessor, who shall have fasted and washed according to detailed instructions, must hold up the object' – Macarius paused again and squinted – 'while saying or singing: "*Santi kapupi wayya jaja minti lalakali*".'

'I say, isn't that a dactylic hexameter?' Priscus broke in. 'Would you say, Alaric, that was an hexameter?'

'It might be,' I said. I looked at Martin, who shrugged.

A big cup of wine, now he accepted it wasn't poisoned, was bringing him back to what passed for his senses. 'It would be necessary to know the quantities in the original language,' he said.

He'd have said more, but I cut in, asking Macarius if he understood the words.

He shook his head. 'They are words from a language unknown to me,' he said. 'But one must recite them three times, and then

476

lie down, looking at the sky with arms and legs outstretched. The enemy will shortly after be annihilated in ways that include burning winds, or fire raining from the sky, or swallowing into the earth, or visitation of demons, or sudden pestilence, or the addition of invincible power to one's own side. It seems to depend on the time of year.'

'Sounds fanciful – though also rather interesting,' said Priscus. He suddenly froze and listened. There was a gentle hubbub of voices outside the tent. He waved at Macarius to go and see what was happening.

'I don't know what you think of that crap document,' he whispered once Macarius was out of the tent, 'but Siroes was no fool. He'd not have come all this way for nothing. What would you say to a good look round that cavern for his object? If Alexandria is destroyed like the Cities of the Plain, or falls into the sea, or whatever, Heraclius and Nicetas can kiss each other's arse before I have them beheaded in the Circus.'

'You as Emperor?' I sneered softly. 'If this stuff does anything at all, you'd be another Caligula.'

'And what of that?' came the reply. 'The Empire's survived more than one demented tyrant. And, with or without that bloody object, I at least could fight off the Persians. If Siroes was right, however, just think what I could do. It wouldn't then be a question of beating the Persians, or defending what we had with the peasant militias you keep crying up in Council. We could go on the offensive against the barbarians. We could bring back the West. We could do all that Siroes was suggesting for the united powers of the world. We could outdo Alexander and Caesar combined. The Empire would become—' He fell silent as Macarius came back into the tent.

I'd watched in a kind of fascinated horror as Priscus had loomed over me and appeared to swell ever larger. It was like back in the dockyard. It stirred other thoughts that I fought to suppress.

'A meeting has been called at the midnight hour for what remains of the Brotherhood Council,' Macarius said. 'There are also reports of lights moving about far to the south.'

477

I pulled myself together. A thought had suddenly occurred to me, and I was eager to share it with Priscus.

'I presume the signal you mentioned earlier,' I said, 'was for the guards you brought up from Alexandria.'

Priscus smiled.

'The idea was that they'd be lurking out in the desert until the signal was given.' He smiled again and nodded. 'They'd then rush in here and see off what was left of the Brotherhood.'

He reached for his drug satchel.

'A strategy Alexander himself might have praised,' I said with a mock toast. 'Did you bother specifying outside which Soteropolis your men should be lurking?'

'What are you talking about, my dear boy?' Priscus answered. He frowned slightly, his face sliding visibly from complacency to concern.

'When you terrorised that map out of poor old Hermogenes,' I said, looking carefully at his face, 'I assume you waited around long enough for him to tell you there were two cities called Soteropolis. You did make sure to specify the right one to your guards?'

I know that Priscus wasn't the only one to have lost out here. But his face was the funniest thing I'd seen in ages. I put my head back and laughed as silently as I could manage. Priscus sat down with a sudden bump and reached for the wine jug.

67

'I don't suppose we could get away with claiming natural causes?'
I asked when I was recovered enough to speak with just a nervous giggle. We all looked at the twisted body on the floor. The
exposed parts of Lucas were now covered in dark blotches. As
for the face – I'd seen more peaceful expressions on the impaling
stakes. Siroes looked much better. But he didn't count for present
purposes. And there was the matter of the garrotte still embedded
in the flesh around his neck and throat.

'Go and tell them,' Priscus said to Macarius, 'that His Majesty
is deep in conference with his guests, and will make himself available for other discussions in the morning.'

'If it really is midnight,' Martin piped up suddenly, 'it's my
birthday. I've made it to thirty-two.' He smiled and looked around.

I smiled a weak encouragement. I was coming down with
a bump after my laughing fit. Even so, it was worth something that Martin had beaten a prophecy by which he'd set
such store – and beaten it in what were not the most favourable
circumstances.

Priscus raised his eyebrows. 'Congratulations,' he said, 'though
I still wouldn't touch the eggy tarts.' To Macarius: 'Now, go and
say whatever's needed to send those fuckers away.' When Macarius
had gone out again, Priscus turned back to me.

'I'm serious about another trip to the Underworld. I'm inclined
to agree there's nothing left down there but a few wog bones.
The *Santi kapupi* stuff we can forget. But once we've chased the
Brotherhood off, I think I will go down for a good look of my
own.' He paused as Macarius came almost directly back in. Again,
he ignored Priscus and looked to me.

'I must inform My Lord,' he said, 'that the Brotherhood Council is assured by His Grace the Bishop of Letopolis that His Majesty has been led astray by the Lord Priscus. They desire an immediate meeting to discuss this and other grievances. They propose to remain outside the tent until His Majesty chooses to show himself.'

Priscus pulled a face and swigged more of the wine. He looked again down at the body of Lucas. 'At least they aren't proposing to come in,' he muttered. He pulled himself together. 'Does anyone know where this other Soteropolis might be?' he asked.

I nodded.

'Well, I suggest we get ourselves over there pretty sharpish,' he said. 'Lucas may not have been their choice as leader. He was, nevertheless, the only one I left them.

'Now, I don't think I ever quite finished my account of the fall of Serdica,' he said to me. 'I got to the part where the ten thousand savages came pouring over the wall. What happened next was, they killed the whole sodding garrison, plus most of the civilian population. The reason I got away was because I kept my wits about me. I took one look at that blonde mob running down the main street at us, and made straight off in the other direction. I got to the far wall. I unbolted the gate myself, and didn't look back until the town was a flickering glow miles behind me. I rode until morning, when I bumped into the relief column sent over by Maurice. You can be sure the account I gave was more heroic than the truth.'

He got up and walked over to the other side of the tent from the leather flaps. He pulled out his knife and quietly opened a long slash in the fabric. I felt the sudden chill of fresh air. A couple of the lamps flickered and went out. Macarius got them relit at once and pushed shades on to them. I looked over at the flaps. There was still a steady murmur of conversation outside. It sounded more impatient than suspicious.

'Will you get your clothes on, Alaric?' Priscus asked, stuffing his cat into a cloth bag. 'Or do you intend riding naked through the desert?'

★   ★   ★

We got perhaps three miles across the moonlit sands before I heard the commotion behind me. I'd been wondering how long it would be before anyone noticed how silent the tent had fallen and walked in. Eventually, I was surprised it had taken so long. We must have made enough noise as we crept through the city of tents above Soteropolis, sniffing our way to where the camels were tethered. But we had got clean away. I was even beginning to think we might get to the other Soteropolis without further incident. I was wrong about that. Looking back from the high dune at the glitter from within the cloud of dust, it might have been the whole Brotherhood in pursuit.

'A few dozen at the most,' Priscus said calmly. 'And since the wind is blowing their dust forward, I'll be surprised if they can see anything at all. They could ride us down over a long chase. But this should be a quick dash. I only hope your geography is better in the desert than it was in the Egyptian quarter.'

He laughed and pushed his camel forward down the other side of the dune. I heard the hiss of the parting sands. Martin clung hard to Macarius on the camel behind mine, squealing softly at every bump. I followed Priscus down. Once on the level, we picked up speed again. Keeping up with Priscus was impossible. His camel raced forward as if they'd known each other all their lives. The wind played cold on my face as we rushed along. As with distance, there is no concept of speed in the desert. But the stones that lay dark on the sandy ground flashed by as if they'd been dropping from the sky.

Twisting your body to look back on a galloping horse isn't something for the inexperienced. I wasn't that good on horseback. On the camel, I didn't dare make the attempt. But I could try not to fall too far behind Priscus. He looked back every so often, and didn't seem worried by what he saw. What would be done with us if we were outrun should have been playing on my mind. But whatever I thought of him in every other respect, Priscus was in charge here, and he knew exactly what he was doing.

The torchlight from what I presumed had been the wrong Soteropolis came in sight without warning. One moment, the sands before us were all dimly white. The next moment, there was a faint glare of yellow just a couple of miles in front of us. Priscus was now swaying backwards and forwards, backwards and forwards, as, very smooth, he forced his camel to go ever faster. He raced ahead, the dozen yards between us rising to twenty and forty. I struggled to keep up, and would easily have been overtaken even by Macarius and Martin together, had not Macarius decided that I should be kept in the middle of the party.

I can't repeat often enough that distances in the desert are hard to gauge. Seeing lights ahead is not the same as being among them. It isn't the same as being within easy reach of them. We raced across the sands, in our ears the thunder of the camel hooves – and the shouting of our pursuers that grew ever closer. We had the advantages of fear and moderate skill and a very good head start. They had every other advantage, and this was beginning to tell.

Then, as I looked ahead, shapes seemed to rise out of nothing from the desert floor. They clustered in a mass, the moonlight glittering from their drawn weapons. Then they fanned out. Without seeing anything for sure, I raced past them. Far ahead of me, Priscus came to a sudden halt. He wheeled his camel round. I went straight past him, and I may have been a quarter of a mile ahead of him before I could get my own beast under control. By the time I could get back to him and Macarius and Martin, battle had been fully joined. I could see little enough in the moonlight. It was a set of confused if rapid skirmishes in which dark shadows reached up to mounted men, who wheeled round in fear, but were too surrounded for any getaway. I could hear the clash of weapons and the screams of men dragged down from their mounts and efficiently butchered. It was over in almost no time at all. Except for the bubbling screams of the dying and a continuing savage growl as if of some supremely powerful beast, the desert was silent all around us.

'Get back on ride,' a female said to me in bad Greek. 'Go on to lights.'

I bowed to the Sister of Saint Artemisia, and tried to find some utterance simple enough for her to understand.

Her face shining with exaltation under the dark smears of what I took for blood, she paid no attention. She waved a dark and dripping sword at me. 'Get back on ride,' she said, pointing at the camel that was turning skittish beside me.

I found the Heretical Patriarch standing on a section of mud-brick wall that hadn't yet fallen level with the desert. About a hundred yards behind me, the Sisters were marching back into the camp, their voices raised together in what sounded like one of the more ferocious Psalms. I got down from the camel again and knelt before him.

'Your Holiness,' I said. I got no further.

Anastasius took me by the hands and raised me up. 'You are safe?' he asked.

I nodded.

He looked at the other two camels. Martin was having one of his shaking fits as Macarius helped him down.

Priscus was looking confused. 'Where are they?' he called to Macarius. He'd been sure we were making for his guards. Anastasius and the Sisters were about as complete a surprise as if the object had dropped into his hands and started working. He looked at the Sisters, who were already tearing madly at the bread and cold meats set out on tables. Just in case more of the Brotherhood should appear, they'd placed their weapons within easy reach. Other than that, there was no evidence of the regular armed support he'd arranged with Macarius.

'There may be much we need to discuss,' Anastasius said, speaking to me again. 'For the moment, let it be sufficient to say that you are safe in the hands of Mother Church. Of course, I discussed your letter with my brother patriarch, John. We were not happy that you had ignored my advice to stay in Alexandria. In view of the emergency, however – endangering, as it did, the whole of Creation – we decided this was a moment for setting aside every difference of creed and to work together. We had a message earlier from the local Bishop, and were planning our attack for the very early morning.'

As he spoke, the Master of the Works came in sight. I nodded to him. He bowed to me. I'd last seen him as I pushed him inside the Church of the Apostles and went after Martin. Other than assuming the whole of the Council had been saved along with Nicetas, I hadn't thought of him since. He now stood before me, looking almost elegant in the cloak that partly covered his robe of office. He bowed again and moved past me. He stopped before Priscus, who was fiddling with the saddlebag on his camel.

'My Lord Priscus,' he said in a loud official voice, 'I bear a warrant for your arrest signed and sealed by His Highness the Viceroy himself. The charges are desertion of your military post and high treason. There are other charges that you can read for yourself. My instructions are to place you in close confinement. Once in Alexandria, you will be examined by His Highness in person prior to being sent on to Constantinople for trial by or before the Emperor.'

Priscus snarled something and went for his sword. But the surprise had been total. Without that, he might have got back on his camel and bolted. No one could have stopped Priscus. Then again, where would he have gone? Even he wouldn't have got far as an outlaw. Even now in the Empire, a warrant of that nature couldn't be ignored. Resistance was futile, and it was impossible to fly.

'You can add sorcery to the charges,' I said with a smothered smile. 'In that saddlebag you'll find a magical text of the highest illegality. He was hoping it would assist him in his treason.' I looked at Priscus.

He stared back more astonished than angry. 'You fucking snake!' he spat. 'You came out here with all this ready planned.'

I made an ironic bow. I did think of a little speech about the Mandate of Heaven – or at least how I'd see him boiled alive in the Circus for what he'd put Martin through. But I'd had enough for one day. A good sit down now, and a cup of something hot, would do nicely. As I turned away, I saw Priscus throw down the sword he'd taken from Siroes, and go and sit quietly on a pile of mud bricks.

'Your Holiness,' I said to Anastasius – and why not concede him the title he claimed? – 'I should much appreciate a doctor or such medical help as you can provide for my secretary.' No one could glue Martin's ear back on. But a dab of opium on those bruised piles would be an immediate comfort.

The sun would soon be up. Now they'd finished vomiting up the feast that had continued through the night, the Sisters were getting ready for prayers. I stood upwind of the camp and looked steadily towards the faint glow on the eastern horizon.

'My Lord is content?' Macarius asked. He stood beside me.

I looked at his closed, impassive face. 'Content is not the word I'd use,' I said eventually. 'But if its rules and purpose continue to evade me, I suppose the game is now over.'

Macarius stepped forward and looked back at me, the faint glow behind him. 'A full understanding is not often given to men,' he said. 'But do you believe the game, as you call it, is over? You must realise that, before it does really end, you are called upon to act once more. No one can force your choice. No one can advise you. But you know what needs to be done. Whether and how you do this has an importance you might imagine, but will never know for sure.'

I stepped to my left and looked again at the eastern sky. The smallest ark of brightness was now peeping above the horizon, scattering the darkness of the night. I hadn't slept in a day, and I felt suddenly very tired. What I most wanted was to lie down and sleep until noon. I'd then be able to think all this through. The politics had been easy, once I'd laid bare the various interest groups involved. But Macarius was right: there was still more to be done. If only I could understand the why of it. Sleep might banish the paralysing confusion I could now feel every time I tried to take thought. But there was no time, I knew. Without shifting his position, Macarius continued looking at me.

'If you will permit me, My Lord,' he said, 'you have played your part very well so far. I was dimly aware of your doings before you left Alexandria. I do not think anyone else could have guessed your intentions. Even if what you might describe as luck gave assistance, it was a clever strategy to get back your secretary and ruin Priscus.'

I continued looking at the horizon. Soon, the light would dazzle and I'd have to turn away. I was thinking of what Priscus had told me in the street outside the Prefecture: *Do ask yourself how an empire survives without men like me. It needs heroes to found it, and poets and artists and philosophers to make it noble. And it needs someone to direct the rack if it's to be kept in order.* But why think of this now? I wondered. There were other words that were more relevant. *You will know what to do,* I'd been told back at the oasis. I looked away from the rising sun and straightened myself.

'We're going back to Soteropolis,' I said quietly. 'Do please arrange an escort if possible. Otherwise I have no doubt the Sisterhood will be more than a match for what little remains of the Brotherhood.'

68

'Can you not feel the evil down here?' Martin asked with a dramatic shiver. 'It radiates as from a second, dark sun.'

I looked up from the fifth scroll of Eratosthenes. The words might have had more impression had I not been hearing their like for the second time in two days. 'Not really,' I said. I leaned back in the rickety chair and took a deep breath. Still watching me, Martin stood in the doorway of the converted tomb. 'You must bear in mind,' I added, 'I have already been down here in far gloomier circumstances.' To say the cavern was now ablaze with light would be an exaggeration. It was, even so, far better lit than on my first visit. And the screams and trills of the Sisters as they went about their business completed my impression of a very different place. 'Such evil as was here,' I said, now reassuring, 'was brought to an end many ages ago. We are here today only to exorcise its memory.'

I suppose I was stretching things with the word 'we'. In truth, while I was the one to explain matters to him, Anastasius was the guiding force down here. He was the one who supervised the clearing of the tombs and the gathering up for burning of the rubbish that littered the cavern floor. He was the one who directed the sweating, joyously shouting Sisters as, inch by inch, they dragged the local representation of Moloch to the chasm edge. I was here, and not in bed, only because Macarius had been insistent again that I was needed – and because I wanted to see if those books were quite so lunatic as I'd at first thought them.

My short answer is that they weren't. What inspiration old Eratosthenes claimed to have found here left no evidence in his text, which, as said, was solidly Epicurean in its approach. The main difference, its numerical basis apart, was that Eratosthenes had taken what for Epicurus were fundamentals and resolved them into different expressions of something more fundamental yet. It was fascinating, and I was glad I'd made for the book rack just as soon as I could convince Anastasius that his own work was a matter for the Church alone, and just as soon as I could give Macarius the slip.

'My Lord.'

Damn! It was Macarius: he must have read my mind.

'My Lord, the preparations are now complete. Your own presence has become essential.'

I scowled, but checked my temper. Though I could feel the tiredness trying to claw its way back into my attention, the return of all Lucas had confiscated after my surrender meant I once again had the means to keep tiredness at bay. I'd never match Priscus when it came to mixing drugs. But half a pinch in wine of dried Lazarus weed, and I was as perky as anyone could wish to be.

'Will you also be taking these books and the box of stones?' I asked. I twisted round and nodded to the now open Library crate. One of the Sisters had smashed it open for me. It had been filled with stones wrapped in lead.

Macarius gave me one of his blank looks. 'Is My Lord asking,' he replied, 'for the various effects of Eratosthenes to be carried back to the surface?' He spoke in a tone presaging an argument.

I grinned and rolled the last book shut. I had not been asking that. But I felt no obligation to explain myself to Macarius. He hadn't really betrayed me to Lucas – or even to Priscus. At the same time, he'd not served me with anything approaching devotion. 'I think they can stay here for the moment,' I said. I carefully replaced the book in its place and followed him out into the main cavern. The Sisterhood had done a fine clearing-up job. The place was swept clean of shrivelled flesh and broken wood. Everything movable was heaped up close by the edge of the chasm. The statue itself was only kept from falling straight into it by a web of ropes ultimately attached to the stone bollards that also held the bridge.

This was all a hundred and fifty yards from where Eratosthenes had made his office. But we stood now only in gloom rather than in punctuated darkness. With Macarius leading the way and Martin hurrying after, I made my now confident way across the floor towards Anastasius. Dressed in their filthy cowls, the less emaciated – and presumably the younger – of the Sisters shuffled about me, gathering up any small objects that had escaped their main sweep. As I approached him, Anastasius bowed deeply.

'On behalf of His Majesty the Emperor,' Anastasius asked loudly in Greek, 'will his Magnificence the Legate resign these objects of the Old Faith to Holy Mother Church?'

As I stopped before him, unknown hands – possibly it was Macarius – reached from behind and pulled off my cloak, revealing the best approximation we'd managed to the robe of an Imperial Councillor.

'In accordance with the law made in the seventh year of the Great Theodosius of blessed memory,' I responded just as loudly, 'these accursed objects, already confiscated to the Sacred Treasury, I hereby resign to the disposal of Holy Mother Church.' I bowed low before him, making sure to keep off my knees; whatever the circumstances might require, however convincingly he might be dressed, Anastasius still wasn't the Orthodox Patriarch. 'Let their fate be oblivion.'

Anastasius lapsed into Egyptian, now walking about the piles of accumulated rubbish to shake holy water over them. At last, it was done. With a dramatic gesture to the Sisters, he stepped back. Again bowing to me and receiving my own response, he stood beside me about six feet from the chasm. Two of the Sisters pushed everything over the edge. There was nothing ceremonial in the motions. The ritual was over. I walked to the edge and looked over. I heard things knock against the walls of the chasm. Once again, I heard no final impact.

Attention had now shifted to the statue, still suspended on the brink. There was the same committal in Greek from Empire to Church, and the same endless chanting in Egyptian. Then this too went over the edge. The Patriarch himself achieved this with a sharp little axe that he took to the retaining ropes. I heard the rush of air as the thing fell and gathered speed. I heard it knock once or twice against the wall. Yet again, there was no final crash. I ignored Martin's whisper about the Pit of Hell. The chasm was deep, I'd allow, but I'd probably seen deeper in the mountains inland from Ephesus.

'It is time now for My Lord to act,' Macarius prompted.

I smiled and took from beneath my robe the sheet of parchment Siroes had brought all the way from Persia. I had skimmed it in the sunshine above. It was just as Macarius had paraphrased it. All I could add was a knowledge of scribal fashions and of how ink and parchment blended together over time. I could tell from this that the document was very old – it might have been contemporary with Eratosthenes: it might have been older still.

'Does My Lord act in this of his own free will?' he asked.

'I do,' I said. Anastasius was watching with surprise as we made up another ceremony on the spot. I tried not to giggle as I went through the responses. When these were over, I looked round for something heavy. All I could see was the topmost nine inches or so of the stone erection. Somehow, this had broken off the statue as it was dragged over to its committal and somehow had escaped the last clearing up. I now lifted it, then wrapped about it the sheet of parchment, securing all with a leather office band Macarius produced as if out of nowhere. I stood on the edge, waiting for every eye in the room to settle on me.

'There is a story,' I said loudly in Greek – if the Sisters didn't understand, there were three men with me who could at least understand the words – 'of a Syrian trade expedition to my own country. This was after my people had displaced the original Celtic inhabitants and before the arrival of the Faith. The Syrians went ashore with strings of coloured glass beads. They returned

490

with pearls of jet black and, where these had been insufficient, with the fair-headed children of their customers.' I paused and looked appreciatively at the two baffled male faces about me. To call Macarius baffled would be saying too much. He just looked stiffer than usual.

'Each side, I have no doubt,' I continued, 'bade farewell to the other in the assurance that it had driven the harder bargain. We know who truly gained and who lost. It is a sure sign of barbarism not to understand the true value of things.' I held up the package of stone and parchment. I waited until even the Sisters had their eyes turned to it. With a contemptuous gesture, I tossed it over the edge. Without bothering to see how it fell, I turned and walked back to where the statue had stood. I stopped here and looked again towards the chasm. I stared at Macarius and pointed at the rope bridge. 'I've done all that was required of me,' I said, now in Latin. 'The rest you can do by yourself.' I watched as he took hold of one of the torches set into the portable brackets, and then as he walked with it over to where the bridge stretched deceptively across the chasm. He held it up and threw it hard towards the middle of the bridge.

I heard the 'whizz', of fire through the air. I heard its soft impact on the wooden planks. I shaded my eyes to avoid the short but intensely bright flare as dry rope and wood turned into ash and took their place in that bottomless chasm. I stared hard with all the concentration I could manage. It was for the shortest moment of which human senses can take account, and it was too brief a moment for me to give any close description of what I saw. But the impression I had was of immense and metallic instruments of torture. They were to the instruments I had seen in Alexandria, or even in Constantinople, as the light in that cavern was to the sunshine far above. If no one ever throws another bridge across the chasm that completes their separation from the world, humanity will not be the loser.

'You may not choose to share it with me,' I said to Macarius as he came and stood beside me, 'but is there anything about this place or these objects that I have not been able to work out for myself?

491

What is it that prompted Leontius and Siroes, and perhaps any number of others down the ages, to risk and to lose all?'

'Why must you always assume,' Macarius replied, 'that, if only it can be clearly asked, every question has an answer?'

'Because it has.' I smiled. 'Every question has an answer. There are no mysteries for those who know where and how to look.' As we walked back to the steps that led to the upper corridor, I looked over to the right. There a single lamp burned brightly in the tomb where Eratosthenes had for seven years looked unblinkingly into the nature of things. He'd been dismissively called the second greatest mind of his age in all that he attempted: the second best mathematician, the second best geographer, the second best general scholar, and so on. I'd held in my hand the crowning achievement of his life. It may have revealed him as an inspired lunatic, or as by far the greatest mind of his age after all – perhaps the greatest of all the Greeks. And my decision had been to leave it where I'd found it. Yes, I'd leave the fruits of his labour in there. If Macarius had insisted, I'd have let him add it to the rubbish thrown into the chasm. But he hadn't, and I wouldn't. Neither, though, would I take them with me. I thought again of Priscus in the dungeon, gloating as he gave his instructions for the use of the rack. I couldn't take thought for those hundreds of the impaled or thousands and tens of thousands of the indiscriminately slaughtered. It was like trying to pay attention to a single flake in a field of snow. But I could think of that boy who'd been broken up and then violated till he died.

'Let the world have liberty,' I said aloud, 'before it steps from the shadows.' I followed the Sisters up the steps. I stopped and turned back. For the first time in five months, I saw Martin and Macarius in an earnest if whispered conversation. I laughed and beckoned them up behind me.

Dirty from the cavern, we emerged blinking into the sunshine of an Egyptian high afternoon. The captain of the guards whom Priscus, it had turned out, had ordered to the right Soteropolis saluted me as I climbed through the entrance and turned back to help Martin. He'd told me of the verbal orders given for my death in whatever skirmish there might be with the Brotherhood. Live rescued captives are better than dead. But Priscus, being Priscus, had wanted to make sure no one could challenge whatever story he eventually made up for Heraclius.

'My son, would you care to witness the final interment?' Anastasius asked.

I nodded. Taking up another pose in robes that, even without the dirt, looked far less impressive in the natural light, I watched as he made his arrangements. The remnants of the Brotherhood were no longer to be seen. Those inclined to lurk behind dunes and heaps of rubbish after the Imperial forces had moved in had run off at the first sound of female battle cries. There was no chance of a counter-attack. Broken in Alexandria, the Brotherhood had been killed off in Soteropolis. The locals drafted in to do the digging were now willing and eager, under the direction of their Patriarch, to undo all that they'd been terrorised into doing.

It took much washing and oiling of granite to get the plug free of sand and tightly back in place. But it was done. As men frantically shovelled sand back into the crater, Anastasius stood over them, pronouncing what he later told me was the most horrifying curse on the place even the heretical Church of Egypt could manage. As if by an afterthought, the bodies of Lucas and of Siroes were thrown into the crater. Siroes was nothing to me. He was just a lesser Priscus; and, because lesser, he'd perished in the contest with Priscus. For Lucas, though, I did feel a certain pity. The man had been a dangerous lunatic. He'd been delighted to think I was dying from the very poison that had instead killed him. If he had made it to Pharaoh, he'd have done no better for the Egyptian people than any other of the native kings had managed. He might easily have been worse. But was it wholly bad that he'd worked – with whatever self-delusion and lack of judgement – for the liberty of his people from an empire that had, since time out of mind, shorn them like a flock of sheep? Whether the questions Macarius had asked of me about my own reaction in like circumstances were serious was of no importance. They were certainly worth considering. We buried Lucas face down, his body – rigid as a wooden statue – still twisted in its death agony.

The crater was filled in. Time and the desert winds could be trusted to restore the obliteration of Soteropolis as a whole. I thought of that girl back in the Egyptian quarter. It was here that she'd assured me I'd find my 'heart's desire'. Well, if it was here, the reserve stock would be underneath the city of tents the other side of the big dune. Since I imagined the whole area would be taken as subject to the Patriarch's curse, getting any of the locals here again with a shovel was out of the question. One day, perhaps, I'd make a second journey – this time with an army of diggers from elsewhere in Egypt, and a regular army of Greeks to make sure the locals didn't make a fuss. But this was it for the moment. All had ended as well as might have been expected in the circumstances. Even so, it wasn't wholly to my taste.

'Come on, Martin,' I said once the crater was filled in. 'I need a good, long drink.'

'Why did she have to do it in this way?' I asked Macarius. 'The lack of simplicity robs her entire work of elegance.'

Macarius turned back from examining his saddlebags. He looked at me and actually smiled. 'What makes you assume she had any direction of what has now passed?' he asked in turn. 'You have called all this a game. Except where they have constrained your own actions, you are ignorant of its rules. Is it not conceivable that even the Mistress herself is constrained? You will have noticed how little control she had over you. Is it not possible that she must answer to powers far greater than her own?'

'Will I see her again?' I asked.

'Is there any reason why you should?' came the answer. 'You have acquitted yourself just as was hoped. I do not think you will ever tell the story now ended exactly as it happened. Certainly, no one would believe you if you tried. But I know you well enough to believe you will take the more credible fragments and work them into a narrative from which you emerge with shining credit. Is that not always the case?'

He climbed onto the camel. I watched him as he rode out to the south. I watched him a long time, until, far distant, he vanished over a sand dune. Being Macarius, he never looked back.

'I knew you'd see reason, my dearest,' Priscus said with one of his brilliant smiles.

We were in my office back in the Palace in Alexandria. On the other side of the closed door, I knew without being able to hear that Martin was fussing over some dereliction of filing that had accumulated in his absence. Priscus sat on the edge of my desk, his legs swinging back and forth.

'I told you it was a simple matter of explaining things clearly to Nicetas,' he continued. I looked at the heap of papyrus he'd dumped in front of me. 'You'll now have to trust me that I didn't have copies made of all this. Forgery of a public document to enrich yourself at the Treasury's expense is not something even Heraclius could overlook in your case. Then there's the matter of your consorting with an obvious sorceress. I'd not be able to prove that in Constantinople. But you know it would come out soon enough in any enquiries made on the spot.

'As my friends in the Intelligence Bureau often say, "There's dirt on everyone, if you only look hard enough".'

I ground my teeth.

'You're a fucking beast and murderer,' I said flatly. 'When I look at you, I'm reduced to wishing, if not perhaps believing, that there is a Final Judgement.'

'If there is,' he said, still smiling, 'I don't think either of us has much to fear. If not in law or in theology, there is in moral philosophy the concept of the set-off. Whatever I have done – whatever I may yet do – is for the benefit of the Empire. Without your efforts, I freely concede, the Empire will not be worth saving. Without mine, however, it cannot be saved.' He dropped his voice, 'Whether I really believed there was anything under Soteropolis worth having, you've made sure it can't be had. That means the Empire must be saved, if at all, as something more like one of your barbarian kingdoms than as the Empire established by the Caesars on the foundations laid by Alexander. We shall need our peasant militias. That will inevitably mean the loosening of control that you and Sergius have been crying up these past two years.

'But, in one form or another, the Empire must and can be saved – and we are the men to do it. Now that you have talked sense into Nicetas, I will give you back these most embarrassing documents. You can also forget any instructions my people in Soteropolis may have misunderstood regarding your safety.'

He stood up and brushed his tunic. I looked again at the documents he'd managed to acquire. Whatever gloss I might put on it to others, there was no doubt I'd been blackmailed into getting Priscus out of trouble. He'd not be going back to Constantinople in chains, but carrying a relic that had now been authenticated by two patriarchs as of the highest potency. According to Anastasius, it had cured the lame and restored sight to the blind. According to Martin, it had wondrously eased his haemorrhoids. Priscus had told everyone he was sure I'd found it in the very house of Joseph. But he would say that, wouldn't he?

And, if I really tried, I might in time even deceive myself. If Nicetas had managed to withdraw the warrants for Egypt – 'reasons of state, you must understand,' he'd sobbed at me while his leg was dressed again – the rest of the Empire had so far been untouched by land reform outside the Asiatic provinces. Without me to drive on the process . . .

I stopped myself. I could deceive myself, but I wouldn't. It would soon be time for the burial of Alexander. Now his head had been found, a funeral could take place at which one Patriarch would officiate and another would be present; a funeral at which Nicetas would repeat the full amnesty he'd ordered as soon as he was back on one of his feet, and which he believed would dry the tears of Alexandria. Some hope, that! Even so, Priscus and I would need to be there to take our places in the still pageantry of Alexandrian and Egyptian government.

'Where is your cat?' I asked suddenly.

Priscus smiled again. 'There was nothing to eat in that prison where you had me confined. I had to bite her throat out and drink the blood. The taste was perfectly horrid. But you never did like cats, did you? After that experience, I think I too might become a doggie man.'

EPILOGUE

Jarrow, Thursday, 4th October 686

Bede brought me some overly ripe pears for lunch. They had a hint of mould about them, but were a pleasant change from bread and milk. When the only teeth you have left are in the wrong place, anything soft is to be welcomed. We sat and reviewed his progress in Greek, which has been most encouraging. I was unable, even so, to keep a slightly melancholic note from the conversation. Getting more advanced texts for him to read than the Gospels is a matter of sending to Canterbury. That's easy. Guaranteeing that I shall live long enough to move him to the stage of self-sufficiency is another matter.

Yes, I've been thinking a lot about death since the coming of autumn. It may have been the piss-poor summer, and then the arrival of frost at night a couple of months early. It may, on the other hand, be those bastard novices. They treat me like some living saint. As often as I step into the refectory to get a refill for my beer jug, they're lining up for benedictions. It wouldn't be so bad if even one of them was worth a second look. But I think I am beginning to repeat myself.

Now, you will recall, my Dear Reader, that I did promise to describe and explain the facts of what happened to me out in the Tyne. You will have noticed the double stack of papyrus heaped up since then, and the fact that I have neither described nor explained anything. If I were younger, I might worry about the decay of my faculties. When I was younger, I always explained myself perfectly well if explanation was what I wanted. Call it an infirmity of age, then, if I have failed now. Whatever the case, I have done all that I

499

can to set the facts before you. On their basis, you may decide as you will.

Speaking for myself, I have decided that whatever I may have seen and heard beneath those dark waters was a trick brought on by lack of air in an aged body. That may seem a feeble explanation. It may even have left a couple of important facts unexplained. But when faced with the apparently miraculous, a reasonable man looks for a natural explanation. One will generally be found. Where not, it hasn't been sought hard enough. Let that be an end of the matter.

However, I did begin my main narrative on 'the day we began to lose Egypt'. Since I end it with Egypt saved – or saved so far as most people judge these things – you may feel doubly cheated. That is your right. My defence, though, is that – little as we could have suspected at the time – the Empire was scarcely yet begun on an age of multiple and interlocking crises from which only now it may be emerging, and emerging with losses that, if irreparable to the Empire as it had existed, may yet be seen as the political equivalent of an amputation of a diseased limb from an otherwise healthy body. Priscus and I thought we had saved Egypt. The Persians still took it from us, and Syria too. Eventually, of course, we did beat the Persians. We did find the second Alexander that Priscus always wanted to be. He didn't so much defeat the Persians as annihilate them. It was as if he'd laid hands on the object. The pressure they had brought, during four hundred years, on the Empire's eastern frontier was completely lifted. Back into every province from which we'd been driven we marched in triumph.

Then we had another letter from the Saracens in bad Greek. We ignored that one. What followed couldn't be ignored.

Other questions may come to mind. My narrative doesn't so much end as reach a sudden halt. What became of us all once we'd left Alexandria? Did Priscus ever get his just deserts? What about Martin? How did Maximin turn out? What did Heraclius think of that less than glorious attempt to redistribute the land of Egypt? Dear me, questions, questions, so many questions! I can answer all of them. And I will answer them if I can evade that threatened canonisation long enough.

But something I will not discuss is the dreams. I must, during the past seventy years, have seen that face a thousand times in dreams. But time, as with a much handled coin, had inevitably blurred over the cold perfection of its beauty. I hadn't expected ever again to see it so clearly in my mind's eye as I find myself now able to do.

No, I will not discuss that. Call it, if you will, another infirmity of age.